A WHISPER OF BLOOD

Edited by Ellen Datlow

BERKLEY BOOKS, NEW YORK

This Berkley book contains the complete
text of the original hardcover edition. It
has been completely reset in a typeface
designed for easy reading, and was printed from
new film.

A WHISPER OF BLOOD

A Berkley Book / published by arrangement with
William Morrow & Company, Inc.

PRINTING HISTORY
William Morrow & Company edition published 1991
Berkley edition / November 1992

All rights reserved.
Copyright © 1991 by Ellen Datlow.
This book may not be reproduced in
whole or in part, by mimeograph or any other
means, without permission. For information
address: William Morrow & Company, Inc.,
1350 Avenue of the Americas, New York, New York 10019.

ISBN: 0-425-13505-5

A BERKLEY BOOK ® ™ 757,375
Berkley Books are published by The Berkley Publishing Group,
200 Madison Avenue, New York, New York 10016.
The name "BERKLEY" and the "B" logo
are trademarks belonging to Berkley Publishing Corporation.

PRINTED IN THE UNITED STATES OF AMERICA

10 9 8 7 6 5 4 3 2 1

Feast upon the imaginative horrors collected in
ELLEN DATLOW'S CRITICALLY
ACCLAIMED ANTHOLOGIES!

A WHISPER OF BLOOD

"A superb anthology . . . extraordinary . . . highly untraditional twists."
—**Gahan Wilson,** *Weird Tales*

"Turn these pages; don't expect to sleep . . ."—*News-Sentinel* (IN)

"Unvaryingly high quality."
—*Publishers Weekly*

"Another fine collection of tales."
—*Booklist*

BLOOD IS NOT ENOUGH

Featuring stories by HARLAN ELLISON, FRITZ LEIBER, DAN SIMMONS, GAHAN WILSON and others . . .

"A stellar vampire anthology . . . superb!"
—*Booklist*

"The variety is dazzling . . . it is as scary and sometimes grisly as any horror fan could desire."
—*Locus*

"Trust me on this, we've got a killer anthology on our hands . . . There's Good Stuff here, heaping doses of it!"
—**Charles de Lint,** *Science Fiction Eye*

"*Blood Is Not Enough* is more than enough if you're in the market for a rich, varied collection of vampire stories."
—**Richard Matheson,**
author of *The Shrinking Man* and *Hell House*

"Horror fans should definitely seek out this collection!"—*Yale Herald*

"A collection of scary beauties . . . The kind of stories that creep up on you in the night, that ambush your mind long after you thought you had forgotten them."
—*Rockland Courier-Gazette* (ME)

Berkley Books edited by Ellen Datlow

BLOOD IS NOT ENOUGH
A WHISPER OF BLOOD

In memory of Blue

I'd like to thank the following people for helping to make this anthology possible: Merrilee Heifetz, David Hartwell, Rob Killheffer, Ginjer Buchanan, Don Keller, and, as always, all the contributors.

Contents

Introduction

In *Blood Is Not Enough*, I wanted to extend the boundaries of what a vampire is—expand the bloodsucker image into the concept of vampirism. I believe I succeeded. With *A Whisper of Blood*, I had intended to see just *how* far I could take the concept without any actual bloodsucking. But my editor, and certain avid fans of the vampire-as-entity who had read and enjoyed the first volume, expressed dismay that I planned to include no actual vampires. So . . . here and there among these metaphorical bloodsuckers lurks a vampire or two. You'll know them when you see them.

Admittedly, some of the stories are a stretch—at least three posit *situations* as vampiric in nature. In "The Pool People," the act of rape has drained the victim of her essential selfhood, she no longer trusts herself or others; in "Teratisms," a family's human monster, and a promise, have robbed the siblings of their own lives, their hopes, even their selves; and in "Folly for Three," the bizarre means of keeping a relationship alive not only drains the participants of any love they may feel for each other but ultimately destroys them as well. "Do I Dare to Eat a Peach?" is about the "State" stealing a man's soul, and in both "The Moose Church" and "Mrs. Rinaldi's Angel," dreams have an enervating effect on the dreamer.

The concept of vampirism can be seen as a metaphor for negative relationships. In these stories, our ideas of love and devotion and loyalty—parental, spousal, friendly, student/teacher, employer/employee—are all perverted in some way, and betrayals abound. The factor of betrayal seems inherent in the idea of the vampire: After all, by showing one hospitality (inviting one into your house) you get bitten. By looking for love (seduction), you get bitten and infected (how appropriate in today's sexual climate). And not only is just one person infected, but the contagion spreads—physically, in the case of the vampire; metaphorically, in other sorts of vampirism—one person's perversion, as in "Teratisms," can corrupt the whole family structure; the ripples of faithlessness in "Infidel" can, it is hinted, spread heresy throughout Christendom; the ruling class's desire to maintain the status quo in "Requiem" forces stagnation upon the entire world.

Anyone picking up this book will have encountered the vampire in fiction before—at least, will have seen *Dracula* or *The Lost Boys*—and so will have already developed some ideas or feelings relating to vampirism. For some, the vampire inspires fear, horror, or terror; for others, the vampire is a seductive creature and promises sex, freedom from ordinary restraint, and immortality. Tapping into the preexisting emotional context that the reader brings to the concept of vampirism, the stories gain an extra dimension, an added edge.

The focus is on the negative relationships themselves, and, in most of the stories here, on the victim. Because of this emphasis on the victim's reaction to the rape, the reader doesn't care about the psychology of the rapist—whether he was abused as a child; or if the dependent aged parent is a ravening monster, the plight of the child in devoting herself to his care is highlighted, rather than the misery of the parent—at least for the duration of the storytelling.

On a recent panel at the World Fantasy Convention, Doug Winter claimed that most horror published today supports the status quo and makes us feel safe. He wasn't wrong. He was talking about *bad* horror fiction. Complacency is, to me, the antithesis of good horror. Effective horror should disturb, perhaps disgust, and, hopefully, linger in the mind of the reader, and like all the best fiction should provoke the reader's self-examination. It can do this by using supernatural elements or psychological ones. The supernatural used to be a comforting way of looking at evil. It came from outside of us and so we weren't responsible for it. I think that the real world has become a much more frightening place, and to many people today it seems easier to believe in the monstrosity of man (after Hitler and Hiroshima) than it is to believe in outside devils who made them/us do it. The prominence of the serial killer in real life and in fiction (particularly the ground-breaking novels by Thomas Harris, *Red Dragon* and *The Silence of the Lambs*) has produced a rash of "psycho-killer" novels and stories. Man has become the monster/demon.

I'm a nonbeliever in the supernatural, which doesn't mean I can't be temporarily frightened by good supernatural fiction. Whether horror can accomplish its purpose is of course dependent on the effectiveness of the storytelling. When I was younger, I was more easily influenced and impressed by the fiction I read: I read and reread Fowles's *The Magus* and Hesse's *Steppenwolf*. They told me things about myself that I might have been better off not knowing but I loved them anyway for making me think. I find there is very little so-called mainstream fiction that can still do that for me. But great weird fiction or horror can occasionally accomplish that. For me, the best horror fiction (or any fiction) works on more than one level—the melody first, to get my attention, the middle and lower ranges to hold it, and to force me to reevaluate the story and, far more rarely, the way I live my life. Horror fiction is meant to disturb complacency and challenge assumptions and I hope the stories in *A Whisper of Blood* will do that for all of you.

ELLEN DATLOW, New York

Now I Lay Me Down to Sleep

SUZY McKEE CHARNAS

Charnas's reluctant vampire, Rose, is a far cry from her famous Professor Weyland. She is not aggressive and means no harm. Despite this, her motivation for becoming a vampire is the same as most other vampires—the desire to cheat death and claim immortality for oneself. Although Rose is one of the few actual vampires in this anthology, she is not by nature a predator and this story is a somewhat gentle piece to soothe the reader into the horror to come.

After Rose died, she floated around in a nerve-wracking fog for a time looking for the tunnel, the lights, and other aspects of the near-death experience as detailed in mass-media reports of such events.

She was very anxious to encounter these manifestations since apparently something loomed in the offing, in place of the happy surcease of consciousness her father had insisted on as the sequel to death. The older she had grown, the more inclined Rose had been to opt for Papa Sol's opinion. Maybe he would show up now trying to explain how he was right even though he was wrong, a bewildered figure of light along with Mom and Nana and everybody?

It would be nice to see a familiar face. Rose felt twinges of panic laced with a vague resentment. Here she was with the gratifyingly easy first step taken, and nothing was going on. Since she was still conscious, shouldn't there be something to exercise that consciousness on?

A siren wailed distantly. Suddenly she found herself walking on—or almost on, for her feet made only the memory of contact—the roof of her apartment building with its expensive view eastward across Central Park. She hadn't been to the park in years, nor even outside her own apartment. Her minute terrace had provided quite enough contact with the streets below. As far as Rose was concerned, these streets were not the streets she had grown up in. She preferred the comfortable security of her own apartment.

Being on the roof felt very odd, particularly since it seemed to be broad daylight and cold out. Far below in the street she could see one of the doormen waving down a cab; he wore his overcoat with the golden epaulets on the shoulders. Rose could have sworn she had taken her carefully hoarded pills late at night, in the comfortable warmth of 14C. Why else would she be wearing her blue flannel nightgown?

Turning to go back to the refuge of her own place, she found an Angel standing close behind her. She knew him—it?—at once by its beautifully modeled, long-toed feet, the feet of a Bernini Angel she had seen in an Italian church on a tour with Fred. Indeed, the entire form was exactly that of the stone Angel she remembered, except that the exposed skin was, well, skin-toned, which she found unsettling. Like colorizing poor old Humphrey Bogart.

"Leave me alone," she said. "I don't want to go."

"You'll go," the Angel said in a drifting, chiming voice that made her ears itch. "Eventually. Everyone does. Are you sure you want to stand out there like that? I wouldn't say anything, but you're not really used to it yet."

Rose looked down and discovered that she had unwittingly backed off or through or over the parapet and now hovered nineteen stories above the street. She gasped and flailed about, for though she had no body to fall—nor for that matter arms to flail or breath to gasp with—sensory flashes still shot along her shadowy, habitual nerve pathways.

Thus the Angel's fingers closed, cool and palpable, on hers and lifted her lightly back onto the roof. She snatched her hand back at once. No one had touched her in years except her doctor, and that didn't count.

But it was not really the Angel's touch she feared.

"I don't want to go anywhere," she said, unable to bring herself to mention by name the anywhere she did not wish to go. "I'm a suicide. I killed myself."

"Yes," the Angel said, clasping its hands in front of its chest the way Dr. Simkin always used to do when he was about to say something truly outrageous. But it said nothing more.

"Well, how does—how do you, um, all feel about that, about people who kill themselves?" She knew the traditional answer, but dared to hope for a different one.

The Angel pursed its perfect lips. "Grouchy," it replied judiciously.

Unwillingly Rose recalled instances from the Old Testament of God's grouchiness. Actually there had been no Bible in her parents' house. She had read instead a book of Bible stories slipped to her one birthday by Nana and kept hidden from Papa Sol. Even watered down for kids, the stories had been frightening. Rose trembled.

"I was brought up an atheist," she said faintly.

The Angel answered, "What about the time you and Mary Hogan were going to run away and enter a convent together?"

"We were kids, we didn't know anything," Rose objected. "Let me stay here. I'm not ready."

"You can't stay," the Angel said. Its blank eyes contrasted oddly with its earnest tone of voice. "Your soul without its body is light, and as memories of the body's life fade, the spirit grows lighter, until you'll just naturally rise and drift."

"Drift? Drift where?" Rose asked.

"Up," the Angel said. Rose followed the languid gesture of one slender hand and saw what might to living eyes seem just a cloud bank. She knew it was nothing of the kind. It was a vast, angry, looming presence of unmistakable portent.

She scuttled around trying to put the Angel between herself and the towering form. At least the face of cloud was not looking at her. For the moment. Luckily there was lots else to look down disapprovingly at in New York City, most of it a good deal more entertaining than Rose Blum.

She whispered urgently to the Angel, "I changed my mind, I want to go back. I can see now, there are worse things than having your cats die and your kids plan to put you away someplace for your own good. Let them, I'll go, they can have my money, I don't care."

"I'm sorry," the Angel said, and Rose suddenly saw herself from above, not her spirit self but her body, lying down there in the big white tub. The leaky old faucets still dribbled in a desultory way, she noted with an exasperated sigh. Her "luxury" building had high ceilings and the rooms were sizable, but the plumbing was ancient.

Her pale form lay half submerged in what looked like rust-stained water. Funny, she had forgotten entirely that after the pills she had taken the further step of cutting her wrists in the bath. The blue nightgown was an illusion of habit.

Not a bad body for her age, she reflected, though it was essentially an Old World model, chunky flesh on a short-boned frame. The next generation grew tall and sleek, a different species made for playing tennis and wearing the clothes the models in the magazines wore. Though her granddaughter Stephanie, now that she thought of it, was little, like Rose herself; petite, but not so wide-hipped, an improved version of the original import wth a flavor of central Europe and probably an inclination to run to fat if allowed.

Good heavens, somebody was in there, also looking at her—two men, Bill the super and Mr. Lum the day concierge! Rose recoiled, burning with shame. Her vacated body couldn't even make the gestures of modesty.

They were talking, the two of them. She had given them generous holiday tips for years to repay them for helping her organize a life that had never required her to leave her apartment after Fred's death and the consequent money squabbles in the family.

Bill said, "Two mil at least, maybe more on account of the terrace."

Mr. Lum nodded. "Forgot the terrace," he said.

She wished she hadn't tipped them at all. She wished her body didn't look so—well—dead. Definitively dead.

"Okay, I can't go back," she admitted to the Angel, relieved to find herself alone with it on the roof again. "But there must be something I can do besides go—you know." She shuddered, thinking of the monstrous shape lowering above her—a wrathful, a terrible, a vengeful God. She needed time to get used to the idea, after Papa Sol and a lifetime of living in the world had convinced her otherwise. Why hadn't somebody told her?

Well, somebody besides Mary Hogan, who had been a Catholic, for crying out loud.

"Well," the Angel said, "you can postpone."

"Postpone," Rose repeated eagerly. "That's right, that's exactly what I had in mind. How do I postpone?"

The Angel said, "You make yourself a body out of astral material: this." Its slim hand waved and a blur of pale filaments gathered at the tapered fingertips.

"Where did that stuff come from?" Rose said nervously. Was the Angel going to change form or disintegrate or do something nasty like something in a horror movie?

"It's all around everybody all the time," the Angel said, "because the physical world and the nonphysical world and everything in between interpenetrate and occupy the same space and time interminably."

"I don't understand physics," Rose said.

"You don't need to," the Angel said. "Astral sculpting is easy, you'll get the hang of it. With a body made of this, you can approach living people and ask them to help you stay. At night, anyway—that's when they'll be able to see you."

Rose thought of Bill and Mr. Lum standing there talking about the value of her apartment. Then she thought of her kids whom she hadn't liked for quite a while and who didn't seem to like her either. Not much use asking them for anything. Maybe Frank, the elevator man? He had always struck her as decent.

"Help, how?" she asked.

"By letting you drink their blood," said the Angel.

Appalled, Rose said nothing for a moment. Down below, a taxi pulled in at the awning and disgorged a comically foreshortened figure. Rose watched this person waddle into the building. "Drink their blood," she said finally. "I'm supposed to go around drinking blood, like Dracula?"

The Angel said, "You need the blood to keep you connected with the physical world. But you can't take it against a person's will, you have to ask. That's the meaning of the business about having to be invited into the donor's house. The house is a metaphor for the physical shell—"

"I'm a vampire?" Rose cried, visions of Christopher Lee and Vampirella and the rest from late-night TV flashing through her stunned mind.

"You are if you want to put off going up," the Angel said with a significant glance skyward. "Most suicides do."

Rose didn't dare look up and see if the mighty cheek of cloud had turned her way.

"That's why suicides were buried at crossroads," the Angel went on, "to prevent their return as vampires."

"Nobody gets buried at a crossroad!"

"Not now," the Angel agreed, "and cremation is so common; but ashes don't count. It's no wonder there's a vampire craze in books and movies. People sense their presence in large numbers in the modern world."

"This is ridiculous," Rose burst out. "I want to see somebody senior to you, I want to talk to the person in—"

She stopped. The Person in charge was not likely to be sympathetic.

The Angel said, "I'm just trying to acquaint you with the rules."

"I'm dead," Rose wailed. "I shouldn't have rules!"

"It's not all bad," the Angel said hastily. "You can make your astral body as young as you like, for instance. But sunlight is a problem. Living people have trouble seeing astral material in sunlight."

For the first time in years she wished Fred were around, that con man. He could have found a way out of this for her if he'd felt like showing off.

"It's not fair!" Rose said. "My G— Listen, what about crosses? Am I supposed to be afraid of crosses?"

"Well," the Angel said, "in itself the cross is just a cross, but there's the weight of the dominant culture to consider, and all its symbols. When western people see a cross, what are they most likely to think of, whether they're personally Christians or not?"

Rose caught herself in time to avoid glancing upward at the shadow giant in the sky. Little charges of terror ran through her so that she felt herself ripple like a shower curtain in a draft. No poor scared dead person would be able to hold her astral self together under that kind of stress.

The Angel began to move away from her, pacing solemnly on the air over the street where a cab trapped by a double-parked delivery truck was honking dementedly.

"Wait, wait," Rose cried, ransacking her memory of *Dracula*, which she and her sister had read to each other at night by flashlight one winter. "What about crossing water? Is it true that a vampire can't cross water?"

"Running water can disorient you very severely," the Angel said over its exquisite shoulder. "You could find yourself visiting places you never meant to go to instead of the ones you did."

Water flows downhill, Rose thought. Down. Hell was down, according to Mary Hogan, anyway. She made a shaky mental note: Don't cross running water.

"How am I supposed to remember all this?" she wailed.

The Angel rose straight into the air without any movement of the translucent wings she now saw spreading from its back. "Just think of the movies," it said. "Film is the record of the secret knowledge of the cultural unconscious."

"You sound like Dr. Simkin, that terrible shrink my daughter sent me to," Rose accused the floating figure.

"I was Harry Simkin," the Angel replied. "That's why I'm doing your intake work." It folded its aristocratic hands and receded rapidly toward the high, rolling clouds.

"My God, you were a young man," Rose called after it. "Nobody told me you died."

The door onto the roof burst open with a crash and two boys lugging heavily weighted plastic bags tumbled out, shouting. Ignoring Rose, they rushed to the parapet. Each one took a spoiled grapefruit out of one of the bags and leaned out into space, giggling and pointing, choosing a passing car roof to aim for.

Rose sidled up to the smaller one and cleared her throat. As loudly as she could she said, "Young man, how would you like to meet a real vampire?"

He lobbed a grapefruit and ducked behind the parapet, howling in triumph at the meaty sound of impact from below but apparently deaf to Rose's voice. Revolting child. Rose bent over and tried to bite his neck. He didn't seem to notice. But she couldn't unwrap the scarf he wore, her fingers slipped through the fabric. So she aimed for a very small patch of exposed skin, but she had no fangs that she could discover and made no impression on his grimy neck.

The whole thing was a ludicrous failure. Worse, she couldn't imagine how it could work, which did not augur well for her future as a vampire. Maybe the Angel had lied. Maybe it was really a devil in disguise. She had never trusted that Simkin anyway.

Worst of all, she was continually aware of the looming, ever-darkening presence, distant but palpable to her spirit, of Him Whom Papa Sol had scoffed at with good socialist scorn. It was all so unfair! Since He was up there after all, why didn't He do something about these horrible boys instead of harassing a poor dead old woman?

Rose didn't want Him witnessing her ineptitude, which might inspire Him to drag her up there to face Him right now. She gave up on the grapefruit-hurling boys and drifted back down to 14C.

It gave her some satisfaction to sift under the sealed apartment door in the form of an astral mist. She floated around admiring the handsomely appointed rooms; she had always had excellent taste.

In the bathroom the tub was empty and reeked of pine-scented disinfectant. Someone had already made off with her silver-backed hairbrush, she noted. But what did that matter, given that her strides were unusually long and slightly bounding, as if she were an astronaut walking on the moon? This could only mean that she was lightening up, just as the Angel had warned.

Frantically she clawed astral material out of the air and patted it into place as best she could, praying that in the absence of blood this astral gunk itself might help to hold her down until somebody came and consented to be a—donor. Her children would come, if only to calculate the considerable value of her things. She was determined to greet them as herself, or as near to that as she could get, to cushion the shock of her request for their donations.

She couldn't see herself in the mirror to check the likeness or to inspect her mouth for fangs. Astral material had a number of limitations, it seemed, among them inability to cast a reflection. She couldn't even turn on the television; her astral fingers wouldn't grip the switch. She couldn't pick up things, the Chinese figurines and fine French clocks that she had brought back from travel and had converted into lamps. Very nice lamps, too. Fred had done his import deals or whatever had been really going on—half the time she had thought him a secret arms trader—but Rose was the one who had had the eye.

My God, she'd been a shopper!

How light she was, how near to drifting—up. No wonder vampires were so urgent about their hunger. By the time Bill the super showed up with two yuppies in tow, Rose felt that for the first time she understood what her daughter Roberta used to mean by that awful phrase "strung out."

Bill was saying, "—first refusal on the lease, that's the law, but if nobody in the old lady's family wants to take it up, then—"

He saw her—the windowpanes, Rose noted, were now dark—and turned red. "I don't know how you got in here, lady, but you'll have to leave."

He didn't seem to recognize her. Of course he wasn't expecting her. Maybe she hadn't done such a hot job with the astral stuff?

She said firmly, "Bill, I have every right to be here, and if these are prospective new tenants you've sneaked in for bribe money, they ought to know that I'm staying."

The young woman said, "Excuse me, but who is this?"

The color drained from Bill's face. He said hoarsely, "What are you doing here, Mrs. Blum? You were dead in the tub, I found you." He waved his arms. "You can't stay here!"

"Let's cut the crap, all right?" the young man said. He thrust money at Rose. Several fifties and three of his fingers went through her forearm.

"Ted, she's a ghost," the woman said, clutching at his coat. "She must be the ghost of the woman who died here."

"Well," Ted said, letting his extended hand float slowly back down to his side. "Tiffany, honey, I think you're right. So, uh, what would you think about living in a haunted, I mean, co-occupying with, um? I'm sure we could work something out, a sort of time-share arrangement? I mean, look at the height of these ceilings."

Rose said, "Sure, we can fix it. All I need is for you to let me drink a little blood now and then. You could take turns."

"Ah, Jesus," sobbed Bill.

Tiffany's eyes bulged. "It's not a ghost," she gasped. "It's a vampire."

"How much blood, exactly?" Ted said, pale but still game.

"I don't exactly know," Rose said. "We'd have to experiment a little at first—"

They fled.

"That's a ten-thousand-dollar finder's fee you cost me!" howled Bill the super, lunging at her.

His breath reached her before he did, and Rose felt her careful astral assemblage fly apart. He had been eating garlic, and the fumes acted on her new body like acid. Her consciousness bounced around like a beach ball in the slipstream of a speeding truck as her body dissolved.

Bill jammed his fist into his mouth and ran, slamming the door so hard behind him that a very nice French Empire miniature fell off the wall.

"Garlic," said a familiar voice. "It's a remarkable food. Completely dissolves the cohesability of astral material."

Grabbing for errant parts of her body, Rose grumbled, "Why didn't you tell me?"

"I tried to cover everything," the Angel said.

"Listen, Dr. Simkin," Rose said. "I can't do this. I'm no vampire. I'm a nice Jewish girl."

"A nice Jewish radical girl, not religious at all," the Angel reminded her. "You named your first cat Emma Goldman."

"We were all freethinkers in those days but so what? A Jew is a Jew, and Jews don't have vampires. I can't do this blood-drinking thing. It's not natural."

The Angel sighed. "It's your choice, of course, but you'll have to go up. Your life review is overdue as it is."

Rose thought of God reviewing her life. "What about you?" she said desperately. "You must be drinking blood yourself, to be sticking around driving me crazy like this. You could spare me some."

"Oh, no," the Angel said, "I do all my work strictly on the astral, nothing physical at all. I don't need weight."

"Why do you look like that?" Rose said. "Harry Simkin didn't look like that, don't think I don't remember."

"Well, I like it," the Angel answered rather shyly. "And I thought it would reassure you. You always had a good eye for art, Mrs. Blum."

"A lot of good it does me now," she said. "Listen, I want to talk to Fred. You know Fred, my husband?"

The Angel cocked its head to one side and rolled its blank eyes. Then it said, "Sorry, he's not available. He's finished his processing and moved on to another stage."

"What stage?" Rose said, feeling a surprising twinge of apprehension for Fred. She remembered all those *New Yorker* cartoons showing fat-bellied businessmen making glum quips to each other in hell, with pitchfork-toting devils leering in the background.

"Don't you think you have enough to deal with as it is?" the Angel countered. "You're bobbing, you know, and your head isn't on straight. It won't be long at this rate."

"I'll find somebody," Rose said quickly. "I need more time to get used to the idea."

"Don't take too long," the Angel said. "Isn't it interesting? This is the first time you've asked me about anybody who's come before you."

"What?" said Rose. "Anybody, who? Who should I ask about? I've been on my own for twenty years. Who cares for an old woman, so who should I care for?"

The Angel, inspecting its fingernails again, drifted silently out through the pane of the closed window.

It was very quiet in the apartment. The walls in these old buildings were very thick, with real plaster. Rose had peace and quiet in which to reassemble herself. It wasn't much fun—no point in making yourself look like, say, Marilyn Monroe if you couldn't see yourself in the mirror—and it wasn't easy, either. At one point she looked down and realized she had formed up the shape of her most recent cat, Mimsy, on a giant scale.

She was losing contact with her physical life, and nobody was likely to come around and help her reestablish it again for a while. Maybe never, if Bill the super went gibbering about what he'd seen in the apartment.

She hovered in front of the family photographs on the wall over the living-room mantel. The light was hard to see by, odd and watery—was it day or night?—but she knew who was who by memory: Papa Sol and Mama; Auntie Lil with that crazed little dog of hers, Popcorn was its name (God, she missed Mimsy, and the others); the two Kleinfeldt cousins who had gone to California and become big shots in television production; Nana in her old-fashioned bathing suit at Coney Island; Uncle Herb; more cousins. She had completely lost track of the cousins.

There was one picture of Fred, and several of the two cute babies who had turned into Mark and Roberta. I should have stuck to shopping and skipped the kids, she thought.

Two pictures showed Rose herself, once amid the cousins now scattered to their separate marriages and fates, and once with two school friends, girls whose names now escaped her. As everything seemed bent on escaping her. She sat in the big wing chair and crossed her astral arms and rocked herself, whispering, "Who cares for an old woman?"

There was no help, and no safe place. She had to hold on to the arms of her chair to keep from floating several inches off the seat. If she didn't get some blood to drink soon, she would float up before that huge, angry face in the sky and be cast into hell on a bolt of black thunder—

The door opened cautiously and a man walked into the apartment. It was her lawyer, Willard.

"Oh, my God," he murmured, looking straight at her. "They told me the place was haunted. Mrs. Blum, is that you?"

"Yes," she said. "What time is it, Willard?"

"Seven-thirty," he said, still staring. "I stayed late at the office."

Seven-thirty on a November evening; of course he could see her. She hoped her head was on straight and that it was her own head and not Mimsy's.

"Oh, Willard," she said, "I've been having the most terrible time." She stopped. She had never talked to anyone like that, or at least not for a very long time.

"No doubt, no doubt," he said, steadying himself against the hall table and putting his briefcase down carefully on the floor. "Do you still keep scotch in the breakfront?"

She did, for the occasional visitor, of which scant number Willard had been one. He poured himself a drink with shaking hands and gulped it, his eyes still fixed on Rose. He poured himself another. "I think I'd better tell you," he said in a high, creaky tone very unlike him, "this haunting business could have serious repercussions on the disposition of your estate."

"It's not haunting, exactly," Rose said, gliding toward him. She told him what it was, exactly.

"Ha, ha, you're kidding, Mrs. Blum," Willard said, smiling wildly and turning a peculiar shade of yellow. He staggered backward against the edge of the couch, turned, and fell headlong. His glass rolled across the carpet and clinked against the baseboard. Rose saw a pale mist drift out of the top of Willard's head as his body thrashed briefly in the throes of what she immediately recognized as a heart attack like the one that had killed Fred.

"Willard, wait," she cried, seeing that his foggy spirit stuff was rapidly escaping upward into the ceiling. "Don't leave me!"

But he did.

Rose knelt by the body, unable to even attempt to draw its still and cooling blood. The Angel didn't show. Willard Carnaby must have gone directly wherever he was headed. She felt abandoned and she cried, or something like it, not for Willard, who had known, as usual, where to go and how to get there with a minimum of fuss, but for herself, Rose the vampire.

After they took the body away nobody came for days. Rose didn't dare to go out. She was afraid she would get lost in the uncertain light; she was afraid she would run into the outwash from some restaurant kitchen and be blasted to such smithereens by garlic fumes that she would never be able to get herself together again; she was afraid of water running in the gutters and crosses on churches. She was afraid of the eyes of God.

She was bumping helplessly against the bedroom ceiling in a doomed panic when someone did arrive. Not Roberta (as she at first thought because of the honey-gold hair) but Stephanie, from the next generation; her granddaughter, who wanted to be—what? An actress. She was certainly pretty enough, and so young. Rose blinked hungrily at her.

Someone was with her, a boy. Stephanie pulled back the curtains and daylight streamed in. She would not be able to see Rose, maybe not even hear her.

Rose noticed something new—a shimmer of color and motion around Stephanie, and another around this boy. If she concentrated hard, while floating after them as they strolled through the place giggling and chatting with their heads together, Rose could see little scenes like bits of color TV taking place within the aura of each of the young people: quick little loops of the two of them tangled in each other's arms in his, and a rapid wheel of scenes in Stephanie's aura involving this boy dancing with her, applauding from an excited audience, showing her off to important people.

Their hopes and dreams were visible to Rose, like sit-com scenes without sound. The walking-on-the-beach scene, a comfortable winter beach with gray skies and green sea and no sand fleas, Rose recognized at once. She had had the same fantasy about Fred. While he was having, no doubt, fantasies like this boy's, of sex,

sex, and more sex; and sex with another girl, some friend of Stephanie's—

"Dump him, Stephanie, he's nothing but a wolf," she said indignantly, out loud.

The boy was too rapt in his hormones to hear. Stephanie frowned and glanced sharply around the room.

"Come on," the boy said. "Who'd know? It would be exciting." Good grief, he was proposing that the two of them make love right here—on the floor, on Rose's antique Chinese carpet! Rose saw the little scene clearly in his aura.

Stephanie hesitated. Then she tossed her honey hair and called him an idiot and tugged him out of the place by the hand. But she came back. She came back alone after dark and without turning on the lights she sat down quietly in the big wing chair by the window.

"I heard you, Gramma Rose," she said softly, looking wide-eyed around the room. "I heard what you said to me about Jeff, and you're right, too. I know you're here. The stuff about the apartment being haunted is true, isn't it? I know you're here, and I'm not scared of you. You can come out, you can talk to me. Really. I'd like it."

Rose hung back, timid and confused now that her moment had come. After all, did she really want her grandchild's presumably fond memories of Gramma Rose replaced with the memory of Rose the vampire?

Stephanie said, "I won't go until you come talk to me, Gramma Rose."

She curled up on Rose's empty bed and went to sleep.

Rose watched her dreams winking and wiggling in her aura. Such an appealing mixture of cynicism and naïveté, so unlike her mother. Fascinated, Rose observed from the ceiling where she floated.

Involuntarily reacting to one of the little scenes, she murmured, "It's not worth fighting with your mother; just say yes and go do what you want."

Stephanie opened her eyes and looked directly up. Her jaw dropped. "Gramma Rose," she squeaked. "I see you! What are you doing up there?"

"Stephanie darling," Rose said in the weak, rusty voice that was all she could produce now, "you can help me. Will you help me?"

"Sure," Stephanie said, sitting up. "Didn't you stop me from making an utter idiot of myself with Jeff Stanhope, which isn't his real name of course, and he has a gossip drive on him that just won't quit. I don't know what I was thinking of, bringing him up here, except that he's cute of course, but actors are mostly cute. It's his voice, I think, it's sort of hypnotic. But you woke me up, just like they say, a still, small voice. So what can I do for you?"

"This will sound a little funny," Rose said anxiously—to have hope again was almost more than she could bear—"but could you stand up in the bed and let me try to drink a little blood from your neck?"

"Ew." Stephanie stared up at her. "You're kidding."

Rose said, "It's either that or I'm gone, darling. I'm nearly gone as it is."

"But why would it help to, ugh, suck a person's blood?"

"I need it to weigh me down, Stephanie. You can see how high I'm drifting. If I don't get some blood to anchor me, I'll float away."

"How much do you need?" Stephanie said cautiously.

"From you, darling, just a little," Rose assured her. "You have a rehearsal in the morning, I don't want to wear you out. But if you let me take a little, I can stay, I can talk to you."

"You could tell me all about Uncle Herb and whether he was gay or not," Stephanie said, "and whether Great-Grandpa really left Hungary because of a quarrel with a hussar or was he just dodging the draft like everybody else—all the family secrets."

Rose wasn't sure she remembered those things, but she could make up something appropriate. "Yes, sure."

"Is this going to hurt?" Stephanie said, getting up on her knees in the middle of the mattress.

"It doesn't when they do it in the movies," Rose said. "But, Stephanie, even if there's a little pinprick, wouldn't that be all right? Otherwise I have to go, and, and I don't want to."

"Don't cry, Gramma Rose," Stephanie said. "Can you reach?" She leaned to one side and shut her eyes.

Rose put her wavery astral lips to the girl's pale skin, thinking, FANGS. As she gathered her strength to bite down, a warm sweetness flowed into her mouth like rich broth pouring from a bowl. She stopped almost at once for fear of overdoing it.

"That's nice," Stephanie murmured. "Like a toke of really good grass."

Rose, flooded with weight and substance that made her feel positively bloated after her recent starvation, put her arm around Stephanie's shoulders and hugged her. "Just grass," she said, "right? You don't want to poison your poor old dead gramma."

Stephanie giggled and snuggled down in the bed. Rose lay beside her, holding her lightly in her astral arms and whispering stories and advice into Stephanie's ear. From time to time she sipped a little blood, just for the thrill of feeling it sink through her newly solid form, anchoring it firmly to her own familiar bed.

Stephanie left in the morning, but she returned the next day with good news. While the lawyers and the building owners and the relatives quarreled over the fate of the apartment and everything in it (including the ghost that Bill the super wouldn't shut up about), Stephanie would be allowed to move in and act as caretaker.

She brought little with her (an actress has to learn to travel light, she told Rose), except her friends. She would show them around the apartment while she told them how the family was fighting over it, and how it was haunted, which made everything more complicated and more interesting, of course. Rose herself was never required to put in a corroborating appearance. Stephanie's delicacy about this surprised and pleased Rose.

Still, she preferred the times when Stephanie stayed home alone studying her current script, which she would declaim before the full-length mirror in the bedroom. She was a terrible show-off, but Rose supposed you had to be like that to be on the stage.

Rose's comments were always solicited, whether she was visible or not. And she always had a sip of blood at bedtime.

Of course this couldn't go on forever, Rose understood that. For one thing, at the outer edges of Stephanie's aura of thoughts and dreams she could see images of a different life, somewhere cool and foggy and hemmed in with dark trees, or city streets with a vaguely foreign look to them. She became aware that these outer images were of likely futures that Stephanie's life was moving toward. They didn't seem to involve staying at Rose's.

She knew she should be going out to cultivate alternative sources for the future—vampires could "live" forever, couldn't they—but she didn't like to leave in case she couldn't get back for some reason, like running water, crosses, or garlic.

Besides, her greatest pleasure was coming to be that of floating invisibly in the air, whispering advice to Stephanie based on foresight drawn from the flickering images she saw around the girl:

"It's not a good part for you, too screechy and wild. You'd hate it."

"That one is really ambitious, not just looking for thrills with pretty actresses."

"No, darling, she's trying to make you look bad—you know you look terrible in yellow."

Rose became fascinated by the spectacle of her granddaughter's life shaping itself, decision by decision, before her astral eyes. So that was how a life was made, so that was how it happened! Each decision altered the whole mantle of possibilities and created new chains of potentialities, scenes and sequences that flickered and fluttered in and out of probability until they died or were drawn in to the center to become the past.

There was a young man, another one, who came home with Stephanie one night, and then another night. Rose, who drowsed through the days now because there was nothing interesting going on, attended eagerly, and invisibly, on events. The third night Rose whispered, "Go ahead, darling, it wouldn't be bad. Try the Chinese rug."

They tumbled into the bed after all; too bad. The under rug should be used for something significant, it had cost her almost as much per yard as the carpet itself.

Other people's loving looked odd. Rose was at first embarrassed and then fascinated and then bored: bump bump bump, squeeze, sigh, had she really done that with Fred? Well, yes, but it seemed very long ago and sadly meaningless. The person with whom it had been worth all the fuss had been—whatsisname, it hovered just beyond memory.

Fretful, she drifted up onto the roof. The clouds were there, the massive form turned toward her now. She cringed but held her ground. No sign from above one way or the other, which was fine with her.

The Angel chimed, "How are you, Rose?"

Rose said, "So what's the story, Simkin? Have you come to reel me in once and for all?"

"Would you mind very much if I did?"

Rose laughed at the Angel's transparent feet, its high, delicate arches. She was keenly aware of the waiting form of the cloud-giant, but something had changed.

"Yes," she said, "but not so much. Stephanie has to learn to judge things for herself. Also, if she's making love with a boy in the bedroom knowing I'm around, maybe she's taking me a little for granted. Maybe she's even bored by the whole thing."

"Or maybe you are," the Angel said.

"Well, it's her life," Rose said, feeling as if she were breaking the surface of the water after a deep dive, "not mine."

The Angel said, "I'm glad to hear you say that. This was never intended to be a permanent solution."

As it spoke, a great throb of anxiety and anger reached Rose from Stephanie.

"Excuse me," she said, and she dropped like a plummet back to her apartment.

The two young people were sitting up in bed facing each other with the table lamp on. The air vibrated with an anguish connected with the telephone on the bed table. In the images dancing in Stephanie's aura Rose read the immediate past: There had been a call for the boy, a screaming voice raw with someone else's fury. He had just explained to Stephanie, with great effort and in terror that she would turn away from him. The girl was indeed filled with dismay and resentment. She couldn't accept this dark aspect of his life because it had all looked so bright to her before, for both of them.

Avoiding her eyes, he said bitterly, "I know it's a mess. You have every right to kick me out before you get any more involved."

Rose saw the pictures in his aura, some of them concerned with his young sister who went in and out of institutions and, calamitously, in and out of his life. But many showed this boy holding Stephanie's hand, holding Stephanie, applauding Stephanie from an audience, sitting with Stephanie on the porch of a wooden house amid dark, tall trees somewhere—

Rose looked at Stephanie's aura. This boy was all over it. Invisible, Rose whispered in Stephanie's ear, "Stick with him, darling, he loves you and it looks like you love him, too."

At the same moment she heard a faint echo of very similar words in Stephanie's mind. The girl looked startled, as if she had heard this, too.

"What?" the boy said, gazing at her with anxious intensity.

Stephanie said, "Stay in my life. I'll try to stay in yours."

They hugged each other. The boy murmured into her neck, where Rose was accustomed to take her nourishment, "I was so afraid you'd say no, go away and take your problems with you—"

Seeing the shine of tears in the boy's eyes, Rose felt the remembered sensation of tears in her own. As she watched, their auras slowly wove together, flickering and bleeding colors into each other. This seemed so much more intimate than sex that Rose felt she really ought to leave the two of them alone.

The Angel was still on the roof, or almost on it, hovering above the parapet.

Rose said, "She doesn't need me anymore; she can tell herself what to do as well as I can, probably better."

"If she'll listen," the Angel said.

Rose looked down at the moving lights of cars on the street below. "All right," she said. "I'm ready. How do I get rid of the blood I got from Stephanie this morning?"

"You mean this?" The Angel's finger touched Rose's chest, where a warm red glow beat in the place where her heart would have been. "I can get rid of it for you, but I warn you, it'll hurt."

"Do it," Rose said, powered by a surging impatience to get on with something of her own for a change, having been so immersed in Stephanie's raw young life—however long it was now. Time was much harder to divide intelligibly than it had been.

The Angel's finger tapped once, harder, and stabbed itself burningly into her breast. There came a swift sensation of what it must feel like to have all the marrow drawn at once from your bones. Rose screamed.

She opened her eyes and looked down, gasping, at the Angel. Already she was rising like some light, vaned seed on the wind. She saw the Angel point downward at the roof with one glowing, crimson finger. One flick and a stream of bright fire shot down through the shadowy outline of the building and landed—she saw it happen, the borders of her vision were rushing away from her in all directions—in the kitchen sink and ran away down the drain.

Stephanie turned her head slightly and murmured, "What was that? I heard something."

The boy kissed her temple. "Nothing." He gathered her closer and rolled himself on top of her, nuzzling her. What an appetite they had, how exhausting!

Other voices wove in and out of their murmuring voices. Rose could see and hear the whole city as it slowly sank away below her, a net of lights slung over the dark earth.

But above her—and she no longer needed to direct her vision to see what was there but saw directly with her mind's eye—the sky was thick with a massed and threatening darkness that she knew to be God: still waiting, scowling, implacable, for His delayed confrontation with Rose.

Despite the panic pulsating through her as the inevitable approached, she couldn't help noticing that there was something funny about God. The closer she got, the more His form blurred and changed, so that she caught glimpses of tiny figures moving, colors surging, skeins of ceaseless activity going on all at once and overlapping inside the enormous cloudy bulk of God.

She recognized the moving figures: Papa Sol, teasing her at the breakfast table by telling her to look, quick, at the horse on the windowsill, and grabbing one of the strawberries from her cereal while she looked with eager, little-girl credulity; Roberta, crying and crying in her crib while grown-up Rose hovered in the hallway torn between exhaustion and rage and love and fear of doing the wrong thing no matter what she did; Fred, sparkling with lying promises he'd never meant to keep, but pleased to entertain her with them; Stephanie, with crooked braids and scabby knees, counting the pennies from the penny jar that Rose had once kept for her. And that was the guy, there, Aleck Mills, one of Fred's associates, with whom love had felt like love.

If she looked beyond these images, Rose realized that she could see, deeper in the maze, the next phase of each little scene, and the next, the whole spreading tangle of consequences that she was here to witness, to comprehend, and to judge.

The web of her awareness trembled as it soared, curling in on itself as if caught in a draught of roasting air.

"Simkin, where are you?" she cried.

"Here," the Angel answered, bobbing up alongside of her and looking, for once, a bit flustered with the effort of keeping up. "And you don't need me anymore. Guardian angels don't need guardian angels."

"Now I lay me down to sleep," Rose said, remembering that saccharine Humperdinck opera she had taken Stephanie to once at Christmas time, years ago, because it was supposed to be for kids. "A bunch of vampires watch do keep?"

"You could put it that way," the Angel said.

"What about Dracula?" Rose said. "Could I have done that instead?"

"Sure," the Angel said. "There's always a choice. Who do you think it is who goes around making deals for the illusion of immortal life? And the price isn't anything as romantic as your soul. It's just a little blood, for as long as you're willing."

"And when you stop being willing?"

The Angel flashed its blank eyes upward. "Your life will wait as long as it has to."

"I'm scared of my life," Rose confessed. "I'm scared there's nothing worthwhile in it, nothing but furniture, and statuettes made into lamps."

"Kid," the Angel said, "you should have seen mine."

"Yours?"

"Full of people I tried to make into furniture, all safe and comfortable, with lots of dust cuzzies stuck underneath."

"What's in mine?" Rose said.

"Go and see," the Angel said gently.

"I am, I'm going," Rose said. In her heart she moaned, This will be hard, this is going to be so hard.

But she was heartened by a little scene flickering high up where God's eye would have been if there had been a god instead of this mountain of Rose's own life, and in that scene Stephanie and the boy did walk together on a winter beach. By the way they hugged and turned up their collars and hurried along, it was cold and windy there; but they kept close together and made blue-lipped jokes about the cold.

Beyond them, beyond the edges of the cloud-mountain itself, Rose could make out nothing yet. Perhaps there was nothing, just as Papa Sol had promised. On the other hand, she thought, whirling aloft, so far Papa Sol had been 100 percent dead wrong.

I never expected to write another vampire story after *The Vampire Tapestry*, but Ellen said, "C'mon, c'mon," and after a while something started (as a story about people walking their dogs, actually, but that's one reason I am so slow to produce work—everything starts somewhere else and the real story has to be teased out into the light). And pretty soon I was working on the old bloodsucker concept with a different perspective than that which produced Dr. Weyland, my 1980 model of the beast.

For one thing, I'm fifty years old and more inclined than I was to contemplate last things. Also, like many of my generation I have numerous elderly relatives, most of them (though not all) female, most of them living alone; so maybe it's not at all surprising that this story became Rose's story. I'm glad it did.

And then, too, the more clearly one recognizes that what's frightening about life in the world is the destructive flailings of people's fears, and the more sophisticated those fears become in a sophisticated age, the more quaintly baroque become such fusty old creatures of superstition as vampires; and one's approach alters accordingly.

On the other hand (not for nothing am I a Libra), I recently did a collaboration with Quinn Yarbro for the purposes of which I woke up Weyland. Now he won't lie down again, and he is a bit light in the quaint and endearing departments. So who knows what coloring my next outing into this territory may take (if indeed there is a next outing that is fit to see print)? That's the nice thing about the career of making up stories—you can always change your mind and tell it the *other* way next time.

Suzy McKee Charnas

The Slug

KARL EDWARD WAGNER

Here is a rather harsh view of those who interrupt the artist at work—I wouldn't even want to speculate as to how close this story is to the author's heart. . . .

Martine was hammering away to the accompaniment of Lou Reed, tapedeck set at stun, and at first didn't hear the knocking at her studio door. She set aside hammer and chisel, put Lou Reed on hold, and opened the door to discover Keenan Bauduret seated on her deck rail, leaning forward to pound determinedly at her door. The morning sun shone bright and cheery through the veil of pines, and Keenan was shit-faced drunk.

"Martine!" He lurched toward her. "I need a drink!"

"What you need is some coffee." Martine stood her ground. At six feet and change she was three inches taller than Keenan and in far better shape.

"Please! I've got to talk to someone." Keenan's soft brown eyes implored. He was disheveled and unshaven in baggy clothes that once had fit him, and Martine thought of a stray spaniel, damp and dirty, begging to be let in. And Keenan said: "I've just killed someone. I mean, some thing."

Martine stepped inside. "I can offer gin and orange juice."

"Just the gin."

Keenan Bauduret collapsed onto her wooden rocking chair and mopped at his face with a crumpled linen handkerchief, although the morning was not yet warm. Now he reminded her of Bruce Dern playing a dissolute southern lawyer, complete with out-of-fashion and rumpled suit; but in fact Keenan was a writer, although dissolute and southern to be sure. He was part of that sort of artist/writer colony that the sort of small university town such as Pine Hill attracts. Originally he was from New Orleans, and he was marking time writing mystery novels while he completed work on the Great Southern Novel. At times he taught creative writing for the university's evening college.

Martine had installed a wet bar complete with refrigerator and microwave in a corner of her studio to save the walk back into her house when she entertained here. She sculpted in stone, and the noise and dust were better kept away from her single-bedroom cottage. While Keenan sweated, she looked for glasses and ice.

"Just what was it you said that you'd killed?"

"A slug. A gross, obscene, mammoth, and predatory slug."

"Sounds rather like a job for Orkin. Did you want your gin neat?"

"Just the naked gin."

Martine made herself a very light gin screwdriver and poured a double shot of Tanqueray into Keenan's glass. Her last name was still McFerran, and she had her father's red hair, which she wore in a long ponytail, and his Irish blue eyes and freckled complexion. Her mother was Scottish and claimed that her side of the family was responsible for her daughter's unexpected height. Born in Belfast, Martine had grown up in Pine Hill as a faculty brat after her parents took university posts here to escape the troubles in Northern Ireland. Approaching the further reaches of thirty, Martine was content with her bachelorhood and her sculpture and had no desire to return to Belfast.

"Sure you don't want orange juice?" She handed the glass to Keenan.

Keenan shook his head. "To your very good health." He swallowed half the gin, closed his eyes, leaned back in the rocker and sighed. He did not, as Martine had expected, tip over.

Martine sat down carefully in her prized Windsor chair. She was wearing scuffed Reeboks, faded blue jeans, and a naturally torn university sweatshirt, and she pushed back her sleeves before tasting her drink.

"Now, then," she said, "tell me what really happened."

Keenan studied his gin with the eye of a man who is balancing his need to bolt the rest of it against the impropriety of asking for an immediate refill. Need won.

"Don't get up." He smiled graciously. "I know the way."

Martine watched him slosh another few ounces of gin into his glass, her own mood somewhere between annoyance and concern. She'd known Keenan Bauduret casually for years, well before he'd hit the skids. He was a few years older than she, well read and intelligent, and usually fun to be around. They'd never actually dated, but there were the inevitable meetings at parties and university town cultural events, lunches and dinners and a few drinks after.

Keenan had never slept over, nor had she at his cluttered little house. It was that sort of respectful friendship that arises between two lonely people who are content within their self-isolation, venturing forth for nonthreatening companionship without ever sensing the need.

"I've cantelope in the fridge," Martine prompted.

"Thanks. I'm all right." Keenan returned to the rocker. He sipped his gin this time. His hands were no longer shaking. "How well do you know Casper Crowley?"

"Casper the Friendly Ghost?" Martine almost giggled. "Hardly at all. That is, I've met him at parties, but he never has anything to say to anyone. Just stands stuffing himself with chips and hors d'oeuvres—I've even seen him pocket a few beers as he's left. I'm told he's in a family business, but no one seems to know what the business is—and he writes books that no one I know has ever read for publishers no one has heard of. He's so dead dull boring that I always wonder why anyone ever invites him."

"I've seen him at your little gatherings," Keenan accused.

"Well, yes. It's just that I feel sorry for poor boring Casper."

"Exactly." Keenan stabbed a finger and rested his case. "That's what happened to me. You won't mind if I have another drink while I tell you about it?"

Martine sighed mentally and tried not to glance at her watch.

His greatest mistake, said Keenan, was ever to have invited Casper Crowley to drop by in the first place.

It began about two years ago. Keenan was punishing the beer keg at Greg Lafollette's annual birthday bash and pig-picking. He was by no means sober, or he never would have attempted to draw Casper into conversation. It was just that Casper stood there, wrapped in his customary loneliness, mechanically feeding his face with corn chips and salsa, washing it down with great gulps of beer, as expressionless as a carp taking bread crumbs from atop a pool.

"How's it going, Casper?" Keenan asked harmlessly.

Casper shaved his scalp but not his face, and he had bits of salsa in his bushy orange beard. He was wearing a tailored tweed suit whose vest strained desperately to contain his enormous beer gut. He turned his round, bland eyes toward Keenan and replied: "Do you know much about Aztec gods?"

"Not really, I suppose."

"In this book I'm working on," Casper pursued, "I'm trying to establish a link between the Aztecs and Nordic mythology."

"Well, I do have a few of the usual sagas stuck away on my shelves." Keenan was struggling to imagine any such link.

"Then would it be all right if I dropped by your place to look them over?"

And Casper appeared at ten the following morning, while Keenan was drying off from his shower, and he helped himself to coffee and doughnuts while Keenan dressed.

"Hope I'm not in your way." Casper was making a fresh pot of coffee.

"Not at all." Keenan normally worked mornings through the afternoon, and he had a pressing deadline.

But Casper plopped down on his couch and spent the next few hours leafing without visible comprehension through various of Keenan's books, soaking up coffee, and intermittently clearing his throat and swallowing horribly. Keenan no longer felt like working after his guest had finally left. Instead he made himself a fifth rum and Coke and fell asleep watching *I Love Lucy*.

At ten the following morning, Keenan had almost reworked his first sentence of the day when Casper phoned.

"Do you know why a tomcat licks his balls?"

Keenan admitted ignorance.

"Because he can!"

Casper chuckled with enormous relish at his own joke, while Keenan scowled at the phone. "How about going out to get some barbecue for lunch?" Casper then suggested.

"I'm afraid I'm really very busy just now."

"In that case," Casper persisted, "I'll just pick us up some sandwiches and bring them on over."

And he did. And Casper sat on Keenan's couch, wolfing down barbecue sandwiches with the precision of a garbage disposal, dribbling gobbets of sauce and cole slaw down his beard and belly and onto the upholstery. Keenan munched his soggy sandwich, reflecting upon the distinction between the German verbs, *essen* (to eat) and *fressen* (to devour). When Casper at last left, it was late afternoon, and Keenan took a nap that lasted past his usual dinnertime. By then the day had long since slipped away.

He awoke feeling bloated and lethargic the next morning, but he was resolved to make up for lost time. At ten-thirty Casper appeared on his doorstep, carrying a bag of chocolate-covered raspberry jelly doughnuts.

"Do you know how many mice it takes to screw in a light bulb?" Casper asked, helping himself to coffee.

"I'm afraid I don't."

"Two—but they have to be real small!" Jelly spurted down Casper's beard as he guffawed. Keenan had never before heard someone actually guffaw; he'd always assumed it was an exaggerated figure of speech.

Casper left after about two in the afternoon, unsuccessful in his efforts to coax Keenan into sharing a pizza with him. Keenan returned to his desk, but inspiration was dead.

And so the daily routine began.

"Why didn't you just tell him to stay away and let you work?" Martine interrupted.

"Easy enough to say," Keenan groaned. "At first I just felt sorry for him. OK, the guy is lonely—right? Anyway, I really was going to tell him to stop bugging me every day—and then I had my accident."

A rain-slick curve, a telephone pole, and Keenan's venerable VW Beetle was grist for the crusher. Keenan fared rather better, although his left foot would wear a plaster sock for some weeks after.

Casper came over daily with groceries and bottles of beer and rum. "Glad to be of help," he assured Keenan as he engulfed most of a slice of pepperoni-and-mushroom pizza. Sauce obscured his beard. "Must be tough having to hobble around day after day. Still, I'll bet you're getting a lot of writing done."

"Very little," Keenan grudgingly admitted. "Just haven't felt up to it lately."

"Guess you haven't. Hey, do you know what the difference is between a circus and a group of sorority girls out jogging?"

"I give up."

"Well, one is a cunning array of stunts!" Casper chortled and wiped red sauce from his mouth. "Guess I better have another beer after that one!"

Keenan missed one deadline, and then he missed another. He made excuses owing to his accident. Deadlines came around again. The one novel he did manage to finish came back with requests for major revisions. Keenan worked hard at the rewrite, but each new effort was only for the worse. He supposed he ought to cut down on his drinking, but the stress was keeping him awake nights, and he kept having nightmares wherein Casper crouched on his chest and snickered bad jokes and dribbled salsa. His agent sounded concerned, and his editors were losing patience.

"Me," said Casper, "I never have trouble writing. I've always got lots of ideas."

Keenan resisted screaming at the obese hulk who had camped on his sofa throughout the morning. Instead he asked civilly: "Oh? And what are you working on now?"

"A follow-up to my last book—by the way, my publisher really went ape-shit over that one, wants another like it. This time I'm writing one that traces the rise of Nazi Germany to the Druidic rites at Stonehenge."

"You seem to be well versed in the occult," observed Keenan, repressing an urge to vomit.

"I do a lot of research," Casper explained. "Besides, it's in my blood. Did I ever tell you that I'm related to Aleister Crowley?"

"No."

"Well, I am." Casper beamed with secret pride.

"I should have guessed."

"Well, the name, of course."

Keenan had been thinking of other similarities. "Well, I really do need to get some work done now."

"Sure you don't need me to run you somewhere?"

"No, thank you. The ankle is a little sore, but I can get around well enough."

At the door, Casper persisted: "Sure you don't want to go get some barbecue?"

"Very sure."

Casper pointed toward the rusted-out Chevy wagon in Keenan's driveway. "Well, if that heap won't start again, just give me a call."

"I put in a new battery," Keenan said, remembering that the mechanic had warned him about the starter motor. Keenan had bought the clunker for three hundred bucks—from a student. He needed wheels, and wheels were about all that did work on the rust-bucket. His insurance hadn't covered replacement for his antique Beetle.

"Heard you had to return your advance on that Zenith contract."

"Where'd you hear that?" Keenan wanted to use his fists.

"My editor—your old editor—brought it up when we were talking contract on my new book the other day. She said for me to check out how you were getting along. Sounded concerned. But I told her you were doing great, despite all the talk."

"Thanks for that much."

"Hey, you know the difference between a sorority girl and a bowling ball?"

Keenan did not trust himself to speak.

"No? Well, you can't stuff a sorority girl into a bowling ball!"

After the university informed Mr. Bauduret that his services would no longer be required as instructor of creative writing at the evening college, Keenan began to sell off his books and a few antiques. It kept the wolves at arm's length, and it paid for six-packs. Editors no longer phoned, and his agent no longer answered his calls.

Casper was sympathetic, and he regularly carried over doughnuts and instant coffee, which he consumed while drinking Keenan's beer.

"Zenith gobbled up *Nazi Druids*," he told Keenan. "They can't wait for more."

The light in Keenan's eyes was not the look of a sane man. "So, what's next?"

"I got an idea. I've discovered a tie-in between flying saucers and the Salem witch burnings."

"They hanged them. Or pressed them. No burnings in this country."

"Whatever. Anyway, I bought a bunch of your old books on the subject at the Book Barn the other day. Guess I won't need to borrow them now."

"Guess not."

"Hey, you want some Mexican for lunch? I'll pay."

"Thank you, but I have some work to do."

"Good to see you're still slugging away."

"Not finished yet."

"Guess some guys don't know when they're licked."

"Guess not."

"Hey"—Casper chugged his beer—"you know what the mating cry of a sorority girl is?"

Keenan gritted his teeth in a hideous grin.

Continued Casper in girlish falsetto: "Oh, I'm so-o-o drunk!" His belly shook with laughter, although he wasn't Santa. "Better have another beer on that one!"

And he sat there on the couch, methodically working his way through Keenan's stock of beer, as slowly mobile and slimy gross as a huge slug feasting its way across the garden. Keenan listened to his snorts and belches, to his puerile and obscene jokes, to his pointless and inane conversation, too drained and too weak to beg him to leave. Instead he swallowed his beer and his bile, and fires of loathing stirred beneath the ashes of his despair.

That night Keenan found the last bottle of rum he'd hidden away against when the shakes came at dawn, and he dug out the vast file of typed pages, containing all the fits and starts and notes and revisions and disconnected chapters that were the entirety of his years' efforts toward the Great Southern Novel.

He had a small patio, surrounded by a neglected rock garden and close-shouldering oak trees, and he heaped an entire bag of charcoal into the barbecue grill that rusted there. Then Keenan sipped from the bottle of Myers, waiting for the coals to take light. When the coals had reached their peak, Keenan Bauduret fed his manuscript, page by crumpled page, onto the fire; watched each page flame and char, rise in dying ashes into the night.

"That was when I knew I had to kill Casper Crowley."

Martine wasn't certain whether she was meant to laugh now. "Kill Casper? But he was only trying to be your friend! I'm sure you can find a way to ask him to give you your space without hurting his feelings."

Keenan laughed instead. He poured out the last of her gin. "A friend? Casper was a giant grotesque slug! He was a gross leech that sucked out my creative energy! He fed off me and watched over me with secret delight as I wasted away!"

"That's rather strong."

"From the first day the slug showed up on my doorstep, I could never concentrate on my work. When I did manage to write, all I could squeeze out was dead, boring, lifeless drivel. I don't blame my publishers for sending it back!"

Martine sighed, wondering how to express herself. She did rather like Keenan; she certainly felt pity for him now. "Keenan, I don't want to get you upset, but you have been drinking an awful lot this past year or so. . . ."

"Upset?" Keenan broke into a wild grin and a worse laugh, then suddenly regained his composure. "No need for me to be upset now. I've killed him."

"And how did you manage that?" Martine was beginning to feel uneasy.

"How do you kill a slug?"

"I thought you said he was a leech."

"They're one and the same."

"No they're not."

"Yes they are. Gross, bloated, slimy things. Anyway, the remedy is the same."

"I'm not sure I'm following you."

"Salt." Keenan seemed in complete control now. "They can't stand salt."

"I see." Martine relaxed and prepared herself for the joke.

Keenan became very matter-of-fact. "Of course, I didn't forget the beer. Slugs are drawn to beer. I bought many six-packs of imported beer. Then I prepared an enormous barbecue feast—chicken, ribs, pork loin. Casper couldn't hold himself back."

"So you pushed his cholesterol over the top, and he died of a massive coronary."

"Slugs can't overeat. It was the beer. He drank and drank and drank some more, and then he passed out on the patio lounge chair. That was my chance."

"A steak through the heart?"

"Salt. I'd bought dozens of bags of rock salt for this. Once Casper was snoring away, I carried them out of my station wagon and ripped them open. Then, before he could awaken, I quickly dumped the whole lot over Casper."

"I'll bet Casper didn't enjoy that."

"He didn't. At first I was afraid he'd break away, but I kept pouring the rock salt over him. He never said a word. He just writhed all about on the lounge chair, flinging his little arms and legs all about, trying to fend off the salt."

Keenan paused and swallowed the last of the gin. He wiped his face and shuddered. "And then he began to shrivel up."

"Shrivel up?"

"The way slugs do when you pour salt on them. Don't you remember? Remember doing it when you were a kid? He just started to shrivel and shrink. And shrink and shrink. Until there was nothing much left. Just a dried-out twist of slime. No bones. Just dried slime."

"I see."

"But the worst part was the look in his eyes, just before they withered on the ends of their stalks. He stared right into my eyes, and I could sense the terrible rage as he died."

"Stalks?"

"Yes. Casper Crowley sort of changed as he shriveled away."

"Well. What did you do then?"

"Very little to clean up. Just dried slime and some clothes. I waited through the night, and this morning I burned it all on the barbecue grill. Wasn't much left, but it sure stank."

Keenan looked at his empty glass, then glanced hopefully at the empty bottle. "So now it's over. I'm free."

"Well," said Martine, ignoring his imploring gaze, "I can certainly see that you've regained your imagination."

"Best be motivating on home now, I guess." Keenan stood up, with rather less stumbling that Martine had anticipated. "Thanks for listening to my strange little story. Guess I didn't expect you to believe it all, but I had to talk to someone."

"Why not drive carefully home and get some sleep," Martine advised, ushering him to the door. "This has certainly been an interesting morning."

Keenan hung on to the door. "Thanks again, Martine. I'll do just that. Hey, what do you say I treat you to Chinese tomorrow for lunch? I really feel a whole lot better after talking to you."

Martine felt panic, then remorse. "Well, I am awfully busy just now, but I guess I can take a break for lunch."

Martine sat back down after Keenan had left. She was seriously troubled, wondering whether she ought to phone Casper Crowley. Clearly Keenan was drinking far too heavily; he might well be harboring some resentment. But harm anyone . . . No way. Just some unfunny attempt at a shaggy dog story. Keenan never could tell jokes.

When she finally did phone Casper Crowley, all she got was his answering machine.

Martine felt strangely lethargic—her morning derailed by Keenan's bursting in with his inane patter. Still, she thought she really should get some work done on her sculpture.

She paused before the almost finished marble, hammer and chisel at ready, her mind utterly devoid of inspiration. She was working on a bust of a young woman—the proverbial artist's self-portrait. Martine squared her shoulders and set chisel to the base of the marble throat.

As the hammer struck, the marble cracked through to the base.

Not much need be said, actually. Every writer—every creative person—lives in dread of those nagging and inane interruptions that break the creative flow. A sentence perfectly crystallized, shattered by a stupid phone call, never regained. A morning filled with inspiration and energy, clogged by an uninvited guest, the day lost. The imaginative is the choice prey of the banal, and uncounted works of excellence have died stillborn thanks to junk phone calls and visits from bored associates.

After all, a writer doesn't have a real job. Feel free to crash in at any time. Probably wants some company.

Nothing in this story is in any way a reflection upon this one writer's various friends, nor does it in any way resemble any given actual person or composite of any persons known to the author. It is entirely a fictitious work and purely the product of the author's imagination.

It has taken me five days to scribble out this afterword.

There's the door. . . .

Karl Edward Wagner

Warm Man

ROBERT SILVERBERG

This story, the first of many that Robert Silverberg sold to Fantasy & Science Fiction *magazine, juxtaposes Aickman-esque tone and subtlety with a satire of suburban manners. In it, he explores the dangerous addiction of an empath.*

No one was ever quite sure just when Mr. Hallinan came to live in New Brewster. Lonny Dewitt, who ought to know, testified that Mr. Hallinan died on December 3, at 3:30 in the afternoon, but as for the day of his arrival no one could be nearly so precise.

It was simply that one day there was no one living in the unoccupied split-level on Melon Hill, and then the next *he* was there, seemingly having grown out of the woodwork during the night, ready and willing to spread his cheer and warmth throughout the whole of the small suburban community.

Daisy Moncrieff, New Brewster's ineffable hostess, was responsible for making the first overtures toward Mr. Hallinan. It was two days after she had first observed lights on in the Melon Hill place that she decided the time had come to scrutinize the newcomers, to determine their place in New Brewster society. Donning a light wrap, for it was a coolish October day, she left her house in the early forenoon and went on foot down Copperbeech Road to the Melon Hill turnoff, and then climbed the sloping hill till she reached the split-level.

The name was already on the mailbox: DAVID HALLINAN. That probably meant they'd been living there a good deal longer than just two days, thought Mrs. Moncrieff; perhaps they'd be insulted by the tardiness of the invitation? She shrugged and used the doorknocker.

A tall man in early middle age appeared, smiling benignly. Mrs. Moncrieff was thus the first recipient of the uncanny warmth that David Hallinan was to radiate throughout New Brewster before his strange death. His eyes were deep and solemn, with warm lights shining in them; his hair was a dignified gray-white mane.

35

"Good morning," he said. His voice was deep, mellow.

"Good morning. I'm Mrs. Moncrieff—*Daisy* Moncrieff, from the big house on Copperbeech Road. You must be Mr. Hallinan. May I come in?"

"Ah—please, no, Mrs. Moncrieff. The place is still a chaos. Would you mind staying on the porch?"

He closed the door behind him—Mrs. Moncrieff later claimed that she had a fleeting view of the interior and saw unpainted walls and dust-covered bare floors—and drew one of the rusty porch chairs for her.

"Is your wife at home, Mr. Hallinan?"

"There's just me, I'm afraid. I live alone."

"Oh." Mrs. Moncrieff, discomforted, managed a grin nonetheless. In New Brewster *everyone* was married; the idea of a bachelor or a widower coming to settle there was strange, disconcerting . . . and just a little pleasant, she added, surprised at herself.

"My purpose in coming was to invite you to meet some of your new neighbors tonight—if you're free, that is. I'm having a cocktail party at my place about six, with dinner at seven. We'd be so happy if you came!"

His eyes twinkled gaily. "Certainly, Mrs. Moncrieff. I'm looking forward to it already."

The *ne plus ultra* of New Brewster society was impatiently assembled at the Moncrieff home shortly after 6, waiting to meet Mr. Hallinan, but it was not until 6:15 that he arrived. By then, thanks to Daisy Moncrieff's fearsome skill as a hostess, everyone present was equipped with a drink and a set of speculations about the mysterious bachelor on the hill.

"I'm sure he must be a writer," said Martha Weede to liverish Dudley Heyer. "Daisy says he's tall and distinguished and just *radiates* personality. He's probably here only for a few months—just long enough to get to know us all, and then he'll write a novel about us."

"Hmm. Yes," Heyer said. He was an advertising executive who commuted to Madison Avenue every morning; he had an ulcer, and was acutely aware of his role as a stereotype. "Yes, then he'll write a sizzling novel exposing suburban decadence, or a series of acid sketches for *The New Yorker*. I know the type."

Lys Erwin, looking desirable and just a bit disheveled after her third martini in thirty minutes, drifted by in time to overhear that.

"You're *always* conscious of *types*, aren't you darling? You and your gray flannel suit?"

Heyer fixed her with a baleful stare but found himself, as usual, unable to make an appropriate retort. He turned away, smiled hello at quiet little Harold and Jane Dewitt, whom he pitied somewhat (their son Lonny, age 9, was a shy, sensitive child, a total misfit among his playmates), and confronted the bar, weighing the probability of a night of acute agony against the immediate desirability of a Manhattan.

But at that moment Daisy Moncrieff reappeared with Mr. Hallinan in tow, and conversation ceased abruptly throughout the parlor while the assembled guests stared at the newcomer. An instant later, conscious of their collective faux pas, the group began to chat again, and Daisy moved among her guests, introducing her prize.

"Dudley, this is Mr. David Hallinan. Mr. Hallinan, I want you to meet Dudley Heyer, one of the most talented men in New Brewster."

"Indeed? What do you do, Mr. Heyer?"

"I'm in advertising. But don't let them fool you; it doesn't take any talent at all. Just brass, nothing else. The desire to delude the public, and delude 'em good. But how about you? What line are you in?"

Mr. Hallinan ignored the question. "I've always thought advertising was a richly creative field, Mr. Heyer. But, of course, I've never really known at firsthand—"

"Well, I have. And it's everything they say it is." Heyer felt his face reddening, as if he had had a drink or two. He was becoming talkative, and found Hallinan's presence oddly soothing. Leaning close to the newcomer, Heyer said, "Just between you and me, Hallinan, I'd give my whole bank account for a chance to stay home and *write*. Just write. I want to do a novel. But I don't have the guts; that's my trouble. I know that come Friday there's a $350 check waiting on my desk, and I don't dare give that up. So I keep writing my novel up here in my head, and it keeps eating me away down here in my gut. *Eating*." He paused, conscious that he had said too much and that his eyes were glittering beadily.

Hallinan wore a benign smile. "It's always sad to see talent hidden, Mr. Heyer. I wish you well."

Daisy Moncrieff appeared then, hooked an arm through Hallinan's, and led him away. Heyer, alone, stared down at the textured gray broadloom.

Now why did I tell him all that? he wondered. A minute after meeting Hallinan, he had unburdened his deepest woe to him—something he had not confided in anyone else in New Brewster, including his wife.

And yet—it had been a sort of catharsis, Heyer thought. Hallinan had calmly soaked up all his grief and inner agony, and left Heyer feeling drained and purified and warm.

Catharsis? Or a blood-letting? Heyer shrugged, then grinned and made his way to the bar to pour himself a Manhattan.

As usual, Lys and Leslie Erwin were at opposite ends of the parlor. Mrs. Moncrieff found Lys more easily, and introduced her to Mr. Hallinan.

Lys faced him unsteadily, and on a sudden impulse hitched her neckline higher. "Pleased to meet you, Mr. Hallinan. I'd like you to meet my husband, Leslie. *Leslie!* Come here, please?"

Leslie Erwin approached. He was twenty years older than his wife, and was generally known to wear the finest pair of horns in New Brewster—a magnificent spread of antlers that grew a new point or two almost every week.

"Les, this is Mr. Hallinan. Mr. Hallinan, meet my husband, Leslie."

Mr. Hallinan bowed courteously to both of them. "Happy to make your acquaintance."

"The same," Erwin said. "If you'll excuse me, now—"

"The louse," said Lys Erwin when her husband had returned to his station at the bar. "He'd sooner cut his throat than spend two minutes next to me in public." She glared bitterly at Hallinan. "I don't deserve that kind of thing, do I?"

Mr. Hallinan frowned sympathetically. "Have you any children, Mrs. Erwin?"

"Hah! He'd never give me any—not with *my* reputation! You'll have to pardon me; I'm a little drunk."

"I understand, Mrs. Erwin."

"I know. Funny, but I hardly know you and I like you. You seem to *understand*. Really, I mean." She took his cuff hesitantly. "Just from looking at you, I can tell you're not judging me like all the others. I'm not really *bad*, am I? It's just that I get so *bored*, Mr. Hallinan."

"Boredom is a great curse," Mr. Hallinan observed.

"Damn right it is! And Leslie's no help—always reading his newspapers and talking to his brokers! But I can't help myself, believe me." She looked around wildly. "They're going to start talking about us in a minute, Mr. Hallinan. Every time I talk to someone new they start whispering. But promise me something—"

"If I can."

"Someday—someday soon—let's get together? I want to *talk* to you. God, I want to talk to someone—someone who understands why I'm the way I am. Will you?"

"Of course, Mrs. Erwin. Soon." Gently he detached her hand from his sleeve, held it tenderly for a moment, and released it. She smiled hopefully at him. He nodded.

"And now I must meet some of the other guests. A pleasure, Mrs. Erwin."

He drifted away, leaving Lys weaving shakily in the middle of the parlor. She drew in a deep breath and lowered her décolletage again.

At least there's one decent man in this town now, she thought. There was something *good* about Hallinan—good, and kind, and understanding.

Understanding. That's what I need. She wondered if she could manage to pay a visit to the house on Melon Hill tomorrow afternoon without arousing too much scandal.

Lys turned and saw thin-faced Aiken Muir staring at her slyly, with a clear-cut invitation on his face. She met his glance with a frigid, wordless *go to hell*.

Mr. Hallinan moved on, on through the party. And, gradually, the pattern of the party began to form. It took shape like a fine mosaic. By the time the cocktail hour was over and dinner was ready, an intricate, complex structure of interacting thoughts and responses had been built.

Mr. Hallinan, always drinkless, glided deftly from one New Brewsterite to the next, engaging each in conversation, drawing a few basic facts about the other's personality, smiling politely, moving on. Not until after he moved on did the person come to a dual realization: that Mr. Hallinan had said quite little, really, and that he had instilled a feeling of warmth and security in the other during their brief talk.

And thus while Mr. Hallinan learned from Martha Weede of her paralyzing envy of her husband's intelligence and of her fear of his scorn, Lys Erwin was able to remark to Dudley Heyer that Mr. Hallinan was a remarkably kind and understanding person. And Heyer, who had never been known to speak a kind word of anyone, for once agreed.

And later, while Mr. Hallinan was extracting from Leslie Erwin some of the pain his wife's manifold infidelities caused him, Martha Weede could tell Lys Erwin, "He's so gentle—why, he's almost like a saint!"

And while little Harold Dewitt poured out his fear that his silent 9-year-old son Lonny was in some way subnormal, Leslie Erwin, with a jaunty grin, remarked to Daisy Moncrieff, "That man must be a psychiatrist. Lord, he knows how to talk to a person. Inside of two minutes he had me telling him all my troubles. I feel better for it, too."

Mrs. Moncrieff nodded. "I know what you mean. This morning, when I went up to his place to invite him here, we talked a little while on his porch."

"Well," Erwin said, "if he's a psychiatrist he'll find plenty of business here. There isn't a person here riding around without a private monkey on his back. Take Heyer, over there—he didn't get that ulcer from happiness. That scatterbrain Martha Weede, too—married to a Columbia professor who can't imagine what to talk to her about. And my wife Lys is a very confused person, too, of course."

"We all have our problems," Mrs. Moncrieff sighed. "But I feel much better since I spoke with Mr. Hallinan. Yes: *much* better."

Mr. Hallinan was now talking with Paul Jambell, the architect. Jambell, whose pretty young wife was in Springfield Hospital slowly dying of cancer. Mrs. Moncrieff could well imagine what Jambell and Mr. Hallinan were talking about.

Or rather, what Jambell was talking about—for Mr. Hallinan, she realized, did very little talking himself. But he was such a *wonderful* listener! She felt a pleasant glow, not entirely due to the cocktails. It was good to have someone like Mr. Hallinan in New Brewster, she thought. A man of his tact and dignity and warmth would be a definite asset.

When Lys Erwin woke—alone, for a change—the following morning, some of the past night's curious calmness had deserted her.

I have to talk to Mr. Hallinan, she thought.

She had resisted two implied, and one overt, attempts at seduction the night before, had come home, had managed even to be polite to her husband. And Leslie had been polite to her. It was most unusual.

"That Hallinan," he had said. "He's quite a guy."

"You talked to him, too?"

"Yeah. Told him a lot. Too much, maybe. But I feel better for it."

"Odd," she had said. "So do I. He's a strange one, isn't he? Wandering around that party, soaking up everyone's aches. He must have had half the neuroses in New Brewster unloaded on his back last night."

"Didn't seem to depress him, though. More he talked to people, more cheerful and affable he got. And us, too. You look more relaxed than you've been in a month, Lys."

"I *feel* more relaxed. As if all the roughness and ugliness in me was drawn out."

And that was how it felt the next morning, too. Lys woke, blinked, looked at the empty bed across the room. Leslie was long since gone, on his way to the city. She knew she had to talk to Hallinan again. She hadn't gotten rid of it all. There was still some poison left inside her, something cold and chunky that would melt before Mr. Hallinan's warmth.

She dressed, impatiently brewed some coffee, and left the house. Down Copperbeech Road, past the Moncrieff house where Daisy and her stuffy husband Fred were busily emptying the ashtrays of the night before, down to Melon Hill and up the gentle slope to the split-level at the top.

Mr. Hallinan came to the door in a blue checked dressing gown. He looked slightly seedy, almost overhung, Lys thought. His dark eyes had puffy lids and a light stubble sprinkled his cheeks.

"Yes, Mrs. Erwin?"

"Oh—good morning, Mr. Hallinan. I—I came to see you. I hope I didn't disturb you—that is—"

"Quite all right, Mrs. Erwin." Instantly she was at ease. "But I'm afraid I'm really extremely tired after last night, and I fear I shouldn't be very good company just now."

"But you said you'd talk to me alone today. And—oh, there's so much more I want to tell you!"

A shadow of feeling—*pain? fear?* Lys wondered—crossed his face. "No," he said hastily. "No more—not just yet. I'll have to rest today. Would you mind coming back—well, say Wednesday?"

"Certainly, Mr. Hallinan. I wouldn't want to disturb you."

She turned away and started down the hill, thinking: *He had too much of our troubles last night. He soaked them all up like a sponge, and today he's going to digest them—*

Oh, what am I thinking?

She reached the foot of the hill, brushed a couple of tears from her eyes, and walked home rapidly, feeling the October chill whistling around her.

And so the pattern of life in New Brewster developed. For the six weeks before his death, Mr. Hallinan was a fixture at any important community gathering, always dressed impeccably, always ready with his cheerful smile, always uncannily able to draw forth whatever secret hungers and terrors lurked in his neighbors' souls.

And invariably Mr. Hallinan would be unapproachable the day after these gatherings, would mildly but firmly turn away any callers. What he did, alone in the house on Melon Hill, no one knew. As the days passed, it occurred to all that no one knew much of anything about Mr. Hallinan. He knew *them* all right, knew the one night of adultery twenty years before that still racked Daisy Moncrieff, knew the acid pain that seared Dudley Heyer, the cold envy glittering in Martha Weede, the frustration and loneliness of Lys Erwin, her husband's shy anger at his own cuckoldry—he knew these things and many more, but none of them knew more of him than his name.

Still, he warmed their lives and took from them the burden of their griefs. If he chose to keep his own life hidden, they said, that was his privilege.

He took walks every day, through still-wooded New Brewster, and would wave and smile to the children, who would wave and smile back. Occasionally he would stop, chat with a sulking child, then move on, tall, erect, walking with a jaunty stride.

He was never known to set foot in either of New Brewster's two churches. Once Lora Harker, a mainstay of the New Brewster Presbyterian Church, took him to task for this at a dull party given by the Weedes.

But Mr. Hallinan smiled mildly and said, "Some of us feel the need. Others do not."

And that ended the discussion.

Toward the end of November a few members of the community experienced an abrupt reversal of their feelings about Mr. Hallinan—weary, perhaps, of his constant empathy for their woes. The change in spirit was spearheaded by Dudley Heyer, Carl Weede, and several of the other men.

"I'm getting not to trust that guy," Heyer said. He knocked dottle vehemently from his pipe. "Always hanging around soaking up gossip, pulling out dirt—and what the hell for? What does *he* get out of it?"

"Maybe he's practicing to be a saint," Carl Weede remarked quietly. "Self-abnegation. The Buddhist Eightfold Path."

"The women all swear by him," said Leslie Erwin. "Lys hasn't been the same since he came here."

"*I'll* say she hasn't," said Aiken Muir wryly, and all of the men, even Erwin, laughed, getting the sharp thrust.

"All I know is I'm tired of having a father-confessor in our midst," Heyer said. "I think he's got a motive back of all his goody-goody warmness. When he's through pumping us he's going to write a book that'll put New Brewster on the map for good."

"You always suspect people of writing books," Muir said. *"Oh, that mine enemy would write a book . . . !"*

"Well, whatever his motives I'm getting annoyed. And that's why he hasn't been invited to the party we're giving on Monday night." Heyer glared at Fred Moncrieff as if expecting some dispute. "I've spoken to my wife about it, and she agrees. Just this once, dear Mr. Hallinan stays home."

It was strangely cold at the Heyers' party that Monday night. The usual people were there, all but Mr. Hallinan. The party was not a success. Some, unaware that Mr. Hallinan had not been invited, waited expectantly for the chance to talk to him, and managed to leave early when they discovered he was not to be there.

"We should have invited him," Ruth Heyer said after the last guest had left.

Heyer shook his head. "No. I'm glad we didn't."

"But that poor man, all alone on the hill while the bunch of us were here, cut off from us. You don't think he'll get insulted, do you? I mean, and cut us from now on?"

"I don't care," Heyer said, scowling.

His attitude of mistrust toward Mr. Hallinan spread through the community. First the Muirs, then the Harkers, failed to invite him to gatherings of theirs. He still took his usual afternoon walks, and those who met him observed a slightly strained expression on his face, though he still smiled gently and chatted easily enough, and made no bitter comments.

And on December 3, a Wednesday, Roy Heyer, age 10, and Philip Moncrieff, age 9, set upon Lonny Dewitt, age 9, just outside the New Brewster Public School, just before Mr. Hallinan turned down the school lane on his stroll.

Lonny was a strange, silent boy, the despair of his parents and the bane of his classmates. He kept to himself, said little, nudged into corners, and stayed there. People clucked their tongues when they saw him in the street.

Roy Heyer and Philip Moncrieff made up their minds they were going to make Lonny Dewitt say something, or else.

It was *or else*. They pummeled him and kicked him for a few minutes; then, seeing Mr. Hallinan approaching, they ran, leaving Lonny weeping silently on the flagstone steps outside the empty school.

Lonny looked up as the tall man drew near.

"They've been hitting you, haven't they? I see them running away now."

Lonny continued to cry. He was thinking, *There's something funny about this man. But he wants to help me. He wants to be kind to me.*

"You're Lonny Dewitt, I think. Why are you crying? Come, Lonny, stop crying! They didn't hurt you that much."

They didn't, Lonny said silently. *I like to cry.*

Mr. Hallinan was smiling cheerfully. "Tell me all about it. Something's bothering you, isn't it? Something big, that makes you feel all lumpy and sad inside. Tell me about it, Lonny, and maybe it'll go away." He took the boy's small cold hands in his own, and squeezed them.

"Don't want to talk," Lonny said.

"But I'm a friend. I want to help you."

Lonny peered close and saw suddenly that the tall man told the truth. He wanted to help Lonny. More than that: he *had* to help Lonny. Desperately. He was pleading. "Tell me what's troubling you," Mr. Hallinan said again.

OK, Lonny thought. *I'll tell you.*

And he lifted the floodgates. Nine years of repression and torment came rolling out in one roaring burst.

I'm alone and they hate me because I do things in my head and they never understood and they think I'm queer and they hate me I see them looking funny at me and they think funny things about me because I want to talk to them with my mind and they can only hear words and I hate them hate them hate hate hate—

Lonny stopped suddenly. He had let it all out, and now he felt better, cleansed of the poison he'd been carrying in him for years. But Mr. Hallinan looked funny. He was pale and white-faced, and he was staggering.

In alarm, Lonny extended his mind to the tall man. And got:

Too much. Much too much. Should never have gone near the boy. But the older ones wouldn't let me.

Irony: the compulsive empath overloaded and burned out by a compulsive sender who'd been bottled up.

... like grabbing a high-voltage wire ...

... he was a sender, I was a receiver, but he was too strong ...

And four last bitter words: *I ... was ... a ... leech. ...*

"Please, Mr. Hallinan," Lonny said out loud. "Don't get sick. I want to tell you some more. Please, Mr. Hallinan."

Silence.

Lonny picked up a final lingering wordlessness, and knew he had found and lost the first one like himself. Mr. Hallinan's eyes closed and he fell forward on his face in the street. Lonny realized that it was over, that he and the people of New Brewster would never talk to Mr. Hallinan again. But just to make sure he bent and took Mr. Hallinan's limp wrist.

He let go quickly. The wrist was like a lump of ice. *Cold—* burningly cold. Lonny stared at the dead man for a moment or two.

"Why, it's dear Mr. Hallinan," a female voice said. "Is he—"

And feeling the loneliness return, Lonny began to cry softly again.

It was January, 1957: my God, a whole lifetime ago. I was in my very early twenties, had just won a Hugo as the best new writer of the year, was producing stories with insane prolificacy, two or three a week. (My ledger entry for that month shows seventeen titles, 85,000 words, and I was just warming up for the *really* productive times a couple of years down the line.)

A phenomenon, I was. And one who took notice of it was Anthony Boucher, the urbane and sophisticated editor of *Fantasy & Science Fiction*. He was a collector at heart, who wanted one of everything for his magazine—including a story by this hypermanic kid from New York who seemed to be able to turn one out every hour. But he wasn't going to relax his high standards simply for the sake of nailing me for his contents page; and so, although he told me in just about so many words that he'd be delighted to publish something of mine, he turned down the first few that I sent him, offering great regrets and hope for the future. What I had to do in order to sell one to him, I told myself, was break free of the pulp-magazine formulas that I had taken such trouble to master, and write something about and for adults. (Not so easy, when I had barely made it to voting age—twenty-one, then—myself!)

The specific genesis of "Warm Man" was a moment at the first Milford Writers' Conference in September, 1956, where Harlan Ellison and I, the two hot young new writers of the moment, were mascots, so to speak, for a galaxy of masters of the field— Theodore Sturgeon, James Blish, Frederik Pohl, Damon Knight, Lester del Rey, C. M. Kornbluth, Fritz Leiber—everyone who was anyone, all of them discussing their lives and their crafts in the most astonishingly open way. During one workshop session involving a Kornbluth story, Cyril had some sort of epiphany about his writing and suddenly cried out in a very loud voice, "Warm!" What that signified to him, I never knew; he declined to share his insight with anyone, though it was obviously a very powerful one. Somehow it set something working in me, though, which very likely had nothing at all to do with whatever passed through Cyril's mind, and out came, a few months later, this tale of psychic vampirism. I sent it to Boucher (who I think had been present at Milford also) and by return mail across the continent came his expression of delight that I had broken the ice at last with him. He ran the story a few months later—May 1957—and put my name on the cover, a signal honor for a newcomer. Boucher was the best kind of editor—a demanding one, yes, but also the kind who is as pleased as you are that you have produced something he wants to publish. He (and a few others back then) helped to teach me the difficult lesson that quantity isn't as effective, in the long run, as quality. Which is demonstrated by this story's frequent reappearance in print over the span of more than three decades since it was written.

Robert Silverberg

Teratisms

KATHE KOJA

Kathe Koja has been building a solid reputation with her enigmatic science fiction and dark fantasy stories for the last few years.

"Teratisms" is a quirky and brutal piece about how even innocence can be ugly and how one family member can enslave or even suck the life out of the others. The family in this story seems cut from the same cloth as the pseudo-family in the film Near Dark.

"Beaumont." Dreamy, Alex's voice. Sitting in the circle of the heat, curtains drawn in the living room: laddered magenta scenes of birds and dripping trees. "Delcambre. Thibodaux." Slow-drying dribble like rusty water on the bathroom floor. "Abbeville," car door slam, "Chin-chuba," screen door slam. Triumphant through its echo, "Baton Rouge!"

Tense hoarse holler almost childish with rage: "Will you shut the fuck *up?*"

From the kitchen, woman's voice, Randle's voice, drawl like cooling blood: "Mitch's home."

"You're damn right Mitch is home." Flat slap of his unread newspaper against the cracked laminate of the kitchen table, the whole set from the Goodwill for thirty dollars. None of the chairs matched. Randle sat in the cane-bottomed one, leg swinging back and forth, shapely metronome, making sure the ragged gape of her tank top gave Mitch a good look. Fanning herself with four slow fingers.

"Bad day, big brother?"

Too tired to sit, propping himself jackknife against the counter. "They're all bad, Francey."

"Mmmm, forgetful. My name's Randle now."

"Doesn't matter what your name is, you're still a bitch."

Soft as dust, from the living room: "De Quincy. Longville." Tenderly, "Bewelcome."

Mitch's sigh. "Numbnuts in there still at it?"

"All day."

Another sigh, he bent to prowl the squat refrigerator, let the door fall shut. Half-angry again, "There's nothing in here to eat, Fran—Randle."

"So what?"

"So what'd you eat?"

More than a laugh, bubbling under. "I don't think you really want to know." Deliberately exposing half a breast, palm lolling beneath like a sideshow, like a street-corner card trick. Presto. "Big brother."

His third sigh, lips closed in decision. "I don't need this," passing close to the wall, warding the barest brush against her, her legs in the chair as deliberate, a sluttish spraddle but all of it understood: an old, unfunny family joke, like calling names; nicknames.

The door slamming, out as in, and in the settling silence of departure: "Is he gone?"

Stiff back, Randle rubbing too hard the itchy tickle of sweat. Pushing at the table to move the chair away. "You heard the car yourself, Alex. You know he's gone."

Pause, then plaintive, "Come sit with me." Sweet; but there are nicknames and nicknames, jokes and jokes; a million ways to say I love you. Through the raddled arch into the living room, Randle's back tighter still, into the smell, and Alex's voice, bright.

"Let's talk," he said.

Mitch, so much later, pausing at the screenless front door, and on the porch Randle's cigarette, drawing lines in the dark like a child with a sparkler.

"Took your time," she said.

Defensively, "It's not that late."

"I know what time it is."

He sat down, not beside her but close enough to speak softly and be heard. "You got another cigarette?"

She took the pack from somewhere, flipped it listless to his lap. "Keep 'em. They're yours anyway."

He lit the cigarette with gold foil matches, JUDY'S DROP-IN. An impulse, shaming, to do as he used to, light a match and hold it to her fingertips to see how long it took to blister. No wonder she hated him. "Do you hate me?"

"Not as much as I hate him." He could feel her motion, half a headshake. "Do you know what he did?"

"The cities."

"Besides the cities." He did not see her fingers, startled twitch as he felt the pack of cigarettes leave the balance of his thigh. "He was down by the grocery store, the dumpster. Playing. It took me almost an hour just to talk him home." A black sigh. "He's getting worse."

"You keep saying that."

"It keeps being true, Mitch, whether you want to think so or not. Something really bad's going to happen if we don't get him—"

"Get him what?" Sour. No bitter. "A doctor? A *shrink?* How about a one-way ticket back to Shitsburg so he—"

"Fine, that's fine. But when the cops come knocking I'll let you answer the door," and her quick feet bare on the step, into the house. Tense unconscious rise of his shoulders: Don't slam the door. Don't wake him up.

Mitch slept, weak brittle doze in the kitchen, head pillowed on the Yellow Pages. Movement, the practiced calm of desire. Stealth, until denouement, a waking startle to Alex's soft growls and tweaks of laughter, his giggle and spit. All over the floor. All over the floor and his hands, oh God Alex your *hands*—

Showing them off the way a child would, elbows turned, palms up. Showing them in the jittery bug-light of the kitchen in the last half hour before morning, Mitch bent almost at the waist, then sinking back, nausea subsiding but unbanished before the immensity, the drip and stutter, there was some on his mouth too. His chin, Mitch had to look away from what was stuck there.

"Go on," he said. "Go get your sister."

And waited there, eyes closed, hands spread like a medium on the Yellow Pages. While Alex woke his sister. While Randle used the washcloth. Again.

Oxbow lakes. Flat country. Randle sleeping in the back seat, curled and curiously hot, her skin ablush with sweat in the sweet cool air. Big creamy Buick with all the windows open. Mitch was driving, slim black sunglasses like a cop in a movie, while Alex sat playing beside him. Old wrapping paper today, folding in his fingers, disappearing between his palms. Always paper. Newsprint ink under his nails. Glossy foilwrap from some party, caught between the laces of his sneakers. Or tied there. Randle might have done that, it was her style. Grim droll jokery. Despite himself he looked behind, into the back seat, into the stare of her open eyes, so asphalt blank that for one second fear rose like a giant waiting to be born and he thought, Oh no, oh not her too.

Beside him Alex made a playful sound.

Randle's gaze snapped true into her real smile; bared her teeth in burlesque before she rolled over, pleased.

"Fucking bitch," with dry relief. With feeling.

Alex said, "I'm hungry."

Mitch saw he had begun to eat the paper. "We'll find a drive-through somewhere," he said, and for a moment dreamed of flinging the wheel sideways, of fast and greasy death. Let someone else clean up for a change.

There was a McDonald's coming up, garish beside the blacktop; he got into the right lane just a little too fast. "Randle," coldly, "put your shirt on."

Chasing the end of the drive-through line, lunchtime and busy and suddenly Alex was out of the car, leaned smiling through the window to say, "I want to eat inside." And gone, trotting across the parking lot, birthday paper forgotten on the seat beside.

"Oh God," Mitch craning, tracking his progress, "go after him, Randle," and Randle's snarl, the bright slap of her sandals as she ran. Parking, he considered driving off. Alone. Leaving them there. Don't you ever leave them, swear me. You have to swear me, Michie. Had she ever really said that? Squeezed out a promise like a dry log of shit? I hope there is a hell, he thought, turning off the car, I hope it's big and hot and eternal and that she's in it.

They were almost to the counter, holding hands. When Randle saw him enter, she looked away; he saw her fingers squeeze Alex's, twice and slow. What was it like for her? Middleman. Alex was staring at the wall menu as if he could read. "I'll get a booth," Mitch said.

A table, instead; there were no empty booths. One by one Alex crumbled the chocolate-chip cookies, licked his fingers to dab up the crumbs. Mitch drank coffee.

"That's making me sick," he said to Randle.

Her quick sideways look at Alex. "What?" through half a mouthful, a tiny glob of tartar sauce rich beside her lower lip.

"That smell," nodding at her sandwich. "Fish."

Mouth abruptly stretched, chewed fish and half-smeared sauce, he really was going to be sick. Goddamned *bitch*. Nudging him under the table with one bare foot. Laughing into her Coke.

"Do you always have to make it worse?"

Through another mouthful, "It can't get any worse." To Alex, "Eat your cookies."

Mitch drank more coffee; it tasted bitter, boiled. Randle stared over his head as she ate: watching the patrons? staring at the wall? Alex coughed on cookie crumbs, soft dry cough. Gagged a little. Coughed harder.

"Alex?" Randle put down her sandwich. "You okay? Slap his back," commandingly to Mitch, and he did, harder as Alex kept coughing, almost a barking sound now and heads turned, a little, at the surrounding tables, a briefest bit of notice that grew more avid as Alex's distress increased, louder whoops and Randle suddenly on her feet, trying to raise him up as Mitch saw the first flecks of blood.

"Oh *shit*," but it was too late, Alex spitting blood now, spraying it, coughing it out in half-digested clots as Randle, frantic, working to haul him upright as Mitch in some stupid reflex swabbed with napkins at the mess. Tables emptied around them. Kids crying, loud and scared, McDonald's employees surrounding them but not too close, Randle shouting, "*Help* me, you asshole!" and Mitch in dumb paralysis watched as a tiny finger, red but recognizable, flew from Alex's mouth to lie wetly on the seat.

Hammerlock, no time to care if it hurts him, Randle already slamming her back against the door to hold it open and Alex's staining gurgle hot as piss against his shoulder, Randle screaming, "Give me the keys! Give me the keys!" Her hand digging hard into his pocket as he swung Alex, white-faced, into the back seat, lost his balance as the car jerked into gear and fell with the force of motion to his temple, dull and cool, against the lever of the seat release.

And lay there, smelling must and the faint flavor of motor oil, Alex above collapsed into silence, lay a long time before he finally thought to ask, "Where're we going?" He had to ask it twice to cut the blare of the radio.

Randle didn't turn around. "Hope there's nothing in that house you wanted."

Night, and the golden arches again. This time they ate in the car, taking turns to go inside to pee, to wash, the rest rooms small as closets. Gritty green soap from the dispenser. Alex ate nothing. Alex was still asleep.

Randle's lolling glance, too weary to sit up straight anymore. "You drive for a while," she said. "Keep on I-10 till you get—"

"I know," louder than he meant; he was tired too. It was a chore just to keep raising his hand to his mouth. Randle was feeling for something, rooting slowly under the seat, in her purse. When he raised his eyebrows at her she said, "You got any cigarettes?"

"Didn't you just buy a pack?"

Silence, then, "I left them at the house. On the back of the toilet," and without fuller warning began to weep, one hand loose against her mouth. Mitch turned his head, stared at the parking lot around them, the fluttering jerk of headlights like big fat clumsy birds. "I'm sick of leaving stuff places," she said. Her hand muffled her voice, made it sound like she spoke from underwater, some calm green place where voices could never go. "Do you know how long I've been wearing this shirt?" and before he could think if it was right to give any answer, "Five days. That's how long. Five fucking days in this same fucking shirt."

From the back seat Alex said, "Breaux Bridge," in a tone trusting and tender as a child's. Without turning, without bothering to look, Randle pistoned her arm in a backhand punch so hard Mitch flinched watching it.

Flat-voiced, "You just shut up," still without turning, as if the back seat had become impossible for her. "That's all you have to do. Just shut up."

Mitch started the car. Alex began to moan, a pale whimper that undercut the engine noise. Randle said, "I don't care what happens, don't wake me up." She pulled her T-shirt over her head and threw it out the window.

"Randle, for God's sake! At least wait till we get going."

"Let them look." Her breasts were spotted in places, a rashy speckle strange in the greenish dashlight, like some intricate tattoo the details of which became visible only in hard daylight. She lay with her head on his thigh, the flesh beneath her area of touch asleep before she was. He drove for almost an hour before he lightly pushed her off.

And in the back seat the endless sound of Alex, his rustling paper, the marshy odor of his tears. To Mitch it was as if the envelope of night had closed around them not forever but for so long there was no difference to be charted or discerned. Like the good old days. Like Alex staggering around and around, newspaper carpets and the funnies especially, vomiting blood that eclipsed the paler smell of pigeon shit from the old pigeon coop. Pigeonnier. Black dirt, alluvial crumble and sprayed like tarot dust across the blue-tiled kitchen floor. Wasn't it strange that he could still remember

that tile, its gaudy Romanesque patterns? Remember it as he recalled his own nervous shiver, hidden like treasure behind the
mahogany boards. And Randle's terrified laughter. Momma.
Promises, his hands between her dusty palms; they were so small
then, his hands. Alex wiping uselessly at the scabby drip of his actions, even then you had to watch him all the time. Broken glasses,
one after another. Willow bonfires. The crying cicadas, no, that
was happening now, wasn't it? Through the Buick's open windows. Through the hours and hours of driving until the air went hu-
mid with daylight and the reeking shimmer of exhaust, and Randle
stirring closed-eyed on the front seat beside him and murmuring,
anxious in her sleep, "Alex?"

He lay one hand on her neck, damp skin, clammy. "Shhhh, he's
all right. It's still my turn. He's all right."

And kept driving. The rustle of paper in the back seat. Alex's
soft sulky hum, like some rare unwanted engine that no lack of fuel
could hamper, that no one could finally turn off.

And his hands on the wheel as silent as Randle's calmed breathing, as stealthy as Alex's cities, the litany begun anew: Florien,
Samtown, Echo, Lecomte, drifting forward like smoke from a secret fire, always burning, like the fires on the levees, like the fire
that took their home. Remember that? Mouth open, catching flies
his mother would have said. Blue flame like a gas burner. What
color does blood burn?

And his head hanging down as if shamefaced, as if dunned and
stropped by the blunt hammer of anger, old anger like the fires that
never burned out. And his eyes closing, sleeping, though he woke
to think, Pull over, had to, sliding heedless as a drunken man over
to the shoulder to let himself fall, forehead striking gentle against
the steering wheel as if victim of the mildest of accidents. Randle
still asleep on the seat beside. Alex, was he still saying his cities?
Alex? Paper to play with? "Alex," but he spoke the word without
authority, in dreams against a landscape not welcome but necessary: in which the rustle of Alex's paper mingled with the slower
dribble of his desires, the whole an endless pavane danced through
the cities of Louisiana, the smaller, the hotter, the better. And he,
and Randle too, were somehow children again, kids at the old
house where the old mantle of protection fell new upon them, and
they unaware and helpless of the burden, ignorant of the loss they
had already and irrevocably sustained, loss of life while living it.
You have to swear me, Michie. And Randle, not Randle then, not

Francey but Marie-Claire, that was her name, Marie-Claire promising as he did, little sister with her hands outstretched.

The car baked slow and thorough in the shadeless morning, too far from the trees. Alex, grave as a gargoyle chipped cunningly free, rose, in silence the back door handle and through the open windows his open palms, let the brownish flakes cascade down upon Mitch and Randle both, swirling like the glitter-snow in a paperweight, speckles, freckles, changing to a darker rain, so lightly they never felt it, so quiet they never heard. And gone.

The slap of consciousness, Randle's cry, disgust, her hands grubby with it, scratching at the skin of her forearms so new blood rose beneath the dry. Scabbed with blood, painted with it. Mitch beside her, similarly scabbed, brushing with a detached dismay, not quite fastidious, as if he were used to waking covered with the spoor of his brother's predilections.

"I'm not his mother!" Screaming. She was losing it, maybe already had. Understandable. Less so his own lucidity, back calm against the seat; shock-free? Maybe he was crazier than she was. Crazier than Alex, though that would be pushing it. She was still screaming, waves of it that shook her breasts. He was getting an erection. Wasn't that something.

"I'm sick of him being a monster. I can't—"

"We have to look for him."

"You look! You look! I'm tired of looking!" Snot on her lips. He grabbed her by the breasts, distant relish, and shoved her very hard against the door. She stopped screaming and started crying, a dry drone that did not indicate if she had actually given in or merely cracked. Huh-huh-huh. "Put your shirt on," he said, and remembered she didn't have one, she had thrown it away. Stupid bitch. He gave her his shirt, rolled his window all the way down. Should they drive, or go on foot? How far? How long had they slept? He remembered telling her it was his turn to watch Alex. Staring out the window. Willows. Floodplain. Spanish moss. He had always hated Spanish moss. So *hot*, and Randle's sudden screech, he hated that too, hated the way her lips stretched through mucus and old blood and new blood and her pointing finger, pointing at Alex. Walking toward them.

Waving, extravagant, exuberant, carrying something, something it took both hands to hold. Even from this distance Mitch could see that Alex's shirt was soaked. Saturated. Beside him Randle's screech had shrunk to a blubber that he was certain, this time, would not cease. Maybe ever. Nerves, it got on his nerves, mosquito with a dentist's drill digging at your ear. At your brain. At his fingers on the car keys or maybe it was just the itch of blood as he started the car, started out slow, driving straight down the middle of the road to where he, and Randle, and Alex, slick and sticky to the hairline, would intersect. His foot on the gas pedal was gentle, and Alex's gait rocked like a chair on the porch as he waved his arms again, his arms and the thing within.

Randle spoke, dull through a mouthful of snot. "Slow down," and he shook his head without looking at her, he didn't really want to see her at this particular moment.

"I don't think so," he said as his foot dipped, elegant, like the last step in a dance. Behind Alex, the diagonal shadows of willow trees, old ones; sturdy? Surely. There was hardly any gas left in the car, but he had just enough momentum for all of them.

I am uncomfortable with afterwords, forewords, and so on because to me a story is useless if it doesn't speak solely for itself. That said, I will note that "Teratisms" is about love, and hunger, and one of the many districts where they intersect.

Kathe Koja

M Is for the Many Things

ELIZABETH MASSIE

Here is another story about a family, although this one is strictly structured in contrast to the chaos of Koja's, and is voluntary. Well, mostly. A perfect example of the adage the road to hell is paved with good intentions.

Mother was dying. Her forehead was splotched and red, and her hair was brittle and dry on the pillow. She sweated without relief, her body like a huge hot cloud on a summer's day, raining steadily, the water collecting in the creases of her flesh and dripping to the folds of the sheet beneath her. The sweat smelled of Vicks VapoRub, and the soiled linens, piled in the corner of Mother's room, added a scent of urine and diarrhea. It was Barbara's job to do the linens, but they were dirtied so quickly now that she had a hard time keeping up.

Grace, feeling ill herself, dabbed Mother's body with the edge of a towel. Mother's breathing had been labored for two days. She was dying. The sense of impending loss and despair roiled in Grace's bowels. Emotions of which she could make no sense were tangled in her chest, causing her lungs to hurt. She shuddered, and wiped the length of Mother's collarbone.

Greg, Grace's brother, came into the room. He stepped lightly on his bare feet, and sat beside Grace on a low chair. Grace gave him the towel. He dabbed Mother's arm. He said nothing. Grace knew he was waiting for her to decide if she could talk about this, or wanted to leave it in silence.

Pain squeezed Grace's vocal cords, and she said, "How can I bear this?"

Greg didn't look at Grace, nor touch her. None of the brothers and sisters knew how to comfort each other. That was Mother's duty. He lifted Mother's massive hand and gently dabbed the moist places between each finger. Then he said, "Stay strong if you can. I've been through this before, and I know what I'm saying. Stay strong."

Grace swallowed, and it hurt.

"Why don't you go to dinner?" Greg said. He put Mother's hand down, then wiped her breast. "I'll take my turn. Mary has made a nice stew. She's upset that no one was on time to the dining hall tonight."

Grace closed her eyes. Several heavy tears joined the sweat on the bed. Then she rose and left the room.

Outside the door, Grace slipped on her clothes and stepped into her shoes. She walked along the hall to the top of the staircase, passing the two open doors of the girls' rooms and the closed door of the nursery. A soft squeak emanated from behind the nursery door, and Grace let her hand touch the wood briefly as she went by. It was Grace's job to do the hourly feeding, but it was only six-thirty. From below was the bland aroma of Mary's cooking, and the sound of Eldon buffing the living-room floor.

At the top of the stairs, Grace's kitten lay in a weak ball. Grace picked it up and squeezed it tightly. It was a shame; this kitty was no good. It had been a nice, healthy animal when Grace had found it in the backyard, but now it was thin and weak and its fur was coming out. Just like all the other kittens Grace had tried to keep as pets. They had been playful and cute and full of energy. Then they each got sick and died. Grace had loved them greatly. And they all died.

Suddenly Grace was flushed with the need to go back to Mother. She dropped the kitten and grabbed the top of the banister, her jaws clenching. Then the sensation passed. Greg was with Mother, it was his turn. And Grace did need to eat. It was almost twenty minutes past dinnertime.

Downstairs, Mary stood in the dining hall, arms crossed, bushy eyebrows a furious dragon across the top of her face. She was the oldest of the children, nearly thirty-nine. She was usually the cook, and always the assigner of chores. She was the rememberer of the rules and the doler of punishments. Mary was the only one of the children to have a room to herself. No one argued with Mary; they complained about her under their breaths at work or in the darkness on their cots at night.

"You're last," Mary told Grace. "You'll have dish duty, then."

Grace said, "That's all right." She slumped to her assigned seat at the long wooden table, poured herself a glass of milk from the carton, and picked up her spoon.

Mary took up a rumpled cotton napkin and looked at it steadily, then sat down across from Grace. "How is Mother?"

"The same."

Mary sighed. "Maybe I'll help you with the dishes," she said. "It will keep me from thinking."

Grace ate a piece of carrot. It caught in her throat. "I wish I'd had time in the infirmary, Mary. Don't you? Maybe then we would know what to do."

Mary shook her head. "Nobody worked in the infirmary, and you don't wish you had. It was bad in there, a lot of sickness we could have caught. Don't you remember Celia Duncan? She died in the infirmary, Grace. Some awful disease. They were right not to let us in there unless we were sick ourselves."

Grace nodded and chewed a bit of cubed beef. Mary cooked just as good as Mrs. Griffith used to. But tonight the food seemed to have no taste.

"You've only been with us a year," said Mary. She paused, then scratched her graying hair. The sound of the buffer stopped, and there was the bumping and scraping as Eldon put the machine back into the front hall closet. "You'll be all right."

Grace wiped her mouth on the cloth napkin and put it back into her lap. "You don't have to help me with dishes."

"Suit yourself."

"Who has devotions tonight?"

"Paul."

"I don't think I can eat all this."

"You don't eat it you get no snack."

Grace sighed and brought another spoonful of stew to her lips. Eldon came into the dining hall. He was just three years Mary's junior, but appeared much older. He was skinny and ugly, with ears that pointed forward like fleshy megaphones and white hair shaved close to his bony head.

"Whole downstairs is done," he announced. There was a pride in his voice. "Could skate on it. Could see your own face if you looked close enough. But I won't be doing upstairs. . . ." He trailed off, then blinked and looked away from Mary and Grace. "Could I at least buff the nursery?" he asked softly.

"No," said Mary.

Eldon's shoulders went up, then down.

Mary said, "Shake the rugs?"

Eldon said, "Yes. All done."

"Barbara and Al and Paul will be in soon from their after-dinner chores. We'll have devotions. A special one for Mother. Why don't you wait in the living room for us, and find a nice verse for Mother in the Bible?"

"But Paul has devotions tonight, don't he?"

Mary frowned, and Eldon became immediately submissive. "Okay," he said. He pulled at one huge ear. "A long verse or a short one?"

"Long," said Grace. Her stew bowl was empty. She held it up and Mary said, "Better."

Grace took her dishes into the small kitchen at the back of the house, and washed the pile that waited there for her. They were nearly all dried and put away when Paul and Al came in the front door. Grace carried the bowl she was drying to the kitchen door and leaned against the frame.

Paul shed his Windbreaker and hung it in the closet between the dining hall and living room. He was thirty-three, with short black hair and brown skin hardened to parchment by the outdoor work he and Al did to earn money for the others. Al stood beside Paul with his hands in his jeans pockets. Al never wore a coat, even in the coldest weather. He kept the sleeves of his T-shirts cut off, and he sported a constant sunburn.

"Mother?" asked Al.

"The same, I think," said Mary. "Greg is with her."

Grace ran the dry rag around and around in the bowl.

Paul set his jaw and his eyes hitched. "Devotions in a few minutes," he said. He turned and went into the living room.

"Barbara out back?" asked Al.

Mary nodded. "Hanging out sheets," she said. "Lots of sheets this past week."

"Want me to get her?"

"That's fine, Al. Tell her it's devotion time, the sheets'll wait."

Al walked past Grace into the kitchen. Grace took the bowl to the cabinet and put it in with the others. Al opened the door leading to the backyard, causing the blinds on the door's window to clap noisily against the glass. He stepped out to the stoop and called for Barbara to come inside.

Grace hurried upstairs for a quick seven o'clock feeding, then came back down to the living room. It was a long, narrow room with a single window facing the street. There were pots of plants that Barbara tried to keep, but most of them were dead or nearly so. The room was kept shaded, because Mary did not like the view of the street. She did not like seeing all the people going about their busy business in their frantic ways; she did not like the bustle of the independents, nor the stiflingly close vicinity of the neighbors. Grace knew Mary kept the shade down so she could imagine she was still at the Home. Mary liked to dust the empty bookshelves and sew up sock holes and think about the Home she had been forced to leave when she was eighteen, twenty years ago.

"Greg going to come down?" asked Paul. He was seated on the flowered sofa beneath the mantel. The Bible was in his lap. Beside him, Eldon pulled at his ear.

"Greg!" called Mary from the base of the steps. "Devotions. Come on, now."

Al sat down beside Eldon. Grace took the floor beside the broken recliner. Barbara, her thin brown ponytail blown askew by the backyard wind, sat on the straight-backed wooden chair by the door, across from the sofa. Mary sat on the recliner.

They all waited in silence, Eldon holding on to his ear, Barbara twisting the end of her ponytail, Paul strumming the pages of the Bible, Grace picking lint from the rug. They did not look at each other.

Greg came downstairs, buttoning his shirt. He entered the living room. "Mother moved a little," he offered, but said no more. He sat on the floor beneath the window.

Paul cleared his voice. "Verses first," he said, and he began. " 'Ye shall find the babe wrapped in swaddling clothes, lying in a manger.' "

Eldon said, " 'Jesus wept.' "

Al said, " 'A bone of his shall not be broken.' "

" 'They came round about me daily like water,' " said Greg.

" 'Jesus wept,' " said Grace.

Paul said, "Nope, already used."

Grace crossed her arms, frustrated. She could barely think. Then she said, " 'I will open my mouth in a parable.' "

" 'And he was with them coming in and going out at Jerusalem,' " said Mary from her chair.

" 'How much then is a man better than a sheep,' " said Barbara. This was one of the few verses that Grace liked, and that she understood. When she heard it she thought of pictures in her Sunday school class long ago, little baby sheep suckling Mother sheep, with Jesus standing by.

Verses done, they all looked at Paul. He opened the Bible to a little torn scrap of paper marking a place. "I found something to read in honor of Mother," he said. He sighed heavily. Nobody liked to be in charge of devotions. But Mary was stern; each took his or her turn. Paul's voice was awkward with the words, and embarrassed. " 'Therefore we are buried with him by baptism into death: that like as Christ was raised up from the dead by the glory of the Father, even so we also should walk in newness of life.' "

Grace listened as intently as she could, hoping this time she might find something that would make sense.

" 'For if we have been planted together in the likeness of his death, we shall be also in the likeness of his resurrection.' "

Paul read on another five minutes. Grace sat and heard the Scriptures, and it was as it had always been, a jumble of old words, a ritual of ancient babble. She did not need to ask the others to know it was the same for them as well. But they were trained to sit and read and quote and listen. In that repetition was the only small sense of calm.

Grace let her gaze wander to the photos and certificates on the mantel over the sofa. There was a picture of Mary back at the Baptist Home, no more than fifteen, wearing an apron and a wan smile, in the huge, smoky kitchen with Mrs. Griffith standing behind her. There was another picture of Al and Paul, twelve and thirteen, just old enough to be allowed to do grounds work, Al sitting on the seat of the Home's tractor, Paul standing on the grass. Behind Paul and Al were George Brennen and Ricky Altis, both fourteen at the time. Both George and Ricky had gone on from the Home, gotten jobs, and had married. They had become independents. They had been able to. Most of the children who had grown up in the Home had been able to. To the right of Al and Paul's snapshot was a photo that had been posed for inclusion in the Home's annual fund drive brochure. In it, a ten-year-old Barbara and an eight-year-old Grace were holding hands and running across the lawn in front of the Administration Building. There were no photos of Eldon. He hated to have his picture taken, and always hid when the Baptist Home board of trustees came out on excursions with their cameras.

"Amen," said Paul.

"Amen," repeated the others.

"Tonight, we'll each have a shorter time with Mother," said Mary. "No more than three minutes each, you hear me? Now, who was first last night?"

Eldon wiggled his hand.

"Then it's you, Barbara," said Mary. "Let's go upstairs."

The seven filed up the steps.

Barbara took off her clothes and went into Mother's room, closing the door behind her. Time with Mother was private, and respected. The others sat on the floor in the hallway. This was the most favored time of the day, yet Mother's illness had given it an urgent touch, and Grace sat quietly, trying to prepare herself. Usually Grace told Mother about her day as she snuggled and sucked on the great white breasts. Tonight, however, Grace thought that she, like Mother, would be without a voice.

They sat and waited. Mary went into the nursery for a minute, then came out and sat down again. The kitten rose from its spot at the top of the stairs and stumbled toward the gathering, then fell several feet short, panting and mewling. Grace didn't want the cat now, she wanted Mother, and so she let the cat lie.

Paul went in after Barbara. Grace had wondered what the boys did in the room alone with Mother, but would never ask. Before Grace had come to live with her brothers and sisters, she had tried to be an independent. She had lived with a man, and he had made her do awful things, like suckle him. She had tried to please him but could not do it, and he beat her. When she tried to kill him, the state put her into a home. Not a good place like the Home, but an ugly place where she had no chores and no devotions and they wanted to talk about her feelings. Grace wondered if Paul and Al and Eldon wanted Mother to suckle them as Grace's man had wanted.

Mary took her turn, and when she came out, her face was ashen. "Not long," she whispered as she zippered her skirt and sat beside Barbara. "She won't eat." Barbara put her head down on her arms. Mary stared at her fingers.

Grace went into Mother's room. As required, she went to the nightstand and chose a nice piece of candy for Mother. She mashed it in her fingers to make it easy for Mother to take, then leaned over the huge, naked body and pressed the candy to the sick lips. Mother did not take the candy, nor acknowledge that it was there. Her eyes did not open. Grace blinked and waited, hoping Mother would awaken and take the offering. But she did not.

Grace dropped the candy to the floor, and crawled onto the mattress with Mother. The cold dampness of Mother's sweat on the sheet made Grace's skin tighten and crawl.

"Today I began a picture of a cat," Grace said, pulling herself more tightly into the body. "It will be a nice one, a picture for you, and you can hang it up in your room." Grace looked up at the wall above Mother's head. On it were sketches that she had done with pencils and crayon crumbs. Pictures of sheep and their babies and Jesus and children doing chores and reading Bible verses and mowing lawns and saying prayers at cot-side and eating meals in the dining hall.

"It is a picture of the kitty I have now. She was a nice kitty, but not so nice anymore. But the picture is what she looked like when I first got her. Gray and white. You'll like it, I think."

Mother said nothing.

Grace closed her eyes and continued with her tale of the day. "Mary made stew, and it was good. Sometimes I wish we could have candy, but candy is sweet for sweet Mothers."

Mother did not move, but Grace could feel a pulse in her huge arm. Grace straddled Mother, and took a breast into her mouth. For a few minutes she suckled in silence. Peace settled on her and she lost awareness of the smell and the sweat and the fact that Mother was dying. Grace's body calmed. This was Mother. This was what they all had wanted. The others had banded together after they left the Home, forming a Home again in this house. They lived as they had learned, doing as they had been taught. But Greg had decided a Mother was the missing element. They had all needed a Mother for so long. After Grace's release from the hospital, she had called the Home and got Mary's new address. She was accepted into the Home of her long-ago brothers and sisters, and into a family that had at last, thanks be to Greg, a Mother.

Grace let go of the nipple, then rolled off the bed. As a parting gesture, she offered another piece of candy, and again, Mother did not take it. Grace stroked Mother's arm and thigh.

Suddenly Mother arched her back and her eyes flew open.

"Mother?"

Mother did not seem to recognize Grace, nor focus on anything. She trembled violently and her throat rumbled. The soft but strong terry towel restraints that were tied about her ankles and neck and shoulders drew taut and caused the bedposts to groan. Mother's mouth dropped open, and she grunted. The massive woman fought the cords. Her eyes spasmed.

She is dying certainly, Grace thought.

Then Mother slumped down again to the bed, and her eyes closed. She was silent, and the shuddering breathing resumed.

Grace went out into the hall. She put on her clothes. Al took his turn with Mother, closing the door behind him.

When the turns were done, Mary directed Eldon to take first watch with Mother during the night while the others slept. She did not believe Mother would last until morning, and it would be wrong for her to be alone when she died.

Mary told the others to brush their teeth and say their prayers and be off to bed. Grace washed her hands for the eight o'clock feeding.

Mary joined Grace at the nursery door. She said, "Why don't I help you this time?"

Grace shrugged. "You don't have to."

"I know I don't. But we'll do it together tonight."

Grace said, "All right."

Grace opened the door and the two went quietly inside.

There was a bed in the center of the nursery, a bedside table, and the rest of the room was bare. No one stayed in this room long enough to need a chair. This room was strictly business. It was a room for tending and cleaning and monitoring. It was dark and quiet and busy, like a little chamber in a honeybee comb.

Mary and Grace moved to the bed. Grace opened the box of candy on the bedside table. She smashed the chocolate between her fingers and held it out.

The figure on the bed strained and caught the candy. Then the mouth opened for more. Grace smiled slightly, then looked at Mary for approval.

"This is good," said Mary. "She's healthy and she eats."

Grace held out more mashed candy, and it was gobbled up. Even Grace's fingers were mouthed clean when she held them close enough.

Grace wiped her hand on her hip, then looked down at the woman on the bed. The woman was filling out nicely. With hourly feedings of good, sweet candy and soft drinks, she was beginning to look like a Mother, with soft, fleshy side rolls and arms like foam pillows. Soon she would be big enough to cuddle, large enough to hide in, soft enough to suckle. This woman, like Mother, was secured to her bed. This woman, also like Mother, had no voice. This was Greg's idea. He was the one to find the women and bring them home; and he was the one who said it was best to remove the tongues. This way, each in turn would be a good Mother. A good Mother who would listen and not scold.

Grace touched the woman's arm. The woman looked at Grace. Her eyes were alive and sparkling, as if mad tears swirled in them. She grunted and pulled at her restraints. Mary smacked her soundly.

"She'll learn," said Mary.

Grace picked another piece of candy from the box and looked at it. Candy tasted good, but Mother's breasts were sweeter. Mother's love was peace.

Grace crushed the candy. She offered it to the woman on the bed, who took it even as her eyes spilled and then brimmed over again.

At two the next morning, Mother died.

My husband, Roger, grew up in a children's home. He and three of his four brothers were put there when their mother died. Roger was six. His brothers were all younger. Roger lived there until he went to college at age eighteen.

Although the children's home was not a nightmare orphanage, the grounds were well maintained, the cottages clean, and counselors were on the payroll, there lacked the warmth and affection and support one would hope to have in a family. The house parents maintained strict discipline and inflexible rules. They never hugged the kids. They never told the kids that they loved them, or even liked them. The children grew up without adult affection, leaving them to either gain it from each other or not at all.

So I imagined that there would certainly be a number of people who, having grown up in this type of institution, would never be able to get beyond the routines and the security of the control the place had over them. And yet, out in the world, trying to re-create what they had known as children, they would also seek the adult tenderness they had never known.

Hey, the search for love is universal, right?

Too bad that search is sometimes deadly.

Elizabeth Massie

Folly for Three

BARRY N. MALZBERG

Malzberg's science fiction has often been tinged with horror, so this story, with its minimalist style, should come as no surprise to those who have been reading him regularly over his career. It effectively conveys the fear of losing control—of a situation, and of one's life.

Good, he said again, this is very good. Just turn a little, let the light catch you. I want to see you in profile, against the light. There, he said, that's good. That's what I want. His voice had thickened, whether with passion or contempt she had no idea. They were still at that tentative state of connection where all moves were suspect, all signals indeterminate.

Ah, he said, you're a piece all right. That's what you are.

I've never done this before, she said. I've never done anything like this before. I want you to know that. She looked out the window, the grey clouds on the high floor hammering at the panes. Way, way up now. For everything there's a first time, she said.

Right, he said, humoring her. Whatever you say. I'm your first. Best in the world. Anything for a hump. He backed against a chair, crouched, fell into the cushions, stared at her from that angle, looking upward intently, checking out her crotch, then the high angle of her breasts, pulled upward within the brassiere, arching. He muttered something she could not hear and raised a hand.

What is it? she said. What do you want?

Come here. I want you to come here right now.

Tell me why.

I don't want games, he said. We'll have time for that later. You want to fool around, play with yourself. Come over here. Move it.

Can't you be a little kinder? I told you, I've never done anything like this before.

You want a commendation? he said. A Congressional Medal of Honor? He cleared his throat, looked at her with an odd and exacting impatience. Everybody has to have a first time, he said. Even I did once. I got through it. You'll get through it too. But you have to close your eyes and jump. Move it over here now.

This isn't the way I thought it would be, she said.

How did you think it would be? Flowers and wine? Tchaikovsky on the turntable? White Russians with straws? This is the setup, he said, this is what a nooner feels like. You don't hang out in bars midday if you're not looking for a nooner.

She looked at him, almost as if for the first time, noting the age spots on his arms, the fine, dense wrinkling around the eyes, which she had not noticed in the bar. Could she back out now? No, she thought, she couldn't. This was not the way it was done. That was all behind her now. I'm on the forty-eighth floor and that's all there is to it and no one in the world except this man knows I'm here. Not the kids, not Harry, not the cops. Okay, she said, I'm coming. She went toward him, trying to make her stockings glide, trying to move the way they moved in this kind of scene on *Dallas*. Maybe she could break him on the anvil of desire. Maybe she could quit him. Maybe—

There was a pounding on the door. Open up, someone in the hall said, open it! Open it now! The voice was huge, insistent.

For God's sake, she said, who is that?

He was trembling. I don't know, he said, what have you put us into? Detectives? Photographers? You got me into this, bitch. He backed away from her. His lips moved but there was no sound.

The noises in the hall were enormous, like nothing she had ever heard. The hammering was regular, once every three or four seconds now, an avid panting just beyond earshot. Like fucking, that's how it sounded. Last chance, the voice said, you open the goddamned door or we break it down.

What have you done? she said to the man. Stunned, absolutely without response, he ran his hands over his clothing, looked stupidly at the belt. This wasn't supposed to happen, she said. This wasn't part of it. *Who is out there?*

Nothing. He had nothing to say. He brought his clothing against him helplessly in the thin off-light in which she had so recently posed. She heard the sound of keys in the hallway. They were going to open the door.

An hour earlier in the bar she had said, Let's go now. I have a room in the Lenox around the corner.

Fast mover, he had said. His briefcase was on his lap, concealing an erection she supposed, one elbow draped over it awkwardly, clutching the briefcase there, the other hand running up and down her bare arm. She could feel the tremor in his fingers. He wanted her. Well, that was *his* problem.

I can be fast when I want, she said. Other times I can be slow. Whatever you say, big boy, I'm on your side. Who can believe these lines? she thought. This is what it's come to now.

Okay, he said. Just let me finish this drink. He raised the cocktail glass. I paid for it, he said, it's mine, I ought to have it.

She pressed his arm. You only think you're paying, she said. *I'm* paying. All the way, up and down the line. In his face she could see the pallor of acknowledgment, a blush of realization. *I've got a hot one here,* that face was saying. Well, that's the idea all right.

Let's go, friend, she said. She pushed away her own glass, clung to him for an instant, then pulled him upright. Let's see how fast you are where it counts. Out in the clean fresh air and then forty-eight stories *up*, that's the right place to put it.

He released her, yanked upright from the stool, took out a twenty, and put it on the bar. We'll see how fast I am, he said. He took the briefcase against his side, gripped the handle. Now, he said. The lust on his face seemed to struggle for just a moment with doubt, then faded to a kind of bleakness as she reached out again and stroked him. Now and now. He rose gravely to her touch. For God's sake, he said. For God's sake—

Now, she said.

They struggled toward the door. The man on the stool nearest the entrance looked up at them, his glasses dazzling in the strobe and said, You too? Every one of you?

She stared. She had never seen this man in her life. Of course, she reminded herself, the salesman with the briefcase was new also. Two strangers, one maybe as good as the other when she had walked in but the salesman was the one she had picked and in whom the time had been invested. No looking back. She said nothing, started toward the door.

Fornicators, the seated man said, infidels. Desolate lost angels of the Lord. Have you no shame? No hope?

Out on the street, the salesman said, Another bar, another crazy. They're all over the place. This city—

I don't want to hear about the city, she said. Please. Just take me to the hotel. Right now. She was appalled by the thought that the man at the bar would come after them. The thought was crazy but there it was. To the hotel, she said. I'm burning up, can't you tell. She yanked at his wrist. Now, she said, let's go.

She began to tug at him, he broke into a small trot. Hey, he said, hey look, it's all right. We've got all afternoon. I'm not going anywhere, we have hours. We have—

I'm afraid he's following us, she said. There, it was out, be done with it. I'm afraid he's going to come after us.

Who? The guy from the bar?

His footsteps, she said, I know them. He's coming up behind us. She turned and pointed, ready for a confrontation right there but of course there was nothing. A couple of secretaries giggling, a man with a dog, a beggar with a sign saying I AM BLIND, that was all. Quickly, she said, before he finds us. I know he's on the way.

She moved rapidly then, dropping her grip, striding out, making the salesman race. Let him struggle, she thought. Let him chase her a little. She was afraid of the man in the bar whether or not he was coming. Desolate lost angels of the Lord. Fornicators, she thought. We're all fornicators but some of us know more than others. There was something to come to terms with in this but she simply could not. All she wanted to do was get to the forty-eighth floor of the Hotel Lenox, take him into that room, get it over with, take him as deep as her brains. Make it happen, make it done. Get it into her. She was burning. Burning.

That morning in the kitchen he had said, I don't know how late I'll be. There's a conference midday and then I have to go out with the accounts exec again. I could be tied up till midnight with this guy, he's a professional drunk. If that's it I'll just get a room in the city and sleep in.

That's nice, she said. That's the third time I've heard that this month. Why bother coming home at all?

Hey, he said, his head tilting to attention, you think I'm lying? You think this is some kind of crap here, that I'm making up a story? Then just say it.

I didn't say a thing.

You think I'm running around? he said. I'm knocking my brains out to keep us in this $250,000 house we can't afford and can't sell and you're running tabs on me? Maybe we ought to have a discussion about that.

We're not going to have a discussion about anything, she said. He looks forty, she thought, and his gut is starting to swell. The sideburns are ragged and at night, the nights that he's next to me, he breathes like an old man, a sob in his throat. He's not going to last but who lasts? What stays? Ten years ago we made plans and every one of them worked out. I'm having trouble getting wet. AIDS is crossing the Huguenot line. The kids are no longer an excuse. We moved here expecting the usual, who was to know the joke was on us? I'm entitled to something too, she said, just think of that.

What does that mean? he said indifferently. He stood, gathered papers, stacked them, and leaned to open his briefcase. You trying to tell me something?

Nothing, she said, nothing at all. Make of it what you will.

Because if that's the deal, two can play you know. I don't have to get a heart attack at forty-two to keep you in a place like this. I can just let it go.

Forget it, she said. I didn't mean anything. It was just an expression. Pushing it, she thought. We're starting to push it now. It used to be easier; now we've got to get closer and closer to the bull.

Everything's an expression, he said. He opened the briefcase, inserted the papers, closed it with a snap. There's no time to discuss this now, he said, maybe later we ought to settle a few goddamned things. Maybe we'll sit down this weekend and talk.

I'll make an appointment, she said.

Enough, he said, enough of this. I'm out the door. You got something to say, maybe you write it down in words of one syllable, we fix it so a simple guy like me can see this. We're practical in the sales department, we only know what's in front of us. You got to spell it out.

Me and my imaginary friend, she said.

Imaginary friend? Is that what you call him now?

You'll be late for the bus, she said. You'll miss your connections and what will happen midday? He stared at her. You've got a schedule to meet, I mean, she said. In four years he won't be able to come, she thought. He'll be a heavy, barking lump next to me and I'll be counting the heartbeats, waiting for the hammer. That's what's going to happen. You bet it would have to be imaginary, she said.

He laughed, a strangulated groan. Too much, he said, you're too much for me. Always were. Always ahead of me. He leaned forward, kissed her cheek, his eyes flicking down indifferently, taking in her body, then moving away, all of him moving away, arching toward the wall and then the door. Keep it going, he said, just take a tip from me and keep it going. He reached toward the door.

Just like I do, he said and with a wink was gone.

She followed him, closed the heavy service door, sat on the

stool, ran her feet in and around her slippers, looking at the clock. In her mind she ran the day forward, spun the hours, turned it until it was one in the afternoon and she would be in the Lenox waiting to be taken. She had worked it all out. But that still left hours, even figuring in the time at the bar and the arrangements to be made there. Too much time altogether. She thought of that.

She thought of it for a long time and of other things, the kids off at school, the difficult arc of the morning already getting passed. What do you think? she said to herself, what do you really think of this? Does it make any sense at all? Is this what we wanted?

Desolation, a voice said. That isn't what you wanted, that's what you've got. So you do the best you can. You make it up as you go along. That's the suburban way of life.

Well, there was nothing to say to that. There almost never was. What she could say would destroy the game. She kicked off her slippers and moved toward the stairs, ready to get dressed, ready to pull herself together. Again. Playing it out.

Two years before that, a Thursday in summer she had said, I can't go on this way anymore, Harry. Can you understand that? It's too much for me, it's not enough for me, it's a greyness, a vastness, I can't take it. I need something else. I can't die this way. She had run her hand on his thigh, felt the cooling, deadly torment of his inanition.

It's not just you, she said. It's everything. It's everybody.

We can work it out, he said. There are things we can do.

We can't do anything. I've thought it through. It's just the situation and it's too much. It's not enough, it's—

It's not just the two of us, he said. There are things to be done.

No shrinks, she said. No counselors. We've had enough of them. We're not getting anywhere.

I don't mean that, he said. There are other things. Things we can do on our own, things that will change.

Oh, Harry, she said, Harry, you have answers, but there *are* no answers, there are only plagues out there and darkness.

So we'll do something, he said, practically. He was a practical man. Because of the plagues, the risks. No one goes out there now if they can help it. I don't want to go out there and neither do you. So we have to work something out.

What? she said. What do you want? What's the answer?

He clutched her hand. We know all about it in the sales game, he said, and I can teach you.

Teach me what?

Masks, he said.

Masks? Halloween?

Repertory theater, he said. That's what we're going to have here. A little repertory theater. So get ready for the roles of your life.

Once she had loved him, she supposed. She must have loved him a lot. In deference to that, then, she laid back in the bed wide-eyed, listened to the tempo of his breathing as it picked up, touched him.

Okay, she said. Tell me more. I'm listening.

Yes, he said. Yes.

In the darkness, as he spoke, it was as if there were now another presence heaped under the bedclothes, an imaginary friend maybe, *her* imaginary friend listening.

He told her what he had in mind.

He sold her on it.

On the forty-eighth floor, she backed against the high window in the hotel room, her eyes fixed on the door, listening to the sound of the key turning. No, she said, no.

The man hobbling toward the door, half-dressed, turned, stared. No what? he said.

No more of this, she said. There's someone out there, she said. There's someone really out there with the key in the lock. We're in over our heads.

She could hear the key turning, turning. It encountered an obstruction, then suddenly it didn't and it was through. The door was moving.

The terror was clambering within her like an animal. He looks forty, she thought, and his gut is starting to swell. He's breathing like an old man. *Over our heads,* she said. I don't know what to do.

He looked at her, speechless. Wait a minute he said. Now just wait—

The door was open. The man from the bar was there smiling, holding a gun now, pointing it. Fornicators, he said, I knew what you were up to. I have the key and I followed you here. Now you're going to pay. You disgust me.

She moved toward the window. Harry was rooted in place.

She looked at the priestly little man with the gun and sadly she looked at her husband, waiting now for whatever would happen.

Curtain, Harry, she said.

There's a passage in Higgins's *The Friends of Eddie Coyle* on marriage. "I got nothing to say about it," the guy says, "there's no way you can understand it unless you've been married; there's no way to explain it." Well, yes, there probably is—my metaphor of fifteen years ago was repertory theater, the donning of masks, the same old reliable faces beneath the inconstant, swooning trappings, but I got bored with this as explanation just about the time that this particular thread of insight seemed to unravel and here is the faithful editor, this book, and this tremulous story to give me a better idea: marriage as psychic vampirism. Of course.

But then again, of course (one hastens to say against the anticipated misunderstandings) everything is psychic vampirism, symbiosis, mutual exploitation: *life* is a form of psychic vampirism; we give unto and take back in different measure and sometimes are unwilling to admit the transaction, call it something else. But then again—and unless you been there, Eddie—there's no way that you can understand this, just no way that you are going to be able to grasp the issue.

"Folly for Three" in an earlier and murkier draft was written in tribute to Cornell Woolrich, whom I knew toward the end of his life and about whom too much has now been written (after many years of too little; "too much" is worse, speaking of vampirism); the story did not, in its Woolrichian mode, make a great deal of sense. Ellen Datlow's services in extracting from the murk the story that this wanted to be were remarkable and (old too late and too late smart) an education. Mutual dependency yet *again*, Eddie old pal.

                                                            Barry N. Malzberg

The Impaler in Love

RICK WILBER

Here's an honest-to-God traditional-type vampire—with a very untraditional urge.

I

Did we frighten your effete God
with that first fevered embrace
that so fed my need that I left you mortal?

You cried for me with pleading hands,
you sought my sudden entrance—
no coy flirtation, no shuttered portal,

there was only a hunger and your firm commands
until I filled your cup, accepted your innocence,
and repaid you with your life.

II

But now, but now—
the sun dies into a cobalt sea,
a reflected spear of its demise
aimed across horizon miles
to beach-edging pines where we stand
as small waves lap a tired shore.

An owl flies overhead on silent, death-hunt wings
to arrow across the narrow beach and bring
shell-stabbing talons to a scuttling crab—
the hermit's claw a feeble gesture of damned—
defiance before it is consumed.

You turn and sweetly smile and say:
"We can still be friends, I'm sure of it,"
and I can only nod and sigh
for what you cannot know of my demands.

I loved you, fragile thing,
and nearly shared it all.
Nearly.

III

I am blessed hard,
angry and hungry and hard to think of how it was
and could have been before your passion set
is this cooling sea of smiles and friendship and talk.

I kept you alive, your rosaried cross and Christ
and simple psalms no more redoubt against my skill
than the hermit's sad claw and crushed chitin.

I kept you alive, I fed from your passion
that sated my own as none had ever done.
I hid my truth to revel in your loins

while your hips thrust to mine
to give rise to desires long dismissed.
Your lips, your tongue defined

our mutual need, and order grew
from the dark chaos that has led me always.
And so I loved you.

I, the fool, loved you in your mortal guile
and set aside a millennium's lessons
for this false hope, all while

knowing it would turn to ruin.
I touched your pale perfection,
pierced your bold smile to enter
and bathe in your warm balm.

IV

But that, dear one, was in another time,
before this silent hour,
this sad and silent hour of mine,
came to you.

Your talk of friendship ends your life,
the cross you bore is lifted now,
your catholic taste has brought this strife
and blame to you.

This sun has set and the hermit has raised
its futile claw against a final consummation
that is, though long delayed, now yours
and mine, to finally share.

This poem began with the middle stanzas after I had watched a darkly beautiful sunset with my wife on a quiet beach in Barbados. We noticed, walking along the Caribbean shore of the beautiful island just as the sun disappeared, some gulls tearing at the partially eaten remnants of a crab at the water's edge. I had been startled several nights earlier by an owl swooping down over my head around midnight in my own backyard in Tampa. Those various scenes tumbled together into useful metaphors that connected with my thoughts on the consuming passions that mark vampirism.

I was determined to avoid the obvious traits and behaviors, the bats and fangs and wooden stakes and garlic. But I was equally committed to having some fun with the sexual drive and innuendo that permeates the vampire legends, so I let that sort of language run rampant. What would happen, I wondered, if a vampire fell in love with a good Catholic girl but she then broke his heart by offering friendship?

Rick Wilber

The Moose Church

JONATHAN CARROLL

Carroll often writes stories within stories—leading the reader into the middle of his characters' lives—and has the rare ability to pique the reader's interest so that one wants to know more about those characters outside the limits of the story. For example, I want to know more about the letter writer in "The Moose Church."

This is one of two stories in which dreaming takes on a sinister aspect.

Judy,

just returned from Sardinia where we'd planned to stay two weeks but ended up driving away after five days because it is one HIDEOUS island, dahling, let me tell you. I'm always suckered by books like *The Sea and Sardinia* or *The Colossos of Maroussi*, where famous writers describe how wonderful it was to be on wild and wooly islands forty years ago when the native women went golden topless and meals cost less than a pack of cigarettes. So, fool that I am, I read those books, pack my bag, and flea (intended) south. Only to see topless women all right—two-hundred-pound German frau/tanks from Bielefeld with bazooms so enormous they could windsurf on them if they only hoisted a sail, meals that cost more than my new car, and accommodations the likes of which you'd wish on your worst enemy. And then, because I have a limp memory, I always forget the sun in those southern climes is so deceptively hot that it fries you helpless in a quick few hours. Please witness my volcanic red face, thanks.

No, I am past forty now and consequently have every right to "Just Say No" to things like these trips from now on. When we were driving back, I said to Caitlin, Let's just go to the mountains for our next vacation. Then low and behold, we came to an inn below the mountains near Graz, next to a small flickering brook, with the smell of woodsmoke and slight dung, red-and-white checked tablecloths, a bed upstairs that looked down on the brook through swaying chestnut trees, and there were chocolates wrapped in silver tinfoil on our pillow. There's no place like home, Toto.

While we were in Sardinia, we spent a lot of time in a café/bar that was the only nice thing about the place. It was called Spin Out Bar and when the owners found out we were American, they treated us like heroes. One of them had been to New York years ago and kept a map of Manhattan pinned on the wall with red marks all over it to show anyone who came in where he'd been there.

At night the joint filled up and could be pretty rowdy, but besides the Nordic windsurfers and an overdose of fat people in floral prints, we met a number of interesting characters. Our favorites were a Dutch woman named Miep who worked in a sunglasses factory in Maastricht. Her companion was an Englishman named McGann and there, my friend, sits this story.

We couldn't figure out why Miep was in Sardinia in the first place because she said she didn't like a lot of sun and never went to the water. She was happy to leave it at that, but McGann thought it germane to add, "She reads a lot, you know." What does she read about? "Bees. She loves to study bees. Thinks we should study them because *they* know how to make a society work properly." Unfortunately, neither Caitlin nor my knowledge of bees extends beyond stings and various kinds of honey we have tasted, but Miep rarely said anything about her books or her bees. In the beginning Miep rarely said anything about anything, leaving it up to her friend to carry the conversation ball. Which he did with alarming gusto.

God knows, the English are good conversationalists and when they're funny they can have you on the floor every five minutes, but McGann talked too much. McGann never *stopped* talking. You got to the point where you'd just tune him out and look at his pretty, silent girlfriend. The sad part was, in between all his words lived an interesting man. He was a travel agent in London and had been to fascinating places—Bhutan, Patagonia, North Yemen. He also told half-good stories, but inevitably in the middle of one about the Silk Road or being trapped by a snowstorm in a Buddhist monastery you'd realize he'd already spewed so many extraneous, bo-ring details that you'd stopped paying attention six sentences ago and were off in your own dream image of a snowbound monastery.

One day we went to the beach and stayed too long—both of us came home in wicked sunburns and bad moods. We complained and snapped at each other until Caitlin had the good idea of going to the bar for dinner because they were having a grill party and had been talking about it since we'd arrived. Grill parties are not my idea of nirvana, especially among strangers, but I knew if we stayed in our barren bungalow another hour we'd fight, so I agreed to go.

"Hello! There you two are. Miep thought you'd be coming so we saved you places. The food is really quite good. Try the chicken. Lord, look at your sunburns! Were you out all day? I remember the worst sunburn I ever had . . . ." Was only part of McGann's greeting from across the room when we came in and walked over. We loaded up plates and went to sit with them.

As both the evening and McGann went on, my mood plunged. I didn't want to listen to him, didn't want to be on this burnt island, didn't relish the twenty-hour trip back home. Did I mention when we returned to the mainland on the overnight ferry there were no more cabins available, so we had to sleep on benches? We did.

Anyway, I could feel myself winding up for one hell of a temper tantrum. When I was three seconds away from throwing it all onto McGann and telling him he was the biggest bore I'd ever met and would he shut up, Miep turned to me and asked, "What was the strangest dream you ever had?" Taken aback both by the question, which was utterly out of left field, and because her boyfriend was in the middle of a ramble about suntan cream, I thought about it. I rarely remember my dreams. When I do they are either boring or unimaginatively sexy. The only strange one that came to mind was playing guitar naked in the back seat of a Dodge with Jimi Hendrix. Jimi was naked too and we must have played "Hey Joe" ten times before I woke up with a smile on my face and a real sadness that Hendrix was dead and I would never meet him. I relayed this to Miep who listened with head cupped in her hands. Then she asked Caitlin. She told that great dream about making the giant omelette for God and going all over the world trying to find enough eggs? Remember how we laughed at that?

After we answered, there was a big silence. Even McGann said nothing. I noticed he was looking at his girlfriend with an anxious, childlike expression on his face. As if he were waiting for her to begin whatever game was to follow.

"Dreams are how Ian and I met. I was in Heathrow waiting to fly back to Holland. He was sitting next to me and saw that I was reading an article on this 'Lucid Dreaming.' Do you know about it? You teach yourself to be conscious in your night dreams so you can manipulate and use them. We started talking about this idea and he made me very bored. Ian can be very boring. It is something you must get used to if you are going to be with him. I still have trouble, but it is a week now and I am better."

"A week? What do you mean? You've only been together that long?"

"Miep was coming back from a beekeepers' convention in Devon. After our conversation in the airport, she said she would come with me."

"Just like that? You came here with him instead of going home?" Caitlin not only believed this, she was enchanted. She believes fully in chance encounters, splendid accidents, and loving someone so much right off the bat you can learn to live with their glaring faults. I was more astonished that Miep'd come with him yet said openly what a bore he was. Was that how a love-at-first-sight bond was sealed: Yes, let's fly off together, darling, I love you madly and I'll try to get used to how boring you are.

"Yes. After Ian told me about his dreams, I asked if I could come. It was necessary for me."

I said to McGann, "Must have been some kind of powerful dream you had." He looked plain, pleasant, and capable but only in a small way—like an efficient postman who delivers your mail early, or the salesman in a liquor store who can rattle off the names of thirty different brands of beer. I assumed he was a good travel agent, up on his prices and brochures and a man who could choose a good vacation for someone who didn't have much money. But he wasn't impressive and he talked forever. What kind of dream *had* he had to convince this attractive and nicely mysterious Dutch woman to drop everything and accompany him to Sardinia?

"It wasn't much really. I dreamt I was working in an office, not where I do work but some other place, but nowhere special. A man walked in who I knew a long time ago but who died. He died of cancer maybe five years ago. I saw him and knew for sure that he had come back from the dead to see me. His name was Larry Birmingham. I never really liked this fellow. He was very loud and much too sure of himself. But there he was in my dream. I looked up from my desk and said, 'Larry. It's you! You're back from the dead!' He was very calm and said yes, he'd come to see me. I asked if I could ask him questions about it. About death that is, of course. He smiled, a little too amusedly I realize now, and said yes. About this time in the dream, I think I *knew* I was dreaming, you know how that happens? But I thought go on, see what you can find out. So I asked him questions. What *is* death like? Should we be afraid? Is it anything like we expect . . . that sort of thing. He answered, but many of the answers were vaguely obscure and confusing. I'd ask again and he'd answer in a different way, which at first I thought was clearer, but in the end it wasn't—he had only stated the muddle differently. It wasn't much help, I'll tell you."

"Did you learn anything?"

Ian looked at Miep. Despite her aloofness and his ten-mile-long dialog it was very obvious that there was great closeness and regard between these two remarkably dissimilar people. It was a look of love to be sure, but a great deal more than that. More, a look that clearly said there were things they knew about each other already that went to the locus of their beings. Whether they'd known each other a short week or twenty years, the look contained everything we all hope for in our lives with others. She nodded her approval but after another moment, he said gently, "I . . . I'm afraid I can't tell you."

"Oh, Ian—" She reached across the table and touched her hand to his face. Imagine a laser line of light or heat going directly across that table, excluding everything but those two. That's what both Caitlin and I felt watching them. What was most surprising to me was it was the first time Miep had either talked or shown real feeling for her man. But there was suddenly so much feeling that it was embarrassing.

"Ian, you're right. I'm sorry. You're so right." She slipped back into her chair but continued looking at him. He turned to me and said, "I'm sorry to be rude, but you'll understand why I can't tell you anything when I'm finished.

"Excuse me, but before I go on, it's hard for me to tell this so I'm going to have another drink. Would anyone like a refill?"

None of us did so he got up and went to the bar. The table was silent while he was gone. Miep never stopped looking at him. Caitlin and I didn't know where to look until he returned.

"Right-O. Tanked up and am ready to go. You know what I was just thinking, up there at the bar? That I once drove through Austria and got a case of the giggles when I passed a sign for the town of

Mooskirchen. I remember so well thinking to myself that a bonkers translation of that would be 'Moose Church.' Then I thought well why the hell not—people worship all kinds of things on this earth. Why couldn't there be a church to Mooses? Or rather, a religion to them. You know?

"I'm rattling on here, aren't I? It's because this is a terribly difficult story for me to tell. The funny thing is, when I'm finished you'll think I'm just as bonkers as my imagined worshipers at the Moose Church, eh, Miep? Won't they think I don't have all my bulbs screwed in?"

"If they understand, they will know you are a hero."

"Yes, well, folks, don't take Miep too seriously. She's quiet but very emotional about things sometimes. Let me go on and you can judge for yourself whether I'm crazy or, ha, ha, a hero.

"The morning after that first dream, I walked to the bathroom and started taking my pajamas off so I could wash up. I was shocked when I saw—"

"Don't tell them, Ian, show them! Show them so they will see for themselves!"

Slowly, shyly he began to pull his T-shirt up over his head. Caitlin saw it first and gasped. When I saw I guess I gasped too. From his left shoulder down to above his left nipple was a monstrously long and deep scar. It looked exactly like what my father had down the middle of his chest after open-heart surgery. One giant scar so wide and obscenely shiny pink. His body's way of saying it would never forgive him for doing that to it.

"Oh, Ian, what happened?" Sweet Caitlin, the heart of the world, involuntarily reached out to touch him, comfort him. Realizing what she was doing, she pulled her hand back, but the look of sympathy framed her face.

"Nothing happened, Caitlin. I have never been hurt in my life. Never been in the hospital, never had an operation. I asked death some questions and when I woke the next morning this was here." He didn't wait for us to examine the scar more closely. The shirt was up and over his head quickly.

"I'm telling you, Ian, maybe it is a kind of gift."

"It's no gift, Miep, if it hurts terribly and I can't move my left arm very well anymore! The same with my foot *and* my hand."

"What are you talking about?"

Ian closed his eyes and tried once to continue. He couldn't and instead rocked up and down with his eyes closed.

Miep spoke. "The night before we met, he had another dream and the same thing happened: This Larry came back and Ian asked him more questions about death. But this time the answers were clearer, although not all of them. He woke up and he says he had begun to understand things that he didn't before. He believes that's why the scar on the inside of his hand is smaller—the more he understands of the dream, the more it leaves him alone. A few nights ago he had another but he woke with a big cut on his leg. Much bigger than the one on his hand."

Ian spoke again, but his voice was less. Softer and . . . deflated. "It will tell you anything you want to know, but then you have to understand it. If you don't . . . it does this to you so you'll be careful with your questions. The trouble is, once you've started, you can't stop asking. In the middle of my second dream I told Birmingham I wanted to stop; I was afraid. He said I couldn't. The ultimate game of 'Twenty Questions,' eh? Thank God Miep's here. Thank God she believed me! See, it makes me so much *weaker*. Maybe that's the worst part. After the dreams there are the scars, but even worse than that is I'm so much weaker and can't do anything about it. I can barely get out of bed. Most of the time I'm better as the day goes on . . . but I know it's getting worse. And one day I won't . . . I know if Miep weren't here . . . Thank God for you, Miep."

I later convinced him to show us the scar on his hand, which was utterly unlike the one on his chest. This one was white and thin and looked years old. It went diagonally across his palm and I remember thinking from the first time we'd met how strangely he moved that hand, how much slower and clumsier it was. Now I knew why.

There's more to this, Judy. But what do you do in a situation like that? When half your brain thinks this is mad but the other half is shaking because *maybe-it's-real*. They asked us for nothing, although I doubt there was anything we could do. But after that night whenever I saw or thought of McGann, I liked him enormously. Whatever was wrong with the man, he was afflicted by something terrible. Either insanity or death dreams were clearly out to get him and he was a goner. But the man remained a bore. A good-natured, good-humored bore who, in the midst of his agony or whatever it was, remained wholly himself as I assume he'd always been. That's the only real courage. I mean, come on, none of us goes into burning buildings to save others. But watching a person face the worst with grace, uncomplainingly, grateful even for the love and help of others . . . That's it, as far as I'm concerned.

Two days later, Caitlin and I decided more or less on the spur of the moment to leave. We'd had enough and weren't getting any pleasure at all from the place. Our bags were packed and the bill was paid within an hour and a half. Neither of us like saying goodbye to people, and as you can imagine, we were spooked by McGann's story. It's not something anyone would be quick to believe, but if you were there that night and seen their faces, heard their voices and the conviction in them, you'd know why both of us were uncomfortable in their presence. But it happened that as we were walking out to the car, we ran right into Miep, who was coming toward the office in a hurry.

Something was clearly wrong. "Miep, are you all right?"

"All right! Oh, well, no. Ian is . . . Ian is not well." She was totally preoccupied and her eyes were going everywhere but to us. Then a light of memory came on in them and her whole being slowed. She remembered, I guess, what her man had told us the other night.

"He had another dream today, after he came home from the beach. He lay down and it was only a few minutes, but when he woke—" Instead of continuing, she drew a slow line across the lower part of her stomach. Both Caitlin and I jumped at that and asked what we could do. I think we both also started toward their bungalow, but Miep shouted, really shouted, "No!" and there was nothing we could do to convince her to let us help. If that were possible. More than that, though, the thing that struck me hardest was her face. When she realized we weren't going to try and interfere, she looked over our shoulders toward their place, where Ian was, and the expression was both fear and radiance. Was it true? Was he really back there, scarred again by death, scarred again because he hadn't understood its answers to his questions? Who knows?

On the boat back to the mainland, I remembered what he had said that night about the Moose Church and how people should be allowed to worship whatever they want. *That* was the look on his girlfriend's face—the look of one in the presence of what they believe is both the truth and the answer to life. Or death.

Our Thoughts,
Ted

"The Moose Church" is a result of a terrible but rather interesting trip to Sardinia. I was so taken by the idea of the story that I decided to use it as the first part of the next novel I will be doing. As to the theme of vampirism, say whatever you will, the ultimate vampire is death.

Jonathan Carroll

Mrs. Rinaldi's Angel

THOMAS LIGOTTI

Ligotti is justly celebrated for his baroque journeys into the unconscious. This story is a little more straightforward and slightly less baroque in language, without, however, losing his unique voice.

Like Carroll's before it, this story, too, is about dreams, but here the dreamer is a collaborator despite himself, inadvertently causing great harm.

From time to time during my childhood, the striking dreams that I nightly experienced would become brutally vivid, causing me to awake screaming. The shouting done, I sank back into my bed in a state of superenervation resulting from the bodiless adventures imposed upon my slumbering self. Yet my body was surely affected by this nocturnal regimen, exercised harshly by visions both crystalline and confused. This activity, however immaterial, only served to drain my reserves of strength and in a few moments stole from me the benefits of a full night's sleep. Nevertheless, while I was deprived of the privilege of a natural rest, there may also have been some profit gained: the awful opulence of the dream, a rich and swollen world nourished by the exhaustion of the flesh. The world, in fact, *as such*. Any other realm seemed an absence by comparison, at best a chasm in the fertile graveyard of life.

Of course my parents did not share my feelings on this subject. "What is *wrong* with him," I heard my father bellow from far down the hallway, his voice full of reproach. Shortly afterward my mother was by my side. "They seem to be getting worse," she would say. Then on one occasion she whispered, "I think it's time we did something about this problem."

The tone of her voice told me that what she had in mind was not the doctor's appointment so often urged by my father. Hers was a more dubious quest for a curative, though one which no doubt also seemed more appropriate to my "suffering." My mother was always prone to the enticements of superstition, and my troubled

89

dreams appeared to justify an indulgence in unorthodox measures. Her shining and solemn gaze betrayed her own dreams of trafficking with esoteric forces, of being on familiar terms with specialists in a secret universe, entrepreneurs of the intangible.

"Tomorrow your father is leaving early on business. You stay home from school, and then we'll go and visit a woman I know."

Late the following morning, my mother and I went to a house in one of the outlying neighborhoods of town and were graciously invited to be seated in the parlor of the long-widowed Mrs. Rinaldi. Perhaps it was only the fatigue my dreams had inflicted on me that made it so difficult to consolidate any lucid thoughts or feelings about the old woman and her remote house. Although the well-ordered room we occupied was flush with sunlight, this illumination somehow acted in a way of a wash over a watercolor painting, blurring the outline of things and subduing the clarity of surfaces. This obscurity was not dispersed even by the large and thickly shaded lamp Mrs. Rinaldi kept lighted beside the small divan on which she and my mother sat. I was close to them in an old but respectably upholstered armchair, and yet their forms refused to come into focus, just as everything else in that room resisted definition. How well I knew such surroundings, those deep interiors of dream where everything is saturated with unreality and more or less dissolves under a direct gaze. I could tell how neatly this particular interior was arranged—pictures perfectly straight and tight against the walls, well-dusted figurines arranged well upon open shelves, lace-fringed tablecloths set precisely in place, and delicate silk flowers in slim vases of colored glass. Yet there was something so fragile about the balance of these things, as if they were all susceptible to sudden derangement should there be some upset, no matter how subtle, in the secret system that held them together. This volatility seemed to extend to Mrs. Rinaldi herself, though in fact she may have been its source.

Casually examined, she appeared to present only the usual mysteries of old women who might be expected to speak with a heavy accent, whether or not they actually did so. She wore the carnal bulk and simple attire of a peasant race, and her calm manner indeed epitomized the peasant quietude of popular conception: her hands folded without tremor upon a wide lap and her eyes were mildly attentive. But those eyes were so pale, as was her complexion and gauzy hair. It was as if some great strain had depleted her, and was continually depleting her, of the strong coloring she once possessed, draining her powers and leaving her vulnerable to some tenuous onslaught. At any moment, during the time my mother was explaining the reason why we sought her help, Mrs. Rinaldi might have degenerated before our eyes, might have finally succumbed to spectral afflictions she had spent so many years fending off, both for her own sake and for the sake of others. And still she might have easily been mistaken for just another old woman whose tidy parlor displayed no object or image that would betray her most questionable and perilous occupation.

"Missus," she said to my mother, though her eyes were on me, "I would like to take your son into another room in this house. There I believe I may begin to help him."

My mother assented and Mrs. Rinaldi escorted me down a hallway to a room at the back of the house. The room reminded me of a little shop of some kind, one that kept its merchandise hidden in dark cabinets along the walls, in great chests upon the floor, boxes and cases of every sort piled here and there. Nothing except these receptacles, this array of multiform exteriors, was exposed to view. The only window was tightly shuttered and a bare light bulb hanging overhead served as the only illumination.

There was nowhere to sit, only empty floor space; Mrs. Rinaldi took my hand and stood me at the center of the room. After gazing rather sternly down at me for some moments, she proceeded to pace slowly around me.

"Do you know what dreams are?" she asked quietly, and then immediately began to answer her own question. "They are parasites—maggots of the mind and soul, feeding on the mind and soul as ordinary maggots feed on the body. And their feeding on the mind and soul in turn gnaws away at the body, which in turn again affects the mind and the soul, and so on until death. These things cannot be separated, nor can anything else. Because everything is terribly inseparable and affects everything else. Even the most alien things are connected together with everything else. And so if these dreams have no world of their own to nourish them, they may come into yours and possess it, exhaust it little by little each night. They use your world and use it up. They wear your face and the faces of things you know: things that are yours they use in ways that are theirs. And some persons are so easy for them to use, and they use them so hard. But they use everyone and have always used everyone, because they are from the old time, the time before all the worlds awoke from a long and helpless night. And these dreams, these things that are called dreams, are still working to throw us back into that great mad darkness, to exhaust each one of us in our lonely sleep, and to use up everyone until death. Little by little, night after night, they take us away from ourselves and from the truth of things. I myself know very well what this can be like and what the dreams can do to us. They make us dance to their strange illusions until we are too exhausted to live. And they have found in you, child, an easy partner for their horrible dancing."

With these words Mrs. Rinaldi not only revealed a side of herself quite different from the serene wise woman my mother had seen, but she also took me much deeper into things I had merely suspected until that day in the room where chests and strange boxes were piled up everywhere and great cabinets loomed along the walls, so many tightly closed doors and drawers and locked-up lids with so many things on the other side of them.

"Of course," she went on, "these dreams of yours cannot be wholly exorcised from your life, but only driven back so that they may do no *extraordinary* harm. They will still triumph in the end, denying us not just the restoration of nightly sleep. For ultimately they steal away the time that might have measured into immortality. They corrupt us in *every way*, abducting us from the ranks of angels we might have been or become, pure and calm and everlasting. It is because of them that we endure such a meager allotment of years, with all their foulness. This is all I can offer you, child, even if you may not understand what it means. For it is surely not meant that you should fall into the fullest corruption before your time."

Her speech concluded, Mrs. Rinaldi stood before me, massive and motionless, her breathing now a bit labored. I confess that her theories intrigued me as far as I could comprehend them, for at the time her statements regarding the meaning and mechanisms of dream appeared to be founded on somewhat questionable assumptions, unnecessarily outlandish in their departures from the oldest orthodoxies of creation. Nonetheless, I decided not to resist whatever applications she chose to make of her ideas. On her side, she was scrutinizing my small form with some intensity, engaged in what seemed a psychic sizing up of my presence, as if she were seriously unsure whether or not it was safe to move on to the next step with me.

Apparently resolving her doubts, she shuffled over to a tall cabinet, unlocked its door with a key she had taken from a sagging pocket in her dress, and from within removed two items: a slim decanter half-filled with a dark red liquid, presumably wine, and a shallow wide-mouthed drinking glass. Carrying these objects back to me, she put out her right hand, in which she held the glass, and said: "Take this and spit into it." After I had done this, she poured some of the wine into the glass and then replaced the decanter in its cabinet, which she locked once again. "Now kneel down on the floor," she ordered. "Don't let anything spill out of the glass, and don't get up until I tell you to do so. I'm going to turn out the light."

Even in total darkness, Mrs. Rinaldi maneuvered well about the room, her footsteps again moving away from me. I heard her opening another cabinet, or perhaps it was a large chest whose heavy lid she struggled to push back, its old hinges grinding in the darkness. A slight draft crossed the room, a brief drifting current of air without scent and neither warm nor cold. Mrs. Rinaldi then approached me, moving more slowly than she had before, as if bearing some weighty object. With a groan, she set it down, and I heard it scrape the floor inches from where I knelt, though I could not see what it was.

Suddenly a thin line of light scored the blackness, and I could see Mrs. Rinaldi's old finger slowly lifting the lid of a long low box from which the luminousness emanated. The glowing slit widened as the lid was drawn back farther, revealing a pale brilliance that seemed confined wholly within the box itself, casting not the least glimmer into the room. The source of this light was a kind of incandescent vapor that curled about in a way that seemed to draw the room's darkness into its lustrous realm, which appeared to extend beyond the boundaries of the visible and made the box before me look bottomless. But I felt the bottom for myself when the whispering voice of Mrs. Rinaldi instructed me to place the glass I was holding down into the box. So I offered the glass to that fluorescent mist, that churning vapor that was electrical in some way, scintillating with infinitesimal flashes of sharp light, sprinkled with shattered diamonds.

I expected to feel something as I put my hand in the shining box, easily setting the glass upon its shallow and quite solid bottom. But there was nothing at all to be felt, no sensation whatever—not even that of my own hand. There seemed to be a power to this prodigy, but it was a terribly quiescent power, a cataract of the purest light plummeting silently in the blackness of space. If it could have spoken it might have told, in a soft and reverberant voice, of the lonely peace of the planets, the uninhabited paradise of clouds, and an antiseptic infinity.

After I placed the glass of wine and spittle into the box, the light from within took on a rosy hue for just a moment, then resumed its glittering whiteness once again. It had taken the offering. Mrs. Rinaldi whispered "Amen," then carefully closed the lid upon the box, returning the room to blackness. I heard her replace the object in its tabernacle of storage, wherever that may have been. At last the lights came on.

"You can get up now," Mrs. Rinaldi said. "And wipe off your knees, they're a little dirty."

When I finished brushing off my pants I found that Mrs. Rinaldi was again scrutinizing me for telltale signs of some possible misunderstanding or perhaps misconduct that I might disclose to her. I imagined that she was about to say, "Do not ask what it was you saw in this room." But in actuality she said, "You will feel better now, but never try to guess what is in that box. Never seek to know more about it." She did not pause to hear any response I might have had to her command, for she was indeed a wise woman and knew that in matters such as these no casual oath of abstention can be trusted, all fine intentions notwithstanding.

As soon as we had left Mrs. Rinaldi's house, my mother asked me what had happened, and I described the ceremony in detail. Nevertheless, she remained at a loss for any simple estimate of what I had told her: While she expected that Mrs. Rinaldi's methods might be highly unusual, she also knew her own son's imagination. Still, she was obliged to keep faith with the arcane processes that she herself had set in motion. So after I recounted the incidents that took place in that room, my mother only nodded silently, perhaps bewilderedly.

I should document that for a certain period of time my mother's faith in Mrs. Rinaldi did not appear to have been misplaced. The very day of our visit to the old woman was for me the beginning of a unique phase of experience. Even my father noted the change in my nighttime habits, as well as a newfound characterology I exhibited throughout the day. "The boy does seem quieter now," he commented to my mother.

Indeed, I could feel myself approaching a serenity almost shameful in its expansiveness, one that submerged me in a placid routine of the most violent contrast to my former life. I slept straight through each night and barely ruffled my bedcovers. Not to claim that my sleep was left completely untouched by dreams. But these were no more than ripples on great becalmed waters, pathetic gestures of something that was trying to bestir the immobility of a vast and colorless world. A few figures might appear, tremulous as smoke, but they were the merest invalids of hallucination, lacking the strength to speak or raise a hand against my terrible peace.

My daydreams were actually more interesting, while still being incredibly vague and without tension. Sitting quietly in the classroom at school, I often gazed out the window at clouds and sunlight, watching the way the sunlight penetrated the clouds and the way the clouds were filled with both sunlight and shadows. Yet no images or ideas were aroused by this sight, as they had been before. Only a vacant meditation took place, a musing without subject matter. I could feel something trying to emerge in my imagination, some wild and colorful drama that was being kept far away from me, as far away as those clouds, remaining entirely vaporous and empty of either sense or sensation. And if I tried to draw any pictures in my notebook, allowing my hand all possible freedom (in order to find out if it could feel and remember what I could not), I found myself sketching over and over the same thing: boxes, boxes, boxes.

Nonetheless, I cannot say that I was unhappy during this time. My nightmares and everything associated with them had been bled from my system, drained away as I slept. I had been purified of tainted substances, sponged clean of strangely tinted stains on my mind and my soul. I felt the vapid joy of a lightened being, a kind of clarity that seemed in a way true and even virtuous. But this moratorium on every form of darkness could only last so long before the old impulses asserted themselves within me, moving out like a pack of famished wolves in search of the stuff that once fed them and would feed them again.

For a number of nights my dreams remained somewhat anemic and continued to present only the palest characters and scenes. Thus, they had been rendered too weak to use me as they had before, seizing, as they did, the contents of my life—my memories and emotions, all the paraphernalia of a private history—and working them in their way, giving form to things that had none of their own, and thereby exhausting my body and soul. Mrs. Rinaldi's theory of these parasites that have been called dreams was therefore accurate . . . as far as it went. But she had failed to consider, or perhaps refused to acknowledge, that the dreamer on his part draws something from the dream, gaining a store of experience otherwise impossible to obtain, hoarding the grotesque or banal enigmas of the night to try to fill out the great empty spaces of the day. And my dreams had ceased to perform this function, or at least were no longer adequate to my needs—that appetite I had discovered in myself for banqueting on the absurd and horrible, even the perfectly evil. It was this deprivation, I believe, that brought about the change in the nature of my dreaming.

Having such paltry sustenance on which to nourish my tastes—frail demons and insipid decors—I must have been thrown back upon my own consciousness ... until finally I came into full awareness of my dreaming state, intensely lucid. Over the course of several nights, then, I noticed a new or formerly obscure phenomenon, something that existed in the distance of those bankrupt landscapes that I had started to explore. It was a kind of sickly mist that lingered about the horizon of each dream, exerting a definite magnetism, a tugging upon the austere scenes that it enveloped from all sides, even hovering high above like an animate sky, a celestial vault that glistened softly. Yet the dreams themselves were cast in the dullest tones and contained the most spare and dilapidated furnishings.

In the very last dream I had of this type, I was wandering amid a few widely scattered ruins that seemed to have risen from some undersea abyss, all soft and pallid from their dark confinement. Like the settings of the other dreams, this one seemed familiar, though incomplete, as if I were seeing the decayed remnants of something I might have known in waking life. For those were *not* time-eaten towers rising around me, and at my feet there were not sunken strongboxes crumbling like rotten flesh. Instead, these objects were the cabinets and cases I remembered from that room in Mrs. Rinaldi's house, except now this memory was degenerating, being dragged away little by little, digested by that mist, which surrounded everything and nibbled at it. And the more closely I approached this mist, the more decomposed the scenery of the dream became, until it was consumed altogether and I could see nothing but that sparkling, swirling vapor.

It was only when I had entered this foggy void that the true sense of dreams, the inherent dread of my visions, was restored to me. Here was a sort of reservoir into which the depths of my dreams were being directed, leaving only a shallow spillover that barely trickled through my nights. *Here*, I say, without knowing really what place or plane of being it was: some spectral venue, a vacant plot situated along the back street of sleep, an outpost of the universe itself ... or perhaps merely the inside of a box hidden away in the house of an old woman, a box in which something exists in all its insensible purity, a cloudy ether free of tainted forms and knowledge, freely cleansing others with its sterile grace.

In any event, I sensed that the usual boundaries of my world of sleep had extended into another realm. And it was here, I found, that the lost dreams were fully alive *in their essence*. Consumed within that barren vapor, which I had seen imbibe a mixture of my own saliva and the reddest wine, they lived in exile from that multitude of unwitting hosts whose experiences they used like a wardrobe for those eerie performances behind the curtain of sleep, forcing the sleeper into the role of both player and witness in the alien manipulations of his memories and emotions, the ungranted abduction of his private history for the wreckless revels of these parasites called dreams. But here, in that prison of glittering purity, they had been reduced to their primordial state—dreams in abstraction, faceless and formless things from the old time that a very old woman revealed to me. And although they had neither face nor form, one of the multitudinous disguises in which I had always known them, their presence was still quite palpable all around me, bearing down upon the richly laden lucidity I had brought with me into a place I did not belong.

A struggle evolved as that angelic mist—agent of my salvation—held at bay the things that craved my mind and soul, my very consciousness. But rather than join in that struggle, I gave myself up to this ravenous siege, offering my awareness to what had none of its own, bestowing all the treasures of my life on this wasteland of abstract dreams.

Then the infinite whiteness itself was flooded with the colors of countless faces and forms, a blank sky suddenly dense with rainbows, until *everything* was so saturated with revels and thick with frenzy that it took on the utter blackness of the old time. And in the blackness I awoke, screaming for all the world.

The next day I was standing on Mrs. Rinaldi's porch, watching as my mother repeatedly slammed the door knocker without being able to summon the old woman. But something told us she was nevertheless at home, a shadow that we saw pass nervously behind the front window. At last the door opened for us, but whoever opened it stayed on the other side, saying: "Missus, take your child home. There is nothing more that can be done. I made a mistake with him."

My mother protested the recurrence of my "sickness," taking a step inside the house and pulling me along with her. But Mrs. Rinaldi only said: "Do not come in here. It is not a fit place to visit, and I am not fit to be looked upon." From what I could observe of the parlor, it did seem that an essential change had occurred, as if the room's fragile balance had failed and the ever-threatening derangement of its order had finally been consummated. Everything in this interior seemed askew, distorted by some process of decay and twisted out of natural proportion. It was a room seen through a warped and strangely colored window.

And how much stranger this color appeared when Mrs. Rinaldi suddenly showed herself, and I saw that her once-pale eyes and sallow face had taken on the same tint, a greenish glaze as of something both rotten and reptilian. My mother was immediately silenced by this sight. "Now will you leave me?" she said. "Even for myself there is nothing I can do any longer. You know what I am saying, child. All those years the dreams had been kept away. But you have *consorted* with them, I know you did. I have made a mistake with you. You let my angel be poisoned by the dreams that you could not deny. It *was* an angel, did you know that? It was pure of all thinking and pure of all dreaming. And you are the one who made it think and dream and now it is dying. And it is dying not as an angel, but as a demon. Do you want to see what it is like now?" she said, gesturing toward a door that led into the cellar of her house. "Yes, it is down there because it is not the way it was and could not remain where it was. It crawled away with its own body, the body of a demon. And it has its own dreams, the dreams of a demon. It is dreaming and dying of its dreams. And I am dying too, because all the dreams have come back."

Mrs. Rinaldi then began to approach me, and the color of her eyes and her face seemed to deepen. That was when my mother grasped my arm to pull me quickly from the house. As we ran off I looked over my shoulder and saw the old woman raving in the open doorway, cursing me for a demon.

It was not long afterward that we learned of Mrs. Rinaldi's death. True to her own diagnosis, the parasites were upon her, although local gossip told that she had been suffering for years from a cancer of some kind. There was also evidence that another inhabitant of the house survived the old woman for a short time. As it happened, several of my schoolmates reported to me their investigations after dark at the house of the "old witch," a place that I myself was forbidden by my parents to go. So I cannot claim that I observed with my own eyes what crept along the floor of that moonlit house, "like a pile of filthy rags," said one boy.

But I did dream about this prodigy; I even dreamed about its dreams as they dragged every shining angelic particle of this being into the blackness of the old time. Then all my bad dreams abated after a while, just as they always had and always would, using my world only at intervals and gradually dissolving my life into theirs.

A few words on the death of the personal vampire. One of the noblest and most tragic figures of the imagination, the vampire has long been reduced to serving some allegorical function in various mundane contexts—psychology, sociology, politics, and so on. The vampire attained his stature through the emotion of fear of a fantastic evil, yet how utterly he has lost it all at the heavy hands of writers and critics whose ceaseless prying has exposed him too often to daylight, murdering his mystery with tabloid revelations as well as talky sessions of analysis.

But if the vampire no longer inspires the emotion he once did, perhaps it is partly his own fault. He lost his mystery entirely because he had so little of it to start. His nature and habits were always documented in detail, his ways and means a matter of public record. Too many laws lorded over him, and all laws belong to the natural world. Like his colleague the werewolf, he was too much a *known quantity*. His was a familiar, most of the time human body, and it was used like a whore by writers whose concerns were predominantly for the body and the everyday path in which it walks. Consequently, the vampire was stripped of all that made him alien to our ordinary selves, until finally he was transformed into merely the bad boy next door. He remained a menace, to be sure. But his focus shifted from the soul to the senses. This is how it is when a mysterious force is embodied in a human body, or in any form that is too well fixed. And a mystery explained is one robbed of its power.

Rest in peace, Nosferatu. None will ever take your place.

Thomas Ligotti

The Pool People

MELISSA MIA HALL

Hall's story deals with an experience seldom written about from the victim's point of view—particularly in horror fiction. The protagonist has been so maimed emotionally that she has lost her sense of self.

---

1. The Pool

The water's so blue it hurts my eyes. On a day like this you have to wear sunglasses or go blind. I'm wearing dark ones, old-fashioned Audrey Hepburn *Breakfast at Tiffany's* sunglasses. The glamorous, heavy-duty I-want-to-be-alone kind. And I'm alone. My cousin has gone to work and left me here by her pool. Her swimming pool. I'll be safe here. I can relax and take it easy. Get a tan on a body that hasn't known a tan since high school. Of course I know sunburns are dangerous. I've slathered my body with sunscreen. I smell like a dream of Hawaii.

This is my summer vacation.

And I'm sitting by the pool.

2. The People

I saw them for the first time in a dream. I'd fallen asleep in the sun. My eyelids bled pink light, then I opened my eyes and my eyeballs fell forward into my lap. I picked them up and put them back in and leaned forward, staring into the water. My hands gripped the side of the pool. The pebble-coarse side slid into smoothness. I touched the surface of the water with the palm of my hand. I felt the ripples. I thought, Molly, you're dreaming, and then I saw them, clear as day, the people. They sat at a table under the water, on the bottom. Fully clothed, they were, their hair streaming out from their heads like seaweed.

Like a show I saw or wanted to see at the Aquarena Watercade

Extravaganza a long, long time ago, when I was little. How I loved the idea of people pretending they weren't really underwater, sucking secret oxygen.

And now, here they are again. Waving.

3. The Pool Man

It's too much sun, seeing people in a pool, waving. I was just remembering a TV commercial. And staring into the water. I should swim. The exercise would be good for me. I'd impress Cara Ann, too. She's so proud of this pool, this house, the lovely landscaping, the life she's made here, without Al.

She wants me to be happy. I open a book instead. The pages are too white. I move over to a circle of shade. I take a sip of tepid Coke. I need ice. I stand up and stretch, lady of supreme leisure.

"The gate was open—"

I drop my book. The intruder looks embarrassed. "Ms. Clovis was expecting me—"

My hand closes over the back of a wrought-iron chair. I can barely breathe. Every time I see them, I feel emptier, looser, gone. But now here is this man. I tighten inside, clench. All men are dangerous. I know that, I know.

He flashes an open billfold like he's from the FBI and stuffs it back into the back pocket of his baggy shorts. "I'm the pool man—at least for today. I'm helping out my big brother, Ben. He owns Sunside Pools—and he's in a bind and I told him, hey, bubba, I'll help you out. I owe him, see? So, just get back to whatever it was you were doing. I won't be long. Well, not too long. It's been a while. You're working on a tan—I see—I know, what tan? Well, never mind, I'll get to work and you won't even know I'm here."

"Cara Ann forgot to tell me—"

She had left a note on the refrigerator I had forgotten to read. I thought it probably said something about what to fix for dinner or when she was coming home. I should've read it.

"I hope you're not planning on swimming. That'll have to wait, I'm afraid, while I do all this. But you can stay out here and keep me company."

He won't stop talking. I stare at him, still uneasy. He's not dressed in a uniform and he's too attractive to be trusted. He has a tan almost as dark as George Hamilton's, which cannot be too healthy, dark eyes, carelessly sexy. He tosses his longish hair back like Miss Piggy and keeps talking, about the weather, music, his favorite kind of food, baseball. He plays with his pool tools like a child.

"What's wrong?"

A fish does this, out of water, gasping. Slowly, I must breathe in and out, slowly. Suddenly there's a wet towel on my face. I push it off and meet the pool man's searching, too observant eyes.

"Lady, you fainted. I've seen that in old movies, but never in real life. Are you okay? Are you sick or something? Should I call Ms. Clovis? She works on that TV show—what is it? I could call her—"

"I'm fine, really."

"Are you sure?"

"No," I say, managing a smile. His white shirt is unbuttoned. He has dark hair on his chest. My head hurts. The white shirt has tiny black dots woven into the cloth. They appear to be moving.

"I think I'd better help you into the house where it's cool."

"Thanks—"

"Bergman, Pete, and you are—"

"Molly Woods."

"Nice to meet you, Molly." He says this with an expectant grin. He acts as if I am sharing some sort of secret joke, but then he sees I don't get it. He leads me into the house. I flop on the nearest chair and motion for him to go back outside. He overwhelms me with the scent of an aftershave mingled with sweat. He keeps looking at me with an expression that frightens me.

"I know, I may or may not be a killer." His hand rests on the sliding glass door. "Trust me, I'm not." He smiles again and his perfect white teeth amaze me. Everyone here has such perfect teeth. Self-consciously, I cover my mouth. My teeth need cleaning desperately.

The door slides shut. I watch him go about his business. He moves in slow motion, carefully. He pauses and considers each action he takes. Something's not right.

I go to the kitchen and get a knife. I sit in the den and watch him out the window. He better not come back in here. The steak knife stays in my lap. I call Cara Ann and ask when she'll be home. "Seven o'clock, like I told you, silly," she says, laughing. "Didn't you read my note?"

I go get the note after I hang up. I read it, keeping the knife always close at hand. It says nothing about a pool man coming.

I look outside and he's bending over the water. Around his neck is a thin gold necklace with a small disc. A tiny round flashlight. He sees something under the water. He stoops down but doesn't use the net. He just stares, shakes his head, and straightens up. He suddenly looks at the house. I know that he cannot see me, but it's as if he does. He smiles.

"I'm leaving!" he yells. "Till next time, Molly—!"

There won't be a next time. He's crazy. But I have the knife.

He comes to the sliding glass door. He knocks on it, still smiling. "Listen, Molly, if you swim, tomorrow, whenever, make sure and take the Polaris out." He points at that white machine thing with the long umbilical cord.

"I know—" I shout.

"And, hey, Molly—I hope you feel better." He seems sincere. "You want to come lock the gate after I leave?"

He doesn't see the knife. I stroke the handle. I'll put it in the pocket of my pink cover-up. I'll carry it with me. He has done nothing wrong.

I follow him out to the gate.

"You living here now?"

"Just visiting."

I glimpse the faint wrinkles at the corners of his eyes. I realize he's probably in his late thirties. Too old to be a pool man?

"You're not local. I could tell that."

I stroke the handle of the knife. I'm perfectly safe. He will not harm me. "No, I'm not. I'm from Tulsa, Oklahoma."

He suddenly leans forward and kisses my cheek. "Welcome to California," he says and the gate clangs shut.

I run back to the house. From the pool I hear strange voices and a bubbling sound. It's a fantasy, just a fantasy. It comes of vacationing. I am used to working and a normal life. Idle time and idle hands create insanity. You think too much. And when you think, you remember.

4. The Dream

The people in the water return to me. I know I'm dreaming, but I'm so happy to see them. I try to say hello, but bubbles come out of my mouth instead of words. I am underwater, too. I start to walk over, to sit down at the table with them. But there aren't any other chairs and it's awkward. I want to see them up close. I force my legs to move. Closer. The water keeps teasing me, pushing me back.

Closer. They don't see me. They don't hear me. Then the man turns toward me and stares right through me. His hair is graying at the temples. The sunlit water twists it out straight. His forehead doesn't match the rest of his face. It's much paler, more innocent and exposed. His eyes widen suddenly, registering my presence. I frighten him. He quickly glances at the woman who has also seen me. She waves her hand. I try to say hello again, then I stop because I see blood, or probably red dye, issuing from her mouth. The woman loses her seat. Released from the chair, which had been holding her in with silky black ribbons, the woman rises through the water. Her legs are gleaming white. The thin white skirt also rises, a flower blossoming backward. The man's face turns upward, following her ascent.

I'm at the table now, looking at the empty chair.

There's a crash or a splash, something that makes the water rumble and stir. The woman has split the surface. She is gone. I sit down in the chair. I am naked. He's watching me, helpless, as the other ones laugh. They're watching me. Everyone sees I'm naked. Two hands come around from the back of the chair, or it is the chair. I think it is the chair. I can't breathe because it is squeezing me. The man's mouth screws up in pain. His chair has hands, too. He can't stop it. And the black ribbons swim around us like snakes. Water moccasins. They hiss, "Watch what we're going to do to her, Mr. Principal, watch us-ss-s." The bubbles keep escaping from my mouth. There is nothing I can say, but if I could, I would. The bubbles fly away, one after another, in a line, like laundry on a line drawn up and away by the wind. One of them I touch with my hand before it escapes; it is rainbow-hued and shining. My hands burn. The ropes twist. What will the children say. Will their eyes go round and spin into shame? Don't look. Don't see.

"It hurts!" I scream or I think loudly and he hears me but one of the other bubbles has settled over his face. It develops into a monarch butterfly.

The hands clutch my middle, the nails biting into my stomach.

"Let go of me—let go—" And then it's dark and I'm in another place, a bad place. But the water's still there, pushing down, and I do not see the table. I'm drowning. "Help me!" My scream melts into a coughing silence. The hands keep holding me down. "Let me go—" I hit the water and it's glass. I hit it but the glass will not break. Safety glass. "I'm not going to hurt you," the other voice says. I keep hitting till my hands hurt because I hurt. The hands hurt.

5. The Vacation

"So, are you having a good time? You need to get out more, do stuff. This weekend I was thinking we could go up the coast or something. I have a friend who has this neat beach house. We could go up there, you know, really get away, watch the ocean."

I could do that. Cara Ann's face brightens when I smile at her. She's encouraged.

"Oh, God, I could use a vacation myself. Listen, at work yesterday, it was just horrible—horrible. It took all day—all because of Serena. Belts. I'm serious. She puts belts on everything she wears. I don't care if it's the most gorgeous suit in the world or the most delicate skirt. Belts, big red plastic belts or awful gold ones. She insists, the star insists. And who am I? Just the lowly costume supervisor. Sometimes, I know, it doesn't matter. And even sometimes the belts aren't so bad. But sometimes, it just makes me sick. To work so hard—" Cara Ann sighs and leans back on the couch.

I lose myself in the contemplation of belts. It's the after-diet-succeeds mania—look at how little my waist is—when you keep cinching the belt in tighter and tighter, regardless of how much it hurts or accentuates the faintest bulge.

"Maybe she lost a lot of weight lately. She's overcompensating." But red plastic?

"And the producer? He's no help. He says, Serena wants belts, she gets belts. I groan. Over a negligee? Won't the viewers think she's gone around the bend or something?"

"Well, maybe she has," I observe, picturing a red plastic belt around a pale pink satin teddy. I laugh. "Maybe her boyfriend has a thing about belts."

"I guess I hate feeling powerless. But it made me sick yesterday. I mean physically ill. I threw-up-my-tacos sick. I don't know, getting sick over a belt? What's wrong with this picture? It's not like I'm working to discover a cure for cancer."

I smooth my ponytail and look outside. The pool's turquoise water catches the fading sun. It is chemically clean and not crippled by an oil slick. But I would rather see the ocean.

Cara Ann notices my switch in attention. "So this pool man, did he have blond hair with faintly green tips and real narrow shoulders. Was his name J. G.? Say about nineteen or twenty?"

"No, he was a lot older and dark. He was slow, real slow, not retarded, but like he wasn't sure of what he was doing."

"Oh, yeah, really good-looking—white, white teeth—smile a lot? Talk a lot?"

"Well, yes."

"What was his name—?"

"Pete Bergman."

"Oh, wow—I knew it—that's P. C. Bergman—God, that Pete—what a kidder." She shakes her short bouncy blond hair and giggles.

"What's the joke?"

"He's an actor. Don't you—didn't you recognize him?"

"Should I?"

"He's on *Santa Fe Stories*—plays a continuing role."

"Oh." I remember the knife and how I was so frightened of him. My cheeks burn and I know I'm blushing, something I've never been able to control and Cara Ann laughs even harder.

"Well, it's not that funny—"

"He's good, I mean, really good. I guess he's practicing for something, researching a role. I know Ben, his brother. He owns Sunside Pools. He told me his little brother was slightly wacko. I met him at a party last year. When Ben started out, Pete actually worked for him, but that was a long time ago. It's too bad his career hasn't ever really taken off."

"But he's still working—"

"On *Santa Fe Stories*? Yes, but I heard his character might be killed off. The last time he left the soap was five years ago—his character got hit on the head by a jealous husband and he wandered off, thinking he was his evil twin brother Raven Blackfoot and Santa Fe never heard of him again till last year when he came back and had a car accident that restored his memory. Then he was Gavin Gold again."

"How do you keep up with all that?"

"VCR. I tape all the episodes on my bedroom set. I've watched that show since I was a kid. Habit and it's the best daytime soap on the tube, period."

Cara Ann fixes herself an iced tea and asks me if I want one.

"No, I'm okay. But tell me why—why do you really like it so much? I've never been able to get hooked on one."

"Continuity. With all the shit I've been through, I just like something that stays relatively the same. Throughout the divorce from Al, the job changes, moving, the custody battle over Teddy, when dad was sick, all the way through them I could watch the citizens of *Santa Fe Stories* and know basically, I was okay because their problems were always so ridiculous and awful that mine seemed to pale in comparison."

A reasonable conclusion. I feel like hugging Cara Ann. "Teddy will be back soon. You miss him, don't you?" Count on me to state the obvious. I should hug her, but I sit across the room from her, frozen. My problems are indistinct. I am in awe of her.

"Hey, this is your vacation, cousin, let's celebrate tonight. You want to?" She comes over to me and pinches me. "Let's go—and if Pete comes again, ask him if Gavin's brain tumor is going to pull the plug on him permanently."

"Are we going to take off this weekend, really—go up the coast?"

"I'll see if I can take some time off. That would be great," she says, but her eyes are suddenly distant and preoccupied. I see her measuring her waist with her hands. Belts. I realize she's just talking and that when it comes time to go, she'll probably have to beg off. She'll tell me I should take off on my own. That I shouldn't be afraid to drive up the coast by myself. She'll tell me about a bed-and-breakfast some friend owns. She'll tell me she'll meet me there a day later. But if I go, I'll have to go alone. And I won't.

I have been here one week.

I am still scared.

6. The Fear

The first thing you do, after some of the shock has worn away, is to deny it happened. Or you decided that whatever happened, happened for a reason, that somehow you did something to deserve it. But mostly, you push it way back under the bed or into the depths of a closet, somewhere that seldom gets cleaned out. I have pushed it as far away from me as I can, but it's still there.

This vacation is supposed to make me feel better, my own brand of therapy. Trying to save money, I suppose. Afraid if I went into therapy, real therapy, the doctor would keep asking me to come back until eventually he'd decide I would need to be admitted to some expensive clinic, that I'd agree and disappear from the rest of my life without a whisper. A safe thing to do.

I could do that. I'm just too tired. I'd like to go to sleep and never wake up.

My mother and father want me to straighten up, be an adult, especially since I'm over thirty. It's way past time. My father's not averse to the idea of psychiatric help but my mother warns me, "It would always be on your record." Maybe she's afraid at some point people will find out and I would thereafter turn into Mrs. Woods's poor loony girl, the one who started off so promising and ended up—well—disturbed.

But I can't get away from it. I don't know what to do. I can't really think about it. There's a wall there, a big, thick stone wall and I don't want it to tumble down on top of me. So I come here to recuperate and there is this pool.

Cara Ann has left me alone to sort things out. Again. She's very patient with me. I think I'm getting better. Maybe I will fix myself a thick chocolate milkshake. Lots of calories. But I can't, I'm just not hungry.

I called Dad last night and he told me an awful joke and I laughed till I cried. Then Cara Ann and I went to a concert of a saxophonist, a rather famous one you see on television from time to time, David Sanborn. But at one point, there was a song that bothered me. It was smoky sweet and trailing down the aisle toward me, it wrapped me up tight and then left, going back the way it had come. I asked Cara Ann what the name of the song was. She didn't know. She said she'd get some tapes for me and maybe we'd find it. But it's here now, the music's in my head.

And I'm looking at the pool.

I like water. Water soothes and refreshes the skin. Sit down in a shower and let it fall on the top of your head. Such freedom. And in a hot tub full of bubbles.

Bubbles.

I see some.

In the water over there.

My feet are in the water. Something dark is coming. Something seems to touch the balls of my feet. I get out of there quickly.

Shadows stretching up and forward. Shadow. Nothing there.

The pool people are still there. I know it. What if I submerge myself. In the water and below me their bodies would rise up to meet me and we would entwine, entangle, and sink down into shadow. Then later, we would float like dead fish in a polluted lake of green glass. Going nowhere. Have you ever noticed how sometimes toxic water glitters with rainbows?

I wish they would show themselves.

I sit down on a white deck chair and wipe the wetness off my legs. I haven't done any swimming in a long while. I used to be deathly afraid of the water since the time a dumb swimming instructor threw me off the high diving board and I almost drowned. What a guy—convinced that scare tactics should be included in lessons for six-year-olds. "Sink or swim!" was his rallying cry, I recall. So I decided to sink. Swimming at that point of my life was as alien an idea as flying.

Eventually, I did learn to swim. Maybe I should take a swim now. I have the beginnings of a healthy tan. I don't need to sunbathe anymore. I could use the exercise.

Maybe tomorrow. Right now I'm just too weak. I feel like an overwatered hanging basket, all the excess water draining out of the bottom, into the pool, into their breathless, sucking mouths.

7. The Actor

"You really didn't know who I was?"

He sits across from me, sipping a glass of iced tea. A lemon wedge bobs in the melting ice and he smiles, again, intent upon some secret joke. Then he laughs. "You've really never seen my show? Or say, I've been in a movie or two. *A Kiss After Death* or *The House of Mirth*—that was on PBS. No? Oh—I know—I was on *Miami Vice* back a few years ago. I had a close-up with Don Johnson. I was a drug lord's bodyguard." Silence. "No? Well, you realize, of course, that this doesn't do much for my ego."

"I'm sorry, honestly, but Cara Ann tapes all of the episodes of *Santa Fe Stories* and I did watch a couple the other night. And you were good—you really seemed to have a handle on your character."

"It's a pile of crap, isn't it? I've been doing Gavin so long I'm thinking shit, maybe *I'm* the real evil twin brother, not Raven Blackfoot."

"Don't put yourself down—" He makes me uncomfortable—fidgeting with his teaspoon and jogging one leg up and down in a nervous, but not totally unattractive movement that makes me too aware of the muscles in his calves. I glance at the pool for solace. The water moves with the wind. "You should be proud of yourself, being a well-known actor and everything. I guess I should read *People* more. I used to watch *Entertainment Tonight* while I graded papers."

He smirks. "Once in a blue moon, right?"

I stare at him weakly. He wants me to flirt. I try a small smile. "It's been really special to meet you—even if it was under dubious circumstance." So, I am flirting. It's not too difficult. I'm wanting him to ask me out. I'd shock Cara Ann, have a date with a TV star. Do I feel stronger? The sun does not go through me.

I'm not floundering. It has not resurfaced. It is far away. Surely, I am stronger.

He brushes my hand. He's wearing a watch with a sporty plastic band instead of a Rolex. I find myself absurdly relieved. Now his hand drifts over mine. Does it show the time in other time zones?

I don't care. I'm glad he decided to drop by. He smiles. His hand caresses mine. Pressure.

"I felt really bad about the other day. Barging in—it's just something I do sometimes. I mean, I've met Cara Ann and I thought it was her day off—it was a joke. I'm in a transitional phase of my career and I needed—"

I pull my hand away and he acts like it embarrasses him. He quickly grips his glass. "Yeah, Cara Ann told me that your character might be killed off, something about a brain tumor?"

He flinches as if I have slapped him. "Come time to move on, you move on," he says curtly. He makes a big deal out of checking the time. "Would you look at that? Duty calls—lunch with my agent. Guess I'd better run." The actor stands, half in and half out of the sun. I'm surprised someone like him would bother with some no-name teacher. Then I catch my self-depreciation and glare at the obscenely cheerful pool. I wonder if I should ask for his autograph? Mom might like it.

"Thanks for dropping by," I say stiffly, also standing. I hold my stomach in and hope I look attractive. "It was a nice surprise."

The pool people are back. Waving at me. Waving in streams of blood. I'm dizzy. I'm going to fall into the water and drown. I will fall; I can't stand still. My arms turn cartwheels. Head over heels, slipping, falling, going down. Gone under.

He catches me. We're sitting at the edge of the pool. He turns me around and studies me with concern. It's like he knows me, for God's sake. Like he's worried. What an actor—or I look really awful. "Should I call Cara Ann? A doctor?"

"I guess I'm just hungry. I'm sorry about that. I just lost my balance. Really, Mr. Bergman, I'm fine. I'll go heat up a frozen burrito in the microwave. I'll be really okay. This is *so* embarrassing—"

He looks away from me, into the pool. He frowns. "It's not that.

It's not that at all." He glances at me. "Talk to me—tell me about it."

Talk to him? My head pounds.

We go inside and I tell a perfect stranger about it and the pool people. He is kind but distracted. He listens patiently and gives me the name of a local psychiatrist. He pities me. He leaves this time without smiling. He says he'll stop by again sometime and maybe we'll have dinner some evening if he can clear his schedule. I don't expect to ever see him again. His eyes are too troubled by the sight of me. I am too real.

And I have to go back to them. I have no choice. They need me.

8. The Movie

Cara Ann has a date with a semifamous chef. She's giddy with happiness. She is certain he'll share the secret of his Double Chocolate Amaretto Mousse. He's Italian-German, a bizarre combination. His accent startles me when he comes to pick her up in his old white Jaguar. He kisses my hand and invites me to come to his restaurant with Cara Ann before I leave to go back home. I am delighted.

My cousin tells me not to wait up for her. As if I'm that stupid.

I go back to the TV in her bedroom and select a few movies to wade through.

I'm watching *Breakfast at Tiffany's* for the tenth time in my life. It's really late. I should go to bed. My eyelids are heavy. It's the scene where Holly is searching for Cat in the rain. I want to die. The rain keeps streaming into Holly's eyes and I start crying "Cat—Cat—" Then it's over but I'm still crying. I have lost something, too. But I can't find it. I will never find it.

I cry myself to sleep.

9. The Nightmare

He is underwater with them. Naked. He has been cut with a razor and the wounds gape open. The black ribbons are now bright red plastic belts and they curl around him. He sits at the table, his head back, the whites of his eyes trained on the watery blue sky and shrouded sun. The actor. And I cannot save him. He has been canceled.

And worse, I do not want to save myself. I sit next to him and slowly, but surely, every breath in my lungs escapes and rises to the surface without me. I know I no longer fight it. My pink legs stretch out before me. It's all over. Someone keeps telling me I'm a whore, a slut, a prostitute, and I realize it does not matter because I am dying.

In a dream you're not supposed to die. But I did.

And in that pool, Cara Ann's pool.

But I do not want to.

Die.

10. The Rescue

We went shopping on Melrose Avenue, Cara Ann and I did. We also hit the other major shopping areas and had a fine dinner at the chef's restaurant. We saw Cher or someone who looks just like her. I told Cara Ann it couldn't be Cher because she lives in New York and Cara Ann confided her showbiz sources had informed her that she was in town working on some hot movie deal. I think she just didn't want me to leave LA without seeing a really famous movie star, bigger than P. C. Bergman. Poor Pete.

I bought some clothes. And I'm going home soon, I think, or maybe I'll never go home. I am very unhappy because it's still there. This vacation has not done me a lot of good. I don't really remember anything about it. Not like I should. Maybe I never will. Maybe I shouldn't. I might stay another week. I might not teach this year.

I haven't heard from the actor, but Cara Ann heard from Ben that I made quite an impression. She didn't say what kind. She might've just said that to make me feel better. She is guilty about the time spent with the chef—Paulo or Paulie. Her little boy, Teddy, comes back next week. It might be nice to stay a little longer.

And it might not.

The weather continues warm. I wrote a postcard to Mom and Dad that actually said, "Wish you were here." What if they're on the next plane?

I'm going to swim today.

I'm wearing the expensive Norma Kamali swimsuit I bought on a whim and that will take me months to pay off. I'm in the shallow end. It's early morning and Cara Ann's gone to work. The air's too cool. My skin shows off a wonderful set of goose bumps. I wade deeper in. Then I see them, the pool people, and they see me. Only this time I hear them. Screaming. Someone has tied them to their chairs. Someone is raping the woman, or trying to. It's just a shadow. God, no, the man, the man is dead. He cannot help her. And look at the woman pushing at the shadow hands and now another shadow falls across her, holding her down with his feet. No one wants to rescue her. No one. But I can. She knows I can see her.

"I'm coming to save you! I'll save you—hold on, I'm coming—" I'll dive in. I can do it. She doesn't know how weak I am, how bloodless and thin. My legs feel like two trembling towers of strawberry Jell-O. But I have to do it.

"Molly!" I turn and see Pete waving at me from the gate. It's locked. Now is not the time—he can't stop me. Idiot's trying to climb over the gate but I can't wait, there isn't time. I point at the pool people and I wade in deeper. I've got to take a good breath and plunge in. He's hurting her. He has one of her breasts; he's squeezing it hard. I can see it so plain. I can see no one cares. But I do.

"I'll tell—everyone will know what an ass you are. Let me go, you sorry bastard—" I'm in over my head and sinking. I'm going way down on butterfly wings laden with weights. I'm a butterfly in an astronaut's suit. I am drowning.

I could swim if I really wanted to. I could die, too. I have a choice. Why doesn't someone help?

"We're just going to fuck you, just like your boss does." They were just kids, bad boys in fake leather, with knives and hard cocks, sixteen, seventeen, eighteen. And I begged them to stop, to let me go. "Please, God, let me go, *please*."

The water swallows me whole. Down at the bottom I see the table's gone; the chairs are gone. The pool people have at last abandoned me. I can rescue no one but myself. A knife in the water, plunging backward. My hand shoots up. Attention class. Any questions?

The man's hand grasps mine strongly. But I'm already climbing out of the pool.

"Are you okay?" he says.

And I kiss him. He touches my face. "You know who they were, don't you?" he says.

I nod.

"My students."

Assault as vampire.

To put the stake through the heart of any vampire, you must first know the identity of the vampire. Denial of assault is subtle and dangerous. The assault is given a sort of power both corrosive and sickening. In order for Molly to rescue herself, she had to first acknowledge what had happened. In doing so, she puts the stake through the vampire and frees herself to live again, no longer allowing the rapists to keep raping her, again, and again, and again.

I wrote this story for all of the Mollys out there and the men like Pete who try to understand them.

And also because butterflies cannot wear astronaut suits, nor should they have to.

Melissa Mia Hall

A Week in the Unlife

DAVID J. SCHOW

Schow's protagonist knows how to get rid of vampires. He's a media creation and has all the answers. . . .

1

When you stake a bloodsucker, the heart blood pumps out thick and black, the consistency of honey. I saw it make bubbles as it glurped out. The creature thrashed and squirmed and tried to pull out the stake—they always do, if you leave on their arms for the kill—but by the third whack it was, as Stoker might say, dispatched well and duly.

I lost count a long time ago. Doesn't matter. I no longer think of them as being even *former* human beings, and feel no anthropomorphic sympathy. In their eyes I see no tragedy, no romance, no seductive pulp appeal. Merely lust, rage at being outfoxed, and debased appetite, focused and sanguine.

People usually commit journals as legacy. So be it. Call me sentry, vigilante if you like. When they sleep their comatose sleep, I stalk and terminate them. When they walk, I hide. Better than they do.

They're really not as smart as popular fiction and films would lead you to believe. They do have cunning, an animalistic savvy. But I'm an experienced tracker; I know their spoor, the traces they leave, the way their presence charges the air. Things invisible or ephemeral to ordinary citizens, blackly obvious to me.

The journal is so you'll know, just in case my luck runs out.

Sundown. Nap time.

2

Naturally the police think of me as some sort of homicidal crackpot. That's a given; always has been for my predecessors. More watchers to evade. Caution comes reflexively to me these days. Police are slow and rational; they deal in the minutiae of a day-to-day world, deadly enough without the inclusion of bloodsuckers.

The police love to stop and search people. Fortunately for me, mallets and stakes and crosses and such are not yet illegal in this country. Lots of raised eyebrows and jokes and nudging but no actual arrests. When the time comes for them to recognize the plague that has descended upon their city, they will remember me, perhaps with grace.

My lot is friendless, solo. I know and expect such. It's okay.

City by city. I'm good at ferreting out the nests. To me, their kill patterns are like a flashing red light. The police only see presumed loonies, draw no linkages; they bust and imprison mortals and never see the light.

I am not foolhardy enough to leave bloodsuckers lying. Even though the mean corpus usually dissolves, the stakes might be discovered. Sometimes there is other residue. City dumpsters and sewers provide adequate and fitting disposal for the leftovers of my mission.

The enemy casualties.

I wish I could advise the authorities, work hand in hand with them. Too complicated. Too many variables. Not a good control situation. Bloodsuckers have a maddening knack for vanishing into crevices, even hairline splits in logic.

Rule: Trust no one.

3

A female one, today. Funny. There aren't as many of them as you might suppose.

She had courted a human lover, so she claimed, like Romeo and Juliet—she could only visit him at night, and only after feeding, because bloodsuckers too can get carried away by passion.

I think she was intimating that she was a physical lover of other-worldly skill; I think she was fighting hard to tempt me not to eliminate her by saying so.

She did not use her mouth to seduce mortal men. I drove the stake into her brain, through the mouth. She was of recent vintage and did not melt or vaporize. When I fucked her remains, I was surprised to find her warm inside, not cold, like a cadaver. Warm.

With some of them, the human warmth is longer in leaving. But it always goes.

4

I never met one before that gave up its existence without a struggle, but today I did, one that acted like he had been expecting me to wander along and relieve him of the burden of unlife. He did not deny what he was, nor attempt to trick me. He asked if he could talk a bit, before.

In a third-floor loft, the windows of which had been spray-painted flat black, he talked. Said he had always hated the taste of blood; said he preferred pineapple juice, or even coffee. He actually brewed a pot of coffee while we talked.

I allowed him to finish his cup before I put the ashwood length to his chest and drove deep and let his blackness gush. It dribbled, thinned by the coffee he had consumed.

5

Was thinking this afternoon perhaps I should start packing a Polaroid or some such, to keep a visual body count, just in case this journal becomes public record someday. It'd be good to have illustrations, proof. I was thinking of that line you hear overused in the movies. I'm sure you know it: *"But there's no such THING as a vampire!"* What a howler; ranks right up there alongside *"It's crazy—but it just might work!"* and *"We can't stop now for a lot of silly native superstitions!"*

Right; shoot cozy little memory snaps, in case they whizz to mist or drop apart to smoking goo. That bull about how you're not supposed to be able to record their images is from the movies, too. There's so much misleading information running loose that the bloodsuckers—the real ones—have no trouble at all moving through any urban center, *with impunity*, as they say on cop shows.

Maybe it would be a good idea to tape-record the sounds they make when they die. Videotape them begging not to be exterminated. That would bug the eyes of all those monster movie fans, you bet.

6

So many of them beleaguering this city, it's easy to feel outnumbered. Like I said, I've lost count.

Tonight might be a good window for moving on. Like them, I become vulnerable if I remain too long, and it's prudent operating procedure not to leave patterns or become predictable.

It's easy. I don't own much. Most of what I carry, I carry inside.

7

They pulled me over on Highway Ten, outbound, for a broken left taillight. A datafax photo of me was clipped to the visor in the highway patrol car. The journal book itself has been taken as evidence, so for now it's a felt-tip and high-school notebook paper, which notes I hope to append to the journal proper later.

I have a cell with four bunks all to myself. The door is solid gray, with a food slot, unlike the barred cage of the bullpen. On the way back I noticed they had caught themselves a bloodsucker. Probably an accident; they probably don't even know what they have. There is no sunrise or sunset in the block, so if he gets out at night, they'll never know what happened. But I already know. Right now I will not say anything. I am exposed and at a disadvantage. The one I let slip today I can eliminate tenfold, next week.

8

New week. And I am vindicated at last.

I relaxed as soon as they showed me the photographs. How they managed documentation on the last few bloodsuckers I trapped, I have no idea. But I was relieved. Now I don't have to explain the journal—which, as you can see, they returned to me immediately. They had thousands of questions. They needed to know about the mallets, the stakes, the preferred method of killstrike. I cautioned them not to attempt a sweep-and-clear at night, when the enemy is stronger.

They paid serious attention this time, which made me feel much better. Now the fight can be mounted en masse.

They also let me know I wouldn't have to stay in the cell. Just some paperwork to clear, and I'm out among them again. One of the officials—not a cop, but a doctor—congratulated me on a stout job well done. He shook my hand, on behalf of all of them, he said, and mentioned writing a book on my work. This is exciting!

As per my request, the bloodsucker in the adjacent solitary cell was moved. I told them that to be really sure, they should use one of my stakes. It was simple vanity, really, on my part. I turn my stakes out of ashwood on a lathe. I made sure they knew I'd permit my stakes to be used as working models for the proper manufacture of all they would soon need.

When the guards come back I really must ask how they managed such crisp eight-by-tens of so many bloodsuckers. All those names and dates. First-class documentation.

I'm afraid I may be a bit envious.

This is a vampire story with no vampires in it.

From punk vampires to porn vampires to gay vampires to vampirism-as-AIDS, vampire fiction has become conventional, a category unto itself. As a genre it is by and large ultraconservative, moribund, demographic, derivative, totally safe, and utterly dull, dull, dull. Grave wavers who wet themselves over today's endlessly recycled bloodsucker might do well to exhume and rediscover the only two fundamental American vampire novels of this century—Richard Matheson's *I Am Legend* and Les Whitten's *Progeny of the Adder.* From them sprang, ultimately, the entire culture of pop vampirism as we know it today.

Distaste for such an adulterated gimmick as traditional vampirism played a big part in the creation of the above-mentioned books. It's the ultimate challenge: *Transcend me if you can.*

It is the oversaturation of vampire lore, and the trivialist's lust to accumulate ever more of it, that is itself a new form of vampirism.

The vampire hunter of unlife is a creature who feeds off *your* hunger to believe in vampires.

David J. Schow

Lifeblood

JACK WOMACK

Womack, known for his science fiction novels, has only been writing short fiction in the last two years. His first story, also horror, was chosen for The Year's Best Fantasy & Horror: Fourth Annual Collection. "Lifeblood" shows how the rituals of religious orthodoxy can be easily perverted to create one's own personal religion—deliberately or unconsciously. Judging from these two stories, Womack is an expert in the psychological obsessions that run our lives and hasten our deaths.

"One of the Pre-Raphaelites, I forget which," the woman said, "buried a manuscript of his unpublished poems with his wife, or perhaps it was his sister, when she died. Several years later he decided he wanted to publish them after all, so he and his friends went to her grave one night and dug her up and retrieved them. Before they reburied her, he combed her hair."

The man and the woman met on Sunday afternoons at the pastry shop on Amsterdam below 111th Street. This particular afternoon, they were talking about love.

"I never realized theologians could be so romantic," he said.

"Those stories were never taught, you know," she said, laughing. "I had to find them, or rather they found me."

They'd been friends for years. They sat there, drinking coffee and sharing a slice of strudel, speaking with the ease and comfort that so rarely lovers, or even brothers and sisters, know.

"A woman I knew in graduate school died a couple of weeks ago," she said. "By the time I heard, the funeral was over. I should have gone."

"I'm sorry," he said. "She must not have been very old."

"Younger than me, actually. I've never told you about her. About what happened. I've always felt responsible for her falling in love."

"Romance, again—"

"It was such a long fall," she said.

"So tell me about it."

"The first time I met Leah was in October of my second year. She lived next door to my friend Alice, in an apartment building on Claremont. When I saw her there in the hall I remembered she was in the class I was taking on Dante. She was very thin and pale, and wore long-sleeved sweaters in the warmest weather. If I'd thought about her at all before then, it was only to wonder whether she was an anorexic or an addict, for I remembered that there were those who called her both. She was neither, in fact. She and Alice already knew each other, and she joined us that evening, and we talked."

"About what?"

"Nothing serious, as I recall. She'd transferred to Barnard from out west for her last two undergraduate years, and like Alice was in the comparative literature department. Leah was extremely intelligent, and so sweet as an angel, or such was the impression she found it impossible not to give. She was so talkative it was easy to tell how shy she truly was. Sometimes she'd say something in such a way, with such offhand yet careful phrasing, that I suspected she'd memorized a number of lines that could serve her well in any social situation, and repeated them as she'd had them told to her.

"Sometime before I left Alice's she went back to her place, to her studies, she said, though shortly afterward we heard her leave. When she'd gone I asked Alice when they'd met. She told me Leah had cut herself one morning, and needed help."

"Cut herself?" The waitress returned to refill their cups. The woman added cream to her coffee, lightening it until its color was as swarthy as her skin.

"She knocked on Alice's door, saying that she'd nicked her hand badly while slicing bread. She held a washcloth on the wound but couldn't get the bleeding to stop. Alice took a towel and wrapped it tightly around Leah's hand. Once the blood stopped Alice saw that it wasn't a deep cut, though she said it looked very frightening until she got used to seeing it.

"She asked Leah if she wanted to go to the hospital to make sure it didn't need stitches but she said it didn't, and that she had gauze in her apartment. Alice went back with her to make sure she'd be all right, for then as always Leah appeared so fragile that she might have broken beneath the gentlest touch.

"Her apartment was clean and neatly furnished, as if she used it only for storage. The bathroom, Alice said, was the coziest room in the place, and when she was telling me this she said she remembered how surprised she'd been to see how much gauze Leah had."

"So she might have been clumsy with knives," he said. "It could have happened before."

"Alice also said the only bread she saw in the kitchen was already sliced," she said. "My suspicions naturally arose. I liked Leah immediately, but for some time afterward the secret agent side of me emerged, and I found myself often attempting to draw theories from what few data I had, but nothing I could imagine seemed likely enough. She and I hit it off well, and we talked often before and after class, and the three of us started going to movies together, to those depressing middle European ones you're always teasing me about. She was so pleasant to be around, even when she was sad, and she seemed so often sad.

"Private, too, intensely private at times. She'd built any number of walls around herself, and only allowed one gate to open at a time. But she let us in, part of the way. Leah said she'd been raised a Catholic, but that now she was agnostic, like me. Perhaps she thought it would make me feel more comfortable; she was very sensitive to the beliefs of others. She told us she'd never gotten along with her family, and that was why she'd moved. Once she made an odd remark, or so we found it at the time, that babies should not be born of men and women, that parents' pain could forever after harm their children. She was safe in that regard, she told us; she could never have her own family to destroy. When we asked her to elaborate, she wouldn't.

"We were certain she was seeing someone. She often went out at night, Alice said, not returning until morning. At first we were rather worried about her, until we realized she always seemed all right upon her return, and that she had been going out for some time before we became concerned. Alice eventually saw the someone she saw. He was a good deal older, and from his bearing and unfashionable dress Alice inferred that he was a former professor of Leah's. She inferred as well that their relationship was more than academic, but Alice couldn't say how much more.

"We imagined that she was content, if not happy, with whatever she had.

"One morning after a discussion on the *Inferno* I noticed a red stain spreading along Leah's sweater cuff, and pointed it out to her. She was quite comfortable around me by then; I think in some ways more comfortable than she was around Alice, because I didn't live so nearby. Without thinking she rolled up her sleeve.

Her arm was so thin, and her skin so translucent, that she looked as if she were starving. One of her cuts had reopened and she bled."

"One of her cuts?"

"Woven into her arm were dozens of thin scars. Small ones, whiter than her skin." The woman replaced her cup within her saucer's basin, and set aside her fork. "She was deliberately cutting herself, you see."

"Why would she do such a thing?"

The woman offered no theory. "When Leah saw me staring at her arm she quickly pulled down her sleeve, and I felt so embarrassed, as if I'd come into her apartment with friends to surprise her, and found her in the bathroom, naked and sick. She behaved as if nothing were amiss, and left at once, saying she needed to talk to her adviser. I intended to mention it to Alice that evening, but never had the chance, because the three of us went out that night. We were taking her to a party because we thought it was good she should get out and meet new people. The most awful thing happened there. I mean that in both senses of the word."

"What was that?"

"Did you ever fall in love with someone at first sight, or watch as it happened to others?" The man shook his head. She sipped her coffee; some spilled onto the table as she lifted the cup to her mouth. "The only experience I could compare it to, not an exact comparison, would be a religious conversion."

"As when one joins a cult, I suppose."

"Not at all. In this there's one messiah, true, but only one apostle as well, and both participants slip in and out of both roles as the drama demands. The surrounding world becomes as gauze around them. Food, drink, sleep, all else is suddenly inessential to life. Nothing becomes so important as being with, and in some ways even attempting to become, the other person. The desire that one blood might beat through two hearts can so swiftly overwhelm."

"I'm as glad I've never experienced it, then," he said, motioning to the waitress that they should receive more strudel. "You make it sound dreadfully obsessive."

"Have you ever heard the old belief that the soul is visible through the eyes?" she asked. "When two people meet and fall in love at first sight I think they do see one another's souls, and know even before they speak that their minds have at once become as one between them, that a true juncture exists. It's an easy enough step in most circumstances to conjoin the bodies, after that. But the last step is most difficult.

"If the souls themselves are enabled to merge, then an apostate such as myself could call it—well—not transubstantiation, I don't believe, but certainly impanation, where a union is affected without loss of respective substance. The triangle is given its point, in a sense. The trinity is complete."

"I gather this is something else you weren't told about in graduate school," he said.

"Call me romantic, if you'd like. Such love can bring the glow of paradise unto the world. But if something goes wrong, it can as easily turn on all the lights of hell. And something did go wrong."

"She met someone. A man?" The woman nodded. "What was he like?"

"From what little I saw, and from all I heard, he was very much like her. Sometimes I've wondered that if they'd only been more dissimilar they might still be together." For a moment the woman stared into the surface of her coffee; the waitress returned with their second helping. "Probably not. If they hadn't been so alike, would they have been so attracted as they were?"

"You're asking me?"

"No," she said. "What was he like? His name was Henry. He was a writer, though I never read anything he wrote. The time or two I'd seen him before he'd struck me as being even shyer than she was, and not nearly so adept at putting it to good use. I gathered he generally avoided social events like the plague. He was older in years than we were, but not by many, and in many ways I suspect that even Leah was truly older.

"They saw one another, and we didn't see them again the rest of the night, and by morning they were inseparable. When I say that even now I feel responsible for their getting together, I know I shouldn't, that it was nothing more than serendipity, but still—"

"You're too quick to blame," he said.

"Too slow, sometimes," she said. "But they were such lonely people after all, and when lonely people meet you can't help but hope they'll be happy."

"Were they happy?" he asked.

"Even coming into class Leah gave every impression of walking on clouds. Those friends of ours who knew Henry told us of the most marvelous transformations in his being, that his voice, his facial expressions, even the way he breathed, changed. So much becomes other so quickly in this sort of relationship. Even the sense of time is subverted, you see. A day may seem to hold a week, or a year. A month might feel no longer than a minute. When two people believe that they've known each other forever, after all, that their meeting itself was at some eternal point preordained, than what is time but something of which there's never enough?"

"Did they stay happy?"

"They wanted to, I'm sure," she said. "After the first few days they were but rarely seen in public together. Alice probably saw them more often than most, in truth, because he stayed at Leah's so often as she stayed at his place, or wherever else it was that she still sometimes stayed, for sometimes Alice would hear him leave, late at night, and then hear her leave soon after, and she'd know she was going to see the other man. That bothered Alice, but there were other aspects that troubled her more."

"Such as?"

"By the end of their first week together he had become so pale as Leah, and even in autumn a tan shouldn't fade so fast. Then, too, the walls in Alice's building weren't especially thick, and sometimes Alice heard more than she wished to hear. She was alone herself at the time, and of course even at the best of times one tries not to think of what your friends might do in bed, even if you truly want to know. Sometimes they were very noisy, and sometimes they weren't, and it was when they weren't that most disconcerted Alice."

"I don't understand—"

"Alice knew the layout of Leah's apartment and knew which of Leah's rooms abutted hers. Some nights as she lay in bed, Alice would imagine that they'd gone to sleep at last, and then realize that they hadn't, that they were in the bathroom. Each night Henry came over a pattern repeated itself. From the midst of silence a low murmur would rise as if from a dream; a sound of pain followed, manifesting itself sometimes as a cry, sometimes as a moan. It never seemed to be Leah's voice that she heard, but then neither of them was loud, and Leah was undoubtedly more subdued because she was more used to it. Then all would be quiet again, until they returned to bed, seemingly with renewed vigor.

"One morning Alice took her trash to the basement. Leah'd already taken hers down, Alice saw, for she recognized a shopping bag she'd seen Leah come in with a day or so before. It was from a medical supply house, and it was filled with what Alice at first took to be red party streamers, disposed of as if after a Valentine's Day celebration. But this was just before Thanksgiving.

"After Thanksgiving I ran into Leah on Broadway, and I could tell she'd been crying, her eyes were so red they looked as if they'd been bleeding. I said let's go somewhere and talk, and she said she had to meet Henry in a little while but readily agreed to come with me, and we went to Café 112. I asked her what was upsetting her so. Do you know how sometimes strangers share with you the sort of revelations friends never share? It can happen, too, with people you know, so long as you don't know them well.

"As she talked to me she spoke in such a way that on one level nothing was said, while on another level all was revealed, or at least much more. She began telling me about the older man she saw, without letting slip any details other than that they'd been together a long time and that they'd met in the same way as she'd met Henry. As a mentor, she said, he'd helped her in innumerable ways, but as she continued to speak I perceived an aspect of their relationship that possibly neither of them saw. If theirs, too, had been love at first sight, and I don't know that it was, then their convergence hadn't quite been true; that perhaps with her compliance his mind took over a part of hers, or even replaced it entirely for a time, and thus it wasn't always Leah who spoke when her lips moved. If we stick with the metaphor I was using earlier, then I'd say that what occurred between them was more of an inadvertently forced consubstantiation.

"Too soon for him, too soon for Leah, he discovered she'd fallen in love with Henry, and he didn't take it well at all. She tried to explain to me as she'd tried to explain to him the realities she understood. He found her relationship with Henry disturbing enough in ways other than how it interfered with their own that he was having none of it. So one night she told him she'd been able to become closer to Henry in a way he was unable, or unwilling, to be.

"As she recalled how that upset him it upset her anew, and she pulled at her hair until she dislodged her barrette. It fell to the floor. I leaned down to pick it up for her, and when I did I saw that her socks had drooped over her ankles. Her legs were thin as her arms, and as laced with tiny white scars. They looked as if for years her nerves had been trying to break free of her skin, that they could no longer be rubbed raw."

The woman drank the rest of her coffee before continuing her tale. He watched her drink, forgetting to eat.

"Both made her better, she told me, and both made her worse, and she thought she knew who helped the most, or rather who hurt the least. But she had no idea how to tell the other of her decision, and so for the moment decided not to decide. The angles of the triangle seemed too perfect to disturb, but she said she knew they had to be. There was, you see, one more complication."

"What?"

"My period, she said. You've stopped having it? I asked, thinking at first I grasped the complications without her telling, unable to imagine that she could have ever been regular, thin as she was. I started, she said.

"What could I do? I took her hands—you can't imagine how cold they were—and held them, and sat with her awhile longer. I waited for her to say more, but surely she knew when she'd said enough. She looked at the clock on the wall and told me she needed to go meet Henry, who lived around the corner. As I walked along with her I felt as if I were accompanying a ghost as she commuted between the houses she haunted.

"Henry stood on the stoop of his building, awaiting her; she smiled so when she saw him, and, taking leave of me, ran to him. They were happy, and that was the most frightening thing of all. When he slipped his arms around her I saw the cuffs his bandages made.

"A day or so after that I went to Mexico with my parents for Christmas. When I returned I called Alice, to see what had happened in my absence. Much, she told me.

"Henry came over one night during the week before New Year's. Leah had stayed out Christmas Eve, but Alice had a hunch she hadn't been with Henry. They didn't say much that she could hear through the wall, and she had somewhere to go herself, and so she left them to their devices. No one can say what happened after that. Maybe Leah related the decision she'd made to him that night, or maybe she already had; maybe she'd already told the one she needed to tell before coming over, and so took this night to celebrate. But something went wrong—immediately or ultimately, who knows—and he was cut too deeply, and didn't get help in time.

"When Alice came home the police were still there. They found Henry in the bathtub, she heard, though not from Leah. Leah sat in the hall, wrapping her arms around herself as if they were bandages, pressing her face against her knees until her legs were bloody. An older man stood in the hall, talking to the officials, and if you didn't know better you might have thought he knew every answer. Eventually he helped her to her feet, and walked with her, down the hall.

"Suicide, they called it, but Henry was no more suicidal than Leah."

The man lay down his fork, feeling hungry no longer. The waitress smiled as she walked by.

" 'No greater grief than to remember days of joy, when misery is at hand,' " she said.

"What's that from?" he asked.

"Canto Five of the *Inferno*," she said. "Poetry can so often help you get to sleep at night."

"What happened afterward?"

"Leah didn't come back to school the next semester," she said. "Possibly so that she wouldn't hear what anyone had to say, but I suspect she'd heard it all before. The next time I saw her was in the spring, here in the pastry shop. She sat by herself in the corner over there, seeming more translucent than before, almost as if, with her compliance or not, she was gradually fading away. I don't think she saw me at all, though I stood before her, and I never saw her again after that.

"Then a couple of weeks ago, she died. Alice found out that she was buried next to Henry, and we wondered about that for a time. It'd be nice to imagine that life can at least be fair to the dead."

"What did she die of?" he asked. "She didn't—"

The woman shook her head. "A virus, we heard. You know how malicious gossip can be. If her older friend retained possession over part of her mind, then I'm certain Henry carried much of her soul away with him. And what was left must have finally given out. Still, she surely did as she thought she had to do. Sometimes I think it's better to be alone, after all. It's safer."

"Check, please," he said; the waitress walked over, moving through the crowd. "But cutting herself like that. How could she have convinced them to go along—"

"I can't speak of the ways of courtship," she said, "but after accepting the trinity, you take communion."

Love slinks pink-footed and sleek,
Scurries through the soul's walls,
Eludes the traps set out to kill it,
At night bites the extremities till they bleed.

Jack Womack

Requiem

MELINDA M. SNODGRASS

What does it mean to be human? This question is one that has haunted SF and horror from H. G. Wells's halfmen in The Island of Dr. Moreau, *through John W. Campbell's alien shapeshifter in "Who Goes There?" The question of what is human is also central to much of Philip K. Dick's work, particularly his novel* Do Androids Dream of Electric Sheep?

The tortured characters in "Requiem" love and appreciate art, and perform music. But they are unable to create. In the context of this story, this alone is what keeps them from being fully human.

Down in the hall someone was enacting the final act of a French farce. *Probably Martin Fletcher,* Barnaby idly thought, using shunt level to avoid any bleed. *Their taste had always run to the absurd.* Main level was feeding properly, pain exploding from the tender flesh of his buttocks as the thin switch continued its steady rhythm. Beneath him Lucinda ground with her hips, timing each thrust to the beat of the tiny bamboo whip. He was nearing climax, and Mary increased the tempo of the whipping. He cursed his newly acquired belly. He felt like a barrel trying to balance on a particularly slippery log. Lucinda caught her legs about his back forcing him down atop her, and he groaned as the heavy meal he had eaten earlier in the evening shifted like a sliding load of ball bearings.

The warm moistness of her cunt closed about his penis squeezing, demanding, and with a white-hot rush he came even as Mary laid one final, triumphant, and very hard blow across his bare, red ass.

Lucinda's throaty sounds of pleasure were punctuated by screams, and bellowed French commands, and the sound of popping champagne corks.

Barnaby grimaced—*So overdone*—and rolled onto his back. And gave a yelp as his tender bottom hit the satin sheets. Lucinda propped herself on an elbow, raked back her long black hair with

133

one hand, and grinned down at him. Her nipples formed rich coffee-colored circles against the tawny skin of her breasts.

"Performance tonight?"

"No, just a rehearsal."

"You must be tense. You don't usually call for the full treatment except for a performance."

He grabbed one swinging breast, and rubbed his thumb across the nipple. "Decided to treat myself."

She rolled away, consulted an ornate white-and-gold clock. "Hour's almost up."

"Do you have to be so cold-blooded? Can't you convince me that it's romance at work here?"

"You don't want romance, Barnaby, you want sluts. For romance you go home to that pretty wife of yours."

"She's frigid."

"Goodbye, Barnaby."

"She doesn't understand me."

"Leave the money on my desk, Barnaby."

"You don't love me."

"That's right, Barnaby."

A few minutes later, and he was out in the chill Santa Fe night. There were a few cars about jouncing and grinding through the monumental potholes that littered the streets like bomb craters. He stuck to the sidewalk, the tough buffalo grass brushing at his pants leg where it thrust through the cracks in the concrete. It wasn't far to the performance hall, and with a star-littered sky overhead, and a brisk wind carrying the scent of burning piñon to his nostrils, he was just as happy to walk.

It also allowed time for the blood to retreat from his inflamed buttocks. The touch of his undershorts against the swollen skin was agony, but it also managed to keep an erection shoving at his zipper. And if he took his time he would be able to sit and rehearse for three hours, serene and relaxed from Lucinda's and Mary's ministrations.

Another car lurched past, and its headlight swept across the mouth of an alley. It was like looking down a black throat with a trashed-out dumpster and several battered garbage cans thrust up like broken teeth. And in the midst of it two shadowy figures were locked in a desperate struggle. Harsh pants and faint whimpers drifted from the alley. Barnaby dug his hands into his coat pockets, hunched until his collar rode up around his ears, and hurried past. It was none of his affair. Had no part in his game. But there was a sick taste on the back of his tongue that lingered for several blocks, and had nothing to do with the cheap wine he had consumed with dinner.

Patricia and Peter were waiting. He muttered an apology for again being late, and seated himself at the baby grand. Peter, his violin tucked beneath his sharp chin, and his brown curls forming a halo about his head, had the look of a mad monk. Patricia was a different sort altogether. Her blue eyes seemed to focus on nothing, and with her long, straight blond hair hanging to her waist she looked like a lost flower child. But there was nothing innocent about the way she gripped her cello between her thin legs. Barnaby's erection bumped urgently against his zipper, and he wished she would stop wearing such short skirts to rehearsal.

Peter made a new mistake this night. So breathtaking in its audacity and creativity that Barnaby almost lost his count. The violinist muttered an apology, but he was staring at the notes with the adoration of an ascetic witnessing the kingdom of God. Patricia had formed a curtain with her hair. Barnaby couldn't read her reaction.

The final trembling chord hung in the air, and Barnaby dropped his hands into his lap. After twenty minutes of playing, and Peter's remarkable addition, he found that his ass had stopped hurting, and the flash of Patricia's pale thigh brought no answering response from his crotch.

"Shall we try it again?" he heard himself ask.

"Sure, and I'll try not to foul up this time."

"No problem."

Patricia shook back her hair, and eyed him, reading more from the innocent two-word remark than he had intended. Sensing perhaps his exultation. Behind her blue eyes lurked the somna, glaring, hostile, very suspicious.

The keys were slick beneath his fingers as they began again. This time it was perfect. Perfect as it was always perfect. As it would have been perfect the time before barring Peter's fascinating gaff. Perfect, soulless, and heartless. And the fault, Barnaby sadly concluded in time with the final chords, was not in the music.

Patricia didn't wait for any quiet banter. She packed her cello in short jerky motions that betrayed her agitation, ducked her head, and hurried from the studio.

"I shouldn't have done that," Peter said contritely.

"No, that's not true. It was magnificent." Barnaby hesitated, then dug out a handwritten score. "Would you mind?"

"Oh, Barnaby, you never give up."

"No."

An "A" hung in the air, then tuned and ready Peter sight-read swiftly and perfectly through the first page. He stopped, bow poised, double chins forming because of his pressure on the instrument.

"Well?"

"It's terrible. Just like the others."

"You see no improvement?"

He considered, replayed a phrase, frowned, caught his lower lip between his teeth. "Some." He dropped the violin to his knee. "Barnaby, why is it so important to you?"

"I don't know, but it is. Vitally important." He swung off the bench and paced the sterile room, shoes squeaking on the linoleum floor. "Sometimes when I'm playing I feel as if I'm on the verge of some great insight, some total understanding that will—"

"What I'm on is the verge of trouble." The snap of the locks on the case echoed off the dingy white walls. "You're a dangerous man to know, Barnaby. You incite a person to risk, and I've taken enough risks for one night."

But they didn't, and that was the problem. Life was a series of endlessly repeating patterns. The thoughts roiled like sullenly boiling poison; but buried deep on the shunt level, safe from any eavesdropping. He slid onto the bench, and ripped out a Mozart piano sonata. Wondering as he played why when using the same seven notes he produced soulless dreck, while Mozart had produced genius, magic. The magic went to work, drawing from deep within him a sensation that was odd and unpleasant and exhilarating all at once. A vise closing somewhere deep within himself.

With a sigh he dropped the lid, a sullen *bang* in the silent room, and left the recital hall.

He has several choices. A late post-rehearsal supper. Home—his mind shied violently from that. He knew what was waiting for him at home. Or Sal's.

Sal's filled with noise, and smoke, and male presence. The waitresses were male wet dreams incarnate. Cute, and buxom, and dumb as rocks. They made appropriate squealing noises when pinched or propositioned, and the rest of the time kept their mouths shut, and served drinks.

Sal, a tall, skinny Italian whose spade beard made him look like a rather befuddled Lucifer, was polishing glasses behind the bar. On the large TV, hung precariously on the wall, the Bears were slaughtering the Patriots at the Super Bowl. Groans, curses, shouted advice, rose from the knot of construction workers, cowboys, and truckers huddled at one corner of the bar.

"The usual?"

"Yeah."

Sal slopped whiskey into a shot glass, and Barnaby tipped it down.

"Neat whiskey will play hell with your liver."

"Well, now that would be a new experience. The descent into the gutter with redemption to follow."

"Hush." Dr. Antonio Garcia's thin, blue-veined hand closed about his upper arm, and forced him away from the bar. "Barnaby, my friend, you are very fey tonight." They settled into a red leather booth. "What troubles you, my friend?"

The score fluttered onto the table between them. The doctor prodded the pages with a cautious forefinger. "Music."

"Yeah, mine."

"Is it good?"

"No, it stinks. Like the piece before it, and the piece before that, and—"

"Why are you surprised?" The Spaniard sighed, and ran a hand across his beautiful white hair. It fell in long waves back from a high white forehead. Which made the darkness of his deepset brown eyes all the more compelling. "Barnaby, my young friend. There are a million things in this world that we can do—"

"Perfectly," he interrupted bitterly.

"As you say, but art is not one of them. The blood of the somnas has thinned and our kind doesn't make music."

"Oh, we *make* music. Like we *make* ball games, and *make* wars, and *make* marriages, but we create nothing." Uneasy interest flared like a point of light from his passive watcher.

"That is not our function—"

"Our function is boredom."

"Not so. We are the vital link between our somnas, and reality. We provide experience, sensation, growth, challenge, but with the dangers filtered by our loyal bodies."

Antonio had assumed his erect tutorial position, finger upraised, his soft, deep voice exploring each word for the maximum effect. Intellectual smugness glowed on his face. For Barnaby this was merely one in an endless repeat of the good doctor's pet philosophy.

"Antonio, you remind me of the Jewish apologists of old time, 1930s. They continued to excuse, and explain Adolf Hitler even as they were led into the gas chamber."

"That is a disgusting analogy! We are not a despised minority being persecuted by our overlords. We are partners in a most unique and special relationship, and we should be grateful for our chance to serve. Without the development of the somna/piggyback relationship there would be no humans on Earth. That great history would have been snuffed out by the actions of a random, malignant virus. As it is we have preserved—"

"Which is my point! We 'preserve,' we experience, but we don't create. And I'm not even sure we're preserving all that well. Look at the fucking streets, the garbage collecting on the sidewalks. And who can blame them. It's a hell of a boring game to be a garbage collector or a member of a street crew. So we get to be doctors and lawyers, and conductors and composers and Indian chiefs. And for what? For What!"

"Barnaby, go home. These distempered freaks do you no good." Hostility and compassion flickered in the dark eyes as Antonio and the somna watched him.

As for himself a band of incandescent pain seemed to be tightening about his temples. With a gasp he crammed the pages into his pocket, and lurched from the booth.

"You'll feel better in the morning."

"Yeah . . . yeah, you're right. I've been working too hard. This opening concert . . . ha ha, burning the candle at both ends . . . ha ha." How easily the words of his role slipped from his tongue. How comforting to have the role to return to. If he didn't he would have to make one. For himself. All by himself.

Laura was waiting. The green shades on the brass student lamp threw a dim light across the darkened living room, and drew highlights from her short cap of light brown hair. Head bowed she sat curled in the corner of the sofa. The line of her neck was a curving song. But it seemed vulnerable, too. Pale and slender, bent like an autumn flower beneath a weight of winter ice. He experienced the same squeezing sensation he had felt during the Mozart. Slipped forward, and kissed her. The short hairs at the nape of her neck tickled his lips.

She flinched, jerked away. "Don't touch me."

He too recoiled from the acid that laced the words. "Laura, love."

"You slime! You son of a bitch!" She spat the words at him from behind the protection of the coffee table. Her voice held only hatred, but her body spoke of unendurable pain as she huddled in upon herself, arms wrapped protectively about her chest.

"What, what have I done? The first night I've been able to get home early, and you start screaming at me."

"You don't like it? Then go back to your bimbos!" She snatched a package of cigarettes from the mantel. It took her five tries to get it lit, and a part of Barnaby admired her ability to suppress her dexterity. It was perfect from the trembling fingers to the cords of her neck etched harshly beneath the fair skin as she sucked in the smoke. "For months I've suspected, but now I have the proof."

A manila envelope slapped onto the brick floor at his feet spilling its contents. Photos. Black and white, grainy, unfocused, but clearly recognizable. His face, looking bloated with the weight that had been laid on him, sheen of sweat, hair matted, eyes screwed tightly shut in ecstasy as Lucinda beat him. Shame lay like a bad taste on the back of his tongue.

"God damn it!" he roared. "I'm under a lot of pressure. And since you're so fucking frigid—"

"Bad choice of words there," she smirked. "Just because I'm not willing to behave like an animal."

"Don't finish. I know it by heart. I hear it every night in bed. *I'm an artist. The physical blunts the soul,*" he mimicked in cruel parody. "Well, if that's the case you ought to be a fucking angel by now."

She dealt him a ringing slap, and he caught her by the wrists, forced her in close. Her head thrashed trying to avoid the kiss that had little to do with love, and a great deal to do with violence.

They staggered about the room locked in this travesty of an embrace. There was a crash, and his soul cringed as a priceless Santa Clara Indian seed pot shattered on the bricks. Dismay loosened his grip, and Laura kneed him neatly in the balls. Pain like a red-hot poker shot from his groin through the top of his head. He collapsed with a keening cry, and held himself.

Laura began booting down the hall toward the bedroom, then froze, turned back, weariness and release etched on her delicate face. Barnaby still hurt. A lot. But the somnas were gone. Exhausted perhaps by the violence of their backs' emotions.

Slowly he rose, came into her arms, laid his head against her soft bosom, felt despair.

They had only a little time. A few seconds becoming minutes becoming (if they were lucky) hours. To spend any way they pleased. His mind stuttered and stopped; *a long walk in moonlight, conversation, playing a duet, making love*. They were like children in a toy store. A multiplicity of delights, joy at having the choice, pain at having to choose. As usual Laura settled the matter.

She slipped from his arms, entered the bedroom. He watched hungrily as her mincing, duck-footed dancer's walk carried her away from him. She would wait, and if there was enough time he would join her there. But now he had to work.

The score was tucked between the pages of a Mozart symphony. Camouflage, or was he hoping that genius somehow rubbed off? He spread the pages, stared wearily at the tiny ink strokes each representing so many hours of anguish. He was sick to death of notes. They haunted his every waking moment.

Why was he so driven? What did he hope to accomplish by this herculean task? To prove that Antonio, and the other philosophers of their age, were wrong? That creativity could exist? And what were the consequences if he were correct?

Worse, what were the consequences for *him* if he failed? Reality was rendered marginally bearable because of this dream. And if he tried and failed—what then? There was no way out. No way to simply say, "I'm tired, I've had enough. I won't go on." Of course he would go on—and on. He had no choice. But it would be an eternity of living with neither hope nor meaning.

He twirled the pen between his fingers. Measure 156. *Miserere.* Mercy. It was a prayer. Pen clenched between his teeth he played the preceding five measures. The notes hung trembling in the shadowy room. They formed a presence in the darkened room rich with the scent of pipe tobacco, Laura's perfume, and old wood lovingly polished with beeswax and lemon oil. *Were they any good?* No, that question could only freeze him. He repeated the phrase. Rediscovering its soul. Or was it his own?

He bent to the paper. *Treble clef—g, e, c—dotted quarter, sixteenth f, back to a.* The scratchings of a pen, the crackle of paper, the occasional fragmentary musical phrase. Forming a miraculous harmonious whole.

* * *

The lone time continued. Barnaby stretched feeling the verte-brae in his spine snapping one by one as he straightened. Carefully he returned the sheets to their hiding place, and buried the memory of his work in shunt level.

He realized, with a start, that while he was sitting and gaping mindlessly at the dull ivory keys of the piano Laura was waiting, and precious private moments were flitting past. He hurried from the study, down the long hall, hesitated before a closed, sealed door. Its twin lay across the hall. Duty warred with resentment. Duty won out. He opened the door into the blue-lit aquatic dim-ness. Gazed at the figure curled protectively about itself, floating, sleeping, dreaming. Elaborate machinery clicked and sighed mea-suring out life in tiny doses. The warmth, wash and ebb of a primal ocean, an eternal womb.

Resentment died to a dull ember, and he felt a wash of pity. He had long ago worn out love. He wondered what the somna would think of that admission? Perhaps be grateful that pity still re-mained. No, such an analysis was beyond it. That was reality, and the somna fed on dreams.

As did he.

He softly closed the door.

Under the goading of his very real personal demon his behavior went from bad to worse. Evenings after rehearsals and perform-ances were spent in screaming battles with Laura. Little progress was made on the requiem for even when lone time occurred he was too exhausted and devastated to work.

He wondered if his watcher had somehow become aware of his secret life, and was using these emotional storms to destroy him. If so it had picked an excellent technique.

Laura opened in *Giselle.*

And the mad scene was unlike any ever seen before. She seemed to float about the stage as if madness had driven out the physical leaving only a fragile, hollow-eyed wraith whose expressive port de bras held a universe of loss, and betrayal. Barnaby ached for her for he *knew* she was dancing out her private anguish.

Behind her the corps de ballet went cleanly, sharply, perfectly through the choreography. It was a tour de force ballet perfection . . . and it held all the soul of a puppet show. Dancing automatons.

But that's because they are *automatons,* thought Barnaby, and felt a stir of fear and resentment from the somna. Molecular programs able to feel pain and pleasure, but unable to replicate themselves. Automatons.

And *you're* automatons too, he flashed at the conductor and orchestra all busily sawing and tooting and gesticulating away. And so are you, he told the audience, as he went slewing about in his seat. And you! And You! And YOU! He was half out of his seat, knee resting on the plush velvet seat cushion, knuckles whitening as he gripped the back of the chair. Around him people stirred, frowned, tittered, shifted nervously.

And so am I.

He collapsed back into his chair. Stared morosely at the stage. Sneered at the willies waltzing about that idiotic prince. Waited for the magic to come again, but Laura had lost whatever had earlier animated her. The final pas de deux could have been a course in weight training.

He had tried to talk about it at the reception afterward. But the people kept drifting away from him, like wraiths, phantoms . . . willies. He blundered about feeling large and gross, but *real* God damn it! Real! And they kept scattering.

"We're just not real." He was perched precariously on a chair, listing from side to side, and he couldn't remember how he got there. White, strained faces stared up at him, and he stretched out his hands, clutching feebly at the air. Trying to grip . . . what? "Don't any of you see it?" he cried. "Laura was real tonight. Oh, it was only for a minute or two, but she was *real*. We should be real like that . . . all of the time."

A hand closed about his wrist, holding him steady.

"Oh, hello, Dr. Garcia."

"Barnaby, stop it. You're upsetting everyone."

"Good. They *need* to be upset." He staggered, slithered off the chair, fell onto it with a hard bump. "I feel strange."

"You're drunk."

"No I'm not. I'm not really drunk. I'm—" He paused trying to think what he was . . . Doing.

"You need to stop thinking about this, Barnaby. You're damaging yourself."

"Good."

"Antonio, let me." Laura's hand was cool against his cheek.

"Laura, no," whispered the doctor. "You're not supposed to be here!"

"Who are you to know where I'm supposed to be?"

His finger thrust out accusingly. "You're ignoring instructions!"

"Yes, no, perhaps, maybe."

Barnaby couldn't tell if she was being facetious or if her neural-paths really were in disarray from this direct disobedience.

"Outrageous. This is atomistic behavior."

"Yes, no, perhaps, maybe," sang out Barnaby, but Laura's only response was a glance filled with blazing anger.

She got him home, dumped him unceremoniously on the couch, and went to check her somna. He sensed rather than heard her return. Huddled into the corner of the sofa, knees pulled to chest, he stared into the yawning pit of the corner fireplace.

"You're leaving."

"Yes."

"On instructions?"

"No." That brought him off the couch. There was again that viselike pressure in his chest, but this had nothing to do with joy. She seemed very small and fragile as she leaned against the door-jamb; a shadowy figure, arms wrapped protectively about her scrawny chest. "This has nothing to do with the soap opera, this is real."

"Why, why?" There seemed to be a swelling in his throat, and the words emerged as a harsh whisper as he forced them past the obstruction.

"I'm afraid."

"But tonight—"

"Was a mistake. I should never have done it. I'm sorry, Barnaby, I'm staying in the womb."

"And if I succeed?"

"You won't. It was a hopeless dream."

"All right, forget succeeding." He gripped her shoulders. "If I finish it?"

"I'll come."

"And if I should succeed?" He enunciated carefully giving her a tiny shake between each word.

"Then it's a different world, isn't it?"

"Is it?"

"You haven't considered the ramifications."

"So Antonio says."

"Good luck, Barnaby." She stood on tiptoes, pressed a soft kiss onto the corner of his mouth.

He hadn't really thought she'd leave. But in the morning both she and her somna were gone. His somna probed, excitement flaring like tiny explosions at this newest twist, then slid back defeated, frustrated, confused by his lack of response.

Seated at the piano late one night, muffled beneath a weight of unhappiness, Barnaby realized that he was experiencing a true emotion. No posturing, no drama, no stirring speeches . . . just loss, and a grinding pain centered once more in the chest.

No wonder man's ancestors thought the heart was the center of all.

You could duplicate mind. Brilliance was easy. He was brilliant. But the heart of man, the soul of man—that was hard.

Laura took up with Rudolfo. The somna agitated, Rudolfo gloated, postured, challenged, Laura drooped. It could have been exciting. The growing rivalry, culminating in violence, the death of the philandering husband at the hands of the handsome, virtuous young lover. But Barnaby refused to play; walking away, focusing on his writing, and wondering if it might not have been a deliberate attempt to be rid of him. Enough damage, and reconstruction would have been necessary. And then he wouldn't be him anymore.

He stopped waiting for the lone times, and wrote whenever his public life gave him time at home. The somna was an angry presence, squatting like an outraged cat in the shadowed corners of a room. But it didn't interfere. Perhaps because after so long as a spectator it was incapable of self-initiated action. Or perhaps because it too believed he would fail.

Only one section remained. The Agnus Dei. He no longer needed the piano, the music ran incessantly through his mind. He also realized he couldn't pen those final phrases with the somna only feet away. As strange as it seemed, after lifetimes of interactive games, this was something that he needed to do alone.

He took out the car, and spent several minutes trying to remember the last time it had been driven. He wondered if in some other enclave, say Fez, a man was busy brushing the dust from his car, and reflecting about how long since it had been driven. The banality of the thought was somehow comforting.

In a few blocks he had left behind the inhabited sections of the city. But the houses continued to straggle across the piñon-covered hills, sad reminders of when Santa Fe had held seventy-five thousand busy, vibrant, productive souls. Now it held ten thousand somnas, and their faithful "backs." Or make that nine thousand nine hundred and ninety-nine. *This* "back" wasn't very fucking faithful.

He wound up the atrocious two-lane highway toward the old ski basin. Reached the pull off that afforded the finest view of the changing aspens in the autumn. No fall of gold spilled down the mountains at this time of year. Instead the bare grey/white trunks of the naked aspens thrust like bones into the dark green masses of the pines.

Barnaby arranged himself on a boulder, felt the bite of the cold stone through his trousers. Opened his portfolio, spread the pages, lifted his pen, poised; waiting for the fanfare, the applause, the breathless trembling gasp of amazement from the multitudes.

The wind sighed down the mountains, tossed the branches of the evergreens with a sound like a distant ocean, fluttered the pages, and passed touching his cheek like a chilly caress.

And he realized that for better or worse he was *alone*.

He was still sitting in frozen frightened stasis when a shower of stones and dirt came skittering down the cliff face on the opposite side of the road. A man followed using a brush and outcroppings with the practiced ease of the longtime mountain climber. He was a big man, with blue eyes that sparkled in a ruddy, wind-chapped face. It was a familiar face. He was the conqueror of Everest.

"Hallo," he said in that clipped, British public-school accent which always sounded fake to Barnaby.

"Hello."

"What are you about?"

"I'm completing a requiem mass," Barnaby replied lightly.

"Oh? Whose?"

"I don't know yet. Could be mine."

"Ah, ha ha, jolly good." E.H. tugged at the turtleneck. "Or mine. I'm tackling Everest next week, don't you know." The smile was back in place as he plowed manfully on with the script.

Barnaby folded his hands primly on the portfolio. "How many times does this make?"

"Uh . . . eh?" The smile faded.

"How many times?"

"Nine," came the sullen response.

"Doesn't it get boring?"

The genial facade was down. For an instant, Barnaby saw despair, and a desperate hunger writhe across the broad, handsome face. Then the mask was back, the somna raging behind the blue eyes.

An accusatory forefinger thrust out. "Y-y-you're damaged!"

Barnaby stood, clutching the portfolio to his chest. "No. What I

am is scared. But it's okay." He smiled, considering, then added
with wonder. "And I'm not bored. I'm curious and anxious and
alive. I'm about to take a risk. Thank you."

He sat, shook the pen to start the flow of ink. The notes flowed
from his soul to the page. He was at peace.

It was absurdly easy to arrange. They were to perform the Verdi
Requiem as the second half of the December concert. During inter-
mission he quietly gathered up the Verdi, and replaced it with his.
By the time the orchestra and chorus had noticed it was too late.
Most of the looks he received were terrified or hostile, but Peter's
lips skinned back a grin that was almost a grimace, and he gave
Barnaby a brief thumbs-up signal.

No rehearsal was necessary. They went through rehearsals
merely to maintain the charade, the vicarious enjoyment for the
somnas.

But it wasn't perfect!

As section followed section errors crept in. Perhaps they were
caused by disruption of the neural-paths because of this awful deviation from instruction. Whatever the cause they were there, and
they did not detract, rather they added to the heartbreaking poi-
gnancy of the work.

The final minor chord hung like a cry in the still air of the audi-
torium. Barnaby bent double, clutching the podium with both
hands in order to stay erect. The vise was back, squeezing at his
chest, because *it had been so beautiful!*

There was no applause. The audience, orchestra, and chorus
went stumbling, almost sleepwalking into the New Mexico night.
They knew, because they could forget nothing, that the music they
had heard and played and sung was original. After three hundred
years of repetition a new voice had been heard.

A few were manic in their joy. Peter capering about with his violin in one hand and bow in the other chanting in a grotesque sing-
song.

"You did it. You did it. You did it."

Barnaby feared that he was damaged, and caught him by the
shoulders.

"Stop it!"

For a long moment he searched Peter's blue eyes, fearing and
not understanding what he read there. "You did it," the violinist
whispered again, and spinning from his grip skipped from the
stage.

Thrusting his baton into his hip pocket Barnaby wandered about the empty stage gathering up scores. Then hesitated, not knowing what to do with them. Finally he paced to the edge of the stage, and let them fall, an ivory waterfall, onto the carpeted floor. His own master score he tucked beneath one arm, and slowly left the stage.

The green room added to his sense of eerie unreality. No chattering crowds, eager well wishers, flushed performers. A bottle of champagne shifted in its bucket, the rattle of the ice loud in the silent room.

Barnaby started back to the stage, but stopped, arrested by a shadowy hatted and coated figure in the darkened wing.

"*Do* you know what you did?" asked Dr. Antonio Garcia.

"Huh?"

"That young man," he gestured toward the empty stage where only moments before Peter had capered. "Seemed to think you had done it. I'm just wondering if you know what *it* is."

The ancient figure seemed to be holding itself with unnatural rigidity. Holding in . . . something.

"Stop being so fucking portentous." He lit a cigarette. "I wrote a requiem. I proved that 'backs' *can* create."

"Which means what?"

"Shit, I don't know." Smoke erupted in two sharp narrow lines from his nostrils. "That I'll write a symphony next?"

Antonio's lined face twisted with anger, quickly suppressed and controlled. "Why a requiem, Barnaby?"

"I don't know. Something meaningful there, you suppose?" A broad grin that brought no answering response from Antonio.

"Yes, Barnaby, there *is* something meaningful there." The words hissed out fueled by his suppressed violence. "You've done for us, you heedless fool. You've upset the balance. Expressed the discontent. You've given us choices. An hour ago our world was secure, our place in it established, defined. Now there is no guiding force."

Barnaby backed away until he came up against the shell. "You're somna," he began.

"Don't speak to me of that thing! You've ruined us! Ruined us! The entire world has changed, and you don't see it! God, what a moron. Well, I can't face your new world, Barnaby. But I can't go back," he muttered as he tottered toward the exit. "But I can't choose. Can't. Can't. Cant." The quavering voice faded, and Barnaby stood frozen with shock.

The somna was a huddled, frightened presence. Barnaby

stepped into the icy night, and it stirred, uncoiling itself from the deepest recesses of his mind. It probed, urged, agitated.

"No," he said aloud, and the word was filled with weariness. "I'm not playing." It slunk back to cower and brood.

The streets were filled with disoriented "backs." Some still trying to play out their somnas' games, but it was like a one-handed man clapping. And Barnaby realized that the network that linked all the "backs" had brought them all the message of his requiem whether they had attended the concert or not. He once more thought of his imaginary counterpart in Fez, and wondered if he understood what had occurred.

Barnaby was starting to, and the understanding terrified him.

Laura was waiting at the house. Cowering on the doorstep. Lost waif. Her hands closed convulsively on his arm as he knelt beside her.

She tried to speak, but only inarticulate sounds emerged. He soothed her with hands and lips and voice. "I love you, Laura," he whispered against her hair.

He rose, stared down at her bowed head. *You've started this, Barnaby, you crazy fucker.*

So does that mean I have to end it? he wailed.

Yes!

I didn't know what I was doing. No answer. *I never meant, never intended . . .*

Choice.

He pressed Laura's shoulders, unlocked the door, walked in. Fear coiled through his mind. Burrowed, sought to hide. He gazed down at the floating somna. White and naked, muscles atrophied from decades of nonuse. For three hundred years they had dreamed life, and their faithful "backs" had experienced every endless nuance, sharing each sensation with their silent, insatiable parasites.

Choice.

Your time has passed. A monitor gave up its grip on flesh with a sticky pop. *It's not malice that motivates me. Just boredom.* The IV's slid from the skeletal arms, and hung like dying seaweed over the edges of the tank. *You've abdicated your right to humanity.*

The somna was writhing now. Wasted muscles jerking as it struggled against the onrush of death. The mouth opening and closing, thick syrupy nutrient bath rushing down the gasping throat.

It was awful, terrifying, and disgusting all at the same time. But he forced himself to watch to the end. After so many years with this

silent watcher it was his final act of service. When the final ago-
nized shudder ended he leaned down, and gently closed the staring
eyes.

And now he knew that humanity had truly passed to them. He
had fashioned and destroyed, created and killed.

It was a contradiction heretofore only achieved by humans.

"Requiem" was written because I was asked to edit an anthology
of New Mexican science fiction authors, and the University of
New Mexico Press insisted that I write a story as well. This kind of
kick in the rear is required before I will write a short piece. I'm a
novelist, and frankly stories intimidate me.

But having agreed to this task I had to find a tale to tell. I have
several and very diverse areas in which I have a passionate interest. One is music—I studied opera at the Conservatory of Vienna.
Another is the area of legal rights for artificially created entities—
androids, robots, AI programs, etc. By wedding these two interests
I suddenly found myself wrestling with the question of creativity.
Can a robot innovate? Does an android have a soul? Can an AI
program dream and desire?

The vampirism element wasn't a conscious decision. Again, I
was grappling with the issues of ownership—human proprietor-
ship of their creations—and it wasn't until the story was completed
that I realized how truly horrific the floating, dreaming human beings actually were.

So that's the saga of "Requiem." Someday I'd like to go back
and figure out what caused the virus that destroyed most of humanity. And how the "backs" built their new society. And if they
killed all the humans. Hmmm, sounds like a novel. Guess I'm
home again. Maybe I'll make another foray into short fiction next
year—if somebody asks me to.

Melinda M. Snodgrass

Infidel

THOMAS TESSIER

I've been a fan of Tessier's since I read Finishing Touches, *a subtle novel of psychological suspense about the loss of innocence, which leads to corruption.*

In "Infidel," Tessier deals with the loss of faith, which—as an invitation allows a traditional vampire to enter one's house—here opens a door for despair to enter the soul.

"And how is me dear old friend Andy these days?"

"He's fine. He's in good health, and he said to tell you he plays golf at least once a week."

"Tsk." Monsignor Comerford shook his head in mock annoyance but couldn't keep from smiling. "It's a grand racket, the parish priest. Marry 'em and bury 'em, and count the weekly take. Tell Andy I said that, would you?"

"I will," Caroline replied.

"Did you know Andy and I were in college together in Dublin? University College. That was ages ago, of course."

"Yes, he told me that's where you met," Caroline said. "And UCD was where James Joyce went too, wasn't it?"

"That's right, Earlsfort Terrace. Great writer, Joyce," the monsignor added perfunctorily, as if he did not quite agree with his own statement. "A fine feel for the city back then, I'll say that much for him."

Caroline reached into her purse. "I took this snapshot of Father Andy a couple of weeks ago," she said as she passed it to the elderly priest.

"Ah, will you look at that chubby little bugger," Monsignor Comerford exclaimed with glee as he took the photograph. "He was always first at the table, now that I think back on it. Mind you, he never shied away from a gargle either, but you'd better not tell him I said *that*. He might worry about his image. Parish priests tend to fret about such things in America."

"You can keep it, Monsignor," Caroline said as he attempted to return the photograph. "It's for you."

"Thank you very much." He set the picture down on his desk, next to the letter of introduction that Father Andy had written for Caroline. "But let's skip that 'Monsignor' business, shall we? Gerry will do nicely." Caroline smiled and nodded. "Good. Now then, how long have you been in Rome?"

"Four days."

It came as a mild surprise for Caroline to be reminded that she was sitting in an office in Vatican City, not in a rectory in some leafy suburb of Dublin. Monsignor Comerford, she knew, had been stationed at the Vatican for nearly two decades, but he was still thoroughly Irish in his appearance, accent, and manner. The pink, well-scrubbed complexion, the curly white hair, the steady cascade of cigarette ash down the front of his black jacket, the gentle sing-song voice—all seemed to belong more in a cluttered Georgian sitting room with peat blazing fragrantly in the fireplace and a big bottle of Powers on the sideboard than in this obscure corner of the papal bureaucracy. Caroline had no clear idea what the Monsignor *did* at the Vatican, but neither did Father Andy.

"And it says here—" tapping at the letter, "—you're a librarian. Is that right?"

"Yes," Caroline answered.

"Very good, and what exactly is it you'd like to do?"

"I'd love to spend some time just looking through the books, the archives. It probably sounds silly, but I've always dreamed of having a chance to explore the Vatican library. I love books and manuscripts, all forms of writing."

Caroline hoped he wouldn't ask if she had been to Trinity or the Bodelian or the Sorbonne, because she hadn't. How could she explain to the priest that it wasn't just books, but the Vatican itself that had drawn her? She really did dream of the Vatican—bizarre images of capture, of anonymous torture, of being trapped forever in an endless maze of barren hallways. Nothing was ever said, there were no signs, but somehow Caroline always knew that she was in the Vatican. At times she wondered if the recurring dreams were a form of sickness, but they never frightened her; on the contrary, she had come to feel almost comfortable with them.

"Is it the dirty books you're after?" Monsignor Comerford's eyes had turned steely. "We've a regular army of these so-called scholars who come trooping through here, most of them American I might add, and all they want to do is study the dirty books. Why we even keep them is beyond me, but nowadays destroying a book is almost a mortal sin. To some folks, anyway."

The monsignor was apparently finished, so Caroline answered his question. "No. History and the history of the faith are my favorite subjects." Faith, she thought, and the loss of it.

"Ah, that's a welcome change." The monsignor beamed at her. "If all the fine young women of the world felt that way, there'd be a lot less bother taking place."

There was a barb in the compliment, for Caroline noticed how the monsignor glanced at her unadorned ring finger. History and books were all well and good, but he believes I should be married and taking care of a bunch of babies, she thought. That was fine with her. Caroline might disagree with Monsignor Comerford as to what a woman should or should not do, but she was actually pleased that he was a priest from the old school. She hadn't come to the Vatican looking for trendiness or progressive attitudes. Her own faith had been blasted by the winds of modernism swirling through the Church in recent years.

"Well, you'd better get started," the monsignor said, rising from his seat. "You can have the rest of the afternoon, just get yourself back here by five. That's when I leave, and I wouldn't want you getting lost."

"Neither would I."

"And if you haven't had enough, you're more than welcome to come back tomorrow. There's so much of that clutter downstairs a person could spend years poking through it all, if he had nothing better to do with his life. And contrary to what you might have heard, none of it is off-limits." The priest paused, then winked at her. "Of course, it's not everyone that gets in."

Monsignor Comerford left Caroline with Father Vincenzo, who was apparently in charge of "the collection." A short, thin man who wore wire-rimmed glasses and spoke excellent English, Father Vincenzo showed her some of the noteworthy documents and volumes in the official library. Air-conditioned, computerized, it was a completely modern operation in a centuries-old setting. And yet, it was a good deal smaller than Caroline had expected. But then Father Vincenzo took her on a tour of the three main levels below ground, where one room grew out of another and the number of them ran into the dozens before she lost count. There were books and manuscripts and tottering heaps of papers piled on every inch of shelf space, from floor to ceiling. Tiny corridors appeared, and then abruptly ended. On the third and lowest level the floor was made up of large stone slabs, long since worn smooth. The rooms were small and boxy, and seemed to have been carved right out of the earth. The passageways were quite narrow and the only lights were strung along the low ceiling with electric cable.

There were no labels, no numbers, no signs, nothing at all to indicate order. If you wanted to find something, where would you start, Caroline wondered. But she was delighted, because she finally felt she had arrived where she was meant to be.

"These are the oldest stacks," Father Vincenzo explained. "Everything valuable or important has been removed, but otherwise it is not very organized."

"There's so much of it," Caroline said.

"Yes, it extends under most of Vatican City. The equivalent of two or three square blocks in New York City, I think." Then a smile formed at the corners of Father Vincenzo's mouth. "You are a book lover. This, I think, is what you came to see."

"Oh, yes, yes. I'm amazed. It's so much like I pictured it in my fantasies." The word seemed too personal, almost sexual in its intensity. Caroline felt her cheeks flush, and all she could do was add weakly, "But more so."

Father Vincenzo brought Caroline back to the stairs in order to show her how easy it was to find the way out, and then he left her alone to pursue her curiosity. She appreciated the fact that he didn't feel it necessary to warn her against damaging, copying, or tracing over anything.

Caroline wandered aimlessly for a while, stopping to look at one item or another, and then moving on. Her knowledge of French and Latin was excellent, and she had a smattering of Italian, but most of the pages on the third level were handwritten, and sooner or later the calligraphy defeated her. Caroline simply could not concentrate, her mind refused to focus. What am I doing here?

Somewhere in a far corner of the third level, Caroline found a battered footstool in one room. She sat down on it, and leaned back against a wall of large, leathery tomes. She was tired, and her feet ached, the usual tourist curse, but she felt very happy. Pennsylvania seemed a billion miles away. She let her eyes close for a moment, and she sucked in the musty air. To Caroline it was like a rare and delicious perfume.

Books were the center of her life, and it had been that way ever since she was a small child. She liked to believe that she could still remember fumbling to open her very first picture book of nursery rhymes—but Caroline knew that was probably more her fancy than an actual memory. Books were mysterious, frightening, thrilling, disturbing, uplifting, nurturing, endlessly available, and always accommodating. Caroline had dated many men over the years, but she had yet to find one who offered the same array of valuable qualities. Most of the time that didn't bother her. If you had to have something other than a relationship for the focal point of your life, what better than books?

Books, and belief. But belief was an increasingly elusive notion. For years it had been a natural part of Caroline's life, but lately it seemed irrelevant, or not even there. Nothing specific had happened to cause this change, yet it seemed as if the deep well of her faith had gradually evaporated to the point where it was now not much more than a thin, moist residue. But you can't control faith, any more than you can choose your dreams.

Caroline stood up and resumed her wandering. In one large room she came across signs of fairly recent activity. There were stacks of bound papers on a table, many more on the floor around it. A prospectus announced the publication of the *Annals of the Propagation of the Faith* in five hundred volumes over a period of twenty years. Caroline knew that the *Annals* were regular reports to the Vatican from Catholic missionaries all over the world. It was a staggering thought. How many centuries of this tedious and obscure paperwork had accumulated by now? And yet, Caroline was sure that some of it must be quite fascinating. However, clipped to the prospectus was a laconic handwritten note, dated November, 1974, which stated that the project was abandoned because of the bankruptcy of the publisher. And of course the Vatican wouldn't squander its own funds on such an improbable commercial venture, Caroline thought, smiling as she left the room.

She walked until she came to the lowest (the floor had a way of gradually winding down into the earth) and most remote corner of the third level. Certainly this was where the overhead reach of electric cable and lights ended. About twenty feet away, just visible in the gloom, was a stone wall that marked the end of the passageway. The books and manuscripts, stacked from the floor to the ceiling on each side, were wedged together so tightly and had been undisturbed for so long that they appeared to have hardened into a solid mass, and Caroline was afraid she would damage them if she tried to remove any one item for scrutiny. She started to turn away, intending to make the long climb back up to the street level, but then she stopped, as she thought she noticed something odd about the far wall.

It was an optical illusion, aided by the feeble light. Yes, she realized, moving closer. There was not one wall, but two, at the end of the aisle. The outer wall, which came from the right, stopped just short of the stacks on the left, and the inner wall receded almost imperceptibly behind it. Caroline approached the gap, barely a foot wide, and peered around the corner.

Total darkness. She reached into it, and felt nothing but cool air. The passage continued. Caroline didn't know what she should do. She wanted to follow it, to find out where it went, but she had nothing to light her way. She could trip and tumble down a hole, or walk into a den of snakes or vermin—too many bad things could happen. Buy a flashlight and return tomorrow.

Yes, but first . . . Caroline slid her foot along the ground and edged herself behind the wall. Just a step or two, she promised, to see if it ends abruptly. Her outstretched hand bumped against something hard, not stone. A metal bar. Caroline gripped it and harsh rust flaked loose in her hand. It had to be a gate, which meant that the passage *did* go on. Caroline shook it firmly once, and the whole thing broke free. It was too heavy and unwieldy to control, so she shoved it away from her. The sound that came in the darkness told her that the gate had hit a wall and then slid down to the left. Firm ground, and a turn.

Caroline worked her way along the narrow passage. The wall swung back to the left, as expected. She moved cautiously around the turn, probing the air with her hand. Caroline stopped. This was as far as she could safely go without a light. She stared at the uniform blackness ahead of her. Beyond this point she could easily get lost in a maze of passageways. Okay, she thought, you found something interesting; come back tomorrow with a flashlight and a sack of bread crumbs.

Caroline hesitated, her mind dancing with possibilities. It could be a long-forgotten catacomb, or a burial chamber that held the mummified remains of ancient Romans. She might even discover some manuscripts that dated back two thousand years. She should discuss it with Father Vincenzo, and together they could organize a proper exploration. But even as Caroline considered this, she found it impossible to turn back. The priest's office was so far away, such an enormous climb—and Caroline felt too tired. The cumulative effects of travel and touring and the miles of walking had finally caught up with her. The dead air didn't help either. She would have to rest for a few minutes before leaving.

As she stood there, leaning against the wall, Caroline began to notice the quality of the darkness. You could say that it had no depth at all, or that its depth was endless. But it was not a perfect darkness, she realized. Somewhere in it, close by or off in the distance, there was—not light, but the subtlest texture of light. I must look like someone on drugs, Caroline thought as she stared ahead. Pupils dilated wide as drift nets to sweep any random photons across the threshold of visibility. I look like a freak, but that's okay because it's a freaky situation. Caroline felt dizzy and disoriented, as if she could no longer tell which way was up, and yet there was nothing she could do—except fall down, if that's what was going to happen—because she was just too tired, too damn tired to care. But she was not wrong. There was light, or something like it.

Caroline was aware of the fact that she was walking. Toward the light, into the dark, it didn't matter which. She felt oddly detached from what was happening, as if her body had decided to move and her mind was simply floating along with it. Probably no one still alive in the Vatican knew of this hidden area, Caroline thought dreamily. Which means, *No one in the world knows where I am now*. But that didn't frighten her. On the contrary, she felt caught up in something of real importance out on the boundary of faith and uncertainty, and dreams.

A suffusion of light infiltrated her right eye, knocking her off balance. It wasn't that strong, Caroline saw as she steadied herself and her eyes readjusted. It was a glow, a hazy cloud of cold light some distance away, too weak to illuminate this place. Yet it had confused her for a brief moment. Caroline crossed the intervening space and walked into the faint light. She looked at a flight of crude stairs that coiled down and away from her, deep into the chilly earth.

For just an instant Caroline's mind slid toward the idea of leaving, but just as quickly it skittered away. Her body had no strength for going back now. It was as if she were caught on an electric current that carried her only forward, and down. And so Caroline descended the wet and slippery steps, pressing her hands against the close walls and bending her head beneath the low rock ceiling. Count the number—but the numbers bounced around like a flock of billiard balls clicking in her brain, and the momentum of her descent increased rapidly, flooding her with apprehension, so she couldn't.

Almost brightness. Caroline's knees sagged as her feet hit bottom suddenly and there was nowhere to go. She had arrived in a small room, really nothing more than a landing. Then she saw the gate, another gate. No, it was a door. Through the bars, a square cell, empty but for the old man lying in the middle of the floor. A clutch of tattered rags. The man looked ancient. What light was this?

Ah, child.

—Who . . . are you?

The words formed in her mind but never escaped her lips. It didn't matter. The old man smiled, and felt, disturbingly, as if he somehow made Caroline's face smile with him.

Mani.

—What?

Caroline's brain swirled sickeningly, and it took an effort of the will to remain on her feet. The old man kept smiling that near-death smile. A sack of dead skin. But the smile, and those eyes, were very much alive. He moved slightly, the muted sound of dusty parchment rustling.

Ma-nee.

The first syllable prolonged, the second quite crisp despite the long vowel. Caroline shook her head slowly.

—No . . .

Manicheus, if you wish.

Impossible, Caroline thought. It was all wrong and she knew she should leave at once, but instead her body sank down on the wall until she was sitting on the bottom step.

—The holy man?

Paraclete. Yes.

—No. Manicheus died in A.D. 275.

Was put to death.

—As a heretic.

Yes, as a heretic.

The old man's laughter simmered uncomfortably in Caroline's brain. This is crazy, she thought, I'm hallucinating, the dreams are pushing up and breaking the surface.

No.

She struggled to recall what she knew of Manicheanism. It was one of many heretical sects that had sprung up in the early years of the Church, and perhaps the most dangerous. The Church had spared no effort to wipe out the Manicheans, although some of their beliefs still lingered on in the despair and cynicism that permeated so much of modern life. They claimed that the universe was made up of two equal forces, light (good) and dark (evil), in eternal conflict. God was good, but God did not reign supreme in this universe. If you put evil on a par with good, then all else is permanently diminished and faith becomes a matter of arbitrary choice. Human beings were just insignificant players in a cosmic struggle without beginning or end. So the gap between the Church and the Manicheans was a vast theological chasm that could never be bridged. But it was an issue of purely academic interest now, or at least it should be, Caroline thought.

—How could you be here?

They brought me back and locked me in this place.

—But why? Didn't they kill you?

Yes, but to them I was a heretic.

—I still don't understand.

The laughter came again, rippling through Caroline's mind in a very unpleasant sensation.

They believed that heretics return to this world, possessing terrible powers. The power to draw the lifeblood of faith out of other souls. To control the feeble human mind. That is why they burned heretics, and tore the bodies to pieces.

But that was another time, centuries ago, and now not even the Church believes in such things. Beliefs change, but do they ever matter?

The Pope had to see me, to see for himself that I really was dead, and so they brought me back from Persia.

—And put you down here and forgot about you?

Oh, they played with me awhile, using their knives and hot irons. Dry laughter, like whistling sand. *But then the old Pope died, and yes, I was forgotten.*

—When did you last . . .

See someone? A charming young novice in the thirteenth century. I haven't been able to move from this spot in about perhaps three hundred years now. Easy to find souls, but not to bring them all the way into this place.

The old man was crazy, Caroline had no doubt. But whatever the truth about him might be, he obviously needed care, and maybe medical attention. He certainly did not belong down in a clammy dungeon. It was a miracle he wasn't already dead. He looked so frail and helpless, and there was such sadness in his eyes.

—I'll get help.

Don't leave me, child.

—What should I do?

The door. Come to me.

Caroline approached the cell door. The hinges looked as if they wouldn't budge. She put her hands around one of the bars in the center of the door, and shook it. The hinges held, but there was some give inside the lock. Caroline shook the door again and the corroded latch crumbled steadily beneath the pressure. Rusty flakes showered down to the floor. The hinges shrieked painfully as Caroline forced the door open.

The old man looked up hopefully as she slipped into the cell and went to him. She wasn't sure what to do next. He looked too weak and fragile to move.

Hold me.

Caroline sat down on the floor beside him, took him by the shoulders, and carefully lifted him up. His head lolled against her shoulder, then slid a little, resting over her heart, and he smiled gratefully. Caroline had no desire to move.

Touch me with your skin.

Caroline stroked his cheek lightly—it felt cool and dry, like one of the old manuscripts she had examined. Regardless of who he was or why he was there, the old man responded to her hand on his cheek. His eyes brightened and his features became more animated. He was certainly old, but so small and shrunken, like some lonely, withered child.

I need to be closer.

Caroline didn't understand. Her mind felt tired, lazy, and remarkably tranquil. She didn't want to move at all. She hugged the old man closer to her.

To your warmth.

Her mind couldn't follow a complete thought anymore. Nothing mattered but the moment, and her part in it. Caroline unbuttoned her blouse and the old man quickly pressed his face to her skin.

More.

Her bra was in the way. Caroline pulled it down, uncovering her breasts. The old man rubbed his face against them, burrowed between them, and then she felt his tongue, like fine sandpaper, seeking her nipple. Caroline was paralyzed with delirium, dazed with a sense of giving. It felt as if her body were a vessel full of precious liquid, a kind of inner sea of living warmth that was now flowing through her skin into him. But there was nothing to replace it, and Caroline's heart quickened with a sudden surge of useless alarm.

—Holy man . . .

Once.

—You brought me here?

In a way, yes.

—You spoke to me in dreams . . .

In dreams you spoke with yourself, and I am what you found.

—You took my faith . . .

What we let go was never there.

—Help me . . .

Become what you become, as I did.

—They were right . . .

Well, yes.

—You became . . .

What they made me.

—God help me . . .

And who is that, child?

Caroline reached up to touch her own cheek and was amazed to find that it already felt as cool and dry as onionskin. Too weak to move, Caroline rested her hand on the man's bony shoulder. She was vaguely aware that she ought to push him away. There was no muscle strength left in her arm. Then Caroline was unable even to remain sitting up, and she fell back flat on the floor. She felt so light there was no pain when her head hit the stone. The old man moved lower and rested his face in the warm softness of her belly. He left no mark on her, for the touch of her skin was enough. An image flickered across her mind—she was buried beneath a million books, and it was not an unpleasant experience. Then the books began to fall, tons of them raining silently down through the darkness, and Caroline fell with them, a fading ribbon of liquid heat that spun and swirled as she flew gloriously out of herself.

She wakes in darkness. Disoriented for a moment, she shoves the dead bones off her bare skin. Now she knows where she is and what comes next. She stands, buttons her blouse, and leaves. She knows the way. So much time has gone by. It's late, and she has a million things to do.

Dona Rintelman got me wondering about what might have been lost or forgotten in the recesses of the Vatican over the course of centuries. This story is for Dona, but it is emphatically *not* about her.

Any similarity between the hold that the world's religions exert on some of their believers, and the legendary power that vampires have over certain hapless human beings, is of course entirely in the mind of the observer. Things always look different from the inside.

Thomas Tessier

Do I Dare to Eat a Peach?

CHELSEA QUINN YARBRO

Tessier's story was about the human embodiment of a religious heresy as vampire. In Yarbro's classic, the State, represented by a few men, metaphorically takes on the characteristics of vampirism when it gives these men the power to brainwash Weybridge and drain him of his personality, his hope, and his will.

Weybridge had been burgled: someone—some *thing*—had broken in and ransacked his memories, leaving all that was familiar in chaos. It was almost impossible for him to restore order, and so he was not entirely sure how much had been lost.

Malpass offered him sympathy. "Look, David, we know you went through a lot. We know that you'd like the chance to put it all behind you. We want you to have that, but there are a few more things we have to get cleared up. You understand how it is."

"Yes," Weybridge said vaguely, hoping that, by agreeing, he might learn more. "You have your . . . your . . ."

"Responsibilities," Malpass finished for him. "Truth to tell, there are times I wish I didn't have them." He patted David on the shoulder. "You're being great about all this. I'll make sure it's in the report."

Weybridge wanted to ask what report it was, and for whom, but he could not bring himself to say the words. He simply nodded, as he had done so many times before. He opened his mouth, once, twice, then made a wave with one hand.

"We know how it is, old man," Malpass said as he scrutinized Weybridge. "They worked you over, David. We know that. We don't blame you for what you did after that."

Weybridge nodded a few more times, his mind on other things. He eventually stared up at the ceiling. He wanted to tell Malpass and the others that he would rather be left alone, simply turned out and ignored, but that wasn't possible. He had hinted at it once,

163

when they had first started talking to him, and the reaction had been incredulity. So Weybridge resigned himself to the long, unproductive wait.

In the evening, when Malpass was gone, Stone took his place. Stone was younger than Malpass, and lacked that air of sympathy the older man appeared to possess. He would stand by the door, his arms folded, his hair perfectly in place, his jaw shaved to shininess, and he would favor Weybridge with a contemptuous stare. Usually he had a few taunting remarks to make before relapsing into his cold, staring silence. Tonight was no different. "They should have left you where they found you. A man like you—you don't deserve to be saved."

Weybridge sighed. It was useless, he knew from experience, to try to tell Stone that he had no memory of the time he was . . . wherever it was he had been. "Why?" he asked wearily, hoping that some word, some revelation, no matter how disgusting, would give him a sense of what he had done.

"You know why. Treating the dead that way. I saw the photos. Men like you aren't worth the trouble to bring back. They should leave you to rot, after what you did." He shook his head. "We're wasting our time with you. Men like you—"

"I know. We should be left alone." He stared up at the glare of the ceiling light. "I agree."

Stone made a barking sound that should have been a laugh but wasn't. "Oh, no. Don't go pious on me now, Weybridge. You're in for a few more questions before they throw you back in the pond. One of these days you're going to get tired of the lies, and you'll tell us what you were doing, and who made you do it."

Weybridge shook his head slowly. His thin, hospital-issue pajamas made him chilly at night, and he found himself shivering. That reminded him of something from the past, a time when he had been cold, trembling, for days on end. But where it had happened and why eluded him. He leaned back on the pillows and tried to make his mind a blank, but still the fragments, disjointed and terrifying, were with him. He huddled under the covers, burrowing his head into the stacked pillows as if seeking for refuge. He wanted to ask Stone to turn the lights down, but he knew the young man would refuse. There was something about nightmares, and screams, but whether they were his own or someone else's, he was not sure.

"You had any rest since you got here, Weybridge?" Stone

taunted him. "I'm surprised that you even bother to try. You have no right to sleep."

"Maybe," Weybridge muttered, dragging the sheet around his shoulders. "Maybe you're wrong, though."

"Fat chance," Stone scoffed, and made a point of looking away from him. "Fat fucking chance."

Weybridge lay back on his bed, his eyes half focused on the acoustical tile of the ceiling. If he squinted, he thought he could discern a pattern other than the simple regularity of perforations. There might be a message in the ceiling. There might be a clue.

Stone stayed on duty, silent for most of his shift, but favoring Weybridge with an occasional sneer. He smoked his long, thin dark cigarettes and dropped the ashes onto the floor. The only time he changed his attitude was when the nurse came in to give Weybridge yet another injection. Then he winked lasciviously and tried to pat her ass as she left the room.

"You shouldn't bother her," Weybridge said, his tongue unwieldy as wet flannel. "She . . . she doesn't want—"

"She doesn't want to have to deal with someone like you," Stone informed him.

Weybridge sighed. "I hope . . ." He stopped, knowing that he had left hope behind, back in the same place his memories were.

Malpass was back soon after Stone left, and he radiated his usual air of sympathy. "We've been going over your early reports, David, and so far, there's nothing . . . irregular about them. Whatever happened must have occurred in the last sixteen months. That's something, isn't it."

"Sure," Weybridge said, waiting for the orderly to bring him his breakfast.

"So we've narrowed down the time. That means we can concentrate on your work in that sixteen-month period, and perhaps get a lead on when you were . . ." He made a gesture of regret and reached out to pat Weybridge on the shoulder.

"When I was turned," Weybridge said harshly. "That's what you're looking for. You want to know how much damage I did before you got me back, don't you?"

"Of course that's a factor," Malpass allowed. "But there are other operatives who might be subjected to the same things that have happened to you. We do know that they are not all pharmacological. There were other aspects involved." He cleared his throat and looked toward the venetian blind that covered the window. It was almost closed, so that very little light from outside penetrated the room.

"That's interesting, I guess," Weybridge said, unable to think of anything else to say.

"It is," Malpass insisted with his unflagging good humor. "You took quite a risk in letting us bring you back. We're pretty sure the other side didn't want you to be . . . recovered."

"Good for me." Weybridge laced his hands behind his head. "And when you find out—*if* you find out—what then? What becomes of me once you dredge up the truth? Or doesn't that matter?"

"Of *course* it matters," Malpass said, his eyes flicking uneasily toward a spot on the wall. "We look after our own, David."

"But I'm not really your own anymore, am I?" He did not bother to look at Malpass, so that the other man would not have to work so hard to lie.

"Deep down, we know you are," Malpass hedged. "You're proving it right now, by your cooperation."

"Cooperation?" Weybridge burst out. "Is that what you think this is? I was dragged back here, tranked out of my mind, and hustled from place to place in sealed vans like something smuggled through customs. No one asked me if I wanted to be here, or if I wanted you to unravel whatever is left of my mind. Cut the crap, Malpass. You want to get the last of the marrow before you throw the bones out." It was the most Weybridge had said at one time since his return, and it startled Malpass.

"David, I can understand why you're upset, especially considering all you've gone through. But believe me, I'm deeply interested in your welfare. I certainly wouldn't countenance any more abuse where you're concerned." He smiled, showing his very perfect, very expensive teeth. "Anyone who's been through what you've been through—"

"You don't know what it was. Neither do I," Weybridge reminded him.

"—would have every reason to be bitter. I don't blame you for that," Malpass went on as if nothing had been said. "You know that you have been—"

"No, I don't know!" Weybridge turned on him, half rising in his bed. "I haven't any idea! That's the problem. I have scraps here and there, but nothing certain, and nothing that's entirely real. You call me David, and that might be my first name, but I don't remember it, and it doesn't sound familiar. For all I know, I'm not home at all, or this might not be my home. For all I know, I never got away from where I was and this is just another part of the . . . the experiment."

Malpass did not answer at once. He paced the length of the room, then turned and came back toward the head of the bed. "I didn't know you were so troubled," he said finally, his eyes lowered as if in church. "I'll tell your doctors that you need extra care today."

"You mean more drugs," Weybridge sighed. "It might work. Who knows?"

"Listen, David," Malpass said with great sincerity, "we're relying on you in this. We can't get you straight again without your help, and that isn't always easy for you to give, I know."

Weybridge closed his eyes. He had a brief impression of a man in a uniform that he did not recognize, saying something in precisely that same tone of commiseration and concern that Malpass was using now. For some reason, the sound of it made him want to vomit, and his appetite disappeared.

"Is something wrong, David?" Malpass asked, his voice sounding as if he were a very long way off. "David?"

"It's nothing," he muttered, trying to get the older man to go away. "I . . . didn't sleep well."

"The lights?" Malpass guessed, then went on. "We've told you why they're necessary for the time being. Once your memory starts coming back, then you can have the lights off at night. It will be safe then."

"Will it?" Weybridge said. "If you say so."

Malpass assumed a look of long-suffering patience. "You're not being reasonable this morning, David."

"According to your reports, I don't have any reason, period." That much he believed, and wished that he did not. He longed for a sense of his own past, of a childhood and friends and family. What if I am an orphan, or the victim of abuse? he asked himself, and decided that he would rather have such painful memories than none at all.

"What's on your mind, David?"

"Nothing," he insisted. There were more of the broken images shifting at the back of his mind, most of them senseless, and those that were coherent were terrifying. He had the impression of a man—himself?—kneeling beside a shattered body, pausing to cut off the ears and nose of the corpse. Had he done that? Had he seen someone do that? Had he been told about it? He couldn't be sure, and that was the most frightening thing of all.

"Tell me about it," Malpass offered. "Let me help you, David."

It was all he could do to keep from yelling that his name was not David. But if it was not, what was it? What could he tell them to take the place of David?

"You look terrible. What is it?" Malpass bent over him, his middle-aged features creased with anxiety. "Is there anything you can tell me?"

Weybridge struck out with his arm, narrowly missing Malpass. "Leave me alone!"

"All right. All right." Malpass stepped back, holding up his hands placatingly. "You need rest, David. I'll see that you get it. I'll send someone in to you."

"NO!" Weybridge shouted. He did not want any more drugs. There had been too much in his bloodstream already. He had the impression that there had been a time when his veins had been hooked up to tubes, and through the tubes, all sorts of things had run into his body. He thought that he must have been wounded, or . . . A light truck overturned and burst into flame as a few men crawled away from it. Had he been one of the men? Where had the accident occurred? He put his hands to his head and pressed, as if that might force his mind to squeeze out the things he needed to know.

Malpass had retreated to the door and was signaling someone in the hallway. "Just a little while, David. You hang on," he urged Weybridge. "We'll take care of you."

Weybridge pulled one of his pillows over his face in an attempt to blot out what was left there. Gouts of flame, shouts and cries in the night. Bodies riven with bullets. Where were they? *Who* were they? Why did Weybridge remember them, if he did remember them?

Another nurse, this one older and more massive, came barreling through the door, a steel tray in her hand. "You calm down there," she ordered Weybridge so abruptly that his fear grew sharper.

There was a chill on his arm and a prick that warmed him, and shortly suffused through him, turning his world from hard-edged to soft, and making his memories—what there were of them—as entrancing as the boardwalk attractions of loop-the-loop and the carousel.

Later that day, when Weybridge babbled himself half awake,

they brought him food, and did what they could to coax him to eat it.

"You're very thin, Mr. Weybridge," the head nurse said in a tone that was more appropriate for an eight-year-old than a man in his late thirties.

"I'm hungry," Weybridge protested. "I *am*. But . . ." He stared at the plate and had to swallow hard against the bile at the back of his throat. "I don't know what's the matter."

"Sometimes drugs will do this," the head nurse said, disapproval in her tone and posture.

"You're the ones keeping me on drugs," he reminded her nastily. "You don't know what—"

The head nurse paid no attention to him. She continued to bustle about the room, playing at putting things in order. "Now, we're not to lie in bed all day. Doctor says that we can get up this afternoon for a while, and walk a bit."

"Oh, can *we*?" Weybridge asked with spite. "What else can *we* do?"

"Mr. Weybridge," the head nurse reproached him. "We're simply trying to help you. If you just lie there, then there's very little we can do. You can see that, can't you?"

"What happened to the *we* all of a sudden?" He wanted to argue with her, but lacked the energy. It was so useless that he almost wished he could laugh.

"That's better; you'll improve as long as you keep your sense of humor." She came back to the foot of his bed and patted his foot through the thin blankets. "That's the first step, a sense of humor."

"Sure." How hopeless it seemed, and he could not find out why.

By the time Malpass came back, Weybridge had enough control of himself that he was able to take the man's kind solicitations without becoming angry with him.

"You're going to get better, David," Malpass promised. "We'll be able to debrief you and then you can get away from all this. If you cooperate, we'll make sure you'll have all the protections you'll need."

"Why would I need protections?" And what kind of protections? he added to himself.

Malpass hesitated, plainly weighing his answer. "We don't yet know just how much you did while you were with the other side. There are probably men who would like to eliminate you, men from their side as well as ours. If we put you under our protection, then your chances of survival increase, don't you see that?" He stared toward the window. "It would be easier if we could be certain that you're not . . . programmed for anything, but so far, we can't tell what is real memory and what is . . . random."

"That's a nice word for it: random." Weybridge leaned back against the pillows and tried to appear calm. "Do you have any better idea of what happened?"

"You were in prison for a while, or you believe you were in prison, in a very dark cell, apparently with someone, but there's no way to tell who that person was, or if it's your imagination that there was someone there." He coughed. "And we can't be sure that you were in prison at all."

Weybridge sighed.

"You have to understand, David, that when there are such states as yours, we . . . well, we simply have to . . . to sort out so much that sometimes it—"

"—it's impossible," Weybridge finished for him. "Which means that I could be here for the rest of my life. Doesn't it?"

Malpass shrugged. "It's too early to be thinking about that possibility."

"But it *is* a possibility," Weybridge persisted.

"Well, it's remote, but . . . well." He cleared his throat. "When we have a more complete evaluation, we'll talk about it again."

"And in the meantime?"

"Oh," Malpass said with patently false optimism, "we'll continue to carry on the treatment. Speaking of treatment," he went on, deftly avoiding more questions, "I understand you're going to be allowed to walk today. They want you to work up an appetite, and you need the exercise in any case."

"The head nurse said something about that," Weybridge responded in a dampening way.

"Excellent. *E*xcellent! We'll tell headquarters that you're improving. That will please the Old Man. You know what he can be like when there's trouble with an operative in the field." He rubbed his hands together and looked at Weybridge expectantly.

"No, I don't know anything about the Old Man. I don't know anything about headquarters. I don't recall being an operative. That's what I'm being treated for, remember?" He smashed his left arm against the bed for emphasis, but it made very little sound and most of the impact was absorbed by the softness.

"Calm down, calm down, David," Malpass urged, once again

speaking as if to an invalid. "I forgot myself, that's all. Don't let it trouble you, please."

"Why not?" Weybridge demanded suspiciously. "Wouldn't it trouble you if you couldn't remember who you were or what you'd done?"

"Of *course* it would," Malpass said, even more soothingly. "And I'd want to get to the bottom of it as soon as possible."

"And you think I don't?" Weybridge asked, his voice rising.

"David, David, you're overreacting. I didn't mean to imply that you aren't doing everything you can to . . . recover. You're exhausted, that's part of it." He reached out to pat Weybridge's shoulder. "I hear you still aren't eating."

The surge of nausea was so sudden that Weybridge bent violently against it. "No," he panted when he felt it was safe to open his mouth.

"The nurses are worried about you. They can give you more IV's, but they all think you'd do better if you . . ." He smiled, making an effort to encourage Weybridge.

"I . . . can't," Weybridge said thickly, trying not to think of food at all.

"Why?" Malpass asked, sharpness in his tone now. "Can't you tell me why?"

Weybridge shook his head, bewildered. "I don't know. I wish I did." Really? he asked himself. Do you really want to know what it is about food that horrifies you so? Or would you rather remain ignorant? That would be better, perhaps.

"You've got to eat sometime, David," Malpass insisted.

"Not yet," Weybridge said with desperation. "I need time."

"All right," Malpass allowed. "We'll schedule the IV for three more days. But I want you to consent to a few more hours of therapy every day, all right?" He did not wait for an answer. "You have to get to the bottom of this, David. You can't go on this way forever, can you?"

"I suppose not," Weybridge said, fighting an irrational desire to crawl under the bed and huddle there. Where had he done that before? He couldn't remember.

"I'll set it up." Malpass started toward the door. "The Old Man is anxious to find out what happened to you. We have other men who could be in danger."

"I understand," Weybridge said, not entirely certain that he did. What if he was not an agent at all? What if that was a part of his manufactured memories? Or what if he was still in the hands of the other side—what then? The headache that had been lurking at the back of his eyes came around to the front of his head with ferocious intensity.

"We're all watching you, David," Malpass assured him as he let himself out of the white-painted room.

Stone regarded Weybridge with scorn when he heard about the increased therapy sessions. "Taking the easy way, aren't you, you bastard?" He lit a cigarette and glowered at Weybridge.

"It doesn't feel easy to me," Weybridge replied, hoping that he did not sound as cowardly as he feared he did.

"That's a crock of warm piss," Stone declared, folding his arms and directing his gaze at the window. "Anyone does what you did, there's no reason to coddle them."

It was so tempting to beg Stone to tell him what it was he was supposed to have done, but Weybridge could not bring himself to demean himself to that hostile man. "I'm not being coddled."

"According to who?" Stone scoffed, then refused to speak again, blowing smoke toward the ceiling while Weybridge dozed between unrecallable nightmares.

The therapist was a small, olive-skinned gnome named Cleeve. He visited Weybridge just as the head nurse was trying to coax him out of bed to do his required walking. "Out for your constitutional, eh, Mr. Weybridge?" His eyes were dark and glossy, like fur or crushed velvet.

"We're going to walk twice around the nurses' station," the head nurse answered for him. "It's doctor's orders."

Weybridge teetered on his feet, feeling like a kid on stilts for the first time. Dear God, had he ever walked on stilts? He did not know. The effort of a few steps made him light-headed, and he reached out for Cleeve's shoulder to steady himself. "Sorry," he muttered as he tried to get his balance.

"Think nothing of it, Mr. Weybridge," Cleeve told him in a cordial tone. "All part of the service, I give you my word." He peered up at Weybridge, his features glowing with curiosity. "They've had you on drugs?"

"You know they have," Weybridge said a little wildly. His pulse was starting to hammer in his neck.

Cleeve nodded several times. "It might be as well to take you off some of them. So many drugs can be disorienting, can't they?" He stared at the head nurse. "Who should I speak to about Mr. Weybridge's drugs? I need to know before we start therapy, and perhaps we should arrange a . . . new approach."

The head nurse favored Cleeve with an irritated glance. "You'd have to talk to Mr. Malpass about that."

"Ay, yes, the ubiquitous Mr. Malpass," Cleeve said with relish. "I will do that at once."

Weybridge was concentrating on staying erect as he shuffled first one foot forward, and then the other. His nerves jangled with every move and his feet were as sore as if he were walking on heated gravel. "I don't think I can—"

Both the head nurse and Cleeve turned to Weybridge at once. "Now, don't get discouraged," the head nurse said, smiling triumphantly that she had been able to speak first. "You can take hold of my arm if you think you're going to fall."

Weybridge put all his attention on walking and managed a few more steps; then vertigo overwhelmed him and he collapsed suddenly, mewing as he fell.

"I'll help you up, Mr. Weybridge," Cleeve said, bending down with care. "You appear to be very weak."

"Yes, I suppose I am," Weybridge responded vaguely. He could not rid himself of the conviction that he had to get to cover, that he was too exposed, that there were enemies all around him who would tear him to pieces if he did not find cover. Who were the enemies? What was he remembering?

Cleeve took Weybridge by the elbow and started to lever him into a sitting position, but was stopped by the head nurse. "Now, we don't want to indulge ourselves, do we? It would be better if we stood up on our own."

"That's a little unrealistic," Cleeve protested. "Look at him, woman—he's half starved and spaced out on the chemicals you've been pouring into him."

Hearing this, Weybridge huddled against the wall, arms and knees gathered tightly against his chest. He did not want to think about what had gone into him. The very idea made him cringe. He swallowed hard twice and fanned his hands to cover his eyes.

"They're necessary," the head nurse said brusquely. "Until we know what's happened to this man. . . ."

Cleeve shook his head. "You mustn't mistake his condition for the refusal of an enemy. From what I have been told, this man is one of our operatives, yet everyone is behaving as if he were a spy or a traitor." He steadied Weybridge with his arm. "When it's certain that he's been turned, then we can do what must be done, but not yet."

The head nurse folded her arms, all of her good humor and condescension gone. "I have my orders."

"And so do I," Cleeve said mildly. "Mr. Weybridge, I'm going to help you back to bed, and then I want to arrange to have a little interview with you. Do you understand what I'm saying?"

It was an effort to nod, but Weybridge managed it; his head wobbled on the end of his neck. "I want . . . to talk to . . . someone." He coughed and felt himself tremble for the strength it cost him.

"Good. I'll return in an hour or so. Be patient." Cleeve gave a signal to the head nurse. "Get him back into bed and arrange for an IV. I don't think he's going to be able to eat yet."

The head nurse glared at Cleeve. "You'll take responsibility for him, then? I warn you, I won't be left covering for you if you're wrong."

What were they arguing about? Weybridge asked himself as he listened to them wrangle. What was there to be responsible for? What had he done? Why wouldn't anyone tell him what he was supposed to have done? He lifted one listless hand. "Please . . ."

Neither Cleeve nor the head nurse paid him any heed. "You'll have to tell Malpass what you're doing. He might not approve."

Cleeve smiled benignly. "I intend to. As I intend to ask for permission to remove Mr. Weybridge from this wing of the hospital. I think we can do more with him in my ward." He turned toward Weybridge. "Don't worry. We'll sort everything out."

"What . . . ?" Weybridge asked, frowning. He felt very tired, and his body ached in every joint. He supposed he was suffering from malnutrition, but there was more to it than that. Even as the questions rose again, his mind shied away from them. There was so much he could not understand, and no one wished to explain it to him. He pulled himself back onto the bed, pressing his face into the pillow, and nearly gagging on the carrion smell that rose in his nostrils. He retched, gasping for air.

"That's enough of that," the head nurse said with unpleasant satisfaction. "When Mr. Malpass takes me off this case, I'll stop giving him drugs, but for the time being, it's sedation as usual. Or do you want to argue about it, Mr. Cleeve?"

Weybridge was sprawled on the bed, his face clammy and his pulse very rapid. His face was gaunt, his body skeletal. He was like something from deep underwater dragged up into the light of day. "I . . . I . . ."

Cleeve sighed. "I'm not going to oppose you, Nurse. Not yet. Once I talk to Mr. Malpass, however—"

The head nurse tossed her head. "We'll see when that happens. Now you leave this patient to me." She gave her attention to Weybridge. "We're too worn out, aren't we?"

Weybridge hated the way she spoke to him but had not strength enough to protest. He waited for the prick in his arm and the warm bliss that came with it. There was that brief respite, between waking and stupor, when he felt all the unknown burdens lifted from his shoulders. That never lasted long—once again, Weybridge felt himself caught in a morass of anguish he did not comprehend.

The walls were thick, slimy stone, and they stank of urine and rats. His own body was filthy and scabbed, his teeth rattled in his head and his hair was falling out. He shambled through that little space, maddened by fear and boredom. Someone else cowered in the darkness, another prisoner—was he a prisoner?—whose?— why?—or someone sent to torment him. He squinted in an effort to see who it was, but it was not possible to penetrate the shadows. He thrashed on his clean, white bed, believing himself in that dreadful cell—if he had been there at all.

Malpass was standing over Weybridge when he woke with a shout. "Something, David? Are you remembering?"

"I . . ." Weybridge shook his head weakly, trying to recapture the images of his dreams, but they eluded him. "You . . ." He had seen Malpass' face in the dream, or a face that was similar. He had no idea if the memory was valid, or the dream.

"We're having a little meeting about you this morning, David," Malpass said heartily. "We're reviewing your case. The Old Man is coming to hear what we have to say."

Weybridge could think of nothing to say. He moved his head up and down, hoping Malpass would go on.

"Cleeve wants you over in his division. He thinks he can get at the truth faster with those suspension tanks of his and the cold wraps. We'd rather keep you here on drugs, at least until you begin to . . . clarify your thoughts. However, it will be up to the Old Man to decide." He gave Weybridge's shoulder another one of his amiable pats. "We'll keep you posted. Don't worry about that. You concentrate on getting your memory in working order."

There was a fleeting impression of another promise, from another man—or was it Malpass?—that winked and was gone, leaving Weybridge more disoriented than before. Who was the man he had seen, or thought he had seen? What had he done? Or was it simply more of the confusion that he suffered? "How soon will you know?"

"Soon," Malpass said, smiling. "Today, tomorrow. They're going to put you on IV for a while this morning. This evening, they want you to try eating again."

"I can't," Weybridge said at once. "No food." He was sick with hunger; he could not endure the thought of food. "I can't."

"The head nurse will look after you," Malpass went on, blithe as a kindergarten teacher. "We're going to take Stone off for this evening, and Cleeve will stay with you. He wants a chance to talk to you, to study your reactions."

"Cleeve?" Weybridge repeated.

"He saw you yesterday," Malpass reminded him sympathetically, his face creasing into a mask of good-hearted concern. "You remember speaking with Cleeve, don't you?"

"Yes," Weybridge said, ready to weep with vexation. "I haven't forgotten. It's the other things that are gone."

"Well, possibly," Malpass allowed. "You don't seem to recall coming here. Or have you?"

"I . . ." Had there been an ambulance? A plane? He was pretty sure he had been in a plane, but was it coming here, or had there been a plane earlier, before he had done—whatever it was he had done? Had he flown then? He was certain that he could recall looking down from a great height—that was something. He tried to pursue the image without success.

"Don't work so hard, you only make it more difficult," Malpass admonished him. "You don't need that extra stress right now. If you get frustrated, you won't be able to think clearly about your treatment and getting better."

"I don't think clearly in any case, frustrated or not," Weybridge said with great bitterness.

"We're trying to do something about that, aren't we?" Malpass said, smiling once again. "You're in the best hands, you're getting the finest care. In time, it will come back. You can be sure of that."

"Can I? And what if it doesn't?" Weybridge demanded.

"David, David, you mustn't think this way. You'll straighten it all out, one way or another," Malpass said, moving away from Weybridge. "I'll drop in later, to see how you're doing. Don't let yourself get depressed, if you can help it. We're all pulling for you." With a wave, he was gone, and Weybridge longed for a door he could close, to keep them all out.

There was a new nurse that afternoon, a woman in her mid-thirties, not too attractive but not too plain, who regarded him with curiosity. She took his temperature, blood pressure, and pulse, then offered to give him a sponge bath.

"I'll take a shower later," he lied. He did not like the feeling of water on his skin, though why this should be, he was unable to say. He knew he was a fastidious person and the smell of his unwashed skin was faintly repulsive.

"It might be better if you let me do this for you," she said unflappably. "As long as you're hooked up to that IV, you should really keep your arm out of water. It won't take long. And I can give you a massage afterward." She sounded efficient and impersonal, but Weybridge could not bear the thought of her touching him.

"No thanks," he said, breathing a little faster. What was making him panic?

"Let me give it a try. Dr. Cleeve suggested that we give it a try. What do you think? Can we do your feet? If that's not too bad, we'll try the legs. That's reasonable, isn't it?"

Both of them knew it was, and so he nodded, feeling sweat on his body. "Go slow," he warned her, dreading what she would do. "If I . . ."

She paid no attention to him. "I realize that you're not used to having a woman bathe you, but after all, your mother did, and this isn't much different, is it?" She had gone into the bathroom while speaking and was running water into a large, square, stainless-steel bowl. "I'll make it warm but not hot. And I'll use the unscented soap. I've got a real sponge, by the way, and you'll like it. Think about what it can be like with a big, soft sponge and warm water."

The very mention of it made him queasy, but he swallowed hard against the sensation. "Fine," he panted.

The nurse continued to get the water ready for him. "You might not think that you'll like it at first, but you will. I've done work with other . . . troubled patients and in this case, you're easy to deal with. You don't make any unreasonable demands or behave badly." She was coming back to him now, carrying the pan of soapy water. "It won't be so hard. I promise." She flipped back his covers, nodding at his scrawny legs. "Feet first, okay?"

He did not trust himself to answer her; he gestured his resignation.

"Left foot first. That's like marching, isn't it?" She laughed as she reached out, taking his ankle in her hand. "The water is warm, just as I said it would be." She lifted the sponge—it was a real sponge, not one of the plastic ones—and dribbled the water over his foot.

Weybridge shrieked as if he had been scalded, and jerked away from her. "No!"

"What's wrong?" she asked, remaining calm.

"I . . . I can't take it. I don't know why, but I can't." He felt his heart pounding against his ribs as he gasped for air. "I can't," he repeated.

"It's just water, Mr. Weybridge," the nurse pointed out. "With a little soap in it."

"I know," he said, trying to sound as reasonable as possible. "But I can't."

"The way you can't eat, either?" she asked, curious and concerned. "What is it about water? Or food, for that matter?"

"I wish I knew," he sighed, feeling his heartbeat return to a steady, barely discerned thumping.

"Can't you figure it out?" She moved the pan of bath water aside. "Can you tell me anything about it, Mr. Weybridge?"

He shook his head. "I wish I could. I wish I could tell someone what it was. I might be able to get rid of it if I knew what it was." His eyes filled with tears and he turned away from her in shame.

"Why would food and water do this to you?" she mused, not addressing him directly, yet encouraging him.

"There was . . . something that happened. I don't . . . remember, but it's there. I know it's there." He brought his hands to his face so that he would not have to let her see his expression. He had a quick vision—perhaps not quite a vision, but an image—of a man with a large knife peeling the skin off someone's—his?—foot, grinning at the screams and maddened profanities his victim hurled at him. Weybridge's skin crawled, and after a short time, he pulled his foot out of the nurse's hands. "I can't," he whispered. "I'm sorry. It's not you. I just can't."

"But . . ." she began, then nodded. "All right, Mr. Weybridge. Maybe we can take care of it another time. It would be sensible to tend to this, don't you think?"

"Sure," he said, relieved that he had postponed the ordeal for a little while.

"What's the matter, though? Can you tell me?" Her expression was curious, without the morbid fascination he had seen in the eyes of Malpass and Cleeve.

"I wish I could. I wish I knew what was happening to me. I wish I . . . I wish it were over, all over." He clasped his hands together as if in desperate prayer. "I've tried and tried and tried to figure it out. I have what are probably memories of doing something terrible, something so ghastly that I don't want to think about it, ever. But I don't know what it was, really, or if it ever really happened, or if it did, it happened to me. There are times I'm sure it was someone else and that I've merely . . . eavesdropped on it. And other times, I *know* I did it, whatever it is, and . . . there are only bits and pieces left in my mind, but they're enough." It was strangely comforting to say these things to her. "I've heard that murderers want to confess, most of them. I'm willing to confess anything, just to know for sure what happened, and maybe, why."

The nurse looked at him, not critically but with deep compassion. "They're speculating on what's real and what isn't: the doctors and the . . . others here. Some of them think you've blocked out your trauma, and others believe that you're the victim of an induced psychosis. What do you think?"

"I don't know what to think. It's driving me crazy, not knowing." He said this quite calmly, and for that reason, if no other, was all the more convincing.

"Do you want to talk about it—I mean, do you want me to stick around for a while and try to sort out what went on when you were—" She stopped herself suddenly and her face flushed.

"Are you under orders?" Weybridge asked. "Are you doing this because they told you to?"

"Partly," she said after a moment. "I shouldn't tell you anything, but . . . they're all using you, and it troubles me. I want to think that you're doing your best to get to the bottom of your . . . your lapses. I don't like the way that Malpass keeps glad-handing you, or the way Cleeve treats you like a lab animal." She had taken hold of the thin cotton spread and now was twisting the fabric, almost unconsciously.

"Are they doing that?" Weybridge asked, not really surprised to learn it.

"They are," she said.

Weybridge nodded slowly, wondering if this kind nurse was just another ploy on Malpass' or Cleeve's part to try to delve into his missing past. He wavered between resentment and hope, and finally said, "Which of you is supposed to be Rasputin and which is supposed to be the saint? That's the usual way, isn't it? One of you convinces the poor slob you're interrogating that you're on his side and the other one is the bad guy, and by pretending to be the guy's friend, you get him to open up." He slammed his fists down onto the bed, secretly horrified at how little strength he had. "Well, I wish I could open up, to any of you. I wish I could say everything, but I can't. Don't you understand that, any of you? I can't. I don't remember." There were only those repugnant, terrifying flashes that came into his mind, never for very long, never with any explanation, but always there, and always genuine, and always leaving him so enervated and repelled that he wanted to be sick, and undoubtedly would have been, had he anything left in his stomach to give up. "God, I don't even know for certain that we're all on the same side."

"Of course we are, David," the nurse protested.

"You'd say that, no matter what," Weybridge muttered. "You'd claim to be my friend, you'd make me want to confide in you, and all the time it would be a setup, and you'd be bleeding me dry, getting ready to put me on the dust heap when you're through with me. Or maybe you want to turn me, or maybe I turned, and you're with my old side, trying to find out how much I revealed to the others. Or maybe you think I was turned, and you're trying to find out."

"What makes you think you were active in espionage?" the nurse said to him. "You're talking like someone who had been an operative. Were you?"

"How the hell do I know?" Weybridge shot back. "Everyone here acts as if I was some kind of spy or intelligence agent or something like that. I've been assuming that I was."

"Suppose you weren't?" She stared at him. "Suppose it was something else entirely."

"Like what?" Weybridge demanded.

The door opened and Malpass stepped into the room. "Hello, David. How's it going?"

The nurse gave Malpass a quick, guilty look. "I'm trying to give Mr. Weybridge a massage," she said.

"I see," Malpass said with sinister cordiality. "What kind of luck are you having?"

"It seems to bother him so . . ." She got off the bed and smoothed the covers over his feet.

"Well." Malpass shook his head. "Tomorrow might be better. There are several things we're going to try to get done this evening, and it would be better if you had a little nap first, David." He motioned to the nurse to leave and watched her until she was out of the room. "Did she bother you, David?"

"She was nice to talk to," Weybridge said with a neutral tone, suddenly anxious to keep the nurse out of trouble. Whatever she was, she was the only person he had met who had been genuinely—or appeared to be genuinely—interested in him as a person.

"That's good to know. It's fine that you're talking to someone," Malpass said, smiling more broadly than before.

"You'll make sure she doesn't get in trouble for talking to me, won't you?"

Malpass' eyebrows rose. "Why, David, what makes you think that she'd be in trouble for a thing like that?"

Weybridge frowned. "I don't know. You're all so . . . secretive, and . . . odd about what you want out of me."

"David, David," Malpass said, shaking his head. "You're letting your imagination run away with you. Why would we want to do such a thing to you? You're sounding like you regard us as your jailers, not as your doctors. We want you to improve. No one wants that more than we do. But can't you see—your attitude is making everyone's job more difficult, including your own. You're letting your dreams and fears take over, and that causes all sorts of problems for us. If I could find a way to convince you that you're creating chimeras . . ."

"You'd what?" Weybridge asked when Malpass did not go on.

Malpass made a dismissing gesture. "I'd be delighted, for one thing. We all would be." He cocked his head to the side. "You believe me, don't you?"

Weybridge shrugged. "Should I?"

"Of course you should," Malpass assured him. "God, David, you'd think that you were being held in prison, the way you're responding. That's not the case at all. You know it's not."

"Do I?"

"Well, think about it, man," Malpass said expansively. "You're being taken care of as thoroughly as we're able. We want you to get better, to get well and be independent. I think everyone here is pulling for you, and . . . well, David, they are all very concerned for you. Everyone hopes that you'll be over this . . . problem soon." He gave Weybridge his most sincere look. "You're a very special case, and we all want to see you get well, entirely well."

"Un-huh," Weybridge said, looking away from Malpass. "And what will happen to me when I get well? Where will I go?"

"Back home, I would guess," Malpass said, trying to give this assertion an enthusiastic ring.

"Back home," Weybridge echoed. Where was that? What was his home like? "Where do . . . did I live?"

"You mean, you don't remember?" Malpass asked, apparently shocked by this question.

"Not really. I wouldn't be asking if I did," he said testily. "And don't coddle me with your answers. That won't help me at all." He folded his arms, taking care not to press on the IV needle taped just below his elbow.

"Well, you live in a small city about . . . oh, eight hundred miles from here. It's on a river. The countryside is rolling hills. The city has a very large textile industry, and most of the agricultural land in the immediate area is devoted to sheep ranching. There's also a good-sized university. You were an assistant professor there for four years. Do you remember any of this?" Malpass asked. "You're frowning."

Weybridge tried to recall such a place and found nothing in his mind that had anything to do with a small city near a river, or a university. "What did I teach?"

"Physics," was Malpass' swift answer. "Astrophysics. You were lured into the private sector to help develop hardware for space exploration. You were considered to be very good at your work."

"Then, how in hell did I end up here?" Weybridge demanded, his voice shrill with desperation.

"That's what we'd all like to know," Malpass said, doing his best to sound comforting. "Your . . . affliction is a real challenge to us all."

"When did I become an intelligence agent, if I was teaching and then doing space research in industry? What was the name of the university where I taught? What city did I live in? What company did I go to work for? Who was my boss?"

"Whoah there, David," Malpass said, reaching out and placing his thick hand on Weybridge's shoulder. "One thing at a time. First, the Old Man has decided that, for the time being, we're not going to give you too many names. It would be distracting, and you might use the information to create . . . false memories for yourself based on the names instead of your recollections. You can see the sense in that, surely."

"I suppose so," Weybridge said sullenly. "But what the fuck does that leave me?"

"In time, we hope it will restore your memories. We want that to happen, all of us." He gripped a little tighter, giving Weybridge's shoulder a comradely shake, doing his best to buck his charge up. "When you can name your university, the head of your department, then we'll know we're getting somewhere."

"Why did I become an agent? Or did I?" He had not intended to ask this aloud, but the words were out before he could stop them. "Is this some kind of ruse?"

"Of course not," Malpass declared.

"You'd say that whether it was or not," Weybridge sighed. "And there's not any way I can prove the contrary." He lowered his head. "The bodies. Where were they? Whose were they?"

"What bodies, David?" Malpass asked, becoming even more solicitous.

"The ones I see in my dreams. The ones with . . . pieces missing. There are some in cells and some in . . . trenches, I guess. It's . . . not very clear." He felt the sweat on his body, and smelled his fear.

"Can you tell me more about them?" Malpass urged. "What do you remember?"

Hands on the ground, just hands, with palms mutilated; a torso with the striations of ropes still crossing the chest; a child's body, three days dead and bloated; scraps of skin the color of clay sticking to rusty chains; a man on a wet stone floor, his back and buttocks crosshatched with blood-crusted weals; a woman, hideously mutilated and abused, lying on her side, legs pulled up against her chest, waiting for death: the impressions fled as quickly as they came. "Not very much," Weybridge answered, blinking as if to banish what he had seen.

"Tell me," Malpass insisted. "You've got to tell me, David. The Old Man has been asking about your ordeal, and if I can give him something—anything—he might decide to . . ." He did not go on.

"To what?" Weybridge asked. "Or can't you tell me that, either?"

"I . . . haven't been given permission," Malpass said in an under voice. "I'll need to get it if I'm going to explain what it is the Old Man needs to know."

This was the first time Weybridge had ever seen Malpass display an emotion akin to fear, and in spite of himself, he was curious. "Why should the Old Man care what I remember? He has me where he wants me, doesn't he?"

"Well, sure, but we don't want you to have to remain here indefinitely," Malpass said uneasily, attempting to make a recovery. "We're all . . . doing our best for you."

Weybridge shook his head. "That's not enough, Malpass. You're holding back too much. I don't want to say anything more until you're a little more forthcoming with me." It was exciting to defy Malpass, so Weybridge added, "I want the lights out at night. I need sleep."

"I'll see if it can be arranged," Malpass hedged, moving away from the bed, where Weybridge sat. "I'll let you know what we decide."

What had he said? Weybridge wondered. What had caused the change in the affable Mr. Malpass? He could not find the answer, though it was obvious that something he had triggered disturbed the man profoundly. "Is there something you'd like to tell me, Malpass? You seem distraught."

"I'm . . . fine, David. You're probably tired. I'll let you have a little time to yourself, before they bring you your supper."

Was it Weybridge's imagination, or was there a trace of malice in Malpass' tone of voice? He watched Malpass retreat to the door and hover there, his hand on the latch. "What is it?"

"Nothing," Malpass said fervently.

"I'm interested in what it is the Old Man wants to know. Find out if you can tell me. Maybe we can all work together if you're not so secretive with me." He was almost light-headed with satisfaction as he saw the door close behind Malpass.

The afternoon hours dragged by; Weybridge remained in solitude, the IV unit by his bed his only company. He would have liked to have something to read, but this had been refused when he asked the first time, and Weybridge had not renewed his request. He lay back against the skimpy pillows and stared up at the ceiling, trying to make patterns and pictures of the play of light and shadow there.

About sunset, Dr. Cleeve entered the room, his pursed mouth giving him the look of an overstuffed bag with a hole in it. "I see you are alone," he said.

"Is that unusual?" Weybridge asked angrily. "Did you think someone else would be here?"

"Under the circumstances, yes, I did," Dr. Cleeve said with great meaning. "The Old Man isn't satisfied with your progress. He's about ready to give up on you, and so is Malpass."

"Give up on me? How? Why?" In spite of himself, he felt worried by this announcement.

"You're not telling them what they want to know, what they need to know. They think you've been turned and that you're simply playing with them to gain your new masters some time."

"That's not true!" Weybridge protested, trying to get to his feet. "It's not possible! I don't know what I did, I don't know why I'm here, I don't even know who you are, or who I am. What do I have to do to make you believe that?" His pulse throbbed in his head and his eyes ached. There were the images, the memories of so much horror that he could not bear to look at them directly, but that proved it—didn't it?—that he was not deceiving them.

"Mr. Weybridge," Dr. Cleeve soothed. "You're overwrought. I can understand how that would be, but clearly you can see that you are not on very firm ground." He reached over and patted Weybridge's arm, just below the place where the IV needles were taped. "I see that your veins are holding up fairly well. That's something. A man in your condition should be glad that we do not yet have to cut down for a vein."

"It . . ." There was a fleeting vision of arms and legs, tattered remnants of bodies, floating on a sluggish current, catching against river reeds, piling up, then drifting on.

"What is it, Mr. Weybridge?" Dr. Cleeve asked intently. "What is happening to you now?"

Weybridge shook his head. "I . . . it's gone now. It's nothing." He felt the sweat on his forehead and his ribs, and he could smell it, hating the odor for its human aliveness.

"Mr. Weybridge," Dr. Cleeve said, folding his arms and regarding Weybridge through his thick glasses, "are you willing to let me try an . . . experiment?"

"How do you mean, 'an experiment'?" Weybridge asked, suspicious in the depths of his desperation.

"There are ways that we can . . . accelerate your mind. We could find out what had truly happened to you, and what you have done. The danger is that if you have been turned, we will know about it, unquestionably, and you will have to face the consequences of your act, but the waiting would certainly be over." He studied

Weybridge with increasing interest. "It would not be difficult
to do, simply a bit more risky than what we have been doing up till
now."

"And what is the risk?" Weybridge asked, wishing he knew
more about Dr. Cleeve—any of them—so that he could judge why
the man had made this offer.

"Well, if the suppressed memories are traumatic enough, you
could become psychotic." He spread his hands in wide mute appeal. "You could still become psychotic just going on the way you
are. It may, in fact, be that you are already psychotic. There's really
no way of knowing without taking certain risks, and this, at least,
would end the suspense, so to speak." He tried to smile in a way
that would reassure Weybridge, but the strange, toothy unpursing
of his mouth was not reassuring.

"I'll have to think about it," Weybridge hedged.

"Let me suggest that you do it very quickly. The Old Man is anxious to have your case resolved, and his way would most certainly
do you permanent damage." Dr. Cleeve watched Weybridge
closely. "If you have not already done permanent damage."

"And we won't know that until we try one of the techniques,
right?" Weybridge ventured, his tone so cynical that even he was
startled by the sound of it.

"It is the one sure way." Dr. Cleeve paused a moment. "It may
not be that you have any choice."

"And it is really out of my hands in any case, isn't it?" He
sighed. "If I say yes to you, or if I wait until the others, the Old
Man—whoever he is—makes up his mind to put my brain through
the chemical wringer. Which might have been done already. Did
you ever think of that?"

"Oh, most certainly we've thought of it. It seems very likely that
there has been some . . . tampering. We've said that from the first,
as you recall." He smacked his fleshy palms together. "Well. I'll
let you have a little time to yourself. But try to reach a decision
soon, Mr. Weybridge. The Old Man is impatient, as you may remember."

"I don't know who the Old Man is. He's just a name people keep
using around here," Weybridge said, too resigned to object to what
Dr. Cleeve said to him.

"You claim that's the case. That's how the Old Man sees it. He
thinks that you're buying time, as I said. He thinks that this is all a
very clever ploy and that you're doing everything you can to keep

us from following up on your case." He shrugged. "I don't know what the truth of the matter is, but I want to find it out. Don't you?" This last was a careful inquiry, the most genuine question the man has asked since he'd come into the room.

"You won't believe it, but I do," Weybridge said, feeling himself grow tired simply with speaking. He had reiterated the same thing so often that it was no longer making much sense to him. "I have to know what really happened to me, and who I am."

"Yes; I can see that," Dr. Cleeve said with an emotion that approached enthusiasm. "You think about it tonight. This isn't the kind of thing to rush into, no matter how urgent it may appear."

As Weybridge leaned back against the pillows, he was feeling slightly faint, and he answered less cautiously than he might have under other circumstances. "If it gets us answers, do whatever you have to do."

"Oh, we will, Mr. Weybridge," Dr. Cleeve assured him as the door closed on him.

There were dreams and fragments of dreams that hounded Weybridge through the night. He was left with eyes that felt as if sand had been rubbed into the lids and a taste in his mouth that drove what little appetite he possessed away from him, replacing it with repugnance.

Malpass did not come to visit him until midday, and when he arrived, he looked uncharacteristically harried. "You're having quite a time of it with us, aren't you, David?" he asked without his usual friendly preamble.

"I've done easier things, I think." He tried to smile at the other man, but could not force his face to cooperate. "I wish you'd tell me what's going on around here."

"The Old Man wants to take you off the IV unit and see if a few days on no rations will bring you around. I've asked him to give me a few more days with you, but I don't know if he's going to allow it. Three of our operatives were killed yesterday, and he's convinced you can tell him how their covers were blown."

"It wasn't me," Weybridge said firmly, and even as he spoke, he wondered if some of those drastic images stored in his mind where the memories had been might be associated with the loss of the other operatives.

"The Old Man doesn't believe that. He thinks you're still following orders." Malpass licked his lips furtively, then forced them into a half smile that reflected goodwill. "You've got to understand, David. The Old Man simply doesn't buy your story. We've all tried to convince him that you're probably nothing more than a pawn, someone who's been set up to distract us, but that isn't making any headway with the Old Man. He's pissed about the other operatives, you see, and he wants someone's head on the block. If it isn't yours, it may have to be mine, and frankly, I'd rather it was yours." This admission came out in a hurry, as if he hoped that in saying it quickly, he would disguise its meaning.

"And you want this over with, don't you, Malpass?" Weybridge asked, feeling much more tired than he thought it was possible to be. "I want it over with too."

"Then you'll agree? You'll let them question you again, with drugs so we're sure you're telling us the truth?" He sounded as eager as a schoolboy asking for a day without classes.

"Probably," he said. "I have to think it over. You're going to have to muck about in my mind, and that's happened once already. I don't want to be one of those miserable vegetables that you water from time to time."

Malpass laughed as if he thought this caution was very witty. "I don't blame you for thinking it over, David. You're the kind who has to be sure, and that's good, that's good. We'll all be easier in our minds when the questions have been answered."

"Will we? That's assuming you find out what you want to know, and that it's still worth your while to keep me alive. There are times I wonder if you're on my side or the other side—whoever my side and the other side may be—and if anything you're telling me is true. If you were on the other side, what better way to get me to spill my guts to you than to convince me that you're on my side and that you're afraid I've been turned. You say you're testing me, but it might not be true."

"David, you're paranoid," Malpass said sternly. "You're letting your fears run away with you. Why would we go through something this elaborate if we weren't on your side? What would be the purpose?"

"Maybe you want to turn me, and this is as good a way as any to do it. Maybe I've got information you haven't been able to get out of me yet. Maybe you're going to program me to work for you, and you started out with privation and torture, and now that I'm all disoriented, you're going to put on the finishing touches with a good scramble of my brain." He sighed. "Or maybe all that has already happened and you're going to see what I wrecked for you. And then what? You might decide that it's too risky to let it be known that you've found out what happened, and so you'll decide to lock me up or turn me into some kind of zombie or just let me die."

"You're getting morbid," Malpass blustered, no longer looking at Weybridge. "I'm going to have to warn the Old Man that you've been brooding."

"Wouldn't you brood, in my position?" Weybridge countered, his face desolate.

"Well, anyone would," Malpass said, reverting to his role as chief sympathizer. "Have you been able to have a meal yet?"

The familiar cold filled him. "No," Weybridge said softly. "I . . . can't."

"That'll be one of the things we'll work on, then," Malpass promised. "There's got to be some reason for it, don't you think? David, you're not going to believe this, but I truly hope that you come through this perfectly."

"No more than I do," Weybridge said without mirth. "I'm tired of all the doubts and the secrecy." And the terrible visions of broken and abused bodies, of the panic that gripped him without warning and without reason, of the dread he felt when shown a plate of food.

"Excellent," Malpass said, rubbing his hands together once, as if warming them. "We'll get ready, so when you make up your mind we can get started."

"You're convinced that I'll consent. Or will you do it no matter what I decide?" Weybridge said recklessly, and saw the flicker in Malpass' eyes. "You're going to do it no matter what, aren't you?"

"I'll talk to you in the morning, David," Malpass said, beating a hasty retreat.

There were dreams that night, hideous, incomplete things with incomprehensible images of the most malicious carnage. Weybridge tossed in his bed, and willed himself awake twice, only to hear the insidious whispers buzz around him more fiercely. His eyes ached and his throat was dry.

Dr. Cleeve was the first to visit him in the morning. He sidled up to Weybridge's bed and poked at him. "Well? Do you think you will be able to help me?"

"If you can help me," Weybridge answered, too exhausted to do much more than nod.

"What about Malpass? Are you going to put him off, or are you going to convince him that my way is the right one?" The tip of his nose moved when he spoke; Weybridge had never noticed that before.

"I . . . I'll have to talk to him." He moved his arms gingerly, taking care to test himself. "I want to do what's best."

"Of course you do," Dr. Cleeve declared. "And we've already discussed that, haven't we?" His eyes gloated, though the tone of his voice remained the same. "You and I will be able to persuade the rest of them. Then you'll be rid of your troubles and you can go about your life again instead of remaining here."

"Will I?" Weybridge had not meant to ask this aloud, but once the words were out, he felt relieved. "Or am I speeding up the end?"

"We won't know that until we know what's been done to you, Mr. Weybridge," said Dr. Cleeve. "I'll have a little talk with Malpass and we'll arrange matters."

"When?" Weybridge asked, dreading the answer.

"Tomorrow morning, I should think," he replied, hitching his shoulders to show his doubt.

"And then?" Weybridge continued.

"We don't know yet, Mr. Weybridge. It will depend on how much you have been . . . interfered with." He was not like Malpass, not inclined to lessen the blows. "If there is extensive damage, it will be difficult to repair it. It's one of the risks you take in techniques like this."

Weybridge nodded, swallowing hard.

"Malpass will doubtless have a few things to say to you about the tests. Keep in mind that he is not a medical expert and his first loyalty is to the Old Man."

"Where is your first loyalty?" Weybridge could not help asking.

"Why, to the country, of course. I am not a political man." He cleared his throat. "I hope you won't repeat this to Malpass; he is suspicious of me as it is."

"Why is that?"

"There are many reasons, most of them personal," Dr. Cleeve said smoothly. "We can discuss them later, if you like, when you're more . . . yourself."

Weybridge closed his eyes. "Shit."

"I have a great deal to do, Mr. Weybridge. Is there anything else you would like to know?" Dr. Cleeve was plainly impatient to be gone.

"One thing: how long have I been here?"

"Oh, five or six weeks, I suppose. I wasn't brought in at first. Only when they realized that they needed my sort of help. . . . That was sixteen days ago, when you had recovered from the worst of your wounds but still could or would not eat." He waited. "Is that all, Mr. Weybridge?"

"Sure," he sighed.

"Then, we'll make the arrangements," Dr. Cleeve said, closing the door before Weybridge could think of another question.

He was wakened that night—out of a fearful dream that he would not let himself examine too closely—by the nurse who had been kind enough to be interested in him and had tried to rub his feet. He stared at her, trying to make out her features through the last images of the dream, so that at first he had the impression that she had been attacked, her mouth and nostrils torn and her eyes blackened.

"Mr. Weybridge," the nurse whispered again, with greater urgency.

"What is it?" he asked, whispering too, and wondering how much the concealed devices in the room could hear.

"They told me . . . they're planning to try to probe your memory. Did you know that?" The worry in her face was clear to him now that he saw her without the other image superimposed on her face.

"Yes, that's what they've—we've decided."

"You agreed?" She was incredulous.

"What else can I do?" He felt, even as he asked, that he had erred in giving his permission. "Why?"

"They didn't tell you, did they? about the aftereffects of the drugs, did they? Do you know that you can lose your memory entirely?"

"I've already lost most of it," Weybridge said, trying to make light of her objections.

"It can turn you into a vegetable, something that lies in a bed with machines to make the body work, a thing they bury when it begins to smell bad." She obviously intended to shock him with this statement, and in a way she succeeded.

"You don't know anything about that," Weybridge said heatedly. "You haven't seen bodies lying unburied in an open grave in a field where the humidity makes everything ripe, including the bodies." He coughed, trying to think where that memory came from. "You haven't been locked in a stone-walled room with five other people, no latrine and not enough food to go around."

"Is that what happened to you?" she asked, aghast at what she heard.

"Yes," he said, with less certainty.

"Did it?"

"I think so. I remember it, pieces of it, anyway." He rubbed his face, feeling his beard scratch against the palms of his hands. Under his fingers, his features were gaunt.

"They'll force you to remember it all, if it happened," she warned him. "Don't you understand? They'll throw you away like used tissue paper when they're done. They don't care what happens to you after they find out what you know. Truly, they won't bother to see you're cared for." She reached out and took him by the shoulders. "If you want to stay in one piece, you've got to get away from here before they go to work on you. Otherwise, you'll be . . . nothing when they're through with you, and no one will care."

"Does anyone care now?" he wondered aloud. "I don't know of anyone."

"Your family, your friends, someone must be worried about you. This place is bad enough without thinking that . . ." Her voice trailed off.

"And where is this place? If I got out, where would I be? Don't you see, I have no idea of who these people are, really, or where we are or what it's like outside. No one has told me and I don't remember. Even if I got out, I would have no place to go, and no one to stay with, and nothing to offer." His despair returned tenfold as he said these things.

"I'll find someone to take care of you until you remember," she promised him, her eyes fierce with intent.

"And feed me?" he asked ironically. "Do you have a friend with an IV unit?"

"Once you're out of here—" she began.

"Once I'm out of here, I'll be at the mercy of . . . everything. Where are we? Where would I have to go for the Old Man— whoever he is—not to find me and bring me back? It might be worse out there." He shivered. "I don't think I can manage. If I could get out, I don't think I'd be able to get very far before they brought me back."

"We're near a river. We're about fifteen miles from the capital, and—"

"What capital is that?" Weybridge inquired politely. "I don't know which capital you mean."

"*Our* capital, of course," she insisted. "You can get that far, can't you? There are names I could give you, people who would hide you for a while, until you make up your mind what you want to do about . . . everything."

"I don't know about the capital," Weybridge repeated.

"You *lived* there, for heaven's sake. Your records show that you lived there for ten years. You remember that much, don't you?" She was becoming irritated with him. "Don't you have any memory of that time at all?"

"I . . . don't think so." He looked at her strangely. "And for all I know, my records are false. I might not have been here ever, and it could be that I haven't done any of the things I think I have."

"Well, letting them fill you up with chemicals isn't going to help you find out. You'll just get used up." She took his hand and pulled on it with force. "Mr. Weybridge, I can't wait forever for you to make up your mind. If they found out I came in to see you and tried to get you to leave, I'd be in a lot of trouble. You understand that, don't you?"

"I can see that it might be possible." He tugged his hand, but she would not release it. "Nurse, I don't want to go away from here, not yet, not until I can get some idea of who I am and what I did. Not until I can *eat.*"

"But you will be able to if you leave. You're being manipulated, Mr. Weybridge. David. They're doing things to you so that you can't eat, so you'll have to stay here. If only you'd get away from here, you'd find out fast enough that you're all right. You'd be able to remember what really happened and know what was . . . programmed into you. They don't care what comes of their little experiments, and they're not going to give a damn if you go catatonic or starve to death or anything else. That's the way they've been treating agents that they have questions about." She paused. "I have to leave pretty soon. It's too risky for me to remain here. They'll catch me and then they'll . . ." She turned away, her eyes moving nervously toward the door.

Weybridge closed his eyes, but the dreadful images did not fade. There were three naked figures, two of them women, twitching on a stone floor. They were all fouled with blood and vomit and excrement, and the movements and sounds they made were no longer entirely human. "I've been thinking," he said remotely, his throat sour and dry, "that I've been going on the assumption that all the pieces of things I remember, all the horrors, were done to me. But I can't find more than three scars on my body, and if it happened, I'd be crosshatched and maimed. I've thought that perhaps I *did* those things to others, that I was the one causing the horror, not its victim. Do you think that's possible? Do you think I finally had enough and wouldn't let myself do anything more?" This time when he pulled on his hand, she let him go.

"I can't stay, Weybridge. If you haven't got sense enough to come with me, there's nothing I can do to change your mind. You want to let them do this to you, I can't stop you." She got off his bed, her eyes distraught though she was able to maintain an unruffled expression. "After today, you won't have the chance to change your mind. Remember that."

"Along with everything else." He looked at her steadily. "If you get into trouble because of me, I want you to know that I'm sorry. If I'm right, I've already caused enough grief. I don't know if it's necessary or possible for you to forgive me, but I hope you will."

The nurse edged toward the door, but she made one last try. "They might have given you false memories. They're doing a lot of experiments that way. Or you could be someone else, an agent from the other side, and they're trying to get information out of you before they send you back with a mind like pudding." She folded her arms, her hands straining on her elbows. "You'd be giving in to them for no reason. Hostages, after awhile, try to believe that their captors have a good reason to be holding them. That could be what you're feeling right now."

"Nurse, I appreciate everything. I do." He sighed. "But whether you're right or not, it doesn't change anything, does it? I can't manage away from this . . . hospital. I'd be worse than a baby, and anyone who helped me would be putting themselves in danger for nothing. And if you're trying to get me back to the other side, who's to say that I'm one of theirs? Perhaps they want me to do more than has already been done."

She opened the door a crack and peered out into the hall. "I've got to leave, Weybridge."

"I know," he said, filled with great tranquility. "Be careful."

"You, too," she answered. And then she was gone.

Weybridge lay back against the pillows, his emaciated features composed and peaceful as he waited for the needles and the chemicals and oblivion.

Short stories are experiments, at least when I write them. I've said that before and it's still true. So here are a few notes on this particular experiment.

Amnesia and related memory failure have always intrigued me. How much of a personality is, in fact, memory? And what happens when memory is damaged or manipulated? How much of personal integrity is a product of conditioning and experience, and how much is bred in the bone?

In this story another factor that interested me was the predatory feeling many helpers have toward their helpees. There is no consensus about who Weybridge really is or what he has actually done, and only his assumption that he was the one perpetrating the terrible acts he may or may not remember gives him the serenity to face oblivion. Everyone else has a personal agenda where Weybridge is concerned; Weybridge, without real knowledge of himself, has no such agenda. For him, it is easier to face extinction than self-knowledge.

There's probably a lesson in there somewhere.

Chelsea Quinn Yarbro

True Love

K. W. JETER

K. W. Jeter's short stories are more explosive than his novels—perhaps because of their compression. He writes about archetypical relationships (in Alien Sex, *a young man's first sexual experience with a prostitute; in* A Whisper of Blood, *the daughter-father relationship) and gives them a horrific twist.*

By perverting normal relationships—those between adult and child and father and daughter—Jeter creates another shocker.

The brown leaves covered the sidewalk, but hadn't yet been trodden into thin leather. She held the boy's hand to keep him from slipping and falling. He tugged at her grip, wanting to race ahead and kick the damp stacks drifting over the curbs. The leaves smelled of wet and dirt, and left skeleton prints on the cement.

"Now—be careful," she told the boy. What was his name? She couldn't remember. There were so many things she couldn't forget. . . . Maybe her head had filled up, and there was no more room for anything else. The mounded leaves, slick with the drizzling rain. Her father scratching at the door, the word when there had been words in his mouth, the little word that used to be her name. . . . The boy's name; what was it? She couldn't remember.

The boy had tugged her arm around to the side, not trying to run now, but stopping to press his other hand against one of the trees whose empty branches tangled the sky.

"You don't want to do that." She pulled but he dug in, gripping the tree trunk. "It's all dirty." His red mitten was speckled with crumbling bark. A red strand of unraveled wool dangled from his wrist.

You do want to . . . That was her father's voice inside her head. The old voice, the long-ago one with words. She could have, if she'd wanted to—she'd done it before—she could've recited a list

197

...ences, like a poem, all the things her father had ever said to her with the word *want* in them.

"There's something up there."

She looked where the boy pointed, his arm jutting up straight, the mitten a red flag at the end. On one end of the wet branches, a squirrel gazed down at her, then darted off, its tail spiked with drops of rain.

The boy stared openmouthed where the squirrel had disappeared. The boy's upper lip was shiny with snot, and there was a glaze of it on the back of one mitten, and the sleeve of the cheap nylon snow jacket. She shuddered, looking at the wet on the boy's pug face. He wasn't beautiful, not like the one before, the one with the angel lashes and the china and peach skin.

"Come on." She had to bite her lip to fight the shudder, to make it go away, before she could take the boy's hand again. "It's gone now. See? It's all gone." She squeezed the mitten's damp wool in her own gloved hand. "We have to go, too. Aren't you hungry?" She smiled at him, the cold stiffening her face, as though the skin might crack.

The boy looked up at her, distrust in the small eyes. "Where's my mother?"

She knelt down in front of the boy and zipped the jacket under his chin. "Well, that's where we're going, isn't it?" There were people across the street, just people walking, a man and a woman she'd seen from the corner of her eye. But she couldn't tell if they were looking over here, watching her and the boy. She brushed a dead leaf off the boy's shoulder. "We're going to find your mother. We're going to where she is."

She hated lying, even the lies she had told before. All the things she told the boy, and the ones before him, were lies. Everything her father had ever told her had been the truth, and that was no good, either.

Her knees ached when she stood up. The cold and damp had seeped into her bones. She squeezed the boy's hand. "Don't you want to go to where your mother is?"

Now his face was all confused. He looked away from her, down the long street, and she was afraid that he would cry out to the people who were walking there. But they were already gone—she hadn't seen where. Maybe they had turned and gone up the steps into one of the narrow-fronted houses that were jammed so tight against each other.

"And you're hungry, aren't you? Your mother has cake there for you. I know she does. You want that, don't you?"

How old was he? *His name, his name* . . . How big, how small was what she really meant. If he wouldn't move, tugging out of her grasp, wouldn't come with her . . . She wanted to pick him up, to be done saying stupid things to his stupid little face, its smear of snot and its red pig nose. Just pick him up and carry him like a wet sack, the arms with the red-mittened hands caught tight against her breast. Carry him home and not have to say anything, not have to tell lies and smile . . .

She had tried that once and it hadn't worked. Once when there hadn't been any other little boy that she could find, and the one she had found wouldn't come with her, wouldn't come and it had been getting dark, yet it had been all light around her, she had been trapped in the bright blue-white circle from a street lamp overhead. And the boy had started crying, because she had been shouting at him, shouting for him to shut up and stop crying and come with her. She had picked him up, but he'd been too big and heavy for her, his weight squirming in her arms, the little hard fists striking her neck, the bawling mouth right up against one ear. Until she'd had to let him go and he'd fallen to the ground, scrambled to his feet and run off, crying and screaming so loud that other people—she had known they were there, she'd felt them even if she couldn't see them—had turned and looked at her. She'd scurried away and then started running herself, her heart pounding in her throat. Even on the bus she'd caught, she'd known the others were looking at her, even pointing at her and whispering to each other. How could they have known? Until she'd felt a chill kiss under the collar of her blouse, and she'd touched the side of her face and her fingers had come away touched with red. The boy's little fist, or a low branch clawing at her as she'd run by . . . The tissue in her purse had been a wet bright rag by the time she'd reached home.

That had been a bad time. The little boy had run away, and she'd been too frightened to try again, scared of people watching when it had gotten so dark, so dark that she couldn't see them looking at her. She'd had to go home to where her father was waiting. And even though he couldn't say the words anymore, to say what he wanted, she knew. One or the other, and the little boy had run away.

She'd stood naked in her bathroom, the tiny one at the back of the house, her face wet with the splashed cold water. She'd raised her arm high over her head, standing on tiptoe so she could see in the clouded mirror over the sink. A bruise under one breast—the little boy had kicked her; that must've been where she'd got it, though she couldn't remember feeling it. Her father couldn't have done that, though her ribs beneath the discolored skin ached with a familiar pain. He wasn't strong enough, not anymore. . . .

"Where are we?"

The boy's voice—this one, the little boy whose mittened hand she held in her own—brought her back. They were both walking, his hand reaching up to hers, and the streetlights had come on in the growing dark.

"This isn't my street. I don't live here."

"I know. It's okay." She didn't know where they were. She was lost. The narrow, brick-fronted houses came up so close to the street, the bare trees making spider shadows on the sidewalk. Light spilled from the windows above them. She looked up and saw a human shape moving behind a steam-misted glass, someone making dinner in her kitchen. Or taking a shower, the hot water sluicing around the bare feet on white porcelain. The houses would be all warm inside, heated and sealed against the black winter. The people—maybe the couple she had seen walking before, on the other side of another street—they could go naked if they wanted. They were taking a shower together, the man standing behind her, nuzzling her wet neck, hands cupped under her breasts, the smell of soap and wet towels. The steaming water would still be raining on them when he'd lay her down, they'd curl together in the hard nest of the tub, she'd have to bring her knees up against her breasts, or he'd sit her on the edge, the shower curtain clinging wet to her back, and he'd stand in front of her, the way her father did but it wouldn't be her father. She'd fill her mouth with him and he'd smell like soap and not that other sour smell of sweat and old dirt that scraped grey in her fingernails from his skin . . .

The boy pressed close to her side, and she squeezed his hand to tell him that it was all right. He was afraid of the dark and the street he'd never been on before. She was the grown-up, like his mother, and he clung to her now. The fist around her heart unclenched a little. Everything would be easier; she'd find their way home. To where her father was waiting, and she'd have the boy with her this time.

Bright and color rippled on the damp sidewalk ahead of them. The noise of traffic—they'd come out of the houses and dark lanes. She even knew where they were. She recognized the signs, a laundromat with free dry, an Italian restaurant with its menu taped to the window. She'd seen them from the bus she rode sometimes.

Over the heads of the people on the crowded street, she saw the big shape coming, even brighter inside, and heard the hissing of its brakes. Tugging the boy behind her, she hurried to the corner. He trotted obediently to keep up.

The house was as warm inside as other people's houses were. She left the heat on all the time so her father wouldn't get cold. She'd found him once curled up on the floor of the kitchen—the pilot light on the basement furnace had gone out, and ice had already formed on the inside of the windows. There'd been a pool of cold urine beneath him, and his skin felt loose and clammy. He'd stared over his shoulder, his mouth sagging open, while she'd rubbed him beneath the blankets of the bed, to warm him with her own palms.

Warm . . . He had kissed her once—it was one of the things she couldn't forget—when she had been a little girl and he had been as big as the night. His eyes had burned with the wild rigor of his hunt, the world's dark he'd held in his iron hands. The kiss had tasted of salt, a warm thing. Long ago, and she still remembered.

She took off the boy's jacket in the hallway. Her shoes and his small rubber boots made muddy stains on the thin carpet runner. Her knees were so stiff now that she couldn't bend down; she had the boy stand up on the wooden bench against the wall, so she could work the jacket's zipper and snaps.

"Where's my mother?" Coming in to the house's warmth from the cold street had made his nose run again. He sniffed wetly.

"She'll be here in a minute." She pushed the open jacket back from the boy's shoulders. "Let's get all ready for her, and then we can have that cake."

The boy had just a T-shirt on underneath the jacket, and it was torn and dirty, with a yellow stain over some cartoon character's face. The boy's unwashed smell blossomed in the close hallway air, a smell of forgotten laundry and milk gone off. She wanted that to make her feel better. The boy's mother was a bad mother. Not like that other boy's mother, the one three or four times ago. She remembered standing by the greasy fire in the backyard, turning that boy's clothing over in her hands, all of it clean-smelling, freshly washed. Inside the collar of the boy's shirt, and in the waistband of the corduroy trousers, little initials had been hand-stitched, his initials. That was what she'd do if she'd had a child of her own; she would love him that much. Not like this poor ragged thing. Nobody loved this little boy, not really, and that made it all right. She'd told herself that before.

"What's that?" He looked up toward the hallway's ceiling.

She pulled his T-shirt up, exposing his pink round belly. His hair stood up—it was dirty, too—when she pulled the shirt off over his head.

"Nothing." She smoothed his hair down with her palm. "It's nothing." She didn't know if she'd heard anything or not. She'd heard all the house's sounds for so long—they were all her father—that they were the same as silence to her. Or a great roaring hurricane that battered her into a corner, her arms over her head to try to protect herself. It was the same.

She dropped the T-shirt on top of the rubber boots, then unbuttoned the boy's trousers and pulled them down. Dirty grey underwear, the elastic sagging loose. The little boy's things (*little . . . not like . . .*) made the shape of a tiny fist inside the stained cotton. (*Great roaring hurricane*) (*Arms over her head*) She slipped the underpants down.

The boy wiggled. He rubbed his mouth and nose with the back of his hand, smearing the shiny snot around. "What're you doing?"

"Oh, you're so cold." She looked into his dull eyes, away from the little naked parts. "You're freezing. Wouldn't a nice hot bath . . . wouldn't that be nice? Yes. Then you'd be all toasty warm, and I'd wrap you up in a great big fluffy towel. That'd be lovely. You don't want to catch cold, do you?"

He sniffled. "Cake."

"Then you'd have your cake. All you want."

His face screwed up red and ugly. "No. I want it now!" His shout bounced against the walls. The underpants were a grey rag around his ankles, and his hand a fist now, squeezing against the corner of his mouth.

She slapped him. There was no one to see them. The boy's eyes went round, and he made a gulping, swallowing noise inside his throat. But he stopped crying. The fist around her heart tightened, because she knew this was something he was already used to.

"Come on." She could hear her own voice, tight and angry, the way her father's had been when it still had words. She tugged the underpants from the boy's feet. "Stop being stupid."

She led him, his hand locked inside hers, up the stairs. Suddenly, halfway up, he started tugging, trying to pull his hand away.

"Stop it!" She knelt down and grabbed his bare shoulders,

clenching them tight. "Stop it!" She shook him, so that his head snapped back and forth.

His face was wet with tears, and his eyes looked up. He cringed away from something up there, rather than from her. Between her own panting breaths, she heard her father moving around.

"It's nothing!" Her voice screamed raw from her throat. "Don't be stupid!"

She jerked at his arm, but he wouldn't move; he cowered into the angle of the stairs. He howled when she slapped him, then cried openmouthed as she kept on hitting him, the marks of her hand jumping up red on his shoulder blades and ribs.

She stopped, straightening up and gasping to catch her breath. The naked little boy curled at her feet, his legs drawn up, face hidden in the crook of his arm. The blood rushing in her head roared, the sound of a battering wind. The saliva under her tongue tasted thick with salt.

For a moment she thought he was still crying, little soft animal sounds, then she knew it was coming from up above. From her father's room. She stood for a moment, head tilted back, looking up toward the sounds. Her hair had come loose from its knot, and hung down the side of her face and along her back.

"Come on . . ." She kept her voice softer. She reached down and took the boy's hand. But he wouldn't stand up. He hung limp, sniffling and shaking his head.

She had to pick him up. She cradled him in her arms—he didn't feel heavy at all—and carried him the rest of the way up the stairs.

Her father was a huddled shape under the blankets. He'd heard them coming, and had gotten back into the bed before she'd opened the door.

She knew that was what he'd done. A long time ago, when he'd first become this way—when she'd first made herself realize that he was old—she had tried tying him to the bed, knotting a soft cord around his bone-thin ankle and then to one of the heavy carved lion's paws underneath. But he'd fretted and tugged so at the cord, picking at the knot with his yellow fingernails until they'd cracked and bled, and the ankle's skin had chafed raw. She'd untied him, and taken to nailing his door shut, the nails bent so she just had to turn them to go in and out. At night, she had lain awake in her room and listened to him scratching at the inside of his door.

Then that had stopped. He'd learned that she was taking care of him. The scratching had stopped, and she'd even left the nails turned back, and he didn't try to get out.

She sat the little boy at the edge of the bed. The boy was silent now, sucking his thumb, his face smeared wet with tears.

"Daddy?" She pulled the blanket down a few inches, exposing the brown-spotted pink of his skull, the few strands of hair, tarnished silver.

"Daddy—I brought somebody to see you."

In the nest of the blanket and sour-smelling sheets, her father's head turned. His yellow-tinged eyes looked up at her. His face was parchment that had been crumpled into a ball and then smoothed out again. Parchment so thin that the bone and the shape of his teeth—the ones he had left, in back—could be seen through it.

"Look." She tugged, lifted the little boy farther up onto the bed. So her father could see.

The eyes under the dark hood of the blanket shifted, darting a sudden eager gaze from her face to the pink softness of the little boy.

"Come here." She spoke to the boy now. His legs and bottom slid on the blanket as she pulled him, her hands under his arms, until he sat on the middle of the bed, against the lanky, muffled shape of her father. "See, there's nothing to be afraid of. It's just nice and warm."

The shape under the blanket moved, crawling a few inches up to the turned-back edge.

The boy was broken, he had been this way a long time, it was why she'd picked him out and he'd come with her. Nobody loved him, not really, and that made it all right. He didn't fight as she laid him down, his head on the crumpled pillow, face close to her father's.

A thing of twigs and paper, her father's hand, slid from beneath the blanket. It cupped the back of the boy's head, tightening and drawing the boy close, as though for a kiss.

The boy struggled then, a sudden fluttering panic. His small hands pushed against her father's shoulders, and he cried, a whimpering noise that made her father's face darken with his wordless anger. That made her father strong, and he reared up from the bed, his mouth stretching open, tendons of clouded spit thinning to string. He wrapped his arms around the little boy, his grey flesh squeezing the pink bundle tight.

The boy's whimpering became the sound of his gasping breath. Her father pressed his open mouth against the side of the boy's neck. The jaws under the translucent skin worked, wetting the boy's throat with white-specked saliva.

Another cry broke out, tearing at her ears. She wanted to cover them with her hands and run from the room. And keep running, into all the dark streets around the house. Never stopping, until her breath was fire that burned away her heart. The cry was her father's; it sobbed with rage and frustration, a thing bigger than hunger, desire, bigger than the battering wind that shouted her name. He rolled his face away from the boy's wet neck, the ancient face like a child's now, mouth curved in an upside-down U, tongue thrusting against the toothless gums in front. His tears broke, wetting the ravines of his face.

He couldn't do it, he couldn't feed himself. She knew, it had been that way the last time, and before. But every time, hope made her forget, at least enough to try the old way. The way it had been years ago.

She couldn't bear the sound of her father's crying, and the little boy's fearful whimper. She knew how to stop it. On the table beside the bed was the knife she'd brought up from the kitchen—that had also been a long time ago—and had left there. Her hand reached out and curled around the smooth-worn wood. Her thumb slid across the sharp metal edge.

She brought her lips to the boy's ear, whispering to him, "Don't be afraid, it's all right . . ." The boy squirmed away from her, but she caught him fast, hugging his unclothed body against her breast. "It's all right, it's all right . . ." He saw the knife blade, and started to cry out. But she already had its point at his pink throat, and the cry leaked red, a drop, then a smearing line as the metal sank and cut.

The red bloomed on the sheets, the grey flooded to shiny wet. The boy's small hands beat against her, then fluttered, trembled, fell back, fists opening to stained flowers.

He didn't fight her now, he was a limp form in her embrace, but suddenly he weighed so much and her hands slipped on the soft skin that had been pink before and now shone darker and brighter. She gripped the boy tighter, her fingers parallel to his ribs, and lifted him. She brought the bubbling mouth, the red one that she had pulled the knife from, up to her father's parted lips.

The blood spilled over her father's gums and trickled out the corners of his mouth. The tendons in his neck stretched and tightened, as though they might tear his paper flesh. His throat worked, trying to swallow, but nothing happened. His eyes opened wider, spiderwebs of red traced around the yellow. He whimpered, the anger turning to fear. Trapped in the thing of sticks his body had become, he scrabbled his spotted hands at her face, reaching past the boy between them.

She knew what had to be done. The same as she'd done before. Her father's bent, ragged nails scraped across her cheek as she turned away from him. She nuzzled her face down close to the little boy's neck. She closed her eyes so there was only the wet and heat pulsing against her lips. She opened her mouth and drank, her tongue weighted with the dancing, coiling salt.

She didn't swallow, though her mouth had become full. Her breath halted, she raised her face from the boy's neck and the wound surging less with every shared motion of their hearts. A trickle of the warmth caught in her mouth leaked to her chin.

A baby bird in its nest . . . a naked thing of skin and fragile bone . . . She had found one once, on the sidewalk in front of the house, a tiny creature fallen from one of the branches above. Even as she had reached down, the tip of her finger an inch away from the wobbling, blue-veined head, the beak had opened, demanding to be fed . . .

The creature's hunger had frightened her, and she'd kicked it out into the gutter, where she wouldn't have to see it anymore. That had been a baby bird.

This was her father. She kept her eyes closed as she brought herself down to him, but she could still see the mouth opening wide, the pink gums, the tongue in its socket of bubbled spit. She lowered her face to his, and let the lips seal upon her own. She opened her mouth, and let the warmth uncoil, an infinitely soft creature moving over her own tongue, falling into his hunger.

The little boy's blood welled into her father's mouth. For a moment it was in both their mouths, a wet place shared by their tongues, his breath turning with hers. She felt the trembling, a shiver against the hinges of her jaw as his throat clenched, trying to swallow. She had to help even more, it had been this way the last time as well; she pressed her lips harder against her father's mouth, as her tongue rolled against the narrow arch of her teeth. The warmth in their mouths broke and pushed past the knot in her father's throat. He managed to swallow, and she felt the last of the blood flow out of her mouth, into his and then gone.

She fed him twice more, each mouthful easier. Between them, the little boy lay still, beautiful in his quiet.

The boy's throat had paled, and she had to draw deep for more.

The sheets were cold against her hands as she pushed herself away from him.

Her father was still hungry, but stronger now. His face rose to meet hers, and the force of his kiss pressed against her open lips.

The blood uncoiled in that dark space again, and something else. She felt his tongue thrust forward to touch hers, a warm thing cradled in warmth and the sliding wet. Her throat clenched now. She couldn't breathe, and the smell of his sweat and hunger pressed in the tight space behind her eyes.

His hands had grown strong now, too. The weak flutter had died, the palms reddening as the little boy had become white and empty. One of her father's hands tugged her blouse loose from the waistband of her skirt, and she felt the thing of bone and yellowed paper smear the sheet's wet on her skin. Her father's hand stroked across her ribs and fastened on her breast, a red print on the white cotton bra. He squeezed and it hurt, her breath was inside his hand and blood and the taste of his mouth, the dark swallowing that pulled her into him, beat a pulsing fist inside her forehead.

She pushed both her hands against him, but he was big now and she was a little girl again, she was that pale unmoving thing rocking in his arms, playing at being dead. She was already falling, she could raise her knees in the dark wet embrace of the bed, she could wrap herself around the little blind thing at the center of her breasts, that just breathed and stayed quiet, and that even he couldn't touch, had never been able to touch . . . the little boy was there, his angel face bright and singing, her ears deafened, battered by that song that light that falling upward into clouds of glory where her mother in Sunday robes reached for her, her mother smiling though she had no face she couldn't remember her mother's face—

She shoved against her father, hard enough to break away from him, his ragged fingernails drawing three red lines that stung and wept under her bra. She fell backward off the bed, her elbow hard against the floor, sending numb electricity to her wrist.

Another shape slid from the edge of the bed and sprawled over her lap. The little boy, naked and red wet, made a soft, flopping doll. She pushed it away from herself and scrambled to her feet.

The bed shone. From its dark center, the depth of the blanket's hood, her father looked out at her.

She found the doorknob in her hands behind her back. Her blouse clung to her ribs, and had started to turn cold in the room's shuttered air. The door scraped her spine as she stepped forward into the hallway. Then she turned and ran for the bathroom at the far end, an old sour taste swelling in her throat.

In the dark, between the streetlights' blue islands, she could feel the leaves under her feet. They slid away, damp things, silent; she had to walk carefully to keep from falling.

There was work to be done back at the house. She'd do it later. She would have to change the sheets, as she always did afterward, and wash the stained ones. She used the old claw-footed bathtub, kneeling by its side, the smell of soap and bleach stinging her nose, her fingers working in the pink water. He let her come in and make the bed, and never tried to say anything to her, just watching her with his blank and wordless eyes, his hungers, all of them, over for a while.

And there were the other jobs to be done, the messier ones. Getting rid of things. She'd have to take the car, the old Plymouth with the rusting fenders, out of the garage. And drive to that far place she knew, where these things were never found. She would come back as the sun was rising, and there would be mud on the hem of her skirt. She'd be tired, and ready to sleep.

She could do all that later. She'd been brave and strong, and had already done the hardest jobs; she could allow herself this small indulgence.

The cold night wrapped around her. She pressed her chin down into the knot of the scarf she'd tied over her hair. The collar of her coat had patches where the fur had worn away. The coat had been her mother's, and had been old the first time she'd worn it. A scent of powder, lavender and tea roses, still clung to the heavy cloth.

At the end of the block ahead of her, the Presbyterian church hid the stars at the bottom of the sky. She could see the big stained-glass window, Jesus with one hand on his staff and the other cupped to the muzzle of a lamb, even though there were no lights on in the church itself. The light spilling over the sidewalk came from the meeting room in the basement.

She went down the bare concrete steps, hand gripping the iron rail. And into the light and warmth, the collective sense of people in a room, their soft breathing, the damp-wool smell of their winter coats.

Where she hung her coat up, with the others near the door, a mimeographed paper on the bulletin board held the names for the altar flowers rotation. Sign-ups to chaperone the youth group's Christmas party. A glossy leaflet, unfolded and tacked, with pledges for a mission in Belize. Her name wasn't anywhere on the different pieces of paper. She didn't belong to the church. They probably wouldn't have wanted her, if they'd known. Known everything. She only came here for the weekly support group.

There was a speaker tonight, a woman up at the front of the room, talking, one hand gesturing while the other touched the music stand the church gave them to use as a podium.

She let the speaker's words flutter past as she sat down in one of the metal folding chairs at the side of the room; halfway down the rows, so she only had to turn her head a bit to see who else had come tonight. She had already counted close to twenty-four. There were the usuals, the faces she saw every week. A couple, a man and a woman who always held hands while they sat and listened, who she assumed were married; they nodded and smiled at her, a fellow regular. At the end of the row was somebody she hadn't seen before, a young man who sat hunched forward, the steam from a Styrofoam cup of coffee rising into his face. She could tell that he was just starting, that this was a new world for him; he didn't look happy.

None of them ever did, even when they smiled and spoke in their bright loud voices, when they said hello and hugged each other near the table with the coffee urn and the cookies on the paper plates.

They had another word for why they were here, a word that made it sound like a disease, just a disease, something you could catch like a cold or even a broken arm. Instead of it being time itself, and old age, and the grey things their parents had become. Time curled outside the church, like a black dog waiting where the steps became the sidewalk, waiting to go home with them again. Where the ones who had known their names looked at them now with empty eyes and did not remember.

She sat back in the folding chair, her hands folded in her lap. The woman at the front of the room had the same bright, relentless voice. She closed her eyes and listened to it.

The woman had a message. There was always a message, it was why people came here. The woman told the people in the room that they had been chosen to receive a great blessing, one that most people weren't strong enough for. A chance to show what love is. A few years of grief and pain and sadness and trouble, of diapering and spoon-feeding and talking cheerily to something that had your father or your mother's face, but wasn't them at all, not anymore. And then it would be over.

That was a small price to pay, a small burden to carry. The woman told them that, the same thing they'd been told before. A few years to show their love. For these things that had been their parents. They'd be transfigured by the experience. Made into saints, the ones who'd shown their courage and steadfastness on that sad battlefield.

She sat and listened to the woman talking. The woman didn't know—none of them ever did—but she knew. What none of them ever would.

She looked around at the others in the room, the couple holding hands, the young man staring into the dregs of his coffee. Her burden, her blessing, was greater than theirs. And so was her love. Even now, she felt sorry for them. They would be released someday. But not her. For them, there would be a few tears, and then their love, their small love, would be over.

She kept her eyes closed, and let herself walk near the edge of sleep, of dreaming, in this warm place bound by winter. She smiled.

She knew that love wasn't over in a few sad years. Or in centuries. She knew that love never died. She knew that her love—real love, true love—was forever.

Stories, when they work, if they work at all, are like lit matches dropped down a well. You don't really see anything except, for a moment, how deep and dark the well is.

I don't know what this story means, other than that it's a story about love and happiness. I don't have much more to say about it, except . . .

1. The words *victim* and *victimizer* are not easily defined. People who do have easy definitions for those words are lying to you, for reasons of their own; and

2. Martyrdom is a seductive endeavor, but then, it should be. After that, there's only silence.

K. W. Jeter

Home by the Sea

PAT CADIGAN

*Cadigan has written at least two other terrific vampire
stories—"My Brother's Keeper" and "The Power and the
Passion." Like Jeter's, this one packs a wallop and you won't
soon forget it.*

There was no horizon line out on the water.

"Limbo ocean. Man, did we hate this when I was a commercial
fisherman," said a man sitting at the table to my left. "Worse than
fog. You never knew where you were."

I sneaked a look at him and his companions. The genial voice
came from a face you'd have expected to find on a wanted poster
of a Middle Eastern terrorist, but the intonations were vaguely
Germanic. The three American women with him were all of a type,
possibly related. A very normal-looking group, with no unusual
piercings or marks. I wondered how long they'd been in Scheveningen.

I slumped down in my chair, closed my eyes, and lifted my face
to where I thought the sun should be. It was so overcast, there
wasn't even a hot spot in the sky. Nonetheless, the promenade was
crowded, people wandering up and down aimlessly, perhaps pretending, as I was, that they were on vacation. It was equally
crowded at night, when everyone came to watch the stars go out.

Of course *we're on vacation,* a woman had said last night at another of the strange parties that kept congealing in ruined hotel lob-
bies and galleries. This had been one of the fancier places, ceilings
in the stratosphere and lots of great, big ornate windows so we
could look out anytime and see the stars die. *It's an* enforced *vacation. Actually, it's the world that's gone on vacation.*

No, that's not it, someone else had said in an impeccable British
accent. It always surprised me to hear one, though I don't know
why; England wasn't that far away. *What it is, is that the universe
has quit its job.*

Best description yet, I'd decided. *The universe has quit its job.*

"Hey, Jess." I heard Jim plop down in the chair next to me. "Look what I found."

I opened my eyes. He was holding a fan of glossy postcards like a winning poker hand. Scheveningen and The Hague as they had been. I took them from him, looked carefully at each one. If you didn't know any better, you'd have thought it had been a happy world, just from looking at these.

"Where'd you find them?"

"Up a ways," he said, gesturing vaguely over his shoulder. He went *up a ways* a lot now, scavenging bits of this and that, bringing them to me as if they were small, priceless treasures. Perhaps they were—souvenirs of a lost civilization. Being of the why-bother school now, myself, I preferred to vegetate in a chair. "Kid with a whole pile of them. I traded him that can of beer I found." He stroked his beard with splayed fingers. "Maybe he can trade it for something useful. And if he can't, maybe he can fill a water pistol with it."

What would be useful, now that the universe had quit its job? I thought of making a list on the back of one of the postcards. Clothing. Shelter. Something to keep you occupied while you waited for the last star to go out—a jigsaw puzzle, perhaps. But Jim never showed up with one of those, and I wasn't ambitious enough to go looking myself.

My old hard-driving career persona would have viewed that with some irony. But now I could finally appreciate that being so driven could not have changed anything. Ultimately, you pounded your fist against the universe and then found you hadn't made so much as a dent, let alone reshaped it. Oddly enough, that knowledge gave me peace.

Peace seemed to have settled all around me. Holland, or at least this part of Holland, was quiet. All radio and TV communications seemed to be permanently disrupted—the rest of the world might have been burning, for all we knew, and we'd just happened to end up in a trouble-free zone. Sheerly by accident, thanks to a special our travel agency had been running at the time. We joked about it: *How did you happen to come to Holland? Oh, we had a coupon.*

A kid walked by with a boombox blaring an all-too-familiar song about the end of the world as we know it and feeling fine. The reaction from the people sitting at the tables was spontaneous and unanimous. They began throwing things at him, fragments of bricks, cups, cans, plastic bottles, whatever was handy, yelling in a multitude of languages for him to beat it.

The kid laughed loudly, yelled an obscenity in Dutch, and ran away up the promenade, clutching his boombox to his front. Mission accomplished, the tourists had been cheesed off again. The man at the next table had half risen out of his chair and now sat down again, grinning sheepishly. "All I was gonna do was ask him where he found batteries that work. I'd really like to listen to my CD player." He caught my eye and shrugged. "It's not like I could hurt him, right?"

Jim was paying no attention. He had his left hand on the table, palm up, studiously drawing the edge of one of the postcards across the pad below his thumb, making deep, slanted cuts.

"I wish you wouldn't do that," I said.

"Fascinating. Really fascinating." He traced each cut with a finger. "No pain, no pain at all. No blood and no pain. I just can't get over that."

I looked toward the horizonless ocean. From where I was sitting, I had a clear view of the tower on the circular pier several hundred feet from the beach, and of the woman who had hanged herself from the railing near the top. Her nude body rotated in a leisurely way, testifying to the planet's own continuing rotation. As I watched, she raised one arm and waved to someone on the shore.

"Well," I said, "what did you expect at the end of the world?"

"You really shouldn't deface yourself," I said as we strolled back to the hotel where we were squatting. If you could really call it a hotel—there was no charge to stay there, no service, and no amenities. "I know it doesn't hurt, but it doesn't heal, either. Now you've got permanent hash marks, and besides not being terribly attractive, they'll probably catch on everything."

Jim sighed. "I know. I get bored."

"Right." I laughed. "For the last twenty years, you've been telling me I should learn how to stop and smell the roses and now *you're* the one who's complaining about having nothing to do."

"After you've smelled a rose for long enough, it loses its scent. Then you have to find a different flower."

"Well, self-mutilation *is* different, I'll give you that." We passed a young guy dressed in leather with an irregular-shaped fragment of mirror embedded in his forehead. "Though maybe not as different as it used to be, since it seems to be catching on. What do you suppose *he's* smelling?"

Jim didn't answer. We reached the circular drive that dead-ended the street in front of our hotel, which had gone from motorcycle parking lot to motorcycle graveyard. On impulse, I took Jim's hand in my own as we crossed the drive. "I suppose it's the nature of the end of time or whatever this is, and the world never was a terribly orderly place. But nothing makes sense anymore. Why do we still have day and night? Why does the earth keep turning?"

"Winding down," Jim said absently. "No reason why the whole thing should go at once." He stopped short in the middle of the sidewalk in front of the hotel. "Listen."

There was a distant metallic crashing noise, heavy wheels on rails. "Just the trams running again. That's something else—why does the power work in some places and not in others?"

"What?" Jim blinked at me, then glanced in the general direction of the tram yard. "Oh, that. Not what I meant. Something I've been wondering lately"—there was a clatter as a tram went by on the cross street "—why we never got married."

Speaking of things that didn't seem important anymore—it wasn't the first time the subject had come up. We'd talked about it on and off through the years, but after eighteen years together, the matter had lost any urgency it might have had, if it had ever had any. Now, under a blank sky in front of a luxury hotel where the guests had become squatters, it seemed to be the least of the shadow-things my life had been full of, like status and career and material comforts. I could have been a primitive tribeswoman hoarding shiny stones for all the real difference those things had ever made. They'd given me nothing beyond some momentary delight; if anything, they'd actually taken more from me, in terms of the effort I'd had to put into acquiring them, caring for them, keeping them tidy and intact. Especially the status and the career. And they sure hadn't stopped the world from ending, no more than our being married would have.

But I was so certain of what Jim wanted to hear that I could practically feel the words arranging themselves in the air between us, just waiting for me to provide the voice. *Well, dear, let's just hunt up a cleric and get married right now.* Add sound and stir till thickened. Then—

Then what? It wasn't like we actually had a future anymore, together or singly. The ocean didn't even have a horizon.

"I think we *are* married," I said. "I think any two people seeing the world to its conclusion together are married in a way that didn't exist until now."

It should have been the right thing to say. Instead, I sounded like a politician explaining how a tax increase wasn't really a tax increase after all. After two decades, I could do better than some saccharine weasel words, end of the world or no.

Say it, then. The other thing, what he's waiting for. What difference does it make? The question I had to answer first, maybe the question Jim was really asking.

The edges of the cuts he'd made in his hand moved against my skin. They felt like the gills of an underwater creature out of its element, seeking to be put back in.

No pain at all. No blood and no pain.

It's not like I could hurt him, right?

Right. It's the end of the world as we know it, and I feel nothing. So we can go ahead now, do all those things that used to be so dangerous. Self-mutilation, bonding rituals, any old hazard at all.

Jim's eyes were like glass.

"Better get into the lobby now if you want to see it."

It was the Ghost of Lifetimes Past; that was what Jim and I had been calling her. She stood a respectful distance from us, a painfully thin blond woman in a dirty white tutu and pink satin ballet shoes. The most jarring thing about her was not her silly outfit, or the way she kept popping up anywhere and everywhere, but that face—she had the deep creases of someone who had lived seventy very difficult years. Around the edge of her chin and jawbone, the skin had a peculiar strained look, as if it were being tightened and stretched somehow.

"The crucifixion," she said, and gave a small, lilting giggle. "They're probably going to take him down soon, so if you want a look, you'd better hurry." Her gaze drifted past us and she moved off, as if she'd heard someone calling her.

"You in the mood for a crucifixion?" I said lightly. It was a relief to have anything as a distraction.

"Not if we can possibly avoid it."

But there was no way we could. Pushing our way through the small crowd in the lobby, we couldn't help seeing it. I vaguely recognized the man nailed directly to the wall—one of the erstwhile millionaires from the suites on the top floor. He was naked except for a wide silk scarf around his hips and a studded collar or belt cinched wrong side out around his head in lieu of a crown of thorns. No blood, of course, but he was doing his best to look as if he were in pain.

"God," I whispered to Jim, "I hope it's not a trend."

He blew out a short, disgusted breath. "I'm going upstairs."

Somehow, I had the feeling that it wasn't really the crucifixion he was so disgusted with. I meant to follow him but suddenly I felt as nailed in place as the would-be Christ. Not that I had any real desire to stand there and stare at this freak show, but it held me all the same. All that Catholic schooling in my youth, I thought, finally catching up with me after all these years, activating a dormant taste for human sacrifice.

Ersatz-Christ looked around, gritting his teeth. "You're supposed to mock me," he said, the matter-of-fact tone more shocking than the spikes in his forearms. "It won't work unless you mock me."

"You're a day late and a few quarts low," someone in the crowd said. "It won't work unless you shed blood, either."

The crucified man winced. "Shit."

There was a roar of laughter.

"For some reason, that never occurs to them. About the blood."

I looked up at the man who had spoken. He smiled down at me, his angular face cheerfully apologetic. I couldn't remember having seen him around before.

"This is the third one I've seen," he said, jerking his head at the man on the wall. The straight black hair fell briefly over one eye and he tossed it back. "A grand gesture that ultimately means nothing. Don't you find it rather annoying, people who suddenly make those grand risky gestures only after there isn't a hope in hell of it mattering? Banning the aerosol can after there's already a hole in the ozone layer, seeking alternate sources of power after nuclear reactors have already gone into operation. It's humanity's fatal flaw—locking the barn after the horse has fled. The only creature in the universe who displays such behavior."

I couldn't place his accent or, for that matter, determine if he actually had an accent—I was getting tone-deaf in that respect. He didn't look American, but that meant nothing to me. All the Americans were getting a European cast as they adopted the local face.

"The universe?" I said. "You must be exceptionally well traveled."

He laughed heartily, annoying ersatz-Christ and what sympathizers he had left. We moved out of the group, toward the unoccupied front desk. "The universe we know of, then. Which, for all intents and purposes, might as well be the universe there is."

I shrugged. "There's something wrong with that statement, but I'm no longer compulsive enough to pick out what it is. But it might be comforting to know that if there is a more intelligent species somewhere, its foibles are greater than ours, too."

"Comforting?" He laughed again. "It would seem that in the absence of pain, no comfort is necessary." He paused, as if waiting for me to challenge him on that, and then stuck out his hand. "I'm Sandor."

"Jess." The warmth of his unmarked, uncut hand was a mild shock. Fluctuations in body temperatures were as nonexistent as blood in these nontimes. Which would only stand to reason, since blood flow governed skin temperature. Everyone was the same temperature now, but whether that was something feverish or as cold as a tomb was impossible to tell with no variation. Perhaps I just hadn't been touching the right people.

"Odd, isn't it?" he said, politely disengaging his hand from mine. I felt a rush of embarrassment. "They wanted to investigate it at the hospital, but I wouldn't let them. Do you know, at the hospital, people are offering themselves for exploratory surgery and vivisection? And the doctors who have a stomach for such things take them willingly. Yes. They cut them open, these people, and explore their insides. Sometimes they remove internal organs and sew the people up again to see how they manage without them. They manage fine. And there is no blood, no blood anywhere, just a peculiar watery substance that pools in the body cavity.

"And hidden away in the hospital, there is a doctor who has removed a woman's head. Her body is inactive, of course, but it does not rot. The head functions, though without air to blow through the vocal cords, it's silent. It watches him, they say, and he talks to it. They say he is trying to get the head to communicate with him in tongue-clicks, but it won't cooperate. *She* won't cooperate, if you prefer. And then there's the children's ward and the nursery where they keep the babies. These babies—"

"*Stop* it," I said.

He looked dazed, as if I'd slapped him.

"Are you insane?"

Now he gave me a wary smile. "Does sanity even come into it?"

"I mean . . . well, we just met."

"Ah, how thoughtless of me."

I started to turn away.

That strangely warm hand was on my arm. "I do mean it. It *was* thoughtless, pouring all that out on someone I don't know. And a stranger here as well. It must be hard for you, all this and so far from home."

"Oh, I don't know." I glanced at the crucified man. "It's all so weird, I think maybe I'd just as soon not see it happen anyplace familiar. I don't really like to think about what it must be like back home." I jerked my thumb at the man nailed to the wall. "Like, I'd rather that be some total stranger than one of my neighbors."

"Yes, I can see that. Though it must be a little easier to be with someone you're close to, as well." He looked down for a moment. "I saw you come in with your companion."

I gave him points for perception—most people assumed Jim was my husband. "Are you from here?" I asked.

"No. As I'm sure you could tell."

"Not really. Is Sandor a Polish name?"

He shrugged. "Could be. But I'm not from there, either."

There was a minor commotion as the police came in, or rather, some people dressed in police uniforms. Scheveningen was maintaining a loose local government—God knew why, force of habit, perhaps—with a volunteer uniformed cadre that seemed to work primarily as moderators or referees, mostly for the foreigners. They pushed easily through the thinning crowd and started to remove the crucified man from the wall, ignoring his protests that he wasn't finished, or it wasn't finished, or something.

"Ite missa est," I said, watching. "Go, the Mass is over. Or something like that."

"You remember the Latin rite. I'm impressed."

"Some things hang on." I winced at the sound of ersatz-Christ's forearm breaking. "That sounded awful, even if it didn't hurt."

"It won't heal, either. Just goes on looking terrible. Inconvenient, too. At the hospital, they have—" He stopped. "Sorry. As you said, some things hang on."

"What do you suppose they'll do with him?" I asked as they took him out. "It's not like it's worth putting him in jail or anything."

"The hospital. It's where they take all the mutilation cases bad enough that they can't move around on their own. If they want mutilation, they can have plenty there, under better conditions, for better reasons, where no one has to see them."

Finally, I understood. "Did you work there long?"

"Volunteered," he said, after a moment of hesitation. "There are no employees anymore, just volunteers. A way to keep busy. I left—" He shrugged. "Sitting ducks."

"Pardon?"

"That's the expression in English, isn't it? For people who leave themselves open to harm? In this case, literally open."

"If it doesn't hurt and it doesn't kill them, and this is the end of it all as we know it," I said slowly, "how can they be leaving themselves open to harm?"

"A matter of differing cultural perspectives." He smiled.

I smiled back. "You never told me what culture you were from."

"I think you could say that we're all from here now. Or might as well be. There's an old saying that you are from the place where you die, not where you were born."

"I've never heard that one. And nobody's dying at the moment."

"But nothing happens. No matter what happens, nothing happens. Isn't that a description of a dying world? But perhaps you don't see it that way. And if you don't, then perhaps *you* aren't dying yet. Do you think if you cut yourself, you might bleed? Is it that belief that keeps *you* from mutilating yourself, or someone else? Do you even wonder about that?"

I looked from side to side. "I feel like I'm under siege here."

He laughed. "But *don't* you wonder? Why there aren't people running through the streets in an orgy of destruction, smashing windows and cars and each other? And themselves."

"Offhand, I'd say there just doesn't seem to be much point to it." I took a step back from him.

"Exactly. No point. No reward, no punishment, no pleasure, no pain. The family of humanity has stopped bickering, world peace at last. Do you think if humans had known what it would take to bring about world peace, that they'd have worked a lot harder for it?"

"Do you really think it's like this everywhere in the world?" I said, casually moving back another step.

"Don't you?" He spread his hands. "Can't you feel it?"

"Actually, I don't feel much." I shrugged. "Excuse me, I'm going to go catch up on my reading."

"Wait." He grabbed my arm and I jumped. "I'm sorry," he said, letting go almost immediately. "I suppose I'm wrong about there being no pleasure and pain. I'd forgotten about the pleasure of being able to talk to someone. Of sharing thoughts, if you'll pardon the expression."

I smiled. "Yeah. See you around." I shook his hand again, more to confirm what I'd felt when he'd grabbed my arm than out of courtesy, and found I'd been right. His skin definitely felt cooler. Maybe *he* was the one who wasn't dying and I had sucked whatever real life he had out of him.

Only the weird survive, I thought, and went upstairs.

* * *

No matter what happens, nothing happens. Jim was curled up on the bed, motionless. The silence in the room was deafening. Sleep canceled the breathing habit, if "sleep" it actually was. There were no dreams, nothing much like rest—more like being a machine that had been switched off. Another end-of-the-world absurdity.

At least I hadn't walked in to find him slicing himself up with a razor, I thought, going over to the pile of books on the nightstand. Whatever had possessed me to think that I would wait out the end of the world by catching up with my reading had drained away with my ambition. If I touched any of the books now, it was just to shift them around. Sometimes, when I looked at the covers, the words on them didn't always make sense right away, as if my ability to read was doing a slow fade along with everything else.

I didn't touch the books now as I stretched out on the bed next to Jim. He still didn't move. On the day—if "day" is the word for it—the world had ended, we'd been in this room, in this bed, lying side by side the way we were now. I am certain that we both came awake at the same moment, or came to might be a better way to put it. Went from unconscious to conscious was the way it felt, because I didn't wake up the way I usually did, slowly, groggily, and wanting nothing more than to roll over and go back to sleep for several more hours. I had never woken up well, as if my body had always been fighting the busy life my mind had imposed on it. But that "day," I was abruptly awake without transition, staring at the ceiling, and deep down I just *knew*.

There was no surprise in me, no regret, and no resistance. It was that certainty: *Time's up.* More than something I knew, it was something I *was*. Over, finished, done, used up . . . but not quite gone, as a bottle is not gone though emptied of its contents. I thought of Jim Morrison singing "The End," and felt some slight amusement that in the real end, it hadn't been anywhere near so dramatic. Just . . . *time's up.*

And when I'd finally said, "Jim . . . ?" he'd answered, "Uh-huh. I've got it, too." And so had everyone else.

I raised up on one elbow and looked at him without thinking anything. After awhile, still not thinking anything, I pulled at his shirt and rolled him over.

Sex at the end of the world was as pointless as anything else, or as impossible as bleeding, depending on your point of view, I guess. The bodies didn't function; the minds didn't care. I felt some mild regret about that, and about the fact that all I *could* feel was mild regret.

But it was still possible to show affection—or to engage in pointless foreplay—and take a certain comfort in the contact. We hadn't been much for that in this no-time winding-down. Maybe passion had only been some long, pleasant dream that had ended with everything else. I slipped my hand under Jim's shirt.

His unmoving chest was cadaver-cold.

That's it, I thought, *now we're dying for real.* There was a fearful relief in the idea that I wouldn't have to worry about him mutilating himself any further.

Jim's eyes snapped open and he stared down at my hand still splayed on his stomach, as if it were some kind of alien, deformed starfish that had crawled out of the woodwork onto his torso.

"You're warm," he said, frowning.

And like that, I was lost in the memory of what it was to feel passion for another human being. What it was to *want*, emotions become physical reactions, flesh waking from calm to a level of response where the edge between pleasure and pain thinned to the wisp of a nerve ending.

I rolled off the bed and went into the bathroom. Behind me, I heard Jim rolling over again. Evidently he didn't want to know about my sudden change in temperature if I didn't want to tell him. A disposable razor sat abandoned on the counter near the sink. If I took it and ran my fingertip along the blade, would I see the blood well up in a bright, uneven bead? I didn't want to know, either.

The exploding star was a fiery blue-white flower against the black sky. Its lights fell on the upturned faces of the crowd on the promenade, turning them milky for a few moments before it faded.

"Better than fireworks," I heard someone say.

"Ridiculous," said someone else. "Some kind of trick. The stars are thousands and millions of light-years away from us. If we see them exploding now, it means the universe actually ended millions of years ago and we're just now catching up with it."

"Then no wonder we never made any contact with life on other planets," said the first voice. "Doesn't *that* make sense? If the universe has been unraveling for the last million years, all extraterrestrial life was gone by the time we got the technology to search for it."

I looked around to see who was speaking and saw her immediately. The Ghost of Lifetimes Past was standing just outside the group, alone as usual, watching the people instead of the stars. She caught my eye before I could look away and put her fingertips to her mouth in a coy way, as if to stifle a discreet giggle. Then she turned and went up the promenade, tutu flouncing a little, as an orange starburst blossomed in the west.

If Jim had come out with me, I thought, weaving my way through the crowd, I probably wouldn't have been doing something as stupid as following this obviously loony woman. But he had remained on the bed, unmoving, long after it had gotten dark, and I hadn't disturbed him again. I had sat near the window with a book in my lap and told myself I was reading, not just staring until I got tired of seeing the same arrangement of words and turning a page, while I felt myself fade. It had been a very distinct sensation, what I might have felt if I had been awake when the world had ended.

The Ghost of Lifetimes Past didn't look back once but I was sure she knew I was following her, just as I knew she had meant for me to follow her, all the way to the Kurhaus. Even from a distance, I could see that the lights were on. Another party; what was it about the end of the world that seemed to cry out for parties? Perhaps it was some kind of misplaced huddling instinct.

I passed a man sitting on a broken brick wall, boredly hammering four-inch nails into his chest. If we hung notes on them, I thought, and sent him strolling up and down the promenade, we could have a sort of postal service-cum-newspaper. Hear ye, hear ye, the world is still dead. Or undead. Nondead. Universe still unemployed after quitting old job. Or was it, really?

The Ghost flounced across the rear courtyard of the Kurhaus without pausing, her ballet shoes going scritch-scritch on the pavement. Light spilled out from the tall windows, making giant, elongated lozenges of brightness on the stone. One level up, I could see people peering out the galleria windows at the sky. When the sun went, I thought suddenly, would we all finally go with it, or would it just leave us to watch cosmic fireworks in endless night?

They made me think of birds on a nature preserve, the people wandering around in the lobby. Birds in their best plumage and their best wounds. A young, black-haired guy in a pricey designer gown moved across the scuffed dusty floor several yards ahead of me, the two chandelier crystals stuck into his forehead above the eyebrows, catching the light. Diaphanous scarves fluttered from holes in his shoulder blades. Trick or treat, I thought. Or maybe it was All Soul's Day, every day.

At the bar island, someone had used the bottles on the surround-

ing shelves for target practice and the broken glass still lay everywhere like a scattering of jewels. I saw a woman idly pick up a
shard lying on the bar and take a bite out of it, as if it were a potato
chip. A man in white tie and tails was stretched out on the floor on
his stomach, looking around and making notes on a stenographer's
pad. I wandered over to see what he was writing, but it was all unreadable symbols, part shorthand, part hieroglyphics.

There was a clatter behind me. Some people were righting one
of the overturned cocktail tables and pulling up what undamaged
chairs they could find. It was the group that had been sitting near
me on the promenade that day, the man and his three women companions, all of them chattering away to each other as if nothing was
out of the ordinary. They were still unmarked and seemed oblivi-
ous to the freak show going on around them—I half expected the
man to go the bar and try to order. Or maybe someone would sweep
up some broken glass and bring it to them on a tray. Happy Hour is
here, complimentary hors d'oeuvres.

The Ghost reappeared on the other side of the bar. She looked
worse, if that were possible, as if walking through the place had depleted her. A tall man on her left was speaking to her as he ran a
finger along the wasted line of her chin while a man on her right
was displaying the filigree of cuts he'd made all over his stomach,
pulling the skin out and displaying it like a lace bib. The skin was
losing its elasticity; it sagged over the waistband of his white satin
pajama pants. The layer of muscle underneath showed through in
dark brown.

I turned back to the group I'd seen on the promenade, still in
their invisible bubble of normalcy. The man caught sight of me and
smiled a greeting without a pause in what he was saying. Maybe I
was supposed to choose, I thought suddenly; join the freaks or join
the normalcy. And yet I had the feeling that if I chose the latter, I'd
get wedged in among them somehow and never get back to Jim.

They were all staring at me questioningly now and something in
those mild gazes made me think I was being measured. One of the
women leaned into the group and said something; it was the signal
for their intangible boundary to go back up again. Either I'd kept
them waiting too long, or they didn't like what they saw, but the re-
jection was as obvious as if there had been a sign over their heads.

I started for the side door, intending to get out as fast as I could,
and stopped short. The boy standing near the entrance to the casino
might have been the same one who'd had the boombox, or not—it
was hard to tell, there were so many good-looking blond boys

here—but the man he was talking to was unmistakably Jim. He hadn't bothered to change his rumpled clothes or even to comb his hair, which was still flat on one side from the way he'd been lying on the bed.

Jim was doing most of the talking. The kid's expression was all studied diffidence, but he was listening carefully all the same. Jim showed him his hand and the kid took it, touching the cuts and nodding. After a few moments, he put his arm around Jim's shoulders and, still holding his hand, led him around the front of the closed, silent elevator doors to the stairs. I watched them go up together.

"Do you wonder what that was all about?"

I didn't turn around to look at him. "Well. Sandor Whoever from Wherever. The man who can still raise the mercury on a thermometer while the rest of us have settled at room temperature. If you start talking about interesting things people are doing in the hospital, I might take a swing at you."

He chuckled. "That's the spirit. Next question: Do you wonder how they get the power on in some places when it won't work in others?"

"In a way."

"Do you want to find out?"

I nodded.

He didn't touch me even in a casual way until we reached his room on the fourth floor. It was the first time I'd ever been higher than the galleria level. The lights in the hallway shone dimly, glowing with what little power was left from whatever was keeping the lobby lit up, and his hand was like fire as he pulled me out of the hallway and into the room.

His body was a layer of softness over hard muscle. I tore his clothing to get at it; he didn't mind. Bursts of light from the outside gave me fleeting snapshots of his face. No matter what I did, he had the same expression of calm acceptance. Perhaps out of habit, covering the secret of his warmth—if the rest of us pod creatures knew he was the last (?) living thing on earth, what might we not do for this feeling of life he could arouse?

Already, his flesh wasn't as warm as it had been. That was me, I thought, pushing him down on the bed. I was taking it from him and I couldn't help it. Or perhaps it was just something inherent in the nature of being alive, that it would migrate to anyplace it was not.

Even so, even as he went from hot to cool, he lost nothing. Receptive, responsive, accommodating—in the silent lightning of dying stars, calm and accepting, but not passive. I was leading in this pas de deux, but he seemed to know how and where almost before I did, and was ready for it.

And now I could feel *how* it was happening, the way the life in his body was leached away into my own un-alive flesh. I was taking it from him. The act of *taking* is a distinctive one; no one who had ever taken anything had taken it quite like I took Sandor.

He gave himself up without resistance, and yet *give up* was not what he was doing, unless it was possible to surrender aggressively. It was as if I wanted him because his purpose was to be wanted, and he had been waiting for me, for someone to provide the wanting, to want him to death. Ersatz-Christ in the lobby had had it wrong, it never could have worked. Humans didn't sacrifice themselves, they were sacrificed to; they didn't give in, they were alive only in the act of taking—

Somehow, even with my head on fire, I pulled away from him. He flowed with the movement like a storm tide. I fought the tangle of sheets and cold flesh against warm, and the violence felt almost as good as the sex. If I couldn't fuck him to death, I'd settle for beating his head in, I thought dimly. We rolled off the bed onto the carpet and I scrambled away to the bathroom and slammed the door.

"Is there something wrong?" The puzzlement in his voice was so sincere I wanted to vomit.

"Stop it."

"Stop what?"

"Why did you let me do that to you?"

He might have laughed. "Did *you* do something to me?"

A weak pain fluttered through my belly. There was a wetness on my thighs.

"Turn on the light," he said. "You can now, you know. It'll work for you, now that you're living."

I flipped the switch. The sudden brightness was blinding. Turning away from the lights over the sink, I saw myself in the full-length mirror on the door. The wetness on my thighs was blood.

My blood? Or his?

The pain in my belly came again.

"Jess?"

"Get away. Let me get dressed and get out of here. I don't want this."

"Let me in."

"No. If you come near me, I'll take more from you."

Now he did laugh. "What is it you think *you* took?"

"Life. Whatever's left. You're alive and I'm one of the fading ones. I'll make you fade, too."

"That's an interesting theory. Is that what you think happened?"

"Somehow you're still really alive. Like the earth still turns, like there are still stars. Figures we wouldn't all fade away at once, us people. Some of us would still be alive. Maybe as long as there are still stars, there'll still be some people alive." The sound of my laughter in the small room was harsh and ugly. "So romantic. As long as there are stars in the sky, that's how long you'll be here for me. Go away. I don't want to hurt you."

"And what *will* you do?" he asked. "Go back to your bloodless room and your bloodless man, resume your bloodless wait to see what the end will be? It's all nothing without the risk, isn't it? When there's nothing to lose, there's really nothing at all. Isn't that right?"

The lock snapped and the door swung open. He stood there holding on to either side of the doorway. The stark hunger in the angular features had made his face into a predator's mask, intent, voracious, without mercy. I backed up a step, but there was nowhere to go.

He lunged at me and caught me under the arms, lifting me to eye level. "You silly cow," he whispered, and his breath smelled like meat. "*I* didn't get cooler, *you* just got *warmer*."

He shoved me away. I hit the wall, and slid down. The pain in my shoulders and back was exquisite, not really pain but pure sensation, the un-alive, undead nerve endings frenzied with it. I wanted him to do it again, I wanted him to hit me, or caress me, or cut me, or do anything that would make me *feel*. Pain or pleasure, whatever there was, I wanted to live through it, get lost in it, die of it, and, if I had to die of it, take him with me.

He stood over me with the barest of smiles. "Starting to understand now?"

I pushed myself up, my hands slipping and sticking on the tiled wall.

"Yeah." He nodded. "I think maybe you are. I think you're definitely starting to get it." He backed to the sink and slid a razor blade off the counter. "How about this?" He held the blade between two fingers, moving it back and forth so it caught the light. "Always good for a thrill. Your bloodless man understands that well enough already. Like so many others. Where do you think he goes when he takes his little walks up the promenade, what do you think he does when he leaves you to sit watching the hanging woman twist and turn on the end of her rope?" He laughed and popped the blade into his mouth, closing his eyes with ecstasy. Then he bared his teeth; the blood ran over his lower lip onto his chin and dripped down onto his chest.

"Come on," he said, the razor blade showing between his teeth. "Come *kiss* me."

I wasn't sure that I leaped for him as much as the life in him pulled me by that hunger for sensation. He caught me easily, holding me away for a few teasing seconds before letting our bodies collide.

The feeling was an explosion that rushed outward from me, and as it did, I finally did understand, mostly that I hadn't had it right at all, but it was too late to do anything about it. The only mercy he showed was to let the light go out again.

Or maybe that wasn't mercy. Maybe that was only what happened when he drained it all out of me and back into himself, every bit of pain and pleasure and being alive.

He kept the razor blade between his teeth for the whole time. It went everywhere, but he never did kiss me.

The room was so quiet, I thought he'd left. I got up from where I'd been lying, half in and half out of the bathroom, thinking I'd find my clothes and go away now, wondering how long I'd be able to hide the damage from Jim—if damage it was, since I no longer felt anything—wondering if I would end up in the hospital, if there was already a bed with my name on it, or whether I'd be just another exotic for nightly sessions at the Kurhaus.

"Just one more thing," he said quietly. I froze in the act of taking a step toward the bed. He was standing by the open window, looking out at the street.

"What's the matter?" I said. "Aren't I dead enough yet?"

He laughed, and now it was a soft, almost compassionate sound, the predator pitying the prey. "I just want to show you something."

"No."

He dragged me to the window and forced my head out. "See it anyway, this one time. A favor, because I'm so well pleased." He pulled my head back to make me look up at the sky. A night sky, very flat, very black, featureless, without a cloud and with no stars, none at all.

"A magic lantern show, yes," he said, as though I'd spoken. "*We* put the signs and wonders in the sky for you. So you wouldn't see *this*."

He forced my head down, digging his fingers more deeply into my hair. Below, in the courtyard, people wandered among a random arrangement of cylindrical things without seeing them. They were pale things, silent, unmoving; long, ropy extensions stretched out from the base of each one, sinking into the pavement like cables, except even in the dim light, I could see how they pulsed.

While I watched, a split appeared in the nearest one. The creature that pushed its way out to stand and stretch itself in the courtyard was naked, vaguely female-looking, but not quite human. It rubbed its hands over the surface of the cylinder, and then over itself. I pulled away.

"You see, that's the other thing about your kind besides your tendency toward too little, too late," he said conversationally as I dressed. If I tucked my shirt into my pants I could keep myself together a little better. "You miss things. You're blind. All of you. Otherwise, you'd have seen us before now. We've always been here, waiting for our time with you. If even one of you had seen us, you might have escaped us. Perhaps even destroyed us. Instead, you all went on with your lives. And now we're going on with them." He paused, maybe waiting for me to say something. I didn't even look at him as I wrapped my shirt around the ruin of my torso. "Don't worry. What I just showed you, you'll never see again. Perhaps by the time you get home, you'll even have forgotten that you saw anything."

He turned back to the window. "See you around the promenade."

"First time's the worst."

The Ghost of Lifetimes Past fell into step beside me as I walked back along the promenade. She was definitely looking worse, wilted and eaten away. "After that," she added, "it's the natural order of things."

"I don't know you," I said.

"I know you. We all know each other, after. Go home to your husband now and he'll know you, too."

"I'm not married."

"Sure." She smiled at me, her face breaking into a mass of lines and seams. "It could be worse, you know. They like to watch it waste me, they like to watch it creep through me and eat me alive. They pour life into us, they loan it to us, you could say, and then they take it back with a great deal of interest. And fascination. They feed on us, and we feed on them, but considering what they are, we're actually feeding on ourselves. And maybe a time will come that will really be the end. After all, how long can we make ourselves last?"

She veered away suddenly, disappearing down a staircase that led to one of the abandoned restaurants closer to the waterline.

As I passed the tower, the hanging woman waved a greeting. There would be no horizon line on the ocean again today.

I had thought Jim would know as soon as he saw me, but I didn't know what I expected him to do. He watched me from where he lay on the bed with his arms behind his head. Through the thin material of his shirt, I could see how he'd been split from below the collarbone down to his navel. It seems to be a favorite pattern of incision with them, or maybe they really have no imagination to speak of.

He still said nothing as I took a book from the stack on the nightstand and sat down in the chair by the window, positioning myself with my back to the room. The words on the pages looked funny, symbols for something I no longer knew anything about.

The mattress creaked as Jim got up and I heard him changing his clothes. I didn't want to look—after all, it wouldn't matter what I saw—and still not wanting to, I put the unreadable book aside and turned around.

The incision was actually very crude, as if it had been done with a jagged shard of glass. I wanted to feel bad at the sight, I wanted to feel sorry and sad and angry at the destruction, I wanted to feel the urge to rush to him and offer comfort. But as Sandor had pointed out, in the absence of pain, no comfort was necessary.

Abruptly, Jim shrugged and finished dressing, and I realized he'd been waiting for something, maybe for me to show him my own. But I had no desire to do that yet.

"I'm going for a walk up the promenade," he said, heading for the door. "You can come if you want." He didn't look back for a response.

"Do you think," I heard myself say just before he stepped out into the hall, "they're everywhere? Or if we could just get home somehow . . ."

"Jess." He almost smiled. "We *are* home."

I followed him at a distance. He didn't wait for me, walking along briskly but unhurriedly, and I didn't try to catch up with him.

The sky seemed darker and duller, the sounds of the people on the promenade quieter, more muffled. The trams didn't run.

I stayed out until dark. The dying-stars show was especially spectacular, and I watched it until Sandor finally got around to coming back for me.

I was sitting on the promenade in Scheveningen on a cloudy day at the end of August. There was no horizon line on the ocean. I started thinking about vampires at the end of the world—vampires because I was sitting next to Ellen Datlow, with whom I share a fascination with vampirism and the many forms it can take, and the end of the world because of the peculiar way sky and sea melted together without even a hint of demarcation, as if there were really nothing out there. Would vampires show up at the end of it all, I wondered, and if so, what kind? Suppose the vampires were the ones who were really alive and the people were the living dead?

Sitting around thinking odd thoughts in various locations is a strange thing to do, I guess, but it's a living.

Pat Cadigan

The Ragthorn

ROBERT HOLDSTOCK
AND GARRY KILWORTH

This may be the most traditional of the stories in the anthology, not for its vampire, which isn't at all traditional, but in its richness of detail. This novelette is a mystery, a historically accurate study, and a classic quest story. A lovely yet chilling grace note with which to culminate this book.

Quhen thow art ded and laid in layme
    And Raggtre rut thi ribbis ar
Thow art than brocht to thi lang hayme
    Than grett agayn warldis dignite

Unknown (c. A.D. 1360)

September 11, 1978

I am placing this entry at the beginning of my edited journal for reasons that will become apparent. Time is very short for me now, and there are matters that must be briefly explained. I am back at the cottage in Scarfell, the stone house in which I was born and which has always been at the centre of my life. I have been here for some years and am finally ready to do what must be done. Edward Pottifer is with me—good God-fearing man that he is—and it will be he who closes this journal and he alone who will decide upon its fate.

The moment is *very* close. I have acquired a set of dental pincers with which to perform the final part of the ritual. Pottifer has seen into my mouth—an experience that clearly disturbed him, no doubt because of its intimacy—and he knows which teeth to pull and which to leave. After the inspection he muttered that he is more used to pulling rose thorns from fingers than molars from jaws. He asked me if he might keep the teeth as souvenirs and I said he could, but he should look after them carefully.

231

I cannot pretend that I am not frightened. I have edited my life's
journal severely. I have taken out all that does not relate forcefully
to my discovery. Many journeys to foreign parts have gone, and
many accounts of irrelevant discovery and strange encounters. Not
even Pottifer will know where they are. I leave for immediate pos-
terity only this bare account in Pottifer's creased and soil-engrimed
hands.

Judge my work by this account, or judge my sanity. When this
deed is done I shall be certain of one thing: that in whatever form I
shall have become, I will be beyond judgement. I shall walk away,
leaving all behind, and not look back.

Time had been kinder to Scarfell Cottage than perhaps it de-
serves. It has been, for much of its existence, an abandoned place, a
neglected shrine. When I finally came back to it, years after my
mother's death, its wood had rotted, its interior decoration had decayed, but thick cob walls—two feet of good Yorkshire stone—had
proved too strong for the ferocious northern winters. The house
had been renovated with difficulty, but the precious stone lintel
over the doorway—the beginning of my quest—was thankfully intact and undamaged. The house of my childhood became habitable
again, twenty years after I left it.

From the tiny study where I write, the view into Scardale is as
eerie and entrancing as it ever was. The valley is a sinuous, silent
place, its steep slopes broken by monolithic black rocks and
stunted trees that grow from the green at sharp, wind-shaped angles. There are no inhabited dwellings here, no fields. The only
movement is the grey flow of cloud shadow and the flash of sunlight on the thin stream. In the far distance, remote at the end of the
valley, the tower of a church: a place for which I have no use.

And of course—all this is seen through the branches of the tree.
The *ragthorn*. The terrible tree.

It grows fast. Each day it seems to strain from the earth, stretching an inch or two into the storm skies, struggling for life. Its roots
have spread farther across the grounds around the cottage and
taken a firmer grip upon the dry stone wall at the garden's end; to
this it seems to clasp as it teeters over the steep drop to the dale.
There is such menace in its aspect, as if it is stretching its hard
knotty form, ready to snatch at any passing life.

It guards the entrance to the valley. It is a rare tree, neither haw-
thorn nor blackthorn, but some ancient form of plant life, with a
history more exotic than the Glastonbury thorn. Even its roots have
thorns upon them. The roots themselves spread below the ground

like those of a wild rose, throwing out suckers in a circle about the twisted bole: a thousand spikes forming a palisade around the trunk and thrusting inches above the earth. I have seen no bird try to feed upon the tiny berries that it produces in mid-winter. In the summer its bark has a terrible smell. To go close to the tree induces dizziness. Its thorns when broken curl up after a few minutes, like tiny live creatures.

How I hated that tree as a child. How my mother hated it! We were only stopped from destroying it by the enormity of the task, since such had been tried before and it was found that every single piece of root had to be removed from the ground to prevent it growing again. And soon after leaving Scarfell Cottage as a young man, I became glad of the tree's defensive nature—I began to long to see the thorn again.

To begin with however, it was the stone lintel that fascinated me: the strange slab over the doorway, with its faint alien markings. I first traced those markings when I was ten years old and imagined that I could discern letters among the symbols. When I was seventeen and returned to the cottage from boarding school for a holiday, I realised for the first time that they were cuneiform, the wedge-shaped characters that depict the ancient languages of Sumeria and Babylon.

I tried to translate them, but of course failed. It certainly occurred to me to approach the British Museum—after all my great-uncle Alexander had worked at that noble institution for many years—but those were full days and I was an impatient youth. My study was demanding. I was to be an archaeologist, following in the family tradition, and no doubt I imagined that there would be time enough in the future to discover the meaning of the Sumerian script.

At that time all I knew of my ancestor William Alexander was that he was a great-uncle, on my father's side, who had built the cottage in the dales in 1880, immediately on his return from the Middle East. Although the details of what he had been doing in the Bible lands were obscure, I knew he had spent many years there, and also that he had been shot in the back during an Arab uprising: a wound he survived.

There is a story that my mother told me, handed down through the generations. The details are smudged by the retelling, but it relates how William Alexander came to Scarfell, leading a great black-and-white Shire horse hauling a brewer's dray. On the dray were the stones with which he would begin to build Scarfell Cottage, on land he had acquired. He walked straight through the village with not a word to a soul, led the horse and cart slowly up the steep hill to the valley edge, took a spade, dug a pit, and filled it with dry wood. He set light to the wood and kept the fire going for four days. In all that time he remained in the open, either staring out across the valley or tending the fire. He didn't eat. He didn't drink. There was no tree there at the time. When at last the fire died down he paid every man in the village a few shillings to help with the building of a small stone cottage. And one of the stones to be set—he told them—was a family tombstone whose faded letters could still be seen on its faces. This was placed as the lintel to the door.

Tombstone indeed! The letters on that grey-faced obelisk had been marked there four thousand years before, and it had a value beyond measure. Lashed to the deck of a cargo vessel, carried across the Mediterranean, through the Straits of Gibraltar, the Bay of Biscay, the obelisk had arrived in England (coincidentally) at the time Cleopatra's Needle was expected. The confused Customs officers had waved it through, believing it to be a companion piece to the much larger Egyptian obelisk.

This then is all I need to say, save to add that three years after the building of the cottage the locals noticed a tree of unfamiliar shape growing from the pit where the fire had burned that night. The growth of the tree had been phenomenally fast; it had appeared in the few short months of one winter.

The rest of the account is extracted from my journal. Judge me upon it. Judge my sanity. There are many questions to which there seem no answers. Who, or what, guided me to previously hidden information during the years? My uncle's ghost perhaps? The ghost of something considerably more ancient? Or even the spirit of the tree itself, though what would be its motive? There are too many coincidences for there *not* to have been some divine, some spiritual presence at work. But who? And perhaps the answer is: *no person at all*, rather a force of destiny for which we have no words in our language.

August 7, 1958

I have been at Tel Enkish for four days now, frustrated by Professor Legmeshu's refusal to allow me onto the site of the excavation. It is clear, however, that a truly astonishing discovery is emerging.

Tel Enkish seems to be the site of an early Sumerian temple to a four-part god, or man-god, with many of the attributes of Gilgamesh. From the small town of Miktah, a mile away, little can be seen but a permanent dust cloud over the low, dry hills, and the steady stream of battered trucks and carts that plough back and forth between the dump site and the excavation itself. All the signs are that there is something very big going on. Iraqi officials are here in number. Also the children of the region have flocked to Tel Enkish from miles around the site. They beg, they pester, they demand work on what is now known as "The Great Tomb." They are unaware that as a visitor I have no authority myself.

August 9, 1958

I have at last been to the site. I have seen the shrine that William Alexander uncovered eighty years ago. I have never in my life been so affected by the presence of the monumental past in the corroded ruins of the present.

My frantic messages were at last acknowledged, this morning at eight. Legmeshu, it seems, has only just made the connection between me and William Alexander. At midday, a dust-covered British Wolesley came for me. The middle-aged woman who drove it turned out to be Legmeshu's American wife. She asked me, "Have you brought the stone?" and looked around my small room as if I might have been hiding it below the wardrobe or something. She was angry when I explained that I had brought only my transcription of the glyphs on the weathered rock. She quizzed as to where the stone was now located, and I refused to answer.

"Come with me," she snapped, and led the way to the car. We drove through the jostling crowds in silence. Over the nearest rise we passed through barbed-wire fencing and checkpoints not unlike those to be found in army camps. Iraqi guards peered into the vehicle, but on seeing Dr. Legmeshu waved us on. There was a sense of great agitation in the air. Everyone seemed tense and excited.

The site itself is in a crater of the tel, the mound on which the temple had been built and over which later generations of buildings in mud had been added. In the fashion of the notorious archaeologist Woolley, the top layer of the tel had been blasted away to expose the remains of the civilisation that had flourished there in the third millennium B.C. It had not been Legmeshu who had been so destructive, but my ancestor, Alexander.

As I feasted my eyes on the beautifully preserved building, she waited impatiently. She told me that the temple was from the period associated with Gilgamesh the King. It was made of refined mud-brick, and had been covered with a weatherproof skin of burnt brick set in bitumen.

"Where had the Alexander stone been set?" I asked, and she pointed to the centre of the ruins. "They had created a megalith structure at the very heart of the temple. The stone that your relative stole was the keystone. This is why you *must* return it. We cannot allow . . ." She broke off and looked at me angrily. If she had been about to make a threat, she had thought better of it.

Her attitude led me to expect the worst from the male Dr. Legmeshu, but I am delighted to say that he could not have been more charming. I found him in the tent, poring over a set of inscriptions that had been traced out on paper. He was leaning on a large slab of rock and when I looked more closely I saw that it was identical to the lintel at Scarfell Cottage.

He was fascinated by the route I had taken in discovering him. The Iraqi government had made formal representation to the British government, five years before, for the return of the "Tel Enkish Stone" to its natural site. Unlike Elgin Marbles, which the British Museum regarded as their right to keep safe, no official in London had ever heard of the Tel Enkish Stone.

The argument had waged within those same "scenes" for years, and had finally been taken up by the press. A picture of one of the other Tel Enkish stones had caught my attention, along with the headline: WHERE IS THE ALEXANDER STONE? Some keen reporter had obviously done his research to the point where he had made the connection.

The museum by that time had established that the stone had been removed by Professor Alexander, who they understood had retired to an unknown location after returning from the Middle East in the late 1890s. The Iraqi government believed none of this of course, thinking that the British Museum had the stone hidden, and relations were soured between the two countries for some years afterwards.

I have told Legmeshu that the stone lies in a quarry, the location of which I shall make known to the museum on my return to the United Kingdom. He has accepted this.

The story of those events, eighty years before, is difficult to ascertain. Alexander had worked on the site with Legmeshu's own great-grandfather. The two men had been close friends, and had made the astonishing discovery of the megaliths at the heart of the mud-brick temple together. There had been eight stones arranged in a circle, standing vertically. Four stones had lain across their tops. A mini Stonehenge. And in the centre, four altars, three to known gods, one . . . one that defied explanation.

"No trace of those altars remain," Legmeshu told me over tea. "But my great-grandfather's notes are quite clear. There were three altars to the three phases of the Hunter God: the youth, the king, the wise ancient. But to whom the fourth altar was dedicated . . .?" He shrugged. "A goddess perhaps? Or the king reborn? My relative left only speculation."

There had been a difference of opinion during that first excavation; a fight; and a death. Apart from what I have written here, the record is blank, save for a folk memory from the inhabitants of Scarfell concerning a tree that grew one winter—a black and evil-looking thorn.

Legmeshu snatched my copy of the Scarfell inscription. He ran his eyes over the signs, the cuneiform script that seemed as familiar to him as was my own alphabet to me. "This is not all of it," he said after a long while. I had realised some time before that the fourth surface of the stone, flush with the brickwork between door and ceiling, had characters on it like the other three. They could not be read of course without demolishing the cottage, which I had not been prepared to do at the time. I told Legmeshu that the fourth side had been exposed over a long period to the toxic air of a northern English factory town and the characters had been all but erased.

He seemed beside himself with fury for a moment. "What a destructive and stupid thing to do, to leave the stone in such a place. It *must* be returned! It *must* be rescued!"

"Of course," I said. "I intend to do so on my return to England. I have only just located the stone myself, after years of studying my great-uncle's notes . . ."

He seemed mollified by this. I have no intention of giving up the whereabouts of the stone however. I lie without shame. I feel obsessively protective towards the stone . . . towards the cottage, and yes, in my adulthood, towards the tree. Somehow they are linked through my great-uncle and to remove or destroy any one of them would be like smashing the Rosetta Stone with a sledge hammer.

Legmeshu seemed to come to a sudden decision, saying, "Follow me," and led me down to the site itself. We came at last to the wide tarpaulin that covered the centre of the temple.

It was an area of mystical energy. I could sense the presence of invisible power. It had an immediate and lasting effect on me. I began to shake. Even as I write—hours after the experience—my hand is unsteady. As I stood there I was in the far past. Fingers of time brushed through my hair; the breath of the dead blew gently against my face. Sounds, smells, touches . . . and an overwhelming, awe-inspiring *presence*—silently watching me.

Legmeshu seemed entirely unaware of these things.

His voice brought me back to the present. He was pointing to the small concrete markers that now showed where the stones had stood, in a circle about twenty feet in diameter. On the floor, clearly outlined in the dry mud, were the twisting impressions of roots.

"It was open to the sky," Legmeshu said. "In the centre of the stones a tree had been grown, quite a large tree by the looks of it. The four altars were oriented east-west. We think there may have been a mud-filled pit below the trunk of the tree, to support its growth."

"And the purpose of the place?" I asked. Legmeshu smiled at me and passed me a small book. I opened it and saw that he had written out the translations from each stone. The particle content of the Alexander stone had just been added and I studied the stilted English. Almost immediately I was aware of what I was reading.

Legmeshu's breathless, "It includes much of the original epic that has been lost, and earlier forms of the rest. It is a momentous find!" was quite unnecessary. I was lost in words:

And behold the waters of the Flood were gone. The mud covered the land as a cloak which stifles. Gilgamesh waited on a hill and saw Utnapishtim, Boatman of the Flood, rise from the plain of mud and beckon. "Gilgamesh I shall reveal to you a secret thing, a mystery of the gods. Hark my words. There is a tree that grows from fire under the water, under the mud. It has a thorn prick, a rose blade on every twig. It will wound your hands, but if you can grasp it, then you will be holding that which can restore youth to a man. Its name is Old Man Who Would Be Young." "How deep is the mud?" Lord Gilgamesh asked. "Seven days and seven nights," answered the Boatman, and Gilgamesh drew breath and swam into the blackness.

When he had cut Old Man Who Would Be Young he swam again to the surface of the mud. Utnapishtim sent a woman with golden tresses to clean and annoint the body of the kingly man. And Gilgamesh possessed her for seven days and seven nights in a fury of triumph, and not for one moment did he let go of Old Man Who Would Be Young. And when the child was born, Utnapishtim gave it at once to Old Man Who Would be Young, so that the first berry appeared on the branches. "Now it will grow," the Boatman said. "And I have told you of the temple you must build and the manner of annointing the flesh."

Now Gilgamesh departed for high-walled Uruk, and when the thorns of Old Man Who Would Be Young pricked his thumbs he was increased of power. And he denied all the old men their touch of the tree, so that their youth was denied them. But when the time came, Gilgamesh alone would place Old Man Who Would Be Young in the proper way, and lie with it in an embrace of seven days and seven nights.

Here then, carved in stone, was a version of the immortality tale of The Epic of Gilgamesh that was quite unlike the story from the clay tablets. And it was an *earlier* version, Legmeshu was quite adamant, a cruder form, with hints of the magic ritual that the later version appears to have lost.

"The stone came from Egypt," Legmeshu said. "This place functioned as a ritual site of enormous importance for perhaps two hundred years. The secret plant seems to have been a thorn, which would account for the pattern of roots on the mud there. I believe this place celebrated immortality. And the fourth altar may be representational: the risen life. So we have Youth, King, Magus, and again Youth."

Legmeshu spoke, but his words became just sounds. He seemed more interested in archaeology than in the astonishing *literary* discovery. To him, legends are only part of the story of the people; they are one more tool, or one more part of the machine that is archaeology. He wants the words intact, as much as he wants the stone intact, but I realise now that he has not been affected by the *meaning* of the words, neither their literal interpretation nor what they imply about culture and ritual in the earliest of civilised times.

Quite clearly my great-uncle was! What other reason could there have been for his dragging away one of the stones—the key stone—and raising, too, a strange and gloomy tree. Did he find the seed of a familiar thorn that in the time of Babylon was known as Old Man Who Would Be Young?

The key! It tells of the growth from fire of a tree. It tells of the child who must be given to the growing sapling. And what other salient information lies on the hidden face of the lintel, awaiting discovery?

August 10, 1958

I can stay here no longer. I wish to return to the site at Tel Enkish but I have received word that the Iraqis are unhappy that I "own" the stone. The time has come to slip away from this country. For a while, anyway. I leave so much unfinished; I leave so many questions unanswered.

June 14, 1965

I had almost come to believe that my supernatural encounter at Tel Enkish was no more than imagination; whimsy. The intervening years have been very barren and very frustrating. (Legmeshu has finally ceased to hound me for the stone, but I still watch my back whenever I am in the Near or Middle East.) Now, something has turned up and I have flown to Cairo from Jerusalem (via Cyprus).

It began two months ago. I was in Jerusalem, initiating the project for which Cambridge has at last agreed to fund me: namely, to identify and discover that true symbolic and mythological meaning of the type of tree that provided the Crown of Thorns at Christ's execution. (A briar wreath, a coif of knotted thistles, a halo of thorn tree twigs? From what species of shrub or tree?) The reference to the "resurrecting thorn" in the work of the unknown writer of Gilgamesh has haunted me for years. Of all the world's great resurrections, Christ's is the most famous. I am increasingly obsessed with the true manner of that raising, and the Crown of Thorns is a teasing symbol, a provocative invitation that came to me while staring at the ragthorn through the window of Scarfell Cottage.

One afternoon, in the university library canteen, a noisy crowded place, I overheard a conversation.

The two men were behind me, speaking in awkward English, obviously a second language to them both. One of them was an Israeli diplomat I recognised; the other was an Arab. I guessed from the dialect of his occasional exclamations in his first language, that he was Egyptian. Their conversation was hushed, but I could hear it quite clearly, and soon became intrigued.

The Egyptian said, "Some diving men, with the tanks on the back—not professional men—tourist. They are swim near Pharos Island, where sunk the old light warnings for ships . . ."

The Israeli took a moment to work out what was being said.

"Light warnings? Light*house*. The Pharos lighthouse?"

The Egyptian said excitedly, "Yes, yes! By ancient city Alexandria. Yes. Find some very old jar. Very old. Thousands years. No sea get into jar. Papers inside. Old papers. Old before coming of Roman peoples. Many more jars in sea, so I am told."

Their voices dropped even lower and I found it was hard to catch what was being said. All I could determine was that the Israeli government are interested in any scroll that relates to its own culture. Naturally, they are prepared to pay a great deal of money and the Egyptian was busy lining his own pockets by bringing this information to the attention of the Israeli Ministry of Culture.

The thought occurred to me immediately: Might there be something in the jars that relates to the *thorn*?

It has been years since Tel Enkish, but once again I have a feeling of fate unfolding: of being watched by the silent past. I am convinced there is something in Cairo for *me*.

June 19, 1965

My contact here is Abdullah Rashid. He is well known to the professors at the University in Jerusalem and has "supplied" objects and information to them for some years.

Professor Berenstein in Jerusalem is a friend of mine and kindly arranged the surreptitious meeting with this man who is in a position to inspect and copy the contents of the jars. This morning, after "checking my credentials," Abdullah came to my hotel. Over breakfast he explained that five of the ancient jars had already been taken from the water and two of them opened in controlled conditions. He is cagey about this knowledge of the contents, but has remarked, cryptically, that he believes there *is* a reference to some thorn tree amongst the first papers to be removed and examined.

The discovery is, as I knew, being kept under tight wraps, and Abdullah was surprised and impressed that I managed to hear about the parchments. It is the intention of the Egyptians to translate the documents and plays themselves, and take full credit before releasing the finds to the world at large. Hence, people like Abdullah are making a great deal of money leaking facsimiles of the parchments.

This is what Abdullah has told me: The discovery so far is of several documents that survived the fire in the Library of Alexandria two thousand years ago. The belief is that before the rioting crowd managed to penetrate the library, strip its shelves, and set the place alight, a number of soldiers loaded saddlebags with whatever the librarians could select to save, and rode from the city to a galley, which pulled offshore. Here, forty glazed amphorae were filled with manuscripts and sealed with wax, linen, more wax, and finally corked with clay. For some reason the jars were thrown overboard near the lighthouse. Perhaps the crew suddenly found themselves in danger and unable to set sail? Nothing more is known of this. Certainly the intention would have been to recover the vessels, once the danger was past, but it must be surmised that there were no survivors who knew of the whereabouts of the jars, or even that they existed. Seawater rotted the rope nets holding them together and then currents carried some of the jars out into the Mediterranean, and stretched them in a line towards Cyprus.

June 20, 1965

Today we saw the recovery operation at work. The shores of Alexandria are always bustling with small craft, mostly feluccas similar to that in which we serenely approached the island. We blended well, since I had dressed in local fashion. It was calm on the blue waters, but the sun bore down on us with unrelenting pressure and its effects have made me quite dizzy. We sailed to Pharos Island, to the northern point, and watched a large rusty dredger assist a team of divers in bringing up the precious artifacts.

Eventually we received our reward. We saw one of the amphorae winched from the water. It was long and slender, encrusted with limpets and barnacles, and dripped a particularly silky, dark green weed, which hung from the bullet-blunt jar like a beard. A crab of gigantic size dangled from this furze by one claw, as if reluctant to release the treasure that had for so long been the property of the ocean.

I asked Abdullah where the amphora would now be taken. He told me, "To the museum." There it would be opened in controlled conditions.

"Is there no chance I could witness the opening?"

He shook his head and laughed. He told me that only certain government ministers and professors would be there. And some technical assistants, who were highly trusted.

Again the laughter as he prodded his chest.

"People like me," he said.

Abdullah's work would be to photograph the opening of the jars, at each stage, then any contents, page by page. Facsimiles would be made from the photographs.

"These facsimiles would be for sale?"

"Not officially of course"—he smiled—"but all things are negotiable, yes?"

June 23, 1965

Abdullah was here, but the news is not good. He has been unable to obtain copies yet, not just for me but for others, as he must not be caught compromising his position at the museum. He has photographed several manuscripts so far.

It is a mixed bag, apparently, and includes two pieces by Plato, a play by Platus called *Servius Pompus*, and twenty pages of a manuscript by Julius Caesar, entitled *His Secret Dialogues with the Priests of Gaul on the Nature of their Magic and Rituals.*

The final piece of parchment contains an even more exquisite original hand: that (it is believed) of Homer himself. It is a fragment of his *Iliad*, and consists of half of the Death of Hector, all the Funeral of Patroclus, and a third or so of the Funeral Games. It is a manifestly ancient hand, and the Egyptians are quite convinced that it *is* the writings of Homer, adding weight to the argument that Homer was one man, and not a collective of writers.

All of this would be enough to excite me beyond tolerance, but Abdullah, aware of the nature of my search, has now told me something that holds me breathless in anticipation: that the *Iliad* fragment contains reference to a "blood thorn."

That is the facsimile I want. I have told him that no matter what else he obtains, he *must* get that fragment of unknown Homer. My enthusiasm has no doubt put up the price of those lines of verse, but I am sure I am being skillfully teased into such a state by Abdullah. He could probably produce the goods now, but is jigging the price up with his procrastination, pretending he is being watched too closely. I can play the game too, and have let him see me packing my suitcase, and looking anxiously at my diary.

October 1, 1965

I am back at the cottage in Scarfell, the place of my birth. I have come here because I *feel* I have been summoned home. I have been at Cambridge for most of the summer, but the voice of something dark, something omnipresent, has called me here . . . home to the cottage, to the wild valley, to the tree.

I have translated much that Abdullah was able to sell me. And indeed, the documents make fascinating reading.

The "new" play by Titus Maccius Plautus (200 B.C.) is hilarious. *Servius Pompus* is completely typical, dealing with a common legionary in Fabius' army who is convinced he is of noble birth, and treats his comrades like dirt. His ultimate discovery that he is slave-born earns him a permanent position: on a cart, collecting the dung left behind by Hannibal's elephants.

The fragment of Caesar is most atypical however and very strange, detailing as it does the legendary and magic matter of the Celtic inhabitants of Europe, and there is a fascinating revelation concerning the coded language that existed within the arrangement of the stones on the landscape.

All that is for another paper. For the moment, it is the Homeric verse that excites me, for in this fragment of the epic cycle of the Greeks on the shores of Asia Minor there is a reference to the resurrection that confirms me in two beliefs: that there has been a deliberate effort to obliterate this knowledge from the world, and that someone—or some *thing*—is guiding my search to build again that knowledge from the clues I am gradually discovering.

The autumn day is dark as I write this, with huge columns of thunderous cloud drifting over Scarfell from the west. I am working by lamplight. I am chilled to the bone. The great rugged face of the fell surrounds me, and the solitary thorn—black against the darkness—seems to lean towards me through the small leaded windows that show its sinister form. That tree has known eternity. I sense now that it has seen me learn of Achilles, and *his* unsure use of the ancient magic.

Here then is my crude translation of the passage of the *Iliad* that is relevant. It is from the "Funeral of Patroclus," Achilles' great friend. While Achilles sulked in his tent, during the siege of Troy, Patroclus donned the man's armour and fought in his place, only to be killed by the Trojan hero Hector. After Patroclus's body had been burned on the funeral pyre . . .

> . . . *then they gathered the noble dust of their comrade*
> *And with ashes from the fire filled a golden vase.*
> *And the vase was double-sealed with fat*
> *Then placed reverently in the hut of the gallant Patroclus,*
> *And those who saw it there laid soft linens*

Over the gold tomb, as a mark of respect.
Now the divine Achilles fashioned the barrow for his friend.
A ring of stone was laid upon the earth of the shore
And clear spring water was sprinkled amongst the stones.
Then rich dark soil was carried from the fields and piled upon
  the stones.
Until it was higher than the storm-soaked cedar.
Prince Achilles walked about the barrow of Patroclus
And wept upon the fertile ground which held his friend
While Nestor, son of Neleus, was sent a Dream from Heaven.
The Dream Messenger came from Zeus, the Cloud-compeller
Whose words reached the ears of the excellent Achilles
Who pulled the blood thorn from the wall of Troy
And placed the thorn tree on the tear-soaked mound.
In its branches he placed the sword and shield of Patroclus
And in so doing pierced his own flesh with the thorn,
Offering lifeblood as his blood for life.

Here, the fragment returns to the story content as we know it: the funeral games for Patroclus and the final reckoning between Achilles and the Trojan champion, Hector. My translation leaves a great deal to be desired. The *metre* of Homer's verse in the original seems very crude, not at all as we have become used to it, and perhaps later generations than Homer have "cleaned up" the old man's act, as it were. But there is power in the words, and an odd obsession with "earth." When Homer wrote them, I am sure he was powered by the magic of Zeus, a magic that Achilles had attempted to invoke.

Poor Achilles. I believe I understand his error. The whole ritual of the burial, of course, was intended to *bring Patroclus back to life!*

His mistake was in following the normal Mycenaean custom of burning the body of his friend upon the pyre. Patroclus never rose again. He couldn't. It is apparent to me that Zeus tried to warn him *not* to follow custom, *not* to place the body of his friend upon the burning faggots, because several lines previously (as the body of Patroclus was laid upon the pyre), Homer had written:

Now in the honouring of Patroclus there was unkind delay,
No fire would take upon the wood below the hero.
Then the excellent Achilles walked about the pyre and mourned
  anew

But through his grief-eyes he saw the answer to the fire
And raised his arms and prayed to all the winds
And offered splendid sacrifice to the two gods
Boreas from the North and Zephyr of the Western Gale.
He made them rich libations from a golden cup
And implored them blow among the kindling
So that the honouring fire might grow in strength and honoured
*   ash be made of brave Patroclus.*

No fire would take and Achilles failed to see the chance that his god was offering him. Zeus was keeping the wind from the flames, but seeing his warnings go unheeded, he turned away from Achilles in a passing pique.

Nothing else in this fragment seems to relate to the subject of the thorn, or its means of operation. Abdullah has promised to send me more material when and if he can, but since nothing has arrived for several months, already I suspect that the knowledge of the lost amphorae and their precious contents is being suppressed.

What can I learn from Homer? That there was a genuine belief in the power of the *thorn* to raise the dead? That some "pricking of the flesh" is important? Achilles pricks his arm: his blood for life. But this is not the only life hinted at in the two references I have so far found: a child was given to the tree, according to the Gilgamesh fragment.

I feel the darkness closing in.

March 11, 1970

The stone lintel is *bound* to the tree! Bonded to it. Tied! It is a frightening thought. This morning I tried to dislodge the stone from its position, scraping at the cement that binds it to the rest of the coarse stone of the cottage. I discovered that the ragthorn's roots are *in the house itself!* It is clear to me now that my great-uncle had a far better understanding of the importance of the tree and stone than I have so far imagined. Why did he drag back the Gilgamesh stone to England? Why did he embed it in the way he did: as part of a door, part of a house. Is the "doorway" symbolic? A divide through which one passes from one world to another? Obviously the hidden side of the lintel contains words of great importance, words that he decided had to be concealed from the curious eyes of his contemporaries.

The stone is not a tomb's marker, it is the tomb itself: the tomb of lost knowledge!

All this has occurred to me recently and this morning I began to extract the lintel from its resting place. I used proper tools and a great deal of brute strength. Imagine my surprise when I discovered that I was scraping through *plant tissue*! A thorny root stabbed out at me, then hung there, quivering and slowly curling. It has frightened me deeply. The whole lintel is covered and protected—on its hidden face—by an extension from the ragthorn that grows at the end of the garden, a menacing and evil presence. I could sever the root to the cottage, but I feel a chill of fear on each occasion that I ponder this possibility. Even now, as I write, I feel I am drawing a terrible darkness closer.

The tree has come to inhabit the house itself. There is a thick tendril of dark root running along the wall in the kitchen.

The chimney stack is webbed with tree roots. I lifted a floor-board and a thin tendril of the ragthorn jerked away from the sudden light. The floor is covered with tiny feelers.

Webbed in tree. And all centering on the stone lintel, the ancient monolith.

No wonder I feel watched. Was it my uncle's doing? Or was he merely obeying the instructions of a more sinister authority?

September 22, 1970

I have received a message from the British Museum, forwarded from my rooms in Cambridge by my research assistant, David Wilkins. He alone knows where I live. He is an able student, a keen researcher, and I have confided in him to a considerable degree. On my behalf he is searching the dusty archives of Cambridge for other references to the "ragthorn" or to resurrection. I am convinced that many such references must exist, and that it is a part of my new purpose to elicit them, and to use them.

"Has the museum any record of William Alexander, or any knowledge of the whereabouts of his papers?" I had asked in 1967, without result.

The new letter reads quite simply thus: "We have remembered your earlier enquiry concerning the effects, records, papers, and letters of William Alexander and are pleased to inform you that a small string-bound, wax-sealed file has been discovered, a fragment of his known effects that has clearly been overlooked during the process of reinstatement of said effects to the rightful owner.

We would be most pleased to offer you the opportunity to break the seal on this file, and to review the contents, prior to discussing a mutually suitable arrangement for their final disposal."

September 25, 1970

I wonder now whether or not William Alexander *intended* this file to be discovered. I would like to think that in his aging bones, he felt someone coming behind, a soul-mate, a follower who would become as entranced with his work as he was himself. Considering what I believe now, however, I think it more likely that he intended at some time to recover the file in person, and perhaps *after* most people believed him gone.

Today I have spoken to my great-uncle. Or rather . . . he has spoken to me. He is as close to me now, as I sit here in my room in the Bonnington Hotel writing these notes, as close to me as if he were here in person. He has left a fragment of his work, a teasing, thrilling fragment.

What did he do with the rest of his papers? I wonder.

The man was born in 1832. There is no record of his death. The year is 1970. It is autumn. I tremble to think of this, but I wonder if a man, born before the reign of Victoria had begun, is still walking abroad, still soaking up the rain and the wind and the sun of the England that birthed him, or of the Bible lands that so captured his heart.

This is a summary, then, of the day's events and discoveries:

This morning I entered the labyrinthine heart of the British Museum: those deep dark corridors and rooms that have been burrowed into the bruised London clay below the building. I was conducted to a small book-lined room, heavy with history, heady with the smell of parchment and manuscript. A man of sober demeanor and middle age received us. He had been working under a single pool of desk lamplight, imprisoned by it like some frugal monk. On my arrival he favoured me with room lighting, so that his desk was no longer a captive of the lamp. He was, despite his dour looks, a cheerful soul, and was as delighted by his discovery of William Alexander as I would become of my discovery of his remaining notes. Alexander, it seems, was an old rogue. He had a formidable reputation. He was known as an eccentric man, of extravagant tastes, and frontiersman's manners. He had shocked the denizens of the nineteenth-century archaeological establishment with his rough Yorkshire speech, his outlandish manners. If it were not for the fact that he produced priceless historical artifacts from lands closed to most Europeans, he might have been ostracized by society from the outset.

He had, it seemed, collected his papers and belongings from his private offices in the deep recesses of the museum, on the 15th March, 1878. His departure had been quite typical of the man. He had placed his files and books upon a handcart and hauled it, clattering, up the levels, dragging it through the reading room disturbing everyone present, through the wide foyer, and out into the day, having caused more than one jowl in the establishment to quiver with indignation. He used to tell my mother, with a hearty chuckle, that if the Victorians were good at one thing, it was displaying indignation.

On passing the Chief Curator on the steps outside, he reached into a bag, drew out a vase of exquisite Egyptian design, and passed it over. When opened, within the neck of the previously sealed vase was a perfectly preserved red rose, its scent a fleeting moment of an ancient summer day, instantly lost as the flower became dust.

Not on the cart that day, however, were thirty sheets of paper, loosely bound between two stiff pieces of cardboard (marked with his initials) and tied with string. He had placed a red wax seal across each of the round edges of the sheaf. On being handed the package, I slit the seals and cut through the formidable string knot with my penknife: shades of an Alexander who lived long before William.

Most of the sheets in the folio are blank. I shall summarise the puzzling contents of the rest.

Sheet 21. This consists of the single word: REVELATION!
Sheet 22. This is written in a more precise hand, but clearly William Alexander's. It reads: "The Bard too! The knowledge passed down as far as ELZBTH 1st. Who censored it? Who changed the text? Two references are clear, but there must be more. There *must* be. Too sweet a myth for WAS to ignore. P—has discovered lost folio, but spirited it away." (Two sheets covered with numbers and letters: a code of some sort?)
Sheet 25. This is headed "The Dream of the Rood." It is one of two sheets that clearly relates to the "thorn" and "resurrection." The margin of this sheet is peppered with words from the Anglo-Saxon language, but the main body of Alexander's text reads like this: *"Sigebeam."* This means Victory tree? The runic character "thorn" is used more prolifically in the allitera-

tive half-lines than seems usual around this point in the poem's body. Then the word *swefna:* "of dreams." Then there are the words *syllicre treow:* "wonderful tree." This phrase is enclosed by the rune "thorn." A dream tree, a tree of victory (victory over death?) *surrounded and protected by thorns.*

"Yes." *The tree of everlasting life.* The tree is the *rood,* of course, the symbol of Christ's cross. But surely "tree" is meant in another sense too? A literal sense. Then, to confirm this, the phrase in the poem "adorned with coverings." Perhaps this means more than it says? Perhaps strips of material? *Rags?*

"I am certain that the message here is the *ragthorn tree.*"

This is the only note on *The Dream of the Rood* in my greatuncle's file, but it proves that *some* albeit cryptic references to the ragthorn remain extant, since this text can be read in any school edition of the poem.

It is clear that an abiding and darker myth concerning the return to life of a soul "buried beneath a tree" has been imposed upon the Christianity of the author (who probably wrote the "Rood" in the eighth century). But was the ragthorn at that time a tangible shrub that could be plucked, planted, and left to resurrect the corpse of the thane or lord buried below? Or was it already a myth by that time in Old England?

The last sheet contains two fascinating pieces of Middle English poetry, dating from the late 1300's, I would think, as one of them is the last stanza of Chaucer's famous poem *The House of Fame,* believed to be unfinished. It is clear that the poem *was* completed, but the last few lines removed, either by Chaucer himself, or by orders of his patron.

Alexander, who must have discovered the parchment, though it is not part of his file, had this to say:

"It is Chaucer's script, no doubt about it. The parchment page is faded, the ink has spread, but I am certain this is the original. Other editions omit the final four lines. Here they are, following the *known* ending:

Atte laste y saugh a man,
Which that y (nevene) nat ne kan
But he seemed for to be
A man of great auctorite . . . (here the known MS ends)
Loo! how straungely spak thys wyght
How ragethorn *trees sal sithe the night,*

How deeth sal fro the body slynke
When doun besyde the rote it synke.

To put those last few lines into more familiar language: Lo, this man spoke of strange things, of ragthorn trees scything away the darkness and how death will creep away from the body if it is buried beneath the ragthorn's roots.

Finally, a single stanza from an English religious lyric, which my uncle found at the same time:

Upon thys mount I fand a tree
Wat gif agayne my soule to me!
Wen erthe toc erthe of mortual note
And ssulen wormes feste in thi throte
My nayle-stanged soule will sterte upriss
On ssulen wormes and erthe to piss.

(On this hill I found a tree
which gave me back my (soul)—
While the world might take note of mortality
And sullen worms feast on *your* throat,
My thorn-pierced body will rise up
To treat the worms and the world with contempt.

This, then, concludes my listing of the sheets bound into what I shall call "The Alexander Folio." How much further in his quest my great-uncle managed to journey is hard to know, but he certainly discovered more than have I. What fire must have burned within him. What a fever of discovery!

How death shall from the body slink when down beside the root it sinks. . . .

That tree. That terrifying tree. It is the route to and from the Underworld for a man who is reluctant to die, who wishes to remain . . . *immortal.*

October 13, 1971
I am being directed, or drawn, towards new discoveries. Is it my great-uncle? Or the tree? If it is William Alexander, then he must be dead, for the spirit of a living man would not work this way. It is only spirits that have been freed from mortality that can guide the living.

This leaves me wondering about whether Alexander attempted immortality—and *failed*.

I suspect that if I searched the grounds of Scarfell Cottage carefully, or dug below the walls, into the space below the tree, I believe I would find his bones. Is he here, urging me to finish what he could not, whispering to me: Do it right, do it right? Or . . . am I influenced by something else, some other spiritual presence?

I can only conclude that if not he, then the ragthorn is my guide. This would beg the question: Why? Why would the thorn wish me to find the clues to its secret power over life and death, its unnatural, no, *supernatural*, force? Unless—and my heart races at the thought—*unless I am its chosen disciple!* Gilgamesh was chosen. No doubt others after him, with Alexander the last. It is possible to fail. Of course it is possible to fail. But I intend to understand, thoroughly, what is expected of me, and succeed where Alexander did not.

A low mist, thick and blunt-nosed, winds through the valley like a soft sentient beast, sniffing amongst the mosses and rocks and leaving damp crags and stunted hawthorns dripping with moisture. Its restlessness finds its way into my spirit. I find writing difficult. There is a feeling on the land of a permanent, mist-ridden dusk. I pace the house, constantly going outside to stare at the ragthorn, perched like some black-armoured mythical bird upon the crumbling drystone wall.

Even inside the house, my eyes continually stray to the lintel, to the evidence of the tree that has it in its tendrilous grasp. My work lies scattered around the house. I am possessed by a desire to leave the place. But I cannot. I have not heard from Wilkins for months. It is a year since I have opened the Alexander folio. Something *must* happen soon. Something must happen.

April 10, 1972

The tree has grown. For the first time in years the ragthorn shows signs of growth, twig tips extending, roots inching farther across the garden, extending below the house itself. It is coming into bud, and it seems to shake, even when there are no winds.

September 17, 1972

An odd fragment has come to light as I worked in Cambridge, searching for the Shakespearean folio owned and hidden by Lionel

Pervis (the P—of the Alexander folio), who I have discovered was my uncle's contemporary. The fragment is a further piece of Middle English, perhaps once part of a collection of Sacred Songs. This fragment, a faded vellum sheet pressed between the pages of a copy of the second edition of *Paradise Lost*, may once have belonged to Milton himself. Certainly, this edition of his book has annotations in his own hand, still clear despite his blindness. One is tempted to wonder whether the dying man was clutching at a truth whose greatness had only been hinted at. He had perhaps discovered this obscure and frightening stanza from a hymn and kept it as an odd symbol of hope and resurrection.

Quhen thow art ded and laid in layme
And Raggtre rut thi ribbis ar
Thow art than brocht to thi lang hayme
Than grett agayn warldis dignite.

When you are dead and buried in lime
And the roots of the Ragthorn form your ribs
You will then be brought back to your home
To greet the world again with dignity.

November 22, 1974

I have at last found a fragment of the lost folio of *Hamlet*, but not from my searches at Cambridge! It was here all the time, in the Alexander papers. One of the apparently blank sheets is not blank at all. I would not have discovered the fact but for a coincidence of dropping the sheets onto the floor and gathering them by the dim light of the hurricane lamp. The shadowy signs of word-impressions caught my attention immediately. The marks were shallow, the merest denting of the heavy paper from the rapidly scrawled writing on the now-lost top sheet. But the impressions were enough for me to use a fine powder of lead, and a wash of light oil, to bring out the words fully.

Clearly, Alexander was privileged to hear the relevant passage from *Hamlet*, from the original prompt copy of the play, and wrote them down. Lionel Pervis would not part with the whole folio itself, and perhaps it is now destroyed.

(Even as I write these words I feel apprehensive. I am certain, those years ago, that I carefully examined these blank sheets and found nothing. I know I tested for secret ink. I *know* that. I would surely have noticed signs of overwriting.)

The fragment of *Hamlet* makes fascinating reading, and tells me much about the method: the actual means by which the process of burial and rebirth must be achieved.

Here is Alexander's account of the discovery, and his copy of the scene that some hand, later, had eliminated from the versions of Shakespeare's play that have come down to us:

> Pervis is a difficult man to talk to. His career is in ruins and he is an embittered man. He has confirmed certain thoughts, however. Added valuable insight. In summary: The most reliable text of *Hamlet* is to be found in the Second Quarto. However, no editor would dismiss entirely the text that appears in the First Folio, though scholars have proved that the First Folio was derived from a corrupt copy of the prompt-book, used at the Globe Theatre.
>
> Pervis' brother is a barrister of repute, in Lincoln's Inn Fields. Was present during the discovery of a hidden room in the cellars of his firm's building, which had been walled up and forgotten. A mountain of documents was discovered in that room, among them several pages of a manuscript of great interest to Shakespearean scholars. Pervis (the barrister) sent these to his brother, in order for the Shakespearean actor to assess their worth in academic terms and asked what monetary value they might have. Pervis (the actor) claimed never to have received the papers and was taken to court by his brother and, though he could not be convicted on the evidence, was widely believed to have stolen the manuscript. It ruined his life and his career.
>
> Pervis later claimed to have been "given" a copy of the manuscript, though it is fairly certain he sold the original to a private collector who will have it now, in some safe in Zurich. Pervis would not release the copy to anyone, but insisted that the new version must first be heard from him, playing Hamlet's ghost at the Old Vic. Victorian society was scandalised and he was refused and demands were made upon him, which sent him into retreat, somewhere in Wales. It was there I managed to track him down. He was by that time a bitter old man. He knew of me, of my reputation for scandalising the society that he believed had dealt him meanly, and with a certain amount of gold was persuaded to part with lines of the text, including reference to the burial place of Hamlet's father, beneath the roots of an *exotic thorn tree*.

(From Act I, Scene V)
Ghost: Thus was I sleeping by a brother's hand,

Of life, of crown, of queen at once dispatched,
Cut off even in the blossoms of my sin,
Unhouseled, disappointed, unaneled,
No reck'ning made, but sent to my account
With all my imperfections on my head.
Aye, quarters to the four winds pointed right
Below the 'bracing ragthorne's needled limbs,
Yet by ironic touch my flesh immured,
Base metal traitoring this but perfect tomb.
O, horrible! O, horrible! Most horrible!
If thou has nature in thee bear it not,
Let not the royal bed of Denmark be
A couch for luxury and damned incest . . .
But howsoever thou pursues this act,
Taint not thy mind, nor let thy soul contrive
Against thy mother aught—leave her to heaven,
And to those thorns that in her bosom lodge
To prick and sting her.

                        Fare thee well at once,
The glow-worm shows the matin to be near
And 'gins to pale his uneffectual fire,
To where my bones lie compassed.

                            Thus to thee

Adieu, adieu, adieu, remember me.

                   (The ghost vanishes)

I have read this speech fifty times now, and still the words thrill me. Since William Alexander had seen this verse, he must surely have seen the clear indications of *method*, the method of burial beneath the ragthorn's "root vault."

"Quarters to the four winds pointed right . . ." The body positioned so that it formed a star, confirmed by that later line: *"where my bones lie compassed."* Obviously not a *set* of compasses, because the angles on such instruments are variable. It has to be the four main points of the magnetic compass: north, south, east, and west.

Then also that warning, not to take metal into the grave.

Yet by ironic *touch my flesh immured,*
Base metal *traitoring this but perfect tomb . . .*

But for the metal, the tomb would have been perfect. (For the raising of the dead?) *Ironic touch.* That play on *irony* and the metal *iron.* Perhaps he had been buried in full armour, or an amulet, whatever, the metal touched his body and imprisoned it within the roots of the ragthorn. The miracle could not take place. Metal had negated the power of wood, a living substance.

I am this much closer to an understanding.

March 18, 1976

My great-uncle is buried beneath the ragthorn. I say this without evidence of bones, or even a final letter from the strange man himself, but I sense it as surely as I feel the tree feeds from the stone.

This afternoon, with a trusted local man called Edward Pottifer, I excavated into the hillside beyond the drystone wall, where the valley slope begins to drop away steeply towards the stream. The ragthorn's roots have reached here too, but it soon became clear where Alexander himself had dug below the tree to make his tomb. We cleared the turf and found that he had blocked the passage with rubble, capping it with two slabs of slate. He must have had help, someone like Pottifer perhaps, because he could not have back-filled the passage himself. I suppose there is no record of his death because he knew it had to be that way. If a man took his body and buried it beneath that tree, it would have been done in the dead of night, in the utmost secrecy, for the church, the locals, and the authorities would surely have forbidden such a burial.

He knew the method, and yet I feel that he failed.

He is still there. I'm afraid to dig into the ragthorn root mass. I am afraid of what I shall find. If he failed, what did he do wrong? The question has enormous importance for me, since I have no wish to repeat his failure.

I am ill. The illness will worsen.

April 12, 1976

I have been studying the evidence, and the manner and nature of the burial is becoming clearer. At Cambridge, Wilkins has sought out all the different meanings of the various key words and I am increasingly convinced that I have a firm knowledge of just *how* the body must be placed in the encompassing, protective cage of roots. The orientation of the body must be north-south, with the arms raised as in a cross to the east and west. There must be no metal upon or within it. The armour is stripped away, the weapons are removed. Metal is counter to the notion of resurrection, and thus I have left instructions that my back teeth are to be removed when I am dead.

May 1, 1976

In preparation for that *time* when it comes, I have now—with the help of Pottifer—dug a passage several feet long into the side of the hill, below the ragthorn. I have finally taken the same route as that followed by William Alexander, but a hundred years has compacted the earth well, and it is no easy task. That we are on the right track is confirmed only by the mixture of slate that appears in the soil, and the fact that the thorn *allows* our excavation to continue in this direction. We press on, striking up, away from the bedrock. We did attempt other passages at first, but with every foot in the *wrong* direction there was a battle to be made with the protecting thorny roots. They snagged at our flesh and pulled at our hair, until we had to abandon those first diggings. The tree knows where it wants to put me.

May 3, 1976

I have found the remains of an infant! Thank God Pottifer was not with me at the time, for it would have shaken him badly. There is a reference in the passage from Gilgamesh: *"and when the child was born, Utnapishtim gave it at once to Old Man Who Would Be Young, and the first berry appeared on the branches."* William Alexander planted this particular shoot or cutting of the tree and would have needed a similar offering. The thought horrifies me, that some mother in a nearby village, or some passing gypsy family, lost their newborn child one Victorian night.

May 10, 1976

Pottifer has made the breakthrough. He came scuttling out of the hole, his face black with earth, his fingers bloody from his encounters with sharp slate and wild thorns.

"Bones!" he cried. "Bones, Professor. I've found bones. Dear God in heaven, I touched one."

He stared at his hand as if it might have been tainted. I crawled into the passage and edged along to the place where he had found my great-uncle. The earth here was looser. The cage of roots was behind me and I could feel into what seemed to be a soft soil. It was possible to work my hands through and touch the dismembered bones and the ribs of the man who lay there. Every bone was wrapped around with the fibrous wormlike rootlets of the tree.

I became very disturbed. I was invading a place that should have been inviolate, and felt that I was an unwelcome intruder into this earthy domain.

My great-uncle had failed to attain resurrection. He had done something wrong and now, I swear, the tree has his soul. It had sucked his spirit from his body to strengthen itself, perhaps to extend its root system, its power over the surrounding landscape? Was this the price of failure, to become the spiritual slave of the tree? Or am I just full of wild imaginings?

Whatever, the embrace of those roots is not a loving one, but one of possession. It is a cruel grip. The tree had hung on to the ash urn of Patroclus because the bones must not be burned. It had not released the flesh of Hamlet's father because there was metal on the body. But *I* am determined to triumph.

When I touched my ancestor's skull, I drew back sharply, then probed again. There were no teeth in the jaws. The skeleton was also oriented correctly, north, south, east, and west.

It was as I withdrew my probing hand from the soft-filled earth chamber that my fingers touched something cold and hard. I noted where it lay, that it was at the top of the leg, close to the spine and clutched it and drew it out.

Edward Pottifer stared at the iron ball in my hand. "That's from an old gun," he said, and at once I remembered the story of my great-uncle's skirmish in the Middle East. Yes. He had been shot and close to death. They had operated on him in the field, but then transported him, delirious, to a hospital in Cyprus, where he recovered. He must have been under the impression that the bullet was removed from his body at that first operation. Of course, his back would have pained him at times, but old wounds do that, without iron in them. That must have been it, for he surely wouldn't have taken the chance, not after finding the method in *Hamlet*.

I did not mean to laugh. It was not disrespect, but relief. He had carried that iron ball into the grave with him. He had removed his teeth, perhaps gold-filled, but not the bullet.

I spoke carefully and succinctly to Edward Pottifer. I told him my teeth were to be removed at death. That my body was to be stripped and *no* metal, not even a cross around my neck, was to be buried with me. My body would be a cross. I marked clearly where my head was to be placed, and how my arms should be raised to the sides. "I will give you a compass. There must not be the slightest deviation."

He stared at me for a long time, his young face showing the anguish he felt. "When do you expect that might be, sir?" he asked me. I assured him that it would not be immediately, but that I was in my fifties now, and a very ill man. I told him to come every day to the house, to make sure I was still alive, and to become familiar with me, and less afraid of me. And of course, I would pay him well for his services. Work was not easy to find in the dale, and the temptations of this offer were too strong for him: I have my grave-digger, and I know he can be trusted.

December 24, 1976

As I write this I am experiencing a sense of profound awe. Young Wilkins is here, and he is frightened and shocked. He arrived at the cottage last night, an hour or so before I was ready to retire. I had not expected him. He had travelled from London that afternoon, and had decided not to telephone me from the station. I understand his reasons for coming without forewarning.

I wonder what it must have felt like for him to be picking through the decaying fragments of several old parchments—brought to Cambridge by Abdullah Rashid, who subsequently vanished!—separating by tweezers and pallet knife those shards of some ancient writer's records that showed any legible writing at all; how it must have felt to be sorting and searching, eyes feasting upon the forgotten words . . . and then to find John the Divine himself!

The writing is fragmentary. The state of ruination of the scrolls is appalling. The Arab traders had already cut each precious document into forty pieces, thinking that by so doing they would increase forty-fold the value of their find. And they were struck by the Hand of Calamity as surely, as certainly, as if Jehovah himself had taken control of their fate. All of them are now imprisoned. Abdullah Rashid is now an exile (perhaps even dead?). Yet he was compelled to come to England, to seek me out . . . to bring his last "gift" (he asked for nothing in return) before disappearing into the night.

I was fated to discover these parchments.

It is the last reference of the ragthorn that I shall discover. No more is needed. It is a fragment that has given me *courage*.

At last I understand my great-uncle's reference to REVELA-TION! He had heard of the lost passage from Revelations of St. John the Divine. Perhaps he saw them? It was enough for him too. Revelation! Triumph!

Oddly, the references to resurrection are not what has frightened Wilkins. If he is afraid it is because he feels that too many of his beliefs are being threatened. He has been sobered by the encounter. But he saw the words "thorn" and "rag" and has brought to me my final, most conclusive proof that there is indeed a lost and forgotten mechanism for the resurrection of the dead, nature's alchemy, nature's embrace, a technique that defies science. No scientist will accept the revivification of the flesh under the influence of thorn, and root, and cold clammy earth. Why should they? But it happened! It has been recorded throughout history; it had begun, perhaps, in ancient Sumeria. There have been deliberate attempts to lose, to deny the fact . . . folios have been scratched out, poems obliterated, classics rewritten . . . the words of the ancients have been edited dutifully, perhaps by frightened servants not of God, but of *dogma* that preaches only the resurrection of the *soul* . . .

Oh, the irony! Oh, the pleasure at what St. John the Divine has told me.

It was all there for us to see, all the symbols, all the truths. The wooden cross, which He himself fashioned in His carpenter's shop, ready for the moment of His thricefold death, drowned, stabbed, and hanged on the tree.

The Crown of Thorns, His mastery over the forest.

The immortal wood, the tree of life, the regenerating forest—of course it can shelter and protect the mortal flesh. There is in the tree a symbol, a reality too powerful for monks with quill pens to dare to fight, to challenge. So they cut it out, they *excised* it. In this way cutting out the soul of John, they cut out the heart from the past.

"He that dies by the wood shall live by the wood."

Perhaps I have the original copy of the parchment, the *only* copy remaining? It was found in a jar, in the hills of Turkestan, and had come into the possession of Abdullah . . . and had done so because it was *meant* to find its way into my hands.

For now I shall record in the journal only part of what St. John said. It is from Chapter 10 of the Revelations. It might have preceded verse 3. It is my great hope. It has confirmed my faith in the rightness of what I shall achieve. A miracle occurred in the house of Lazarus.

> *And I looked into the Light, and Lo, I saw Him command a thorn tree to spring from the roof of the house of Lazarus. And the tree had seven branches and on each branch there were seven times seven thorns. And below the house seven roots formed a cradle around the dead man, and raised him up so that again his face was in the light.*
>
> *So cometh the power of the Lord into all living things.*
>
> *And again He cried: That ye might rise anew and laugh in the face of Death, and blow the dust from thy lungs in the eyes of Death, so that ye can look on Hell's face and scorn the fires and rage upon the flames and rise thee up.*
>
> *And Lo, I saw how the thorn withered and died and the Angel of the Lord flew from its dust.*
>
> *And He cried out in the voice of the Immortal King:*
> *The Lord is in all things and He is in the One Tree.*
> *He that dies by the wood shall live by the wood.*
> *He that dies by the thorn shall live again by the thorn.*

April 15, 1978

Pottifer was here. I sent him to the tree, to begin to clear the chamber. The pain in my chest is greater than I can bear sometimes. I must refuse the sensible remedy of moving to London, to be closer to the hospital that can relieve such things, and extend my life, even though they cannot cure me.

Pottifer is very calm. We have kept the secret from the village and not even his family knows. He has managed to clear the root chamber whilst keeping the failed bones of my ancestor undisturbed below a thin layer of soil. As long as I am within that quivering cage of thorns I shall succeed. I shall live again.

There is a great danger, however. I believe now that the tree took William Alexander, body and soul, for its own. Perhaps that is its exacted compensation for the failure of its disciples, to possess *all* that remains, not just the flesh, but the spirit also?

I *know* I have it right, and I can depend on Pottifer, completely, just as my great-uncle must have depended on such a man. Pottifer is devoted to me, and obeys me implicitly.

September 11, 1978 (extract)

The moment is very close. I have now acquired a set of dental pincers with which to perform the final part of the ritual. Pottifer has seen into my mouth and knows which teeth to pull.

September 20, 1978

Pottifer is with me. I am certainly going. How vigorously the body clings to life, even when the mind is urging it to relax in peace. There is no longer any pain. Perhaps the closeness of death banishes such mortal agonies. I can hardly move, and writing is now an effort of will. This will be the final entry in my journal. Pottifer is very sad. I admire him. I have come to like him very much. His great concern is to get my body into the chamber before the *rigor* of death stiffens my limbs. I have told him to relax. He has plenty of time. Even so, he need wait only a few hours for the rigor to pass. I have thought of everything. I have missed no point, no subtlety. When I am gone, Pottifer will end this journal and wait for one year and one day before returning to Scarfell Cottage. These papers, I am sure, will not be there. They will be in my own hands. If they *are* still in evidence, Pottifer is to send them to young Wilkins, but I am absolutely certain that I will be here to decide their fate, just as I have decided my own.

Adieu, or rather *au revoir*.

September 21

This is Pottifer. The docter told me to rite this when he was gone. I berried him as he told me to, and no dificulties. He said there must be no mistakes and spoke on the tree saying it sucked men dry of there souls who make mistakes. His last words to me were Pottifer I must face Hell and look on its face like Saint John tells. He seemed very fearfull. I give him a kiss and said a prayre. He shouted out in pain. You do not understand I must first look on Hells face he shouted you must berry me face down.

I said to him, you are a good man docter, and you shall *not* face Hell. You shall face Heaven as you diserve. Saint John does not need your penance. Do not be fearful of Hell. You are to good and if you come back I shall be your good friend and welcome you straight.

Then he died. His fists were clenched.

He is in the earth now and all that I have is his teeth, God bless him. I wanted to put a cross but the thorns have grown to much and there is green on tree and I do not like to medle to much since there is more growth and very fast. No one has seen the tree so green and florished for a long wile not since that time in the last centry so the tales go.

P.S.

This is Pottifer agen. I have got some thing more to say. Some thing odd has hapened. It is more that one year and one day. The docter is still in the ground. I was in the pub and a man came in and asked for a drink. He said he was the royal poet. I think he said his name was John Betcherman. He had been walking near Scarfell and had seen the tree. He had felt some thing very strange about the place he said. A strong vision of death. Someone screaming. He was upset. He asked about the cottage but I said nothing. He wrote a poem down and left it on the table. He said there I have exercised this terrible place and you have this and be done with it. Then he left. Here is the poem. It makes me feel sad to read it.

> *On a hill in highland regions*
> *Stands an aged, thorny tree*
> *Roots that riot, run in legions*
> *Through the scattered scrub and scree:*
> *Boughs that lap and lock and lace*
> *Choke the sunlight from that place.*
>
> *Deep below its tangled traces*
> *Rots the corpse of one unknown*
> *Gripped by roots whose gnarled embraces*
> *Crush the skull and crack the bone.*
> *Needled fingers clutch the crown*
> *Late, too late to turn facedown.*

There were these two British writers, one lived in the country, the other in the city. The country writer loved to visit the city and partake of brandy and Greek kebabs in the local hostelry. The city writer liked to visit the country and guzzle ale and barbecued steak under the apple trees. The two writers needed an excuse for these indulgences, and so they invented one, and this excuse was called "collaborating on a story" . . . It soon emerged that the story was to be about a legendary tree, which they both vaguely recalled from the tales their grandfathers used to tell them of mystery and myth. Soon they were delving with suppressed excitement into old documents at the British Museum and began to come up with some frightening discoveries.

The first of these finds was in studying the original text, in Anglo-Saxon, of the Old English poem "The Dream of the Rood." The marrying of the "tree" (crucifixion cross) and the "thorn" (a runic character) was too elaborately regular to be an accident of metre or alliterative language. Other discoveries followed, and the story gradually surfaced, like a dark secret from its burial mound.

The tall, hairy-faced writer, his eyes shining in the near darkness of the British Museum at five o'clock on a winter's evening, said, "We've got something here, mate." The short, clean-shaven writer, his hands full of trembling documents, answered with true English understatement, "You're not wrong, mate." So between them they began writing the history of the terrible "ragthorn tree."

Then again, they could have invented the whole thing, like these bloody storytellers do. As their old grandfathers used to say, "Why spoil a good story by sticking to the truth?"

Robert Holdstock
Garry Kilworth

Contributors' Notes

Pat Cadigan

Pat Cadigan is the author of two science fiction novels, *Mindplayers* and *Synners* (Bantam), and numerous SF and horror stories, several of which have been nominated for awards. Most of these stories are collected in *Patterns*, published by Ursus Imprints. She lives in Kansas with her husband, artist and book designer Arnie Fenner, and their son Bobby.

Jonathan Carroll

Jonathan Carroll has lived in Vienna almost twenty years. He rarely includes a biography, because he feels that too often authors' biographies are more interesting than the work itself. His latest book is *Outside the Dog Museum* (Doubleday).

Suzy McKee Charnas

Suzy McKee Charnas started out writing a couple of feminist, sociological-type science fiction novels in the seventies (*Walk to the End of the World* and *Motherlines*), moved into fantasy-horror in the eighties with *The Vampire Tapestry* and *Dorothea Dreams*, and is currently working on the fourth of a series of young adult fantasy novels about growing up in a magical version of New York City; but she can't seem to shake completely free of the vampire thing (of course not; she doesn't really want to). She just had a play put on in San Francisco's Magic Theatre, adapted from "Unicorn Tapestry," and is in the process of looking for another production. Meantime, "Boobs," a werewolf story, has won the Nebula Award and was nominated for the Hugo (her first nomination and she's very pleased with it). She is also working, as ever, on the trilogy-completing volume that follows *Motherlines*, although by the time she finishes the damn thing who knows whether it will follow at all? And she has this idea for another play. . . .

Melissa Mia Hall

Melissa Mia Hall is from Forth Worth, Texas. She finished her first novel when she was thirteen. She's been a short story writer for ten years and has been published in anthologies such as *Razored Saddles, Post Mortem, Masques III* (with Douglas E. Winter), *The Seaharp Hotel, Skin of the Soul,* and *Dead End: City Limits.* She's also written a novel, *Touchwood,* and has been a book critic, teacher, bookseller, photographer, advertising copywriter, and screenplay collaborator.

Robert Holdstock

Robert Holdstock was born in Kent, U.K., in 1948. He worked in medical research before becoming a free-lance writer in 1975. He has published several novels including *Eye Among the Blind, Necromancer,* and *Mythago Wood,* which won the World Fantasy Award. Its companion volume, *Lavondyss cavon,* was published in 1988, and a collection of fantasy stories, *The Bone Forest,* was published in 1991. He lives in London.

K. W. Jeter

K. W. Jeter is again living in Los Angeles, after years of being away; he finds it to be a congenial hell. A new science fiction novel, *Madlands,* was published in 1991 (St. Martin's), and a new horror novel, *Wolf Flow,* in 1992 (St. Martin's). A four-issue miniseries, entitled *Mr. E,* appeared from DC Comics in the spring of 1991. The art is by John K. Snyder and the project will be "For Mature Audiences Only," very much a part of the kinko-pervo side of the graphic novel genre.

Garry Kilworth

Garry Kilworth is the thickness of a shadow away from fifty years of age and has been writing professionally for fifteen years. He has published thirteen novels, four children's novels, and seventy-one short stories. His semi-permanent home is in rural Essex, England, but he has traveled and lived abroad for much of his life. At the moment he resides in Hong Kong. He has a passion for the short story, revealed in his collections *The Songbirds of Pain* and *In the Hollow of the Deep-Sea Wave*. His next collection, *In the Country of Tattooed Men*, is due out from Grafton Books, England, this year.

Kathe Koja

Kathe Koja lives in Detroit with artist Rick Lieder and her son. She has stories in *The Pan Book of Horror*, *Still Dead*, *The Ultimate Werewolf*, and other anthologies; her first novel, *The Cipher*, inaugurated the new Dell horror line, called Abyss, in 1991.

Thomas Ligotti

Thomas Ligotti was born and lives in Michigan. He has been transcribing nightmares into fiction since 1981 and his short fiction has appeared in the magazines *Fear* and *Weird Tales*, and in the anthologies *Fine Frights*, *Prime Evil*, *Best Horror From Fantasy Tales*, *Best New Horror*, and *Heroic Visions II*. His collection, *Songs of a Dead Dreamer*, was originally published in an edition of three hundred copies by Harry O. Morris's Silver Scarab Press in 1986. It has subsequently been brought out by Carroll and Graf in a hardcover trade edition.

Barry N. Malzberg

Born July 24, 1939, Barry N. Malzberg sold his first story in November 1965, his first science fiction story (a short-short to Fred Poh for *Galaxy*) on January 11, 1967. Since then he's sold a lot more short stories and more than a few novels as well, but has been distinctly less prolific since about 1979. Two political stories will appear shortly or simultaneously in *Alternate Presidents*, an original anthology edited by Michael Resnick and Martin Greenberg; recent short stories also appear in *Stalkers, Cold Shocks, What Might Have Been, Full Spectrum, Fantasy & Science Fiction, and Omni*. He thinks that Michael Shaara, Walter Tevis, John William

Corrington, Alfred Bester, and Stanley Elkin are probably the best American writers of the late century.

Elizabeth Massie

Elizabeth Massie was born in 1953 and has been a teacher for sixteen years. She lives in the Shenandoah Valley in Virginia and is married with two children. Her stories have been published in *The Horror Show, Grue, Iniquities,* and *Deathrealm,* and in the anthologies *Women of Darkness, Borderlands, Obsessions,* and *Dead End: City Limits.* She has also written a television special, "Rhymes and Reasons," which was produced and distributed by PBS and won a 1990 Parents' Choice Award.

David J. Schow

David J. Schow has a pyramid of chromed skulls on his TV set. His wardrobe is predominantly black, his sunglasses are quite dark, and he only comes out at night. He is known primarily in the horror field for his powerful, award-winning short fiction, and for editing *Silver Scream,* arguably the first splatterpunk anthology. His novel debut was *The Kill Riff,* his "rock 'n' roll horror novel," and he has recently completed *The Shaft,* his "sex and drugs horror novel." In 1989 he branched out into films and television, scripting the unsavory activities of such social lions as Leatherface and Freddy Krueger. His short fiction has been collected in *Seeing Red* (Tor) and *Lost Angels* (Onyx).

Robert Silverberg

Robert Silverberg was born in New York City, and has lived in the San Francisco Bay Area for many years. His first book, *Revolt on Alpha C,* was published in 1955. He is the winner of four Hugo awards and five Nebula awards as well as most of the other significant science fiction honors. He is the author of over one hundred books and an uncounted number of short stories, which have appeared in such magazines as *Omni, Playboy,* and *Penthouse,* and have been widely anthologized. Among his best-known book titles are *Dying Inside, The Book of Skulls, Gilgamesh the King, Lord*

Valentine's Castle, Born with the Dead, and *Nightfall* (with Isaac Asimov). He currently edits *Universe,* an anthology of original science fiction, with his wife, Karen Haber.

Melinda M. Snodgrass

Melinda M. Snodgrass was born in Los Angeles, California, and now lives in New Mexico. After studying opera in Vienna, she returned to New Mexico and became a lawyer. Three years later she quit law to write. She was executive script consultant on *Star Trek: The Next Generation* for two seasons. Her script "The Measure of a Man" was nominated for the Writers' Guild Award for outstanding achievement in writing. Her prose work includes the *Circuit* trilogy (Berkley/Ace), the *Wild Card* anthologies (Bantam), *Queen's Gambit Declined* (Warner), and two mainstream novels. She is currently working on the first *Wild Card* novel and writing television scripts.

Thomas Tessier

Thomas Tessier is the author of several novels of horror and suspense, including *The Nightwalker, Finishing Touches, Rapture,* and most recently, *Secret Strangers.*

Karl Edward Wagner

Karl Edward Wagner was born and grew up in Knoxville, Tennessee. He has lived in Chapel Hill, North Carolina, since 1967. He is a former psychiatrist and a full-time writer since 1975. His first novel, *Darkness Weaves,* was published in 1970 and he has written or edited over forty books since then, including his collections *In a Lonely Place* and *Why Not You and I?* and (as editor) the annual *Year's Best Horror Stories* (DAW). He is the winner of four British Fantasy Awards and two World Fantasy Awards. He is currently working on *The Fourth Seal,* a medical chiller for Bantam, *Satan's Gun,* a horror novel for Tor, a graphic novel with artist Kent Williams for DC, and a bunch of overdue short stories that will someday make up his third horror collection.

Rick Wilber

Rick Wilber's poetry has appeared in a variety of mainstream and science fiction magazines in the United States and Great Britain, including *Asimov's*, *Cencrastus* (Scotland), *Irish America*, *Gryphon*, *Quilt*, *Free Lunch*, *Spitball*, *Onionhead*, and *Omnibus*. His first collection, *Clearances*, was published by American Studies Press in 1991.

His short stories have appeared in *Asimov's*, *Analog*, *Pulphouse*, *Fiction Quarterly*, and other magazines, and in several anthologies, including the *Chrysalis* series, *Alien Sex*, and *Subtropical Speculations*.

He teaches journalism at the University of South Florida and frequently writes for the *Tampa Tribune*, where he also edits *Fiction Quarterly*, the short story and poetry Sunday supplement of the newspaper.

Jack Womack

Jack Womack is the author of three novels, related by blood and set in the very near future: *Ambient*, *Terraplane*, and *Heathern*. Born in Kentucky, he lives near the pastry shop, in New York City.

Chelsea Quinn Yarbro

Chelsea Quinn Yarbro sold her first story in 1968. Since that time she has published more than forty books and fifty short stories—including the St. Germain and Olivia historical vampire novels. Currently, she is working on a series of occult mysteries, the Charlie Moon series, which is being published by Berkley.